NOMADS

BY BENJAMIN KANE ETHRIDGE

Bats tittered for their direction. Jackals growled their obeisance. And somewhere nearby, just at the corners of Duncun's vision, perverse people prayed for the creatures to find release. Duncun, his body a twisted throne for a twisted monster, could only remain there before the gaping maw between the worlds, and listen to the Children sing.

Pull the muscle from its kernel Bring us the Feast Eternal! Power scorned is weakness born— It is, it is, it is.
Loam the tread, tread the loam Slit throat chorus on your tome
Passage sought, darkness wrought— It is, it is, it is.
Tear apart the ever weeping skies Suck the eyeball fruit, free its lies
Pain endured, treasure absurd— It is, it is, it is.

Icy tears, larger than Duncun thought his tear ducts capable of creating, drafted out the sides of his eyes and cooled his hot face. He called for Alisyn. He wasn't mad at her anymore. He loved her. He wanted to show her how afraid he'd been. It wasn't too late. If he could survive this long, with this many sickeningly compound fractures, perhaps it wasn't his time. But he had to get out of this place before Cloth returned.

"Help," he rasped and broke down weeping. "Fer chrissakes, help me."

The pub was quiet and would remain so. People didn't pay attention to it; they walked by all day as though this was the single least important location in the universe. But while the pub was quiet, the gateway was anything but.

"Please help!" Duncun shouted, louder than he thought himself capable of now.

Then he heard a response. Far inside the tunnel, claws scraped against the obsidian space below and started to move.

To one of my favorite authors and best friends I've ever had, Michael Louis Calvillo.

You never had a chance to read this novel, Michael, but your love and devotion for BLACK & ORANGE was my principal motivating factor in continuing this series.

This one is for you, brother!

ACKNOWLEDGMENTS

I would first like to give a big thanks to both Gavin Lees and Jim McLeod for guiding me in all things Scottish. Any errors or inconsistencies in that regard are completely this Southern Californian author's fault and reflects in no way on their superb instruction.

Thanks also to Matt Dixon, the fellow who provided the amazing cover art for *Nomads* and for the supplemental short story collection, *Reaping October*, which features one of the Cats of Delkilth. Amazing work as always, Matt! You rock, sir.

All of my writer, editor and publishing colleagues know who they are. Thanks for all the support and guidance.

A big embrace to my wife and children for inspiring me, and to my parents and sister for always being in my life. I'd probably be writing exceptionally depressing tech thrillers if I didn't have such wonderful people to color my interior worlds and brighten the shadows. I will love you all, to the last moment.

PROLOGUE

Two Weeks Ago

Where was Kauph Courre? Where was the heart of the Harvest?

The refrigerator had cut a square of blinding light into the loft and allowed her to see the scrap of notebook paper lying next to a grimy lantern and oily box of matches. Fia tapped it with idle interest. "What's Kauph Courre mean?" she asked. "It's not Gaelic, is it?"

"No, it's drunken," Douglas replied, voice squeezed by his bent posture. "Always write down what I dream. That night I had one too many Wee Heavys. I tell ye, I'm through with that devil's piss." He chuckled self-consciously, and glass clinked as he withdrew the bottles. The refrigerator snapped shut. A square afterimage cut through him as he stood there in the dark, popping off the caps with a bottle opener. "You sure you don't want me to try the lantern again? Nobody's gonnae see anythin' up here."

"Nah, it's for the best—don't want any inappropriate shadow puppets on yon window. This isn't a show for all of Thorny Bank." Another self-conscious laugh. The dusty floorboards squeaked as his shape drifted closer. Even with scarce detail Douglas moved like a timid mouse sniffing cheese. There was fear in every inch of him.

"Here." A cold bottle slid into Fia's hand. She didn't like ale but had made the suggestion to loosen the resolve of her best friend's father. Douglas must have felt mightily low agreeing to come up here, Fia just out of Secondary, and him old enough not only to be the dad she never had, but perhaps granddad; he must have felt like a first rate pervert. Fia didn't feel that way. She'd once lied to his daughter Lara, told her she preferred older men. It was only for shock value at the time, just to get a gasp out of her friend, but now she was intensely committed to the idea. Like some sort of powerful magic, her little lie had become an enormous truth.

Fia's eyes were adjusting to the dark. Th loft was stuff to the gills with indistinguishable odds and ends collected over a marriage that should have ended years ago. It made her feel sorry for Douglas—this was his little hideaway from his wife, and yet complete escape wasn't possible, even here. Fia never wanted to be a prisoner in her own house when she got older, especially not confined to a dirty space over a garage.

Sipping on the bitter brew, she watched as blue lights from a passing car swept through the old window. It made her think of a lighthouse beam through fog. Douglas slurped down most of his ale now. Fia set hers, almost full, down on the carpenter's desk and moved toward him.

He went rigid at her approach. "Now there, what're you doin'?"

She put her fingertips on his chest and slowly clawed downward. This was already exciting her. Douglas was a fine older man, no doubt.

"I'm gonnae get another one. You want—?"

Too late to get away. Fia's fingers curled around his belt and she brought him one lumbering step closer. She angled her lips up to his face. He turned slowly away but this didn't deter her. She kissed the stubbly neck and heard him groan a little. "Fia," he breathed, *"you're just seventeen."*

"And legal."

"But Lara…"

"Let's not talk about her right now," she replied and continued to devour the scratchy plane of his throat up to his ale-wet lips.

Douglas committed to those lips. He was good at this. Better than she might have imagined, with how distant a real sex life must have been for him. Earlier that night, he'd given her an extended justification for what would happen tonight. His wife Susan was in Lanark, visiting her mother, stricken with pneumonia last Tuesday. It was clear Douglas felt bad about being so opportunistic, but at the same time he noted, in his own dovish way, that he and his wife really hadn't been intimately close since Lara was born.

"I want you." His voice trembled with excitement, and now Fia could feel the male part of Douglas take over. He groped her breasts hungrily and kissed them through her sweater. She squeezed his body into hers.

"Lay out the blanket."

He abruptly disconnected from her and half-disappeared into the loft's space.

"Hurry—wait, do you have johnnies?" Fia already had one in her purse, in case, but didn't want to let her intentions become *that* obvious.

"I have some," Douglas replied.

She slid her phone out from her hip pocket. From one menu option to the next, she scrolled through to the camera's settings and turned off the shutter sound. *This was so fun!*

Floorboards protesting, Douglas spread out a blanket that could have been any color. It was a dark void on the gray floor lit by the quiet light of the streetlamps outside.

"Good?"

"Great," she replied.

Eagerly, he tore off his suit. His slacks clunked on the floor with the sound of his belt buckle. Fia had to do some catching up and unzipped her jeans. She noted Douglas's turbid gut and turned her eyes down.

She was naked now and Douglas stood on the blanket, waiting. Before her thoughts could flow in another direction, she pulled him down on the blanket. She took him in her hand and realized he already had the condom on. "Oh, good boy," she told him. Douglas rested on his back, letting her straddle him. His entire body was quivering.

This probably wouldn't last long, Fia decided. She poised above him. "Are you cold?"

"No, love, just, you know…"

"I know," she cooed and kissed his chest. It tasted like his aftershave. She loved his aftershave. It had an ashy smell to it. Perfect for their Armageddon.

Fia grunted as he went inside her. He was longer than her last boyfriend Jamie, though not as wide. It was an adjustment for her body at first. Pulses went through him and into her. *Definitely wouldn't be long*, she thought again and rocked her hips. At the same time she readied the camera phone. Douglas's head was thrown back. He wasn't looking up at her, just had a face full of open-mouthed shock. He may well have been avoiding her for the high voltage guilt sent through the metal band around his finger.

The floorboards squeaked sensuously. Fia slid up a bit and leaned back. Through her camera's new night-vision app, she watched the glowing green stalk enter between her legs. The photo looked dirty enough, scandalous, internet-ready. She next took a series of body and head shots. Douglas lifted his face at the camera's light and she got a perfect one of his face.

"What are you doing?" he demanded.

She didn't dare stop moving, but she set the cell phone away from them. "I wanted to remember this. I'll...delete them, if you want me to."

Douglas's body had gone still on seeing the camera, but as she rocked on him some more, his sudden stress faded. She didn't know if the matter of the camera was completely closed but he must have let it go for now. With a great sigh, he grabbed onto her ass and began to enjoy the moment again.

Downstairs the side door whined open. They froze.

"You up there, fuck-faced again?"

Fia recognized the voice. She'd heard the braying sound of it too many times on her way to school. Douglas's wife Susan had driven Fia to school since she and their daughter Lara were in primary together. The woman was by all accounts a brute. She'd walloped Lara for minor infractions at school, took uncensored joy in it even, and had once given Douglas a fat lip while he was apologizing for coming back late from a Union meeting.

"You there?" Susan yelled up again.

Douglas held onto Fia's hips as though he were the frightened child. He was starting to go limp inside her, and it felt disturbing, but Fia didn't dare get off and take a chance with these floorboards.

A trash can lid opened and shut. Footsteps rang sharply on the concrete.

Douglas beckoned Fia to lean forward so he could whisper. With a reek of ale breath, he said, "She won't come up here. Can never find the hall switch."

A moment later the stairs creaked with his wife's falling steps. The creaking stopped. "Turn on the damned lantern!"

They waited there, sex statues.

"Mother's pulled through again. I thought we'd celebrate... am I talkin' to myself? Or are ye too fucked already for the pub?"

Fia heard Douglas swallow.

The stairs creaking turned to a dry moaning as his wife entered the loft. "Christ, I know you're up there. Damned car is here. You're passed out. Probably choked on your own upchuck, bastard. Can't see a thing in this place. Come on! Wake!" Susan stood in the doorway, trying to adjust her eyes.

"Douglas," she snapped.

His whole body convulsed. Fia dug her nails into one of his wrists.

Susan walked toward them, stopping only a couple feet away from where they lay. She irritably patted at the wall for guidance and stepped away from them. Suddenly, something flashed—the screen of the cell phone—just as Susan kicked it halfway across the room.

"What in—?" Susan glanced around before heading for where she thought the unknown item had gone, then stepped aimlessly around for a moment and bumped into immovable invisible things while searching, each impact louder than the next. Fia could see the cell phone's faint glow in a corner. It'd turned onto its face.

"Douglas," Susan said again, his name rotten on her tongue. She grappled onto the carpenter's desk. "Ah, here now. Maybe if you'd replace the light in the fan, I wouldn't have to endure this shite..."

Susan turned her back to them. A box rattled with matches as she opened it. She struck one and a flame jumped to life in her hand. She cupped it protectively and paused before nudging Fia's ale out of the way of the lantern.

"Still cold," she remarked. "Ah, ya bastard..."

The match flame dipped down inside the lantern. She turned the knob for the propane and the mantle ticked, ticked, ticked, glowing on and off. It didn't take and the match went out. Susan lit another match and tried again. The same thing occurred but she tried it a while longer. She thumped her fist on the desk as the match burned her fingertips. "—hell with this," she grumbled and touched the ale bottle to soothe the burn. "You're up here, you can go straight to hell, Doug."

She stomped loudly down the stairs.

It felt like Fia had been holding her breathe until the truck fired up and the garage rumbled shut. Intense darkness had resumed. She thought about dressing and grabbing her cell phone, calling it a night.

"Don't suppose you want to try again?" Douglas's voice sounded thin, different somehow. With how close they'd come to being caught—he still wanted to go for it. They'd hardly shaken the jitters from their bodies, his wife not even a couple blocks away, and *to hell with it*? This wasn't in his character.

Because I've already changed him, Fia thought, *not ashamed of being proud.*

The faulty lantern flared briefly. For a moment she saw Douglas leaning back on one arm, his head sadly bowed.

"Of course I wannae." She slid off the side of him. "But I'm getting cold. You get on top."

He moved out of the way and Fia rested on the warm spot his body had made on the blanket. Gradually, he moved over her and his legs clamped hers shut at the knees. "You've got my legs pinned, love. Little difficult like that, I'n't it?"

Something bitter ruptured in her mind as a pair of ruthless hands viced around her throat. A pocket of dusty loft air stuck in her lungs expanded, no place to go. Dark stars whirled overhead and burned spots into her mind. The lantern malfunctioned a few more times, backlighting Douglas's body hovering over her. His eyes—Fia couldn't tell if they were the same, she was losing this battle, she was dying, and this monster was just trying to save his ass. Regret started pouring down. *I shouldn't have taken those fucking photos! I should have never gone after Lara's father. Why couldn't I just let it go?*

"Thanksgiving to the Eternal Feast," said a voice, which didn't belong to Douglas.

The lantern pulsed and suddenly burst into full light. The loft came into view, just as it was slipping away from her vision. She'd gouged up Douglas's arms without having realized it. For an agonizing moment she stared askance into his bone white face and into his eyes, one black and one orange. Her body arched in one last effort and then fell.

Right after, the lantern went out, for good.

I am what they call the Messenger in some places, the Interloper in others. Both titles carry great importance with some people, although I can't imagine why. They've put me on a higher plane of existence, but I'm not a god. I watch the two worlds and read minds. I attempt, in the only way I know, to help my Nomads lessen their burden. I must protect them every day and guide them into every Halloween. If I have a duty in this universe, it is only that.

The Nomads, Patty Middleton and Teresa Celeste, have blood-ties to the Old Domain, but being raised on Earth, they know little of its nature, which is why they depend on my letters. Patty and Teresa were on another continent, busy preparing for Halloween, with no idea about the monster that walked the Thornliebank streets of Glasgow. I, however, saw the wicked thing, striding through the storm cloud shadows, wearing the body of Douglas Stevens, that poor dead girl's claw marks still stinging on his arms.

That monster inside the man was named Chaplain Cloth.

Douglas's presence of mind was funneling into the giant malevolent hole that had opened inside him, and though he had long been an acolyte of the Church of Midnight, I sense he'd never really believed in the tales of Cloth. For Douglas, the Church had been nothing more than a great networking group for his labor union ties, not a religious institution that could replace his Catholic upbringing.

As I watched him in that frantic moment of murder, his thoughts spoke loudly: Help me, *Lord God! The Devil has come and possessed my body!*

But this wasn't the case at all. No.

As Chaplain Cloth often coined, the Devil was just a cover song.

The farther he walked the more certain his destination became. Before he'd even become a regular, Douglas had long dreamed about the Marigold pub. More than the pub itself, he had dreams about its storeroom and what lay beyond its worn door behind the bar of dark stained wood.

It was a few weeks ago, Katherine, the bartender's niece, had come out of the storeroom hysterically crying and broke a bottle of gin with one of her flailing hands. She'd been in an even mood only minutes ago, but when her uncle Jon finally calmed her down she started spouting what most took as nonsense. According to her there were thousands of rats in the storeroom—maybe even bats from the pitch of the sounds—and it was so cold back there she got freezer burns from the door's handle.

The Marigold had seen better days, so the rats could have very well been present, not a thousand, but enough. And some of those kegs could be rightly cold. So the easily grasped explanations didn't help Katherine's case too much. She had come to live with Jon last year because of a mental breakdown, and though she was unquestionably homely, she still had to fight off a long string of late night drunks. She'd threatened many times before to quit—so everybody took this as a dramatic justification for her inevitable departure.

But not Douglas. When he was eleven years old, before he'd even set foot in any pub, let alone the Marigold, he'd had a terrible nightmare that began with a blonde woman sobbing outside an open freezer door. He even recalled the bottle of Bombay Sapphire she backhanded and sent tipping over. Other things happened in the dream, later on, that caused Douglas himself to wake up screaming and sobbing like the woman had. He couldn't recall most of it, so he began writing down anything he could remember from the dreams. Rarely did the fragments make sense or contain new information, but he kept writing them anyway, for almost fifty years now.

He still remembered the first note he ever scrawled: *a body must be broken to be perfect for me.*

A crisp breeze kicked up and stung his face. He felt it, the monster inside did not. Douglas took out Fia's phone. It was in his best interest to smash the device on the sidewalk. Everything blurred for a second. His fi played over the phone's keys like they were on a mission. Th moved independently of him. He didn't even look at the glowing screen to see what his possessed hand was doing...what the monster was doing.

Just like now, Douglas didn't feel like he owned that last horrible encounter back in the loft. He started wondering if he'd really even been the one who killed his daughter's best friend, Fia. His would-be lover. His savior.

You cannot take credit for killing her, answered a voice in his head. It was a calm voice, which was terrifying because this must have been how insanity began, not a shout, but a whisper. Walking down the cold, wet, mirrored streets of lamplight and starlight, Douglas found himself probing further. He turned off the cell phone and stuck it in his pocket. Rather than ask the obvious, the who-the-hell-are-you question, he instead asked, why would you kill Fia?

I had to see. See what?

The voice was positively placid. If your will was stronger than my will, the girl'd still be alive. But you were weak. She was weak. So it happened that way. Not a very cheery moment in time for either of you, *but now you know.*

Douglas's muscles twitched at odd, opposing angles and his bones quivered at unusual frequencies. They were in transition, he realized.

Who in God's name are you?

Let's go in, said Chaplain Cloth, *pushing open the door of the Marigold.*

The smallish pub had most of its tables and bar crowded with patrons. Douglas attempted a glance to the storeroom door. Out of habit, it was always the first place he looked when he walked into the Marigold. His eyes wouldn't move there this time; Cloth focused on something else: the studded wooden club mounted over William Gray's typical table.

The club was a recurring item in Douglas's past dreams but he'd never thought much about it though. Come to think of it, he'd never even written the bludgeon down in his notes. Now he (they: him and this Cloth person) headed straight for William's table.

Douglas had never gotten used to how large William's face was, or how thick his arms were, how the silver watch he wore looked like a struggle of steel against ever-widening flesh. The man was freakish in size, with a personality to match.

A young student pushed back in his chair from the table. "You can suck my boaby, William," he said. His face was drunken red and eyes bloodshot.

William tapped over the kid's king piece on the chessboard. "Oh sober yourself up. You play with a handicap, disnae mean you have to *be* handicapped. Now bring me another one of these sorry rum and Cokes."

"Get sodded." The kid slapped the high backed chair forward and made for the bar. William laughed merrily like a fairy tale giant who'd just gobbled up a child. Carefully, he went to setting back all the pieces on his board.

Douglas/Cloth stood before him. William lifted an eye for a moment. "You what they call *gothic*?" He redirected the faces of the knights. "That's a place three blocks from here."

When they didn't answer, William looked up and a goofy smile formed on his large mouth of crooked coffee teeth. "Oh shit, what are you doing with all that face paint on, Doug? You look like a damned clown."

"I have a fever," said Cloth/Douglas.

"That so? Well, the medicine's behind the bar, you twat."

"Can I play?"

"No," answered William matter-of-factly. "You suck at chess. I'd rather sit here and pick my ass. Go on with you, Doug. I'm not in the mood."

"I've gotten better."

"It'd have to be a *lot* better." William turned his face sideways, smile fading to mild disgust. "You've done a messy workup on yourself. You got two different contact lenses. Fever my arse. Are you on speed or somethin'?"

"I'd like to play." Cloth/Douglas sat. "And I'd like to borrow that, just for tonight, then it can go back on the wall."

William followed his gaze to the trophy club mounted on the wall. He huffed in disbelief. "You've got lead paint on the brain too."

"What if I beat you in less than ten minutes?"

"The fuck you will. Even sober, that'd be piss and swill."

"If I win, you have to let me take the club tonight." William looked alarmed. "The hell you will."

"Are you scared of losing? Don't worry, I won't put a scratch on your precious club. I promise."

"Why do you want it?"

"Just do it, William," someone shouted. A few tables around them had grown interested.

With a sigh, William checked his big watch, and then, he moved a knight out. "Go then, shit talker."

Cloth bent over the chess board, studying it.

"Hurry up," William said with a smirk that hinted already of victory. "You'll sing praises through your arsehole about me tomorrow, or I'll stomp that powdered face of yours."

Cloth had already positioned his knight. William didn't think about the next move and sent out a pawn. The two exchanged moves fiercely, each piece snapping on the table. Douglas watched his hands move: controlled. Cloth systematically lost their queen, and then a bishop, and a rook, while only picking up William's two bishops. It didn't look to be enough to bring down his defenses.

Five minutes had already passed.

The big man wore a slobbery rum and Coke grin. "You know, fair Douglas, there are good sacrifices of your pieces and bad sacrifices of your pieces and then," he began snickering, which turned into an obnoxious chortling, "then there's out and out genocide!"

A few others hooted with him, but Cloth continued to play. Douglas watched as William swept up another rook in his mitt. Without pause, Cloth moved a bishop and declared, "Check."

"Sad," tisked William and moved out of check. Cloth moved his knight. "Check mate."

William had been reaching for his queen, but realized he'd made a mistake going to claim that last rook. He studied the checkered table. After a few minutes he shook his tremendous head.

"We were playing too fast," he concluded. "Yes. Too fast. Clearly."

Cloth turned the brass key to remove the glass over the trophy, set the pane gently on the ground near the table, and then took down the club. William watched, crestfallen, like a man watching his own open-heart surgery. Cloth rested the club on the table to admire it. The black and orange eyes twinkled in the bronze plate hammered into the side of its handle. "That was fun."

The moment was awkward. William seemed near to tears. Cloth slipped the phone out of Douglas's pants pocket and hummed a few bars of some unknown song.

"Douglas?" a woman's voice said from their shoulder. Cloth turned.

From within himself Douglas stared at his wife.

Red eyed, gray-black hair in wild disarray, Susan stood there, trembling, shaking her head. "You—that was you in those photos from Fia's phone. Wasn't it?" With a questioning look around her, she grasped his shoulder and her teeth ground together. "Wasn't it? You tell me, you prick."

Douglas cowered inside his own mind. Susan had slapped him silly once after a football game for running their car into the tree in their front yard. Her slaps had hurt more than some men's fists and he could still imagine the points of her knuckles. "What are you talking about, dear?" Cloth's voice sounded sarcastic on Douglas's lips.

Susan snatched his ear and pulled his head toward her angry, whispering lips. "After so many times I could have been unfaithful to you...you great, bastard, shitface fuck! She's a *child* and clearly did this to get at me, not to—"

"I sent the photos."

Susan let go of him and took a step back in shock. "What?"

"I thought you'd enjoy some of the angles." Cloth/Douglas picked up Fia's cell phone and tossed it. The phone struck Susan's chest and fell to the floor. Douglas wailed from inside, but it was a yawn under a waterfall. He'd remembered messing with the phone outside the pub but had no idea that Cloth had been sending the photos to Susan.

Now Susan took another step back, so appalled and drunk she couldn't find the words at first. "I'm going to take you for everything, Douglas. You won't even get your woodworking tools."

"Oh get sodded. Stick this up your cobwebby cunt and spin, you jealous hag." He shoved the club toward her. Susan swept it away from him with a disgusted gasp. He ignored the murderous look in her eyes and turned back to his chess partner. "Now there, William, was that a good game or what?"

William shouted a protest that was too late. The club connected first with Douglas's middle back, knocking his body forward, the chess table tipping into William's enormous gut. The glass pane from the trophy smashed somewhere on the ground, below the violence.

"Funny now? Think it's funny now?" Susan screamed. "Fuck you, hag," he blared through the blinding pain;

Cloth laughed merrily in his mind.

Another strike, this one less accurate, glanced off Douglas's arm and Susan struck the table behind her, sending three men bolting from their chairs and pretzel mix scattering in the air. Douglas slipped off his chair just in time to encounter a blow to the face.

Immediately, Douglas faded inside his own mind, the last images in his life, his blood speckled wife bringing the club down harder and harder, as though to drive a railroad spike. He whimpered, became a clear pinpoint in his subconscious, and then blinked to nothing.

The corporal flesh belonged to the chaplain now.

His face fluttered with nerve damage. He could hear the clatter of the club on the floor and next the sounds of Susan's capture, her earsplitting yells as somebody hauled her out of the pub.

"Can you breathe, Doug?" someone asked. "Burning up in here," he said. "Why is it so hot?"

"He said he had a fever before," William stated, somewhere in the darkness.

"He's not looking good. Bloody hell, are those his teeth lying everywhere about?"

"Pretzels."

"So hot...I'm dying here," said Cloth. "Get some ice for his head, for chrissakes."

"Ice maker's broken."

"What?"

"Remember, the gin spilled in the back of the machine when Katherine went loony. Hasn't worked since."

"That's why my rum and Cokes have been flat all night. For fuck's sake..."

"Yes, let's worry about your fuckin' drink."

"Hey, fuck you."

"I feel like I'm going to black out from the heat, lads," said Cloth. "Can you put me near the storeroom?"

"She got your back good, Doug. Dun't think we should move you. You'll be fine here, just don't try and talk for now."

"Please, do this for me."

Jon the bartender piped up. "What is he on about? Nobody's going in *there*."

"Do it," instructed William. His guilt was palpable in the silence. "Just open up the cold room, Jon. Whatever makes him comfortable, while we wait, just crack the door a little."

Cloth pushed up on his hands and straightened his back. "My back's okay, I'm just so...hot."

"See there," demanded William, "he just needs help. None of us's doctors. Help me, Jon."

"Fuck," Jon breathed. "Someone call yet?"

"Aye," someone distant answered.

They lifted up his pummeled body, William grabbing under his arms and Jon taking his ankles, and carried Cloth behind the bar. He made no sound—he had enough damage to this human shell to invoke the transition—they just had to get him inside the storeroom. Jon pushed back on the door and a blast of unnaturally frigid air caused him to yell out in alarm. William lost hold of Douglas. The mangled body hit the floor, nose and remaining front teeth striking first, and at the moment he made contact, the gateway to the Old Domain tore open the back wall.

Douglas's internal bleeding forged a river for Chaplain Cloth to fully arrive into this world. Muscles laced together, younger and stronger, and fat cells shrunk and tightened. Bones fed off the blood's commanding design and grew denser.

In the mirror over the bar he could see it all. Douglas's faded salt and pepper hair lost its curl and went straight and shined like black glass. Skin that was already pale, lost its imperfections, its moles, its coarse arm hair, and turned to a shark-belly white.

Jon leapt over Douglas's transforming body and scrambled over the bar. William moved nimbly behind like a man two hundred pounds lighter.

Scores of pumpkin vines rushed out after the two men and coiled around the room. A flutter of rubbery black terrors erupted with it, diving for the bewildered humans running for the door. William tripped and twisted his ankle. His chin slammed down on a vine and he bit his tongue bloody. Nobody turned back for him.

Chaplain Cloth stood. An immaculate black suit knitted around his body, sewn from the darkness. The suit accentuated his white skin, making it look healthier than it deserved; he wore his new flesh like a man in his earlier thirties. An orange handkerchief roared up from his breast pocket and Cloth plucked at it merrily. He strolled out into the pub's main area, which had become a mess of upturned tables and thick jade vines already budding with pumpkins.

William Gray fought to get untangled from the vines, huffing and puffing, near to cardiac distress. Cloth whistled for his attention and he stopped. There were large tears sliding from William's eyes down the slopes of his wide cheeks.

Cloth bent, seized a rook piece on the ground and held it up. "Care for another go?"

After only a second's thought William turned for the door, bounding expertly over some of the larger vines, and ran outside. Cloth followed after and turned over the sign in the window to closed.

None of them would remember the events of that night, nor would anybody return to the pub. The Old Domain decided what it wished to reveal and what it wished to withhold from the world of man. The monster with the black and orange eyes could only leave behind nightmares and mysteries.

For now.

Chaplain Cloth turned over the rook in his white hands, thinking about how much it resembled a column. "Must I forever play this game the same way?"

He headed back to the gateway in the storeroom, where he would wait and gain his strength for Halloween. Before soaking into the void, he flicked the chess piece into the shadows.

OCTOBER 26TH THIS YEAR

ONE

Teresa spotted the agent. The Arc was a wiry Caucasian man with a fully shaven head, made blue by his thick hair follicles. On his chin hung a black goatee, thin in the middle, the sides of it like drooping horns. Making a show of not looking in her direction, he placed an iPad on his lap and began to poke it every which way. A droning female voice echoed throughout the airport. *Gate 511 departures please standby for gate change. Gate 511 departures please standby for gate change.* The Arc turned out his arm and looked at his expensive wrist watch.

Teresa picked up a fashion magazine with a young anorexic woman in a purple dress, which had scarcely enough fabric for a napkin. Teresa lifted the magazine to the level of her mouth. "There's one across from the currency exchange," she told Patty. Patty had her shoulder to Teresa, her face secreted by rich golden hair. Unlike her partner, Patty really was reading a magazine. "The Church?" she asked.

If only, thought Teresa. "Office of Arcane Phenomenon." *Patty didn't look up from her magazine but her right eye*brow lifted. "It isn't him, is it?"

"No it isn't *him*. Is that why they found us? Did you tell—?"

"Hardly, and I don't appreciate your tone, by the way." Patty swatted a thin magazine page aside.

"Stop being so sensitive." Teresa took a Hershey's kiss from her pocket. "I'm going to have a walk."

"And the Messenger's letter?"

Popping the kiss in her mouth, "No, you go grab it. Regroup at Air France, latest departure. I'll unfold the other Arcs into the airport."

"Not if Byron's with them you won't."

Teresa shoved the fashion magazine sideways into the overstuffed rack. "I'm not as impressed with him as you."

"Gimme a break." Patty walked farther into the gift shop aisle and disappeared around a cardboard display of Los Angeles Lakers T-shirts.

Teresa headed through the other side of the store toward the large rain-slashed windows of the international terminal. The downpour colored the outside world in dark rending blues where the cloud cover intensified and where the sunlight struggled to penetrate. The slapping sounds of water descending on LAX registered like an assault, a war. It didn't help the bleak mood Teresa already found herself in at this time of year.

Halloween was coming.

She walked briskly through the crowds, eyes flitting back and forth to make the other agents. The Messenger had long ago provided them with photographs and backgrounds of all OAP agents, but they would likely be in disguise now. Fortunately the bald man's unique goatee had given him away, for he normally wore his hair shoulder length. Dumb of him not to cut the chin growth, especially since it looked so unattractive.

The other agents might not have any of the same giveaways, but Teresa would find them. All of them.

Even Byron Telamon.

There were several shelves of stuffed animal jack-o' lanterns in the gift shop. Patty thought about the term *stuffed animals* and studied the fang bearing pumpkins once more. Just looking at them made the scar tissue twitch in her right calf. The soleus muscle injury was supposed to be fully recovered, but her mind didn't always agree with her body. The jack-o'-lanterns glared on.

Stuffed animals.

Animals…yeah, that's about right.

Patty rubbed the painful pits of her eyes. She'd had about three hours of sleep, the thoughts of last Halloween on her mind, as well as the missions of the past eight months in Australia, Japan and then in the States. The total of Church assassinations had to be a record for them this year, although it wasn't something Patty felt proud of. No, in fact, it was the type of thing that kept her up through the witching hours of the night, staring up at the ceiling in one of their bad motels, reliving every ghastly moment in atrocious detail. Every memory stirred something in her, like a razor broth in her stomach. Patty Middleton had a self-realization she hadn't imagined before.

I'm a mass murderer.

Teresa always told Patty to keep focus on the cold truth about Halloween and hopefully that would keep her sane, make the killing easier. The mantra normally worked. Patty knew what those stuffed animal pumpkins on the shelf really could be—a psychotic shard of awareness lodged in Western society's mind, one that didn't hurt until somebody removed it. The holiday had always been a colossal cover-up and on the entire world, still worked its secretive magic well.

At one time she'd thought the same way about Halloween as the next person. But ten years ago that view had stopped for Patty Middleton, the day a fifty-year-old woman named Teresa Celeste showed up on her parents' doorstep with instructions in hand—a letter written by the same mysterious person who'd sent communications to Patty's family for years, always warning them that after their daughter's tenth birthday she would be leaving them, forever.

That person, the Messenger, had written such letters since well before Patty was born, before even Teresa was born, and long before that, for the unknown number of other Nomads who'd come and gone throughout the centuries. Yes, generations had done the bidding of a handwriting ghost, to preserve the ignorance of what Halloween was, following every instruction of every letter.

One such letter had been planted in this very airport. Finding it was inevitable, because it would find them, not the other way around. There would be no leaving it behind either, because the letter would appear and reappear until they opened it. So it waited out there. Patty could feel it like an impending doom.

You're being silly, *she chided herself.* Think of the letter as ongoing research.

A bit of guilt washed over her. For two months now, behind Teresa's back, she'd been researching like a mad woman to discover any leads on the Messenger's whereabouts. It may have been in vain, but as Patty became older and the deaths she dealt piled up endlessly, the only solution that presented itself was clear. She had to find out who this Messenger was. Then, with his or her cover blown, maybe Patty Middleton and Teresa Celeste would no longer be indentured servants, no longer Nomads.

Lost in these dark-hopeful thoughts, Patty bumped into someone. She was an older lady—seventies, skeleton-fragile, in a knitted pink-purple-green sweater that only an elder would wear—a lump of terror fisted in Patty's throat. In another decade Teresa would be seventy. She would be just as fragile and as weak as this woman was, with drooping skin and red rimmed eyes that looked exhausted behind the cataract gauze. How would advanced age work in their nomadic type of life? Patty couldn't imagine the Messenger would keep Teresa to fight on Halloween into her seventies. Teresa would have to stop being a Nomad someday. *Right?*

The old lady stretched for an I ⊚ L.A. coffee mug and looked askance to the register. The red-faced man behind the counter pretended not to see her and languidly stirred ramen noodles in a Styrofoam cup stained orange.

Patty touched the woman's shoulder. "Ma'am, do you need help?"

Her rheumy eyes sparkled. "Oh thank you, Miss."

Patty held up one finger to confirm and the woman mimicked her. "Yes, need just one."

Patty stepped on a lower shelf for a boost but at five foot one she still had quite a distance to make up. The mugs were obviously overstock, meant to be moved down to another shelf and still stranded high above. Patty's fingers grazed the mug— and her frustration instinctively caused her to seek the cold core in her brain, the place that brought ghost matter from the Old Domain into this world.

No, she thought. No mantles here. She made another attempt

and actually pushed the mug farther away. Well maybe... *Teresa would be upset for building something so unnecessary and impulsive. They normally wouldn't draw ghost matter to create a mantle unless they were practicing or defending the*
Heart of the Harvest.

Still though, Teresa wasn't here and Patty reminded herself that she wasn't, nor would she ever be the same as her partner. Patty drew the ghost matter and created a perfect square mantle, a little less than the size of a nickel, to push the mug closer to her fingertips. The mug slid forward and she let the mantle dissolve. Something odd wavered through her mind. It was impossible to tell if this happened every time she built a mantle because memory of the sensation was immediately lost once you stopped—building a mantle was always a new experience.

She grasped the mug's handle and brought it down. The lady, too short and bent to notice the mug's short voyage into Patty's hand, thanked her profusely and at once fell into a lengthy account about her step-granddaughter's infatuation with Los Angeles. Patty didn't hear any of it though. Movement outside the shop had taken her attention.

A tall, well-built Latino man came toward the gift shop, his footsteps swift and his right hand planted on his hip, under his sports coat. Patty recognized him as an Arc—one of those OAP agents from the Messenger's photographs. His hair was shaggier than it had been in the photo and his intense blue eyes were now an intense, fake looking green from colored contact lenses.

"Excuse me, ma'am." Patty gave the lady a gentle squeeze on the shoulder and ducked out of the store.

The man gained on her. The government agents were not their enemies, but were not friends either; the Nomads had no allies except for the Messenger. That was law to them. In such a public place, this had to be done right.

Patty touched the cold place in her mind again and drew ghost matter. She had to make sure the mantle hit home with mild force or it could kill him. Not all the Arcs seemed to know, or perhaps even believe in the Nomads' ability. This one obviously didn't or he wouldn't have been charging after her like this. And he wouldn't see the mantle coming. As far as Patty knew, mantles were invisible to everybody in this world except for her. Not even Teresa, with all her experience and years of building, could see their structure. Coordinated movement of mantles was possible though, regardless of sight—Patty's brain had an instinctual map of the atmosphere and the mantle cut through it like a foreign body.

The invisible projectile left her so quickly, it fluttered her hair. Out of the corner of her eye she saw the silver pane increase speed toward the agent. Then a tremendous clap echoed in the hall and cries of surprise followed. Patty spared one look over her shoulder and saw the Arc trying to pull himself up with the unsolicited aid of two teenage guys. He was begging them off and trying to get moving again. "Man, your nose is bleeding," one guy in a sideways Raiders hat pointed out.

Patty quickened her pace into the flowing airport. She'd lost the agent, but there would be others. Time to move quickly. She'd messed around long enough.

Get the letter. Get back to Teresa.

How in the hell had the Arcs found them?

Patty tried to think back to the weeks leading up to today. The Messenger sent them to raze one of the Church of Midnight's oldest chapels out in the Mojave Desert. It wasn't much of a job really. There were no Bishops, no Inner Circle in residence, and, not surprisingly, the three acolytes living in the old mining shafts had little idea about the Church of Midnight's true function. They weren't even really thugs, just a few squatters hoping for another contribution check from the church. It was a sign of the times for the slowly expiring Church, because there was a lot of history and relics still in the Mojave chapel and in years past there might have been well over five or six hundred church members living there. Patty almost felt it a shame to bring a thousand boulders crashing down on top of all of it.

Killing the acolytes wouldn't have made much a difference, and that had been extremely difficult for Teresa to sign off on, but Patty did manage to convince her to spare the three men. They drove the dumbfounded group back to civilization (if Vegas could be considered such) and released them. It wasn't much of a victory for Patty but she was glad to enjoy a blood free campaign for a change.

Patty scanned the Traveler's Aid Office, and let a frustrated sigh go. The Arc was somewhere north of her, mixed in with the crowd, fighting his way through. She'd tagged his body with that mantle. When the mantle got closer, she'd feel it.

Now what to do?

She sat down on a planter. A punk rocker sat on the edge nearby, outfitted in a leather vest, his arms flowing with tattoo sleeves, his ears with wide holes and his head with a disarrangement of spiked green and blue hair. A treacherous acne shadow went from his left temple down the side of his jaw, ending at a pointed chin. He yanked at his vest, which made a squeaky sound that was anything but intimidating. After a moment, he shifted his weight and passed some gas.

Lovely.

This must have been his personal goodbye to Patty. When he stood, Patty noticed a black envelope resting just behind where he'd been sitting. She picked it up and took a closer look at the envelope. Dust and grime smeared its surface. Clearly this thing had been somewhere for a long while before Johnny Rotten sat on it. Even at the adhesive seam there appeared to be a tangle of smashed cobwebs. Patty used her finger to tear through the envelope. The vellum crunched as she lifted the note out. Some of it flaked away like a potato crisp.

Glasgow. Book a flight for tomorrow. Our communication has been compromised.

—Messenger

At the bottom of the parchment, a blob of dark brown traced the edge. It looked a lot like blood but it could be a coffee stain for all she knew. She peered closer at it, studying its color.

"Hey you!"

Patty's mind gripped a mean, razor lined mantle and sent it speeding out.

Teresa brought her own mantle and the two intercepted

each other in a cascade of red-gold sparks that only Patty saw.

Teresa moved her head back and raised her eyebrows. "Whoa there, no more Sour Patch Kids for you."

Patty rubbed her chest and smugly handed over the note. "Sorry. Look there. I think there's some blood on the bottom."

Teresa carefully regarded the discoloration. "Might be."

"It might be the Messenger's blood."

Teresa handed back the note. "Glasgow, huh? Haven't been there in years."

"You don't think we should even try to look into it? What could it hurt?"

"The Messenger wouldn't be so careless to leave blood on a note. You know that by now. It's probably just some random stain."

"We could still analyze what made the stain. This could be our chance to do some tracking. I mean, after Halloween of course..."

Teresa stood with a wince. She rubbed her left knee and gritted her teeth. Patty realized just then that Teresa wore the blue blouse she'd gotten her for Christmas. She'd been apprehensive about the deep neckline of the blouse, because it was a little too "young woman" looking, according to her. Patty thought she looked great in it, even if it was too nice to wear with just ratty jeans and tennis shoes, but then Teresa had never been one to go out of her way to impress others.

"I think we should look into a flight," said Teresa. "Let's go. Maybe on the way you can explain to me how the OAP found us."

"I told you I don't—"

"There," yelled a lady's voice up the ramp. "She's the one." The old lady from the gift shop stood there. Dried blood trailed down the side of her face. A TSA representative spoke into a walkie-talkie and hurried toward them, leaving behind the woman and the store cashier, both dumbfounded.

All passengers standby at designated gates. All passengers standby at designated gates. Thank you.

Teresa and Patty took off into the crowd. They rounded a hall and their feet echoed down a tile corridor.

"Where are the other Arcs?"

"Western corridor," Teresa huffed. "I hope."

Across the expanse of the international terminal Patty caught sight of the gift shop from earlier. Pieces of flaming debris littered the ground outside of the side exit. Among other goods, some of the stuffed animal pumpkins lay there, darkened and smoldering. Several TSA and police officers were siphoning the crowd around the mess.

Teresa's eyes widened. "What did you do Patty?"

"Nothing," she said, running ahead. "I didn't do anything."

"They'll have all the exits. We better hide."

Patty saw a bathroom. "There."

Teresa hawked over her as Patty knuckled her eyes, trying to crush the tears away. She said softly, "It happened again, didn't it? With the mantles...the explosions?"

Instead of answering, Patty readjusted her weight on the side of the toilet lid. Teresa had one foot behind the pipe and one on the lid. For now that seemed to give her enough balance. There were a few other women in the bathroom, all of them using the opposite bank of stalls. Toilet paper banged in circuits. A cell phone had gone off.

"Something is causing this, Patty. Maybe you've worn yourself out and you can't control them like you used to."

"I don't know. It doesn't feel any different."

"Maybe other things are making you tired. You've been hard at work for the past couple months. I'm not stupid. You're always looking for internet service, coming back to the room late. After all this time, you have to know—you *have* to understand that we'll never find out who the Messenger is." When Patty didn't say anything, Teresa added, "Or is this about that chapel in the desert? I gave you what you wanted. We let those acolytes go free."

Patty snorted. "Yeah, we're practically saints. I don't know how we managed to find it in our hearts not to pull down another building on unsuspecting people."

"Church of Midnight," Teresa corrected.

The mantle surrounding them had a small aperture for

air at the top. The field of ghost-matter brought from the Old Domain obscured them and muffled their voices, but it was too heavy to push—so they couldn't just walk out of the airport undetected. Besides which, if someone happened to bump into something invisible, that would draw even more attention to them. Hiding inside the mantle was necessary. That's what Patty kept telling herself. It wouldn't accidentally blow them up. *That old woman might have died. If she'd been closer to the mantle's explosion maybe...*

"Do you have control of this one?" Teresa asked, as though reading Patty's thoughts.

"God, just fuck off."

Patty felt her jaw ring smartly. Teresa had never slapped her before. Her first impulse was to hit back, but her shock only allowed for her to glare back at her partner. There was no apology in Teresa's pretty almond eyes. No guilt in her sun-weathered, sixty-year-old face. "You better decide what the hell it is you're doing wrong with building mantles, or you will screw us one day, Patrice. Royally. I'm goddamn serious about this."

"You done lecturing?"

"That was the preface."

Patty touched her stinging cheek. "You don't have the—"

"I have *every right*," Teresa finished. "You—"

Just then Patty's mind clenched. She could feel the mantle from earlier, just outside the door. Using it as a mirror to cast images into her brain, she had a view of the hall outside the bathroom. Several TSA and four Arcs stood at the ready. One Arc held his credentials up for another man to read. The words *Homeland Security* could be heard in the mix of hurried explanations.

"You see them?" asked Teresa.

The door to the women's restroom whined as it opened. "Security. Please come out of the restroom," said a man's voice.

Byron.

Patty closed her eyes rather than look at Teresa's self-satisfied expression.

He went on, "We need everybody out. Please do so quickly." Two toilets flushed. Doors opened. Murmurs followed. "This way," said Byron politely. "Thank you for your help, your cooperation, your speed."

The door shut. For a moment, there was only silence.

Stall doors opened as his footsteps fell in the hollow space. "We had a guy come to us. Church of Midnight—" A stall door kicked open across the room. "—said you two were over in Vegas. Sold us the info. He's come to us before with some buzz. Not what you'd call a devout follower, but he was plenty pissed that you caved in his little desert nest."

"How'd they know?" Patty whispered.

"You can't figure it out? Shit, the whole time in the car you were talking about the Wynn hotel when we took those dumbasses to the city. I knew we should have just buried them."

Patty gripped her forehead and shook her head.

"I got to review the casino security tapes myself," Byron noted. Another door squeaked open. "You're a pair of stunning broads, I must say. Easy to pick you out. It was nice to see you again, and so nearby, at that. The department almost had one of my guys tail you here but I knew you'd notice. So I took the liberty. I think I'm still the only fellow who can sneak up on you two…" Byron laughed but there was nothing real on it. "Come on girls, just some questions. You know I have your backs."

Their stall rattled.

Something slim and metallic came through the space between the door and its frame. The lock easily popped out and the door bumped the mantle. Patty narrowed its width, but the damage was done. Byron stood outside, strong and tall and with unbreakable good looks. Marble veins of premature gray streaked his dark hair. It made him all the more sexy, damn him anyway. He had his firearm holstered, but the loop had been drawn off and his hand poised over the handle. Patty found herself hating his tight smile, even though she loved it sometimes. "Yoo-hoo?" he said. He poked a lock-picking device back into his coat pocket.

They remained still, for whatever good that would do them now.

"Pete," Byron said into a mic in his lapel. "Kill the lights."

The restroom door opened, a man leaned in and hit the

bank of light switches.

Byron took a spectral pen light from his other pocket and shined it into the stall. The light reflected off the ghost matter in a wide gold and blue star that settled at once around their shapes, and although there would be no clarity, two figures could be seen behind the watery prism.

"You owe me," he said. "For the last two years, after all I've done for you girls, you owe me big time. One little interview with the Nomads to appease the department. Just one. What do you say?"

TWO

Evil had its eyes on Camden Amherst. He stared up into the sky. The stars were black punctures in an endless orange inferno. Upon him, a smothering feeling set in. Burning, and stinging, and wrenching, and flattening flesh over a brittle layer of bone: that's what Camden had been reduced to in the presence of this enormous thing. He looked away, fighting for a breath, just one pitiful squeeze of one lung, something, anything, to put out the burn and restore his clarity, and if he could not seek that one breath, he prayed to pass out and wipe those black stars from his black mind, oh but fuck it all, *what was the point*? We were all just so many death-tears cried into a tangerine soup poured into the fissures of every fissure, filling even the cellular structures of all matter in existence with that intense bright evil, and Camden imagined what they could be on the other side of the other side, the reverse of what he was seeing, not black on orange, but orange stars on a black sky—inflamed cysts poking through blistering pitch.

Then he realized that breathing wouldn't be necessary, that he'd succeeded in pulling his sight away, and his thoughts and his memories.

Away.

Away from It.

Now he was at a table. Not *at*. On. On a table. Somewhere he heard his father bellowing about "fucking up his prepositions!" His ears stung at the memory of his father's quick cuffings. It made him cry. He missed that pain. He missed, oh God, did he miss his father. He missed living in a world with such an elegant, simple structure—you only had to make one person happy, not the entire world, not the whole bloody world…

At the table he laid upon, Camden could hear voices from those seated at each blackened chair. They were real voices. Each syllable rang so real it felt like blasts of icy water in his face, sobering him from his terror—nothing that real sounding could be cruel—these were intelligent voices. They meant to help him. Didn't they?

The voices came from people in the chairs but he didn't see anyone sitting on the sun bright cushions. The conversations were casual sounding, carrying the air of adult sophistication, but the words weren't English, or any other language with which Camden was familiar. Babblings. Droolings. Cackling and swallowing and wheezy coughing. Some of the bizarre words bounced like hiccups and others dived down into bass notes, like the smashing of pipe organ keys. And it all sounded civilized. Proper. The chaotic mumbling had organization to its statements, questions and answers.

And then something spilled over his chest. Camden reactively pawed at himself. He glanced down. Through a surgical opening in his torso, his guts dangled over his sides like gray jungle snakes. Unseen hands lifted one loop of intestines and some invisible blade delicately sliced a segment off. He gasped.

It was a weak sound, and it reminded him he wasn't the hero people thought he was.

A murmured question followed.

He understood what was asked but heard no specific words.

"No please, have it, please, enjoy it," he told the phantom.

Enjoy me.

Camden sent out the same message to the rest of the table, but they were way ahead of him. Both of his maimed legs wobbled and danced at the end of the table as though two opposing forces wrestled to get the choicer bits. Something critical was said about the bubbly fat around the thigh.

"I apologize. It's that I wanted to exercise more, this past year—"

A question floated above him. He tried to track where it came from. The dining room was dark, so terrifying and dark. "What was that?"

Camden's eyes were soundly plucked from his head. A few moments later he could hear the squishing sound of teeth chewing through them. They gagged and began spitting out pieces of eyeball.

"Wasn't much for carrots."

The joke came out lopsided, because an unseen hand suddenly grabbed his jaw and ripped it through his face. Something jagged and covered in a bitter acid sawed through the back of his tongue. Shock had Camden pinned, and pain waited somewhere. It was abject, but wasn't dead. It would eventually arrive. It would be abrupt—

Now.

He wanted to twist his body and scream. There was nothing left of him physically, he'd given all of himself away, and he couldn't make a move. Yet the ghosts asked for more. They weren't pleased with what he had to offer.

There should be more.

Why couldn't he have provided more?

Camden asked for forgiveness and they growled at him. He apologized for apologizing. Shame gave him a new form. He was a garden slug, running with slime and earth and stupidity, and he had nothing to offer the universe. He was a parasite sucking on the heart of a madman.

Shivering in the darkness, a bony finger flicked his ear and he bolted up. Chaplain Cloth leaned over him, one eye black, one eye orange. "We need to chat, Archbishop. Your Church has crumbled and I no longer have any use for you hunting the Heart of the Harvest. My Children and I will attend to that task, but there is another way your congregation can help us. Let's begin with your Priestess of Midnight."

"What…" he swallowed. "What about her?"

Cloth smiled. Evil had its eyes on Camden Amherst.

"Fuckin' hell!" Camden shot up in his dampened sheets. He crushed his hand against his face and pulled air greedily through his nostrils. Despite the absurd, grotesque things that had occurred, there hadn't been a moment in the dream when he questioned reality. Now though, with true reality returned, he felt inclined to question the cold stone and brick room, the glossy black furniture, and beside him the redhead prostitute still sleeping off the champagne, one breast above the dark sheets, a cherry nipple pert from the drafty chamber. It all looked like an amateur's first painting. After a second, Camden averted his eyes. He imagined he wouldn't like it if somebody stared at him while he slept.

For a moment he buried his face in his hands and then, one at a time, Camden swung his legs off the bed. He propped his head up on one hand, trying to wake more fully. His beard felt scratchy and uneven. He needed to sculpt it a bit and tie it with some new bows. People liked that. Bows in his beard made him looked amiable, not exactly like a leader but like a silly heart you could confide in; otherwise he looked gruff and unapproachable.

Was that your goal? *He wondered.* To be Uncle Chuckles? Or an influential Archbishop of Midnight?

Fuck.

A chill broke out over his body. Chaplain Cloth had spoken. To him. To Camden Amherst. The orders were clear now. He just had to communicate with the other sect of the church. But it wasn't like he could just pick up the phone and call them. Contacting the Church of Morning wasn't a light job. *It meant killing people to provide conduit bodies.* Camden didn't want to order someone dead again so soon after his last interworld meeting. Years had gone by and he was able to overlook a few dead acolytes, but now it just felt...cruel. Unjust. And above all, with their numbers dwindling, counterproductive.

He tapped his lips in thought. Rather than using conduit bodies, maybe he could inform the Church of Morning in another manner? What though? He decided he would avoid the matter for the moment.

Absently, Camden petted the prostitute's red-gold hair. The onyx marble nightstand had four different types of champagne bottles, his cell phone and a torn johnny wrapper. She didn't care where he chose to stick his cock, but she'd been picky about the champagne. One after the other, Camden finally had one sent up that pleased her, but he couldn't imagine she'd had more than half a glass.

He snatched his phone off the nightstand and called his domestic head, Fraser Thompson.

"Archbishop, good morning," a voice quickly answered. "Do you want a rundown of your engagements today?"

Camden scratched again at his beard. "Sure."

"Holly Thorpe needs ye to check the plumbing in her chamber—"

"And we can't have our maintenance do that?"

"Ye promised her specifically. Remember?"

"Oh?"

"And Margaret Daubes, Ted Brodsky and Gill Crane want to learn how to administer the Gauntlet on testers. They have been instructed prior but like how ye explain the rites rather than the Priestess."

Camden puffed in annoyance. "Alisyn isn't very descriptive, I know. Okay then. Anything else?"

"Yes. The demonstration ye wanted to give Mina on how yer marrow blossoms open at two different frequencies. She wanted to test the balance of the different petals."

"Am I some guinea pig with straw sticking to its ass? Doesn't that damn apothecary have a text she can read on the subject? The balance of my blossoms is terrific. My lungs feel fine."

"I related that already for ye."

"Didn't satisfy the nag, eh? Can I put her off?"

"Of course, Archbishop. And I would," replied Fraser, "but I will remind ye of the promise to stop by in a couple of days."

"Christ," Camden said and sighed, "well, add that too."

"Ye also committed to lunch with Duncun Stedden, Richard Bizzer, Sarah—"

"Set up a group lunch," Camden finished. "Anything else?"

"Letters of release for ten—sorry, twelve people." Fraser paused. "And I still say ye let me sort out their differences. We can't afford more defections. Our numbers of acolytes have fallen into a sorry state and more than half of these people are Inner Circle. This is a deep problem for us, Archbishop."

"I don't want people who don't want us. I will write the letters. No retaliations unless they break their oath of silence."

"I understand."

"Oh, can you send down breakfast for my friend?"

"Of course. And ye, Archbishop?"

"Not hungry. I'll make up for it later at lunch. Please try to find the Priestess of Midnight when you get a moment."

"At once," said Fraser. Camden thought he heard a trace of disappointment in his right hand's voice, but it was too subtle to be certain.

They hung up and Camden stared at the lump in his bed. He used to be able to have women in the Church come to him, *willingly*. Since the congregation had thinned over the past decade he now had to resort to high class tramps. He had to play by the rules of a normal man again. Strange. Ascending to this status had been the high point of his church career, and now he wished he didn't have the title. It brought his powerlessness more to light.

Aye, they don't know how strong I really am.

"Because you don't ever show them, you arse," he whispered.

Camden took a deep breath and opened his mind to the calling of Cloth's children. Millions of infinitesimal marrow blossoms opened inside his lungs and filled with power. The children sang about the Eternal Feast and the thanksgiving to that feast. Today, they sang also of the gateway to the Old Domain. When the sacrifice was made, it would open wide. The two Columns would fit in its threshold and the way would be open forever, worlds flowing through worlds.

The Columns...that reminded him. Last week Fraser had shown him the article about the Pillar of Ginsau brought to the St. Mungo Museum. Two Midnight Historians and their know-it-all apothecary Mina had confirmed this relic as having the best potential to support this world's side of the gateway. Much had been written about the Pillar of Ginsau in the archive of the Archbishops, and the pillar had been in the hands of the Church back in the late fourteenth century. Now it was in Glasgow, right in their neck of the woods. By the photos, the column looked quite huge though. How they would ever be able to steal such a thing, especially with their limited capabilities, was up for massive deliberation between Camden and his advisors. Ten years ago, maybe, *but now? No way.*

One thing at a time though. The dream.

Chaplain Cloth.

As much as Camden would have liked to do it all on his own, the Church of Morning needed to know what Cloth had told him. It wasn't right to hoard information to gain status over the other church sect; these were dangerous times and knowledge had to be shared between the two churches.

Camden looked around for a scrap of paper on the nightstand and in its drawers. Nothing. He didn't want to bother Fraser again. The man was probably halfway up the stairs now and would have to double back.

Camden got an idea. Perhaps it was as easy as picking up his phone.

What the hell, he thought. I can get another phone, and I haven't used the blossom like this in a while...

He put a text message into his cell phone, trying to keep his English simple since Kennen's reading comprehension of this world's script was limited.

Archbishop Kennen,

Chaplain Cloth has spoken to me in dream. The Priestess of Midnight must be granted the power of All-Sight. Our apothecary will see to this. Keep this device as a gift, one Church to another.

—Camden

After studying world maps in the Tomes of Eternal Harvest, Camden was deft with regional placement now. He knew where in the Old Domain he would send the cell phone and that was to a place in the Peninsula of the Rotting Eye, in the palace, in the private chambers of the Archbishop of Morning, Vasoth Kennen.

Camden stared into the phone's screen and then took the whole phone into his sight, and then into his mind's eye. With relentless concentration, he gripped the device harder. The marrow blossoms in his lungs opened wider, black and orange petals vibrating with the transference of power. Cloth's children sang a bloody chorus in his mind. By way of his thoughts, he pushed, pressed, forced—the phone into the Old Domain. The phone sizzled around its edges and left this world in a flicker, only a faint smoldering plastic odor remaining.

A throbbing bubble in Camden's head threatened to pop. He massaged it until the pain passed. There were a few scars just above his hairline from his first attempts at pushing matter into the Old Domain. He learned quickly how to keep his own molecules where they belonged, so his face and body wouldn't end up looking like haggis. Some previous Bishops had the misfortune of cellular mutilation, and all because they were too impatient to learn how to balance their marrow blossoms. Camden knew how to wait. That was a quality he owned and one that he was most proud of.

His stomach growled and let go a runaway gurgle. Maybe he could do with some food after all. *Better let Fraser know before he got too ahead of himself.* Camden looked around for his phone for a second, checked the nightstand and the floor, and then remembered where he'd just sent the phone and shook his head in disbelief.

"For fuck sake, I'm getting old," he said.

The chapel beneath Newark Castle in Port Glasgow could hold several thousand people comfortably. It was an immense place that had started as only a single occupant tomb beneath the castle's cellar. The Church of Midnight knew about the tomb because it belonged to Archbishop Maxwell, one of the most notorious men in the church's legacy. In 1597 Sir Patrick Maxwell constructed a new north range replacing the earlier hall, and in secret, excavated beneath the castle, creating a dungeon for his lovers, and at times, the numerous children he spawned from them.

The castle, like so many others, eventually fell into the hands of preservation groups. This proved more fortunate than if a distant relative still claimed the land, for some twenty years ago, more than half of the site's private donors of Historic Scotland were also part of the Church of Midnight. It wasn't difficult to keep secret; those who raised too many questions or grew suspicious would later be discovered floating in the Clyde, so much fish food.

Expanding from the dungeon, the newly made chapel went seven hundred feet underground, at a severe slope, engineered to prevent water intrusion and farther erosion of the ancient foundation. Because of this, some people called the Port Chapel the Leaning Tomb.

Camden merely called it home.

The eastern tunnel led to a long bank of trees off Greenock Road. One had to enter and exit with care not to be seen. Just like last night, they blindfolded the prostitute, and took her outside where an acolyte waited to drive her back to her street corner.

"Call me, love," she cried out through the trees.

Unlikely. However, had she been looking Camden in the eyes, *could he have said no?*

Camden solemnly watched as they shut the hatch in the tree trunk. Dirt and leaves drifted down into the darkness. An earthy perfume settled in his nostrils. It should have reminded him of the harvest season. It should have called to him and filled his heart with hope. It only made him think of decay, of failure. He prayed to invoke an appropriate passage to reflect his feelings, but the Tomes of Eternal Harvest sat dusty in his mind, just as they did in his personal library. He must have been the worst Archbishop in history.

Fraser appraised him from within one of the few bubbles of light shining down through the root system overhead. He didn't have to say anything. Camden knew Fraser well enough to read his emotions with little effort.

"She said she was lonely," explained Camden.

"They always do."

Both men startled at the sound of the Chapel bell. An awakened God moving its filthy vocal cords, the dreary sound rolled throughout the underground.

Fraser glanced over in panic. "Ye didn't tell me there'd be another meeting with the Church of Morning."

Camden listened to each toll in disbelief. "What the fuck? They allowed the channel to come through without my consent?"

Fraser looked stricken. "I...can find out which Inner Circle was posted in communications."

"It doesn't matter now. Bugger!" Camden took off down the hallway, clenching his fists. "There wasn't supposed to be a meeting. I sent a message, personally. I told that arsehole all he needed to know. Kennen's doing this to outshine me."

Fraser followed him, lockstep. "The Archbishop of Morning has to be put in his place. He does not rule our church, as I often point out."

"I've no time for a lecture about this Fraser. Where are the corpses we used at the last meeting?"

"They're in cold storage, half frozen—"

"Well get to thawing!"

"What of new sacrifices?"

"No! We have bodies. Use them." Camden yanked open the stairwell door. He bolted up a flight of stairs, feeling his knees creak with each step. Fraser fled down another corridor. Dozens of Inner Circle darted from their rooms, the men adjusting neckties and belt buckles, the women straightening their black business attire. Camden continued up another flight and took a left down a torchlit hallway that hung with smoke due to the poorly maintained ventilation shaft. His eyes burned with the smoke and it made him angrier, for the shaft's debris should have been cleared out earlier that week. People weren't doing their jobs.

Someone grasped his arm and Camden reacted quickly. The marrow blossoms inside his lungs clenched. Even with pulling back, Camden's touch scalded the acolyte.

"Ah ya—!" a younger man with oily black hair cradled his arm and took a step away, looking down. "I am so sorry, my Archbishop...You said we could go over the historical series of Tomes."

"Did you hear the bell toll, acolyte?"

"Aye."

Camden squinted at him. "Who are you?"

"Thomas Vingel."

"Obviously I don't have time, Thomas."

The man nodded. "Of course you don't. My apologies."

"At least not right now," Camden answered. "What series were you interested in?"

Wild excitement flooded the man's blue eyes. "The creation of the Voyeur! I understand it was the Clan of Sickness that created the beast in a laboratory in the Old Domain and—"

Camden touched Thomas's shoulder. The man flinched but made no other movement. "We will translate this series later. It's a good one you've chosen. I will have Fraser put you on my ledger."

"Thank you."

"I have to go." Camden took off running. The Chapel bell rang again through the hall.

On and on, his head spun with the inception of one fact: Camden Amherst couldn't do this anymore. He couldn't lead in this manner. There wasn't enough of him to go around. He was failing a church that had been around since the erection of Stonehenge and it would be his fault when it crumbled to dust. All his.

He arrived at the Priestess of Midnight's chambers and knocked loudly. He could see the feeble light cast under the door, so he knew Alisyn was inside. "Did you hear the bell?"

"Of course I heard it."

"Aren't you coming to the meeting?" he asked. "We never arranged it."

"Yes, but—"

"We aren't at the beck an' call of the Church of Morning. Tell them to piss off."

"Alisyn, open the door."

"I would ignore them, if I were you, Camden. You've taken this *Midnight seeks the Morning* thing a wee bit far."

"Alisyn, please."

"I'm busy Camden."

"Alisyn!"

"Shhhh, you'll wake the bairn."

With a silent growl, Camden turned away and headed back downstairs. A frenzy of people tried to get organized in the hallway outside the great conclave chamber. Up ahead gurneys of black wrought-iron squeaked on their old wheels. Dead bodies rested under orange sheets. They were taken into the great chamber, followed by a wheeled tote of equipment.

"Think the Church of Morning would do all this hoppin' aroun' for us, if we called a meeting on them?" said someone in line.

"Shit," another said in disgust.

Camden turned to see the source of the comments but couldn't match the voices with all the torchlit faces.

Fraser arrived and stood near the chamber threshold. "We lost pressure in our chiller system, the ammonia has been contained but the bodies were not completely frozen."

Camden trudged over and leaned against the cold stone wall. He could smell the odor of death worming through the air like gaseous vomit.

"Are ye okay, Archbishop?"

Camden shook his head. He saw how this worried his friend and he brought out his most winning smile. "Yes, I'm well. I'm fine. Being an eejit, is all. I—Chaplain Cloth spoke to me this morning."

Fraser straightened and a shadow crawled over his face. "He's entered this world already?"

Camden's insides twisted. His swallow tasted like pumpkin guts. "Cloth is in Thornliebank somewhere. He came through the body of our labor union plant."

A couple of nearby faces in the hallway turned at this, looking sick.

"Doug?" Fraser tried to wrap his tongue around the name. "He came through Doug Stevens?"

"Aye."

Fraser ran a hand over his mole spotted, half bald head. His black suit seemed to drop around his body, three sizes too big. The look of it deepened Camden's melancholy. There was little money anymore to buy the Inner Circle new clothes. All the Columbian deals had soured three years ago and had never come back in full operation. The clients were too afraid…that damned Patrice Middleton had people just as scared of her as they were of Chaplain Cloth.

The bell sounded again, more urgently.

Fraser patted Camden on the shoulder. "I'm going to help set things up. Shouldn't be long."

"Aye," said Camden.

Fraser left him in the hallway with all his Inner Circle followers. Despite there being close to sixty people present and their incessant cataloging of wants and needs, Camden felt far away and alone, on an island of his own making.

When Camden entered the council chamber Fraser already had five acolytes testing the equipment on each cadaver. Camden sat in the elegant wrought iron throne and twisted at his beard, wishing he'd showered earlier. He stared at the dead occupants of the chairs on the other side of the empty fire pit, each with a wasp-like machine suspended over them and small marionette strings running down to their exposed nerves. A dirty blond haired man in his twenties, his throat cut to the spine; a woman of similar age and hair color, her throat, ironically, not cut deeply enough—the insulated wire attached to her vocal cords had to be forced through the wound; there was an older man, mid-sixties, with a full head of dark and silver hair, his body less pale than the others; next was a thin man in his forties, decomposing faster than the others—an acolyte had shot him in the stomach several times when the throat cutting failed at first; and last, sitting there, slumped over, a teenage girl, mousy brown hair, a look of surprise painted forever on her homely face—Camden didn't like looking at her when her corpse was fresh, but now it was worse.

Each conduit corpse of the Old Domain Bishops had a table near their chair and on that table rested the brutal looking phonograph that their vocal cords had been connected to. Camden watched as an acolyte tried to heft one of the heavy devices up on the table of the teenage girl. She watched, deadeyed, mouth gaping, oh my God, *I'm dead.* The table shuddered as the acolyte got the edge of the device onto it.

"Do you need any help?" asked Camden.

Finished with connecting his corpse, another acolyte rushed over to help. She had long, raven black hair, almost the same deep color as Alisyn's but not as thick. Her brown eyes had that look of youth in them, a look of many things yet to see. "I have it, Archbishop," she said with a dignified bow.

Camden fell back in his throne. *Can I ever be of use again?*

The slate discs placed on the phonographs spun and crackled with loud white noise for about ten minutes. Camden waited for the conduits to find their mental connection to the people in the other world. Four sets of dead lips began to froth and make sounds and their limbs shook manically.

They would announce themselves to start the council.

The dirty blond corpse: "Archbishop of Morning, Kennen." His female twin: "Bishop Paliz of Azaraith."

The older man's arms lifted, clamps on the exposed muscle fibers flexing noisily. Despite the awkward motor skills, he brought his hands together and he said, "Bishop Magra of Bat Canyon."

Decomposing man: "Bishop Theren of Lastground."

The Mousy Teenager sucked in a wet breath, then said, "Bishop Relgard of Castletomb."

Kennen's conduit, the dirty blond, took on a petulant expression through its sagging, ulcerated face. "I hope this has some large standard of importance to bear, especially keeping us waiting this long. As you know, I am busy with my mother. She has fallen ill after a long battle of disease."

Camden cautiously began, "You called the meeting—"

"I received your funny message device. A stupid use of power."

"You don't like Samsung, I take it."

"What?"

"I thought you'd like another item for your collection."

"Let us talk of your communion with Cloth." Archbishop Kennen's voice sounded clotted, like someone drowning in blood. "You claim he has a new plan to find the Heart of the Harvest, and forgive me if this sounds...unkind, but why would he only commune with you?"

"He has come over, Archbishop, and the gateway rests in my city."

Kennen sounded flummoxed. "I have pressing matters to attend to with my mother and I cannot allow you to miss yet another opportunity, as your Church is wont to do, as of late. You need our help preparing your Priestess of Midnight."

A stirring went through the crowd of Inner Circle seated behind Camden. His people wanted him to stand strong. They had no idea the power the Church of Morning possessed. They would bite their lip too, *in my shoes*, thought Camden.

"What do you suggest?" he asked calmly.

"Chaplain Cloth wishes the Priestess to acquire the ability of All-Sight and use it to locate the Heart of Harvest. This is a very difficult incantation. You have no real good idea what that means, do you? I can see by your stupid face you don't." The corpse laughed and a gout of blood burst from its left eye and something bluish ran from the side of the rotting lips. Head lolling left and right, the corpse glanced around the room. "Anybody here know?"

The young acolyte who'd spoken to Camden earlier raised her hand and the corpse's hungry eyes found her at once. "Ah, tell us, cottage pie."

"For All-Sight, the Priestess must behold an Apex Goblin. I am not certain for what duration…"

"My, what beauty," Kennen said with relish. "She doesn't live in a world where such a beast exists, and yet she knows, so sweet that she is. These are the types of followers I can expect when the worlds unite? And how well can I expect your obedience to me when the time comes?"

"I would serve the union of churches—the Eternal Church, Archbishop."

"Of course you would. Come here woman."

"What does this have to do with the All-Sight incantation?" Camden asked, panic rising in his throat.

The acolyte moved closer to the corpse and bowed her head. He dropped a vein-busted hand down his slacks and pulled out a purple-blue, frost-bitten penis. "Indulge me a moment. Do you forfeit humility for the Eternal Church?"

She looked away in horror.

"This is enough," Camden said. "We were speaking of other matters."

"We were speaking about whether your church can follow

through. This is a simple matter. Do you even know what it means to command an obedient slave?" asked Kennen.

"She's no slave."

"They all are."

"Can we just—"

"In a moment, Archbishop, in a moment!" Kennen chuckled and wagged the warped phallus back and forth. "I want your little Miss here to suck the dead seed out of this conduit body. Get down here woman. Now!"

"You don't have to," Camden told the acolyte. "Really Kennen, this is absurd!"

"Will you show me your worth?"

The girl nodded. Camden expected to see tears, but this young woman's face had become like stone.

"Then, please me!"

The acolyte took two purposeful steps forward and dropped to her knees. She grabbed the moldering head of the penis and put it in her mouth. Camden watched in revulsion, waiting for her to turn away and vomit, but the girl bobbed on the corpse with a wild passion. The other conduits chortled up blood as they watched. Pieces of the member sloughed off in her fist, the scrotum drooping and disconnecting in oily gray and red wads. It was only a moment before the entire organ became a grisly mush.

The dirty blond corpse grinned with a fitting rictus. "Still limp. Alas, I have no sensation across the worlds, but it is nice to see who your followers really answer to, Archbishop Amherst."

"Stop that!" Camden took to his feet. *Why won't she listen to me? The poor fool!*

The young woman slowed but didn't relent.

With a pat on the back, the corpse released her from her duty. The acolyte backed away and began to vigorously spit on the floor.

"Go wash up," Camden told her.

This order she obeyed at once, scrambling up to flee the chamber.

The Archbishop of Morning's conduit couldn't stop smiling. "It's funny. She has no idea how much *worse* it would be to really suck my cock. This corpse is far handsomer than I am in the flesh."

The other conduits laughed again.

Camden felt dizzy with self loathing. "Fuckin' hell, can we please continue?"

"As that little whore so kindly offered, the Priestess must *see* an Apex Goblin, but they only exist in the Old Domain. Does anybody know how this can be achieved from someone in the Blind World?"

Camden didn't like the Old Domain's nickname for the Earth, and always felt his hackles rise when he heard it. *Then say something to the son of a bitch!*

No words formed on Camden's lips.

A runnel of bloody spit cascaded over Kennen's chin. "Bishop Paliz, do you have any ideas?"

After some thought, the wires in the dead woman's throat bounced. "We need to prepare a *gram'vling* elixir—"

Camden interjected, "I have apothecaries for that. We need only to search our other chapels for the components."

"What other chapels?" snapped Kennen. "The Nomads have buried your entire following. *Blood on the Tomes*, am I ever glad I called this meeting."

"We have storehouses of components in Hamilton and in Edinburgh."

"And they likely won't be adequate for the elixir."

There was a following silence that should have been natural with the corpses, but the situation made it highly unnatural. They didn't trust the Church of Midnight to anything anymore. Would the Church of Morning peer into every move they made from now on? Camden clenched his fists atop his knees and bit a small hole into his lower lip.

"It will be a cocktail of marrow seed oil and several brains of a Lungbat," the corpse for Bishop Paliz replied. "The elixir can transport the Priestess over on ethereal frequency, via the cerebral cortex, administered in the eyes."

"I will send over the components tonight to your apothecary," said Kennen. "The Priestess will likely be directed to Blakandor Forest, where an Apex Goblin is noted to live." He paused and added, "You are certain this is Cloth's will? The last time we tried this, the Interloper largely prevented my own Priestess from using the same All-Sight ability to the fullest. Forgive my boldness, but if the Church of Morning failed at this tactic, what makes you think your church will fare better?"

Camden didn't know how to answer that. First off, the audacity of the question made him livid. Second off, Archbishop Kennen was absolutely correct. He didn't know that Alisyn's handling of the ability would get them closer to Heart of the Harvest or not.

"Bearing witness to an Apex Goblin will give the Priestess a terrifying insight into both of the worlds," Kennen remarked. "Is she ready for such a rite?"

"Alisyn will be ready," Camden stated without hesitation. He hoped it didn't sound like a lie.

Alisyn Dunning perched over the small pine box. She stooped a little to sniff at the lid. There was no scent other than the pine and even that had faded over the last ten years. Her fingers glided across the polished surface. Inside, in the dark, her child waited. All those years ago and still it vexed her. Maybe it had been a mistake to put her newborn son in the box—maybe Camden'd had a right to his child too. He hadn't been pleased when she told him it had to be done, but he made no attempt to stop her either.

She was only fourteen at the time she had his baby and that'd been entirely her fault; she lied about her age, she seduced Camden—the baby was necessary, but the timing was wrong to give birth to the True Son. He would be born on the Day of Opening, just as his father had. Still, something about Camden's child was very special, and a soft susurration in her ear, one that smelled of rot and old blood, told her this child would be able to be reborn on Halloween. Alisyn had all the hopes of a young girl when she first sealed the baby away, but now, as a young woman, she thought differently; she doubted the infant survived all these years in a box, like some kind of hibernating bear cub. Even though this reality couldn't be clearer to her, she wasn't ready to accept failure yet. That was something she and

Camden had always had in common.

Her fingers drummed against the wooden box again. *Could he hear it?*

She contemplated, for what seemed like the billionth time, just opening it and being done with wondering. Bones, dust and nothing else: that's what she would find. The baby had died long ago from starvation, maybe even oxygen deprivation. Its tiny corpse rested in this box and *you've been too cowardly to open the box and face it.*

She tugged on the latches. She didn't dare shake the box. No, the timing was always, always wrong.

At least Camden had felt like the right father. He was born on Halloween and his son's soul felt as though it could fill that shallow pit inside her. The other children that followed didn't make her feel the same way. That's why she'd held out hope that one day the time would come. Either the True Son would be born to a different father, or the sleeping baby would begin crying in its box, telling her it was time…

If only she had somebody to tell her the answer. Something told her that praying to Chaplain Cloth wouldn't just be a waste of time, but also dangerous for her son's welfare.

Cloth would not want a True Son born into the universe. He wouldn't want to contend someday with the Lord of Masks.

From under the box Alisyn took up some baby photographs. The first photograph: the child's eyes were closed, the skin badly bruised and splotchy. The product of a rape, she never gave him a name. He was stillborn. This child, she knew, would not be the one, but she still wanted to remember him. The second photograph was taken from outside the hospital nursery, a slight glare on the window from the camera's flash. Camden had arranged an adoption, never questioning who the father had been. Occasionally Alisyn fell into a deep depression looking at this photo. Even though the girl wasn't the True Son, it hurt too much not to know her.

These babes were all conceived through ignorance. After consulting the Tomes, particularly the series involving the Lord of Masks, Alisyn realized that father and son must be born or conceived while the gateway grew on Halloween, the

Day of Opening. The texts were never conclusive, and often contradictory in fact, so she tried to keep her loins bursting with seed as often as possible.

Camden had been downright prudish with her lately, but she'd come across two other men besides him who might be worthy. Duncun Gibbs, a fellow Glaswegian, and Ronald Montel from Melbourne. With Ronald being out of the country, she hadn't spoken to him in a while now, which left Duncun, who just last week had accused her of having gravidophilia, the false belief of pregnancy.

Nevertheless, Duncun still had potential. He was actually a little more aggressive than the type of man she usually approved of. Duncun was transfixed on Japanese women and let his hunger show through without censor. Alisyn was half Japanese and half Scottish, but that didn't seem to lose any value with Duncun. The last time she went to his Anime-plastered flat, they fooled around, got naked—she tried to pin him down, keep his business in where it belonged, but he threw her off his lap and climaxed on her thigh. He grabbed her by the throat, gently applied pressure to the inception of strangulation, just to show what he could do to "sneaky bitches in heat" like her. Then he brought out his gravidophilia claim.

Her biological clock was a timer fixed to plastic explosives right about now, but just as she'd worked up the power to go find her mobile and call Duncun, a solid knock came from the chamber door.

"Alisyn," said Camden. "I'm coming in." She sighed. "Watch where you step."

"Aye, you don't need to keep reminding me."

Just past the threshold Alisyn had buried the bodies of her stillborn children, and a few she'd kidnapped and sacrificed without Camden's knowledge. Their bones blessed the stone and mortar floor and made her chamber a place of fertility and power, so the Tomes told.

The heavy banded door swung open and Camden's stocky form filled the doorway. He wore one of his newer suits, its ebony shine smooth from the candlelight in her room. Other than shutting the door quickly behind him, he gave no other indication of the surprise seeing her naked on the floor, but his eyes did light on the box sitting near her. He took a wide step over the coffin bricks in the floor.

She regarded him for a moment. Would her doubts about Camden Amherst ever go away? Lately he'd seemed so overwhelmed and spineless that she couldn't possibly imagine him being the father of the True Son—and yet, something about the baby in the box gave her hope. *Why was that?*

"An' whit wid you like for your birthday?" Alisyn removed her bathrobe off the bedpost. Not knowing where the robe's belt was, she left it open.

"The Day of Opening is gift enough."

"Boring. You say that every year. I thought we might open the box together an' see our son reborn to life. Wid that no' be a better gift?"

"Ah," said Camden. There was no humor in his eyes. "You say that every year as well, but never bring yourself to do it."

Alisyn glared at him.

"I have things to discuss with you. The Church of Morning will be sending over some components today—and what are you doing?"

She lifted her leg and put one foot on the bed. She tore away at the soft toenail of her big toe. Its thickness had been bugging her. Camden was obviously moved at the spectacle between her legs, the open invite of flesh there, because he'd lost his train of thought.

"What are you doing?" he asked again, eyes boggling.

"Grooming," she said. "Did you wash yourself after that hooker? I'm not having you sticking her filth in me."

"That woman was interested in a deal with the church. Nothing more."

"Did you fuck that one?"

"Rubbish. Like you'd care anyway." Camden shook away the spell over him. She'd known him since she was fourteen, and now, at twenty-four, she still got him hard pretty easily. She doubted any wee tramps he found walking the streets could bring about such a reaction so quickly. Alisyn liked that. Even though she supposed she shouldn't like it, she still did. Carefully, she tapped at the split between her legs with her thumb. She wasn't even particularly turned on by him any more, but enjoyed watching how quickly a man could abandon everything at the mere sight of her birth canal. So much impious power there and so easy to utilize...

Camden sat on the bed. "I didn't come here for this. You think I just use your body as I please? Has it ever been that way?"

Alisyn closed her bathrobe and moved closer to him. "Not enough to my liking," she joked.

Camden's beard smelled of cherries in a cedar bowl. Never mind her recent frustrations with him, it was always nice to take in his scent. In many ways, they were best friends that had always bordered on worst enemies. Passion at both ends of the spectrum. She liked that about him too.

"Let's talk about the ability of All-Sight. Do you know this incantation?"

She didn't, but didn't let on. "Whit about it?"

Camden then described a dream he had with Chaplain Cloth and a directive for her to gain an ability to see both worlds in her mind's eye. She would need to work with the apothecary to gaze into the Old Domain and look upon a creature known as the Apex Goblin. It reminded her of a fragmented story in the tomes, *Liar's Lust*, but she couldn't recall the story including specific rites. "Is this something you think you are ready for?" he asked.

Not answering, she slid off the bed and crossed the room to stand before her shelves of specimen jars of semen and blood. She'd taken precautions so that Camden did not know what men they'd come from. He wasn't the jealous type, but she still needed his commitment. She already had most of the Church hating her, she didn't need him to start as well.

"I feel too empty to endure the apothecary."

"Mina is boorish but that's no real reason here. You just feel sorry for yourself."

She narrowed her eyes at him. "As though I shouldn't? I can mind a rather harsh looking illustration of myself in the chapel bathroom, with a particular inscription. Do *you* recall what it was Archbishop? It was only last month."

Camden turned red. "I still mean to have that removed.

I've just been—occupied."

"*Queen Cunt*," she supplied musically. "These are our followers, Camden. I didn't see you even try to discover the origin of the artwork."

"How would one go about that?" he asked, exasperated. "Keeping yourself nestled away in your chambers all day doesn't make for much of a charismatic leader. You are in a position to be hated or loved, Alisyn."

"I choose neither. I'd rather be left alone."

Camden gave her a sharp look. "The gateway has opened in Glasgow. The Nomads are on the way here to kill the lot of us. It disnae matter if you feel empty or feel sad or feel like dancing up and down. They're coming. If we don't fight them, if we don't win, you'll not be around any longer to feel empty. And I'll not be around to hear you complain on it."

Alisyn pulled her robe tight. She didn't want him enjoying her body anymore.

"I love you, dear," he went on. "I want you to live to see better years and give you many wains. That is why we need to perfect our plans and set them in motion."

"A baby?" she asked, ignoring the latter. "Is that whit you said?"

He blinked several times and stuttered.

"Your seed?" Alisyn let her robe fall open and went to him. She grasped his shoulders awash in joy. "You won't resist again? I have promised that the next baby will be spared if it isn't the one. You believe me, don't you?"

"Aye, aye, of course," he finally said, "but we cannae talk about the future until we're certain we have one. Understand?"

She pressed her lips into his mouth. He received them, dryly at first, and then hungrily kissed her back. They kept kissing for a while. Alisyn knew it would not escalate into anything else. Not today. It wasn't the right time. Camden knew about timing, just as she did. They would show their bond and devour each other's taste, but bringing new life wasn't on the agenda. Kissing was delightful as always, and yet, her mind wasn't on pleasure. As usual it returned to the one thing she didn't want to think on.

The box beneath her bed with the patient baby waiting inside.

THREE

The agents parked in an Inglewood strip mall. Patty noted the businesses present, a barber shop, smoke shop, water store and a dentist. The barber shop had its lights on but nobody sat in any of the chairs. The smoke shop had too many loud neon advertisements plastered on its windows to see if anything lived beyond its doors. About ten cars here, but no real signs of life. This seemed to be the trend everywhere they went, all over the globe. In regard to the world being destroyed by the creatures of the Old Domain, the world seemed to be doing a fine job of that wholly on its own. At least the rain had broken up a bit and some California sunshine peeked out from the apertures between the storm clouds above. Byron ushered the Nomads from the red Ford Focus, through a break in a dying hedgerow, to the front door of Dr. Grinny's Dental Practice. Teresa gave Patty a sidelong glance, as though to say, are we really doing this? When Patty gave her no noticeable answer, Teresa's own expression changed to a *let's* just go.

And they could. Th could go whenever they wanted. Th men certainly couldn't stop them. Byron was right.

Th did owe him for saving their ass two Halloweens in a row. Without the information he'd provided, Chaplain Cloth might have put Patty and Teresa in a bind that got the Heart of the Harvest killed and maybe themselves as well. Normally the Nomads did not feel compelled to repay debts because they operated outside of such things. However, Patty assumed Teresa thought it a relatively easy way to appease Byron for now and then hope he never tracked them again. Patty, on the other hand, had other reasons for agreeing to the meeting and hoped it wouldn't cause too much of a stir with Teresa.

Byron leaned up against a concrete column as his partner, Denis, unlocked the security lock from the front door. Byron chomped on some gum. Occasionally he snapped a purple bubble and it would have been obnoxious to Patty had the sun not backlit his black hair and made him look so stunning with that marbleized gray running through the temples. Byron blew a bubble that nearly touched his nose. It popped and he chomped it down again.

Teresa slipped her arms together with a look of impatience. "Which one of you is Mr. Grinny?"

"That'd be him," he said, moving his head to gesture at his partner.

Denis smirked. "Come on, people, let's hurry. I don't know how long we can stay here before the department sends someone to find us."

They walked through an unlit reception area, down a hallway, each room still possessing a dental chair, though no other equipment was present. Eerie multicolored light filtered through overhead stained-glass skylights depicting calming vistas and oceans with jumping dolphins.

"Torture rooms?" Patty asked. "I suppose those windows are supposed to keep your mind off the pain while the dentists hammer a tooth out?"

Byron brushed past her, smelling of a subtle earthy smelling cologne. "The local anesthesia takes your mind off the pain, Pat. Those windows just give you something to look at while you wait for the drilling to stop."

He spread his hand against a door to hold it open. The two women and the other agent filed into a break room. A dead plant on the sink made the air smell faintly of a swamp. All but Byron sat down at a long table with bad plastic chairs that squeaked with the slightest movement. Denis methodically placed a notepad on the table with a small voice recorder. After he fi arranging everything, he thumbed one side of his strawberry blond mustache and then pinched his nostrils.

"Why didn't we go to the Whittier office?" Teresa asked. Denis gave Byron a penetrating stare. "They know that location? Our main office, Agent Telamon?"

Byron's look was blank. "I didn't tell them, if that's your insinuation."

"Yeah, it is."

"We knew about it before you even moved furniture in," said Patty. "Our source doesn't leave many stones unturned."

Denis looked stunned. "Source? The Messenger?"

Teresa fished in her blouse pocket for a Hershey's kiss but couldn't find one. "Is this already the interview?"

Byron headed for the door. He took out some ear-buds for his iPhone and fit them in his ears.

"A moment, Ms. Celeste." Denis's face visibly flushed. "What do you think you're doing?"

"Listening to Sam Cooke," said Byron. "Patty's got me hooked on him."

Patty shot him a smile.

"And you're doing this now, why?"

Byron shrugged one arm at his partner. "If you gotta go, you really got to, right?"

"Byr—"

"I'll be back in two flushes. Relax, you got this, bro."

The door closed with Denis Boyle's mouth hanging open.

Patty gave Teresa a look of satisfaction. "He has an odd way about him, doesn't he?"

"On the planet I'm from it's called being an asshole," replied Denis, "Okay look, obviously this is not an official interrogation."

"Unless your budget cuts have been very severe." Teresa propped her head up with a fist and eyeballed the man. "We're only doing this because of how much help Byron has been. Honestly, I don't know what you want to accomplish. Most will consider the things we say paranoid-schizophrenic nonsense."

Denis's eye sockets were ringed in darkness, his nose veined with burst capillaries from drinking too much. The man looked one cup of coffee away from death. "I appreciate this, especially since I know that you don't have to leave me alive if you don't want to."

Teresa smiled faintly. "We want to."

"That's good news on top of more good news. My intrepid

partner has told me you've single-handedly sacked most of the Church of Midnight chapels."

"Your partner talks too much." Teresa glanced at Patty. "As does mine."

"Before I start, off the record, I want to know what happened at the airport today. If you have any idea at all? Was an explosive planted in the gift shop?"

"No," said Teresa. It was somewhat the truth.

"I have to take your word. There wasn't any evidence recovered. We looked for fragments and came up with zipperoo." Denis folded his bright red hands together and knocked his big thumbs together. "This wouldn't make sense in most cases but we're dealing with the Old Domain. The Church of Midnight may be nearly wiped out, but the main man hasn't gone anywhere."

"And he won't go," Teresa replied, "Chaplain Cloth will last longer than our sun will burn. The explosion wasn't his doing though, or anybody from the Church of Midnight for that matter."

"Like we said in the car earlier, we don't know how it happened," said Patty.

"Let's start with what we know then." Denis cleared his throat and pressed down the record button. Patty kept her focus on him, but in her mind she cut a mantle through the wall to check on Byron. He was opening a bathroom stall and had a slip of paper in his hand. Enough, she thought, *I'm not going to spy on the man in the bathroom.* God, she was becoming just as paranoid as Teresa. Patty let the mantle dissolve. Denis was looking through his papers and telling the recorder what date it was and who accompanied him for the interview.

"You two constantly move around the world all year long and follow directives by an unknown person you call the Messenger. Every Halloween, a gateway, or portal, whatever, opens to another world. This place you call the Old Domain. The gateway cracks open slightly but if a sacrifice is fed to it, it opens wider. There is a threat that if the gateway is opened long enough, our world will merge with the Old Domain. This event has been going on since humans first came to be, perhaps before. Am I right so far?"

"Sure," Teresa said, leaning into the table, restlessly.

"The entity known as Chaplain Cloth and his Church of Midnight seek this sacrifice and you two are obligated to protect it until Halloween ends. Every year the sacrifice changes to a different person. These sacrifices are known as the Heart of the Harvest. You've saved most of these Hearts but have also lost a few." Patty looked away, feeling a slight tension headache coming on.

"I don't understand something though," Denis admitted. "What about these sacrifices you lost? If over the centuries the Church has kept on chipping away, why hasn't the gateway opened permanently yet? It must be wider now than it was, said in 1910 or something."

Teresa pressed her lips together a moment. "Most Hearts of the Harvest are not strong enough to open the gateway permanently. Once, back with my previous partner, he and I encountered such a potent sacrifice, but that was one in a million."

"This is the partner whose body was found in a bar just outside Colton?"

Teresa looked at him a long moment and then closed both hands into fists. She gently rapped on the table with both, trying to will herself to keep speaking. "We were separated that night...I didn't know that his body was found."

"I'm sorry," said Denis abruptly. "I can look up where his remains went, if you like."

"No." Teresa straightened. Patty touched her shoulder, and she shook her head. "Go on please."

"All right, so, for the most part, the Heart isn't enough to keep the gateway open forever?"

"Not lately, it would seem."

"Why even bother with the Heart of the Harvest then?"

Nearly interrupting him, Patty said, "Just because it doesn't stay open long, doesn't mean the gateway can't let in all sorts of evil shit from the Old Domain."

"Evil shit?"

"No other words for it."

"Fair enough, but let me ask you this then. Is there another way to keep the gateway open forever, besides using the Hearts as sacrifices? How can Chaplain Cloth merge our worlds if the gateway's always snapping shut on him?"

Teresa smoothed her hair back into a temporary ponytail and let it fall. She did that when she felt cornered or annoyed. Patty was all too familiar with the gesture and it always put her on alert. To her surprise, however, Teresa's tone was even.

"I have read the Tomes of Eternal Harvest from start to finish several times," she said. "Over the years I found several addendums in the chapels we raided. A bishop by the name of Cole Szerszen described a pair of columns that might have the power to hold the gateway open indefinitely. One for this world, one for the Old Domain. The concept appears several times and is alluded to in other Tomes—nothing rock-hard specific. Can the actual columns be out there somewhere? Absolutely. Do I think they are? I lean toward maybe."

"Maybe, huh?"

"That was from the addendum we found in the desert?" Patty asked Teresa.

She nodded.

Denis searched frantically through his papers, perhaps sensing his time with them had suddenly grown limited. He hit pause on the recorder. "This is really good...you don't know how much this means to our department. The orbital anomaly ten years ago only took us so far with the Federal review, especially since the largest piece of photographic evidence we have has gone missing."

Patty's blood went chill. "Which photo?"

But she knew. Byron had told her about it once. Back on Halloween of 1964 someone snapped a Polaroid of Chaplain Cloth. Decades later the Office of Arcane Phenomenon recovered the photo. Byron told her that none of their researchers could actually look directly at the photo without becoming violently ill; their lab had to study it through a mirror. Even that gave them migraines.

"I never saw the evidence, so I couldn't say," Denis said. "But it had to be someone with access to the lab."

Teresa moved a train of silver-brown hair off her shoulder

and cracked her knuckles. She seemed about to say something, then cracked her knuckles again.

The door opened with a shove and Byron rushed in holding a portable GPS. "We have to go ladies. Our boss is on the way."

Denis went rigid. "What? They're coming? How did Jeffery find this location?"

"I don't want to hang around to ask him. You?"

Denis clawed his keys from his pocket. "Get my things. I'll pull around to the back."

Byron watched his partner bluster out of the room. Patty and Teresa stood and searched for an exit. With the ease of a man just wandering into the kitchen for his morning joe, Byron took a coffee mug in the sink, filled it with water. "Look, it's tough to get my people to believe what Halloween really means. And yet, scare someone into thinking they're going to lose their job and they'll believe the Pope's a ninja."

"Are we going or what?" asked Teresa.

"I need to get my people pumped. They're motivated about rooting up new evidence. You didn't really think I'd let the department have all your juicy details, did you?" Byron casually took Denis's recorder from the table and dropped it into the mug. "Man, these things are always busting."

Teresa noted it. "And Denis was so excited."

"Well you girls are exciting," said Byron with a grin. "He'll get over it. Come on, I'll walk you to the back."

Byron took out the recorder, put it in his suit pocket and picked up a notepad from the table. He showed them down the hallway to a fire exit in the back of a dusty coat room. The door opened to a whitewashed alley surprisingly free of graffiti and litter. Sunlight spilled down relentlessly and the air filled with the smell of rain cooking off the surrounding streets.

"You said you wanted evidence," Patty said with a sidelong look to Teresa. "Do you want something to wet your whistle better than hearsay?"

"Always," said Byron.

Patty took out the letter from the Messenger and handed it to him.

"What the hell are you doing?" demanded Teresa, who tried

to intercept it but was too late. Byron looked down the alley one way, then the other before reading the message. He nodded. "Glasgow, eh? The Church is actually pretty intense over there right now. Probably the only place in the world where they are—you two gonna keep me worried?"

"Have to make it fun," Patty said.

Byron tucked the note into the notepad under his arm. "What's this about communications being compromised?"

Teresa gestured wildly around them. "*This*, us being here. We don't share information with anybody except our annual contact. That's how it's always been. This is putting the Heart in danger."

Patty felt Teresa's stare burning through her neck, but went on anyway. "Notice the stain at the bottom of the letter?"

Byron nodded. "Sure did. Is it blood?"

"I was hoping you could tell us."

Teresa shook her head. "It's a ridiculous waste of time. The Messenger will not be found through DNA."

Byron noticed the silent discord. "Hey, I won't show anyone else. I was forensics for a few years, and worked for a graphologist—I could maybe link the handwriting to someone, if this guy or gal has a past of any kind. I can deliver this information if you give me any leads to the gateway's location this year. I know you two have ways of finding out. This information will not be leaked to the department. It's personal business."

"You say that every year, Byron." Teresa locked eyes with him. "And every year we tell you the same thing: *you don't want to find the gateway*. Trust me. You really don't."

"I really do. I have to find it before Halloween, before it starts moving all over the place." What Byron said made no dent, so he bent back and stretched his arms, cringed at what seemed like a muscle-pull. "Or I could give the letter back and forget I saw it?"

"Fine with me," said Teresa.

The red Ford Focus swung around the corner of the alley.

"The Messenger knows exactly where the gateway is," said Patty. "I guarantee it. Help us find the Messenger and we'll go to the gateway together."

Byron looked at her skeptically.

"Fine, do the blood analysis," said Teresa quickly. "Make Patrice happy. The end result might make an impression on her. Come on Patty. We're walking."

"Are you sure you don't want a ride?" asked Byron. "Yes, she is," answered Patty, rolling her eyes.

The car pulled up with a very intense looking Denis behind the wheel. The window rolled down and his voice matched the hysteria in his face. "What's going on? Where are they going?" Byron sat down beside him in the passenger's seat. "They've told me the location of this year's Heart of the Harvest. Looks like we're headed to Puerto Rico, buddy."

"No shit?"

"*Shit*," Byron replied.

Cars, trucks, buses, and occasionally bicycles flowed past the Nomads. They waited for a taxi to break that flow and send them on their way back to LAX. Patty rubbed her temples, thinking about standing in those long lines for security, waiting in those hard chairs at the terminal. She wasn't looking forward to the all-too-familiar scene and hoped it took a long time for a taxi to find them.

Her partner, on the other hand, looked more at ease. Teresa counted clouds, a subtle childish joy still in her sixty-year-old gaze.

"I don't feel like the airport today," Patty told her.

"Yeah, I'm through with them too. Necessary evil though, right?"

Patty looked down and sighed.

"Still, the letter doesn't say we have to book the flight today. We've spent so much time in the sky the last three years, I feel like we're a couple of grounded birds. I rather like it from this vantage." Teresa pushed some of her gray-slashed almond hair out of her dark blue eyes and looked harder into the distance, searching. "Let's get a room and leave on the first available flight tomorrow."

Teresa normally wanted to be ahead of schedule. With the best frequent flyer programs to which the Messenger had enrolled them, they could easily book a flight the night before, but it still wasn't unusual for Teresa to have them set out three or four days before a target date.

While completely perplexed by this change of heart, Patty wouldn't argue in the slightest. Relieved, she blissfully gazed up to the sky with her partner, feeling that the world had suddenly grown a thousand shades brighter.

"So beautiful."

"Patty, I want you to understand something." Teresa paused and Patty looked at her as she chose her words. "I do like Byron, but I think we need to still be careful of him."

"He destroyed the interview tape though. He didn't have to do that. Come on Teresa—he's on our side."

"Did you see how easily he lied to his partner about going to Puerto Rico? That was a little too convincing."

"So?"

"It's not the first time. Remember how he could sense our mantles the one time, and then denied it? And what about when he didn't recall anything about his parents after telling us earlier that his father was in the Army and his mother was a librarian? He's secretive."

"And we aren't?"

"This is where you have to listen to your older, wiser partner. I've met people who have allergies to telling the truth."

"He's not one of them."

"As I said, *I like him*. But he's a big distraction for us—sometimes it's easy to forget what's going on while he's around. That's a good and bad thing, obviously."

"I don't see how it could be a bad thing."

"My partner Martin was the same way. He always took his mind off of the job. He could pull me out pretty easy too. Not so surprising they found him in a bar...typical." Teresa snorted at some unsaid memory and then draped her hand over her blue blouse. She didn't often mention the permanent mantle in her chest, the one that Martin had placed there to contain a cancerous tumor in her lung. That was part of the reason Martin wore himself out one Halloween and got himself killed. From time to time, Patty looked inside Teresa to check the mantle, but it was strong, a superior creation. Martin had really cared about her. He had to know that he wouldn't be strong enough to face Cloth, not after endeavoring upon something so complex, but Patty knew why he did it. For Teresa, she'd have done the same.

"You miss having him as a partner?" Patty carefully asked. "Another life, hon. That was a different Teresa Celeste, a different world. Having Patty Middleton as a partner has been a whole lot safer for me, that's for sure. Got to admit though, every single time we get one of those letters I can't help but look for some type of sign I'll be released from my duty—that's nothing against you."

Patty put her hand up, as though to reassure her she understood.

"There's no use hiding it any longer. I'm not so great at building mantles now." Teresa went on, "and I haven't been a good marksman since my eyes went sketchy...Don't have the speed I once possessed...Why would the Messenger still want me around?"

"To keep me company," said Patty wryly.

Teresa gave her a playful shove and looked to the sky again. "What would a year in my life be like without everything focused on Halloween? I'm too used to it now. I don't think I could live that way. I'd have to know who the Heart of the Harvest was, where the gateway would be each year. I couldn't let the day pass in complete ignorance."

"You don't trust me to go it alone?"

Teresa half-smiled. "The Messenger always keeps a pair of Nomads around, as far as I know. So, I don't trust whatever partner you'd end up with. I don't think I could *live it up* while you and some rookie tackled this all on your own."

"The Church of Midnight isn't much of a threat anymore."

"Compared to Cloth, they never have been. He's what always worries me."

Patty could only nod at this.

"You're not a silly teenager anymore, but when you get older you'll realize how much of a kid a twenty-one-year-old really is. I never listened either, for what it's worth."

"Yeah...wait, are you justifying slapping me earlier?"

"Sure I am, you little snot."

Patty laughed.

"I'm being serious about Byron though. The Messenger doesn't want us making new relationships for a reason. People can get hurt. People you *love*."

Byron Telamon's different though, *thought Patty. She sensed* the blood of the Old Domain in him. She figured Teresa had too, but didn't want to bring it up. As much as Teresa wanted to be released for duty and could discuss it at length, she didn't want to be replaced.

"Have you really asked yourself why he's after the gateway so badly?"

"We've kept him at arm's length," said Patty. "He probably wants to see it for himself. His whole job revolves around the gateway, just like ours."

"He's nearly obsessive over finding it."

"The paranoia is strong in you."

Patty spotted the taxi turning the corner down the street and signaled. With a gentle tap to Teresa's leg, Patty stood from the bench and stretched.

The cabbie, with a curious salon-styled hairdo and one crucifix earring, pulled half of his hulking form out of the cab. Out of breath he said, "LAX?"

"Yes, to get our bags. Then we're going to a hotel. A nice one." Patty opened the door for Teresa.

"The Messenger hasn't given us our annual allowance yet," grumbled Teresa.

"Hey, old lady," Patty said, getting inside the cab, "live it up a little."

Byron rubbed at his throbbing hands. He wanted to soak them in warm water, and his feet while he was at it. A nice bath. Some salts. Some bubbles. Sam Cooke's greatest hits. Maybe one of those sticks of Indian incense. He had to unwind. He had to find a way to put his mind on the future rather than the present. That worked for him when he was approaching a fit. Since he was a kid, tuning out had always worked to a degree.

The tingling beneath his knuckles felt like acid bubbling at the bone. Oh, how he wished it was. Acid would eat through him and there would be an ending to all this shit. But there was no ending. Just pain, delirium, the fit, and then a couple days of respite. Last time it happened really bad, sometime back in June, he slept for a day and had to call in for another. This time of year he had to skip resting and relaxing.

The gateway... Cloth...

He had to find them this time around. That was the only true relief.

Byron realized that he might be a Nomad just like Patty and Teresa, even if broken—some people were born with handicaps and his was a broken connection to the Old Domain that had put him in a constant state of sickness. He only knew that the cure was in the gateway. Would Cloth give it to him? Or would he have to kill Cloth for it?

Was that possible?

Byron's thoughts returned to the here and now. Denis was still pissed at him. His partner steered the car erratically, changing lanes, cutting off a few conservative drivers. Too much stress rubbed off. Denis Boyle would benefit from a contact high, especially now of all times. The man was making Byron jittery and when Byron became anxious, he thought about the stabbing, stinging, frying feelings beneath his fingernails, between his toes, deep in his underarms.

Then it manifested: a cutting surge like a band saw went from the soles of his feet and hit his spinal cord. He grimaced and closed his eyes.

Mind over matter? But the mind *was* matter...

"Damn it," said Denis. "That interview wasn't long enough. I wanted to ask them about those invisible things they pull from the Old Domain."

Byron drummed his fingers on the window. "Mantles?"

He knew exactly what they were: particles drawn across the threshold of both worlds or what Teresa once referred to as Ghost Matter. Byron could not draw mantles yet, he hadn't had the mental training, but he understood the act with a great level of intimacy, in the way he supposed a person with amnesia still understood how cold and hot felt.

Denis spluttered. "Yeah, mantles…how could I forget about that? Hey, you grabbed my recorder right?"

Byron pulled it out of his pocket. A couple of beads of water dropped off the bottom but Denis was too busy driving to notice.

"Can you transfer it to your computer?" asked Denis. "My sound card is still wacky."

"Good idea."

After all, Byron thought, even water-logged, the recorder might still work. This gave him a chance to corrupt the file, if needed. As far as the Nomads were concerned, it was better to keep his partner and the rest of the department both interested and ignorant; the more he could control information about them and the Church of Midnight, the better for his plans.

That letter was serendipitous. The blood analysis may or may not lead to the Messenger, but he still had other options if that didn't pan out.

Make the truth a lie, make a lie the truth.

The trick was to keep in the good graces of the Nomads and still be able to use the resources of the OAP. One might have to give though. Would it be worth it to lose the Nomads' trust? To lose Patty's trust? Or did he really just want good health?

In peace?

Being healthy would mean unlocking a real life.

Fuck, *his spine hurt.*

Byron nudged open the glove compartment and took out the cigar he put in there on the way to the airport. Last night he'd slit it open and trash-canned half the tobacco for some purple hair chronic, the most pungent marijuana in his possession. The receptionist, Heather Somebody or other, at Operations had one of those weed licenses and got him all the good hydroponic shit.

Denis glanced over. "You ain't lighting up in here again man. Just forget it."

Byron turned on the radio. After some blaring static, Spanish commercials, and a hair-band song, he found some Sublime. Byron lit the end of the cigar with care-giving precision. Denis stabbed at the window button to get fresh air. "We have to find a way to get a meeting with Jeffrey, you know, if we're going out of the country. We won't make much of a case for ourselves if you're all red-eyed and loopy on drugs."

"What drugs? Weed?" Byron took a deep inhale. It watered his eyes, instantly put his mind elsewhere, just where he wanted it.

Away. Far.

Away.

Denis frowned. "Okay, then, I take it we're not going to talk about Puerto Rico now."

Better get this over with. Byron opened the ashtray and tapped the end of the cigar. *"Why'd you want to go there anyway?"*

"What?"

"I couldn't tell you when the Nomads were still in earshot, but I've known for a while they're headed to Glasgow. I have a feeling they're meeting the Church there."

"But you said the Nomads were enemies of the Church…"

"Hey, Denis, man, look," he took another toke, blew out the gray blue smoke, his throat tightening, "I don't have all this stuff straight—I'm just as confused as you are. The Nomads might not have been upfront with me before. I don't take it personally."

"How'd you find out about Glasgow? You never mentioned anything before."

Byron offered him the blunt.

"—the hell away from me with that crap." Denis tried to steady the car. "Are you going to tell me?"

"Huh?"

"Glas-*fucking*-gow, you prick."

"I have a Church contact. If the intel he provided me turns out to be true, we'll have an opportunity to ask the Nomads anything we want. For the first time ever, their mantles won't be an issue. We'll have the upperhand."

"And how?"

"There's a place where they can't use their power. It's a small area called a Void, and I have the general boundaries in the city mapped out."

"You'd have us drag them to a place where they can't use mantles? I mean, I thought you were their friend."

"I'm your friend first, buddy. Besides, like I said, they might be consorting with the Church, which *doesn't* make them our friends."

Denis shook his head for a long time. Byron watched him, actually became mesmerized for a moment, thinking maybe the guy would shake his head forever, an endless loop, a broken record, a robot powered by disbelief.

They stopped at a light. Sharp tremors cut through Byron's gut and made him feel close to losing control of his bowels. Nausea brought an acidic taste into his mouth and tears bloomed in his eyes. His teeth creaked together, driving pressure into his forehead, sure to give him a migraine later.

The convertible next to them pounded with rap music and made the frame of their car buzz. Byron stripped off his seatbelt, rolled down the window and leaned out.

"What are you doing?" hollered Denis, slapping the wheel. "Ah fuck you, man! Shit!"

Byron yelled over to the booming car. "Hey you! Hey you guys!"

The driver glared at him from under a gray beanie and his girlfriend, in her oversized sunglasses, looked away, embarrassed.

"Hey!"

"What?"

"*Tuuuuurn* that shit up, son!" Byron let out a wicked howl. The teenager raised his eyebrows and looked at his girlfriend. They both started cracking up. Byron pounded the hood of the car and loosened his tie. "Come on, ain't got all day!"

"Get your ass back in here!" Denis snarled.

Shaking his head with a smile, the guy adjusted his stereo, but only a little louder. His girlfriend giggled and slapped her white-white thighs.

Nearly falling out of the car, Byron offered his marijuana cigar. "You want this blunt, dude? I'm good. I'm in a suit, homey, what the hell do I know, right?"

The light changed to green. The girl said, "Don't take that," but the guy took the blunt anyway.

Denis peeled out. In the rearview mirror, Byron saw the kid sniffing the smoke and the mere sight of him doing that, looking like some kind of zitty bloodhound, just about made him lose it. He dropped back into the seat and stifled the giggles, and all the while his partner was disgusted, which made it funnier.

"Hey," Byron finally said, "I got rid of my shit. Aren't you happy about anything?"

Denis pulled over in a parking lot of a defunct gas station. He put the car in park and irritably pulled up the parking brake. "What in the hell is the matter with you? You're totally out of control."

Byron looked down at himself and checked his hands. "I'm pretty serene, you have to agree. Stress free." He reached for the radio and Denis slapped his hand away.

"You need to stop."

"No," said Byron sagely, "you need to *start*."

His partner deflated in his seat and closed his eyes. "Can we just pull it together? The department isn't exactly trigger-shy about another round of layoffs. There're rumors Phil joined a military contractor overseas. He's gone from the office more than you are lately. Know anything about that?"

"Dunno shit." Byron put back his seat and tried unsuccessfully to get comfortable. "I do know that Phil gives me a headache."

"Perish the goddamned thought, but you're next in line for his job."

Byron cringed. To this day, he still didn't even know how he got the job at the Office of Arcane Phenomenon. He couldn't even recall how he'd heard of the agency. He lied to them about working for the FBI and had never even been part of the Department of Homeland Security in any way, shape or form. He doctored his resume, just for the deranged reason that he thought he could get away with it. And he did; he somehow still passed security clearance. The day he met his superior, Phil Jeffery, the man looked at him oddly and said, "We've met before, haven't we?"

They hadn't, but Byron made something up right then and there, and it became the truth in the next moment. That had been happening to him ever since he began fighting the pain. Things got twisted around him sometimes, but he was getting better at trying to untwist them preemptively.

Getting better, but he was still far from mastering it. A tear rolled down the side of his cheek and he quickly clawed it away. Denis studied him with concern. "What's the matter man? You have that disc problem again?"

If only. Byron reached back to rub his spine. "*Something fierce.*"

"Why didn't you say so before?"

He shrugged. "I'm a little depressed too, tell ya the truth."

"Ok, where's my tablet of paper? I just need to make some notes about this interrogation so I can fill out the 12-72. You're saying Glasgow now? I don't know how we're going to sell this to Phil. Where's my paper?"

"Tablet's in the back."

Denis took out a pen from the cup holder and turned to the back of the car. While he searched, Byron moved his foot carefully, pushing the tablet fully under his seat. He was not in the mood for making up another round of lies about the Messenger's letter tucked inside.

"I don't see it back there."

"You can grab one off my desk when we get back. I've got a ton."

"You should have," said Denis, turning the ignition, "you never take notes." As he dropped the car into gear, he looked over at Byron. "You going home then?"

"I have to go to the lab."

"Why?"

"Because I want to fuck one of the assistants who works there, that's why."

"Whoa there, old boy. TMI."

Byron began wishing he hadn't given that blunt away. "You're making me crazy right now, just drive."

Denis chuckled, almost seeming proud of the idea. "We sound like a married couple now."

Maybe at one time, thought Byron, but a divorce is coming. *His government job couldn't last forever.*

Not like this.

FOUR

The Heart of the Harvest grows and matures on October 31st. This process springs from an old power, a remainder of an era lost to myself and to the monster known to his church as Chaplain Cloth. As far as I know, there is no common link in heritage to people who yield the sacred fruit. The fruit chooses to grow in someone much for the same reason an isolated plant stretches for light—it is the mindless, yet often fortuitous will of nature.

This is to say, the two worlds need to unite, for better or for worse. Nature doesn't care about sacrificing what it takes to meet that need. Nature is a risk taker, both a winner and a loser. The Courre brothers are an interesting case study in this design. More than several times I'd seen the Heart of the Harvest grow simultaneously in those who shared a womb, but I'd never seen two siblings born at completely different times produce the fruit. Not until Kauph and Bre Courre.

And that was not the only mystery. Nobody in the Old Domain had grown the fruit in thousands of years, mainly because the potency of the sacrifice wasn't as strong. Up until now, the Blind World, or Earth as its English speaking people called it, had always produced the Hearts of the Harvest.

Now this.

This strangeness.

Two Hearts growing in the Old Domain.

One in an older brother, one in a younger brother. Nature's way of reacting to an imbalance.

That imbalance, I was more certain of. Patrice Middleton had shaken the foundations of the universe, from the Blind

World to the Old Domain, and perhaps beyond. Her power had become too great and so the fingers of chaos planted its seeds elsewhere to counter her aggression to the design.

With massive hubris and ill-conception, I believed I was ready for this new development. I had my eyes firmly on Kauph Courre. His brother Bre was another, more unfortunate circumstance. By the time I realized he too carried the sacred fruit, it was too late to spirit him away into hiding.

The Church of Morning abducted Bre Courre around eight years of age. Fortunately for me, and unfortunately, I suppose, for Bre, his fruit grew abnormally and after a brief blooming, proceeded to rot inside his body. The decomposition of the fruit was another first, as far as I knew. I'd certainly never seen or read about anything quite like that before; the sacred fruit dissolves on November 1st, the day after maturation, or, in less cheerful circumstances, if harvested and fed to the Children. Those were the only two manners of decay with which I was familiar. Rotting? Fermentation? Never. On my best days the strangeness of it all still confounds me and gives me endless worry about the many things I have yet to learn.

I came to understand that the residual power of the fruit would ferment inside Bre until his dying day. Most of the Church of Morning feared this potential, and some believed the power could be harnessed somehow, but after several attempts to offer him to the gateway, it was discovered that the Children would not feast upon a fermenting source of power. It was a grave disappointment to all, but a relief to me.

Eventually Bre was taken for a broken historical apparatus, and around the Church's territories that was how the local tales told of him losing his birth name and becoming known as "He Who Might Have Saved the Worlds."

She'll be the cleanest invalid in the old Domain, thought Bre as he turned through the doorway, buckets sloshing over his shoulder yoke.

From the boiler house he had over two hundred lava sprites smashed to coals to fire the boiler. Twenty buckets of steaming hot water. Ten trips up and down Cobweb Hill. All for the Archbishop of Morning's enfeebled mother, Pel'Hahr. Bre could only assume the luxurious bath meant the Archbishop felt guilty for being wrapped up the last two days in Church business.

Bre approached the other buckets of water, his knees trembling as he squatted closer to them. Despite his efforts to remain silent, he grunted and half expected to hear Archbishop Kennen curtly snap his name.

Kennen had given Bre Courre two nicknames. Phrey, which rhymed with Bre but in the undead tongue happened to be slang for "a ghoul's filthy uterus," and also the second more obvious label of *Slave*. Today it seemed he had no patience to address Bre as either. Instead Kennen glared at him and then massaged the bruises along his arms from the conduit hook-up of earlier today.

His meeting with the Church of Midnight had not been long, but whatever had transpired in the conclave hollow had unsettled him. Bre suspected it was because lately Kennen could not be bothered with the Blind World and at the same time he'd lost faith in the Church of Midnight to deliver the Heart of the Harvest. That lack of control ate at him more every year.

Kennen bent over his spicer witch mother, dabbing her temples with a luminous red sponge reaped from Olathu Ocean. Bre gently unhooked each bucket from his yoke. He pushed the buckets against the others, most of which would go unused. There had been no other further instructions, so Bre would wait, head bowed. This never lasted long. Kennen would not see his slave idle unless he was too preoccupied.

With the exception of the occasional sloshing of the bucket and the witch's soft snoring, silence hummed inside the stuffy cottage, still outfitted with all of the witch's dusty jars, pouches, ladles, knives and laboratory tables. The two room home sat off the side of the Palace of Morning in a long shadow cast from the palace wall. Built from the husk of a dead boulder troll, the rooms always managed to be humid inside, despite the shadow coverage. When Pel'Hahr had still been coherent she insisted on staying in her own home and unless she needed to gather supplies for spells, rarely set foot outside. Kennen, newly raised to Archbishop status, had the palace built next to the cottage and respected her wishes to stay there, even when she fell unconscious from a blood disease.

Many things had shaped the Archbishop before Bre became indentured to him, and he came to know that Kennen was as much a slave to his mother as Bre was to him. Though Kennen never spoke of it, Bre had heard other slaves in communal cells back in the palace tell stories of the Archbishop's past, the kind only a fool would repeat in his presence. But if those stories were true, before his complete devotion to his witch mother, Kennen had given much to the cause of uniting the worlds.

After losing his wife to a sacrifice, his Priestess to the Blind World, his sons to a treacherous uprising, Kennen now only had his mother left. She'd been in poor health most of Bre's life and when hope seemed lost completely Kennen would always explain that, "She sacrifices calmness of body because she knows her destiny—her duty to the Churches united, the Eternal Church. We must pay back that sacrifice with diligence, Slave, or we have failed the very universe."

The Archbishop tossed a sponge in the bucket with a curse. He pushed back his deep orange hood, hemmed with shimmering black runes, oily whispers of magic. It was never pleasant to behold Kennen's brutish, reconstructed face, mostly because Bre couldn't read the bizarre expressions through the fleshy welds, staples and stitches. Years of donating flesh to his mother's illness had created a faceless human than the rotting visage of a shark devil.

Kennen scratched thoughtfully behind one ear badly in need of re-stitching. The greenish ear flopped back and forth on three tiny black sinews about to snap. He'd wanted to avoid more staples, since his face had more than two hundred already, but it looked like he'd soon have little choice.

Kennen stood, an orange tower looming over Bre. "She needs another blood cleansing. Bring all of them."

"The entire lot?"

Kennen's eye that sat a little lower than the other glared especially hard. "That's what *all* means, doesn't it?"

Bre made no rejoinder. He was off. Out the bile painted door. Up the rusted path. He hurried to the palace medical cache, making certain to say hello to his favorite pair of bleeding trees. It was bad luck to forget to say hello. He ran faster and ignored the pangs of his empty stomach. It was bad enough Kennen would be outraged they had so few Tick Goblins cleared for cleansing, but Bre didn't want to be slow returning on top of it. He expected some unjust outburst today and it was better to foresee which one came, rather than to be blindsided. How Bre was treated didn't matter right now anyway.

Keeping the spicer witch alive was all that did.

Tick Goblins quickly hibernate when left untouched. Those that have not fed are the size of a child's playpen ball, their bulbous backs writhing with a translucent yellow skin webbed in thin scarlet blood vessels. After feeding they become twice larger and change to an unsightly purple-red. In this state several thin sex organs punch through the dermal layer at the upper joints of the small black legs and arms.

Having studied the creature rigorously, Bre didn't mind handling the Ticks while they slept; they rested upon porcelain cooling plates in their divided crate like a dozen dormant eggs from an enormous animal. The crate had to be covered and thoroughly shaken to bring them out of hibernation. With such a proclivity for deep slumber, it was a wonder how the Ticks survived in Greshi Marsh where a host of other goblin races would happily devour their parasite cousin.

With the last crate of Tick Goblins in hand, Bre hurried back to the witch's cottage. The scintillation of the millions of human teeth that comprised the northern watchtower created a river of gold and silver auroras on the path of rusted golemstones. Bre went recklessly through the rare play of light without pausing and then through the two bleeding trees whose trunks bent inward as though to hold each other. Hello again, he quickly thought to the trees. They'd been his companions since childhood. Some days, the shade of their white velvet leaves did feel like an embrace, and the blood red sap that continually leaked from their gray bark smelled of the childhood forest home he'd known with his brother Kauph. He was glad he never took the trees for granted. They unlocked the door to his mental freedom, provided reprieve from the sweat and toil, and took him back to that person he began life as. It may have been silly or immature, but they reminded him it was possible for someone to love Bre Courre, despite everything else.

When he got back to the cottage, Kennen had the witch's faded peach robes up past her graying nipples. Her body was unnatural. It held the pallor of an aged woman, but the shape and smoothness of a younger woman in full blossom. Sometimes when Bre was alone and aroused, he'd imagine the witch straddling him, her slim hips working faster, the coif of silver pubic hair slick with perspiration, the round breasts bouncing subtly and then fiercely, those marble colored nipples hard and soft to touch. It shamed him, but with no real interaction between the female slaves in the palace, the witch was all the fantasy he had.

Kennen's busted face turned and caught him staring. It wasn't the first time, but lust was one of the few traits Kennen trusted and understood; he never questioned it. His eyes then lowered to the crate. "One? I thought we had more."

"This is all we've tested, master," Bre replied, frozen in his tracks. "The others haven't been cleared yet."

The Archbishop personally tested all the Tick Goblins for disease. He didn't want to take the chance that a test surrogate would deceive him or be less likely to catch a particular strain of disease that he and his mother would acquire. Out of the last few batches, he'd rejected three ticks and contracted several viral illnesses, one that left Kennen bed ridden for a little more than two and a half weeks with high fever, tremors and bloody stool. That certainly would have ended his mother Pel'Hahr.

Bre waited for the Archbishop to throw something at him or at least shout in anger, but Kennen appeared more focused than usual. Desperate even. Rather than belabor his disappointment, he snatched the crate from Bre, placed his black bruised thumbs tightly over the lid and began to violently shake it. Stress and inquiry fluctuated through his disturbing scowl. He shook it, inspected the crate for sound, shook it again, inspected, shook, and on.

Then the soft sucking sounds came from inside the crate, a needy refrain.

Kennen set down the crate on the floor and pried off the lid. The egg-shaped ticks shifted in their little partitions. He took one delicately by the top, the fleshy outer wall of the stomach sagging like the skin of a scrotum. Kennen gave the thing another shake, to bring it fully awake, and then dropped the tick between his mother's breasts. The hollow black teeth on the tick's belly sunk in and began to draw blood. Once the tick was removed, they would retain its waste fluid for a transfusion. The blood went through a treatment process in the tick's digestive system and purified it of disease and increased antibodies and overall plasma strength.

Leaning over, Kennen squinted in confusion at the tick, which flexed greedily on his mother. "Why is it drawing so quickly?" he asked. He bent over closer and studied the side of the tick. The blue phalluses that gorged with blood had green spots over their slimy flesh and tiny spines at their tips. "What *are* those?"

When Bre didn't answer immediately, the Archbishop caught him by his neck and shoved his face down, inches from the feeding creature. "What is that?"

Bre stammered in terror, "This one isn't from Greshi Marsh..."

"No," Kennen replied, almost comically, "no it fucking well isn't. Why did you bring me a Brogish?"

The Tick Goblins found near Lake Brogish had three chambered stomachs and were far less predictable in feeding habits than others of its species. Bre recalled the Archbishop testing this one though, in case they needed a quicker transfusion. Kennen probably recalled this as well but, as usual, had to shift blame to Bre to vent his frustration.

"I should have given you a reminder," Bre said. Kennen erupted in a bitter laugh and rubbed his eyes.

"It wasn't diseased though, master. It's clean. We just need to watch it closely I think."

Kennen released his neck. Bre could feel the cuts left behind from the man's broken fingernails. "That's not a chance I'm willing to take. We need to get this thing off her. Now!"

"Too dangerous at the onset of feeding. I'd let it go a little longer, master." Bre folded his hands on his lap and bowed slightly.

"Would you?" Kennen turned back to his mother. Her flesh was inflamed and pink around the Tick Goblin. For a second it seemed he'd take Bre's advice, because the Archbishop just stood there, heaving, his mangled face abject from the moment, akin to a farmer observing his yield. Then something threw Kennen into a panic. "No, no, no, no—*too* much!"

He went to release the tick. Pinching the base of each sex organ would cause the Tick Goblin to believe a mate had initiated intercourse and it would detach from its host. Kennen's fingers were deft but the tick remained.

"It's not unlatching."

Perhaps these Brogish variety would mate even while they fed…

"I'll put my hand under it," Bre offered. This would get the tick to remove its teeth and sink them into new flesh. There wouldn't be enough teeth to hold it to Pel'Hahr then and Bre could remove it. This was how they used to do it before they figured out the sex organ stimulus.

Kennen considered this. Sweat popped on his forehead and some of it dripped sideways and laterally on the weird slopes of his skin.

Bre took the initiative and stepped forward, hand ready to slip under the tick. He'd never had a Tick Goblin like this on his hand, and the others feeding on him had burned like all the blood in his arm turned into molten steel, but there was no time for hesitation.

"Away! You'll ruin our chances." Kennen shoved him aside and put his own fingers under the tick. He jimmied at the tick's body and it wouldn't move. "*Blood on the Tomes*," he cursed and from the poultice shelf he snatched a lean bronze surgical knife. Carefully, Kennen worked the knife underneath the tick.

On the opposite side of the creature, a barbed proboscis whipped out and sunk into Pel'Hahr's throat. Blood dashed the fibrous cottage wall behind the witch's head.

Kennen froze. He watched in dread as a slim line of hemorrhaging ran down from Pel'Hahr's neck only to be immediately sucked back up.

The Archbishop yelped and drew the knife to slash at the proboscis. Bre caught his wrist. Kennen's power brought Bre's whole body forward.

"Don't!" he cried. "Archbishop, please! It'll spawn a nesting child from the severed part left under the skin."

The proboscis chugged like a hose from a well pump. What little color the porcelain-white witch had possessed before rapidly fled.

"Give me that," Bre said, grabbing for the knife. "I'm going to remove it."

Kennen turned quickly. Bre stepped back in time to receive a razor fine cut through the shoulder. He glanced at the unintended wound and then back to the Archbishop.

"If you kill her, *Phrey*," heaved Kennen, "this will be the last thing you do."

Bre took the knife. He believed his master's warning, but it was much less potent than those of the past. Kennen didn't want an excuse for punishment this time. He wanted Bre to succeed and that was all.

Working quickly, Bre opened the blood-bloated belly with a cut from the head to the end of the digestive tract. The inside of the goblin looked identical to the marshland variety except for the extra stomach chamber. Bre hoped its defensive systems worked in the same sequence. Two lateral cuts through the broccoli shaped top of the spinal cord disabled the main nervous system to prevent a frantic response to internal pain, and next with the knife's serrations he sawed through the black and orange cords of its auditory system. This would deafen it to any sounds it could interpret as threats. Now, he had to detach the nineteen muscle groups in the saddle-jaw that pushed out the teeth.

The Archbishop stood behind as Bre went skillfully about the task. He flinched when he felt Kennen put pressure on the freely bleeding cut in his shoulder. Bre was certain this was more of a show of nervous energy than Kennen's concern for him, but it was nice to think otherwise.

Bre finished the teeth and found a large muscle ligature that connected to the proboscis. It was denser than the other tissue and the knife's blade seemed to dull on it. Bre had another go and just when his arm really got working, the proboscis withdrew with a bloody hiss. The three chambered stomach sucked inward, trembled, and then exploded all over the witch's gray body.

Not to mention him and Kennen.

Shocked to the core of his being, Bre stood there, knife in hand, hyperventilating. Kennen drew three fingers through the blood sheen over his horrid face and left behind wiggling trails. His other hand dropped from Bre's shoulder wound.

Kennen grabbed a rag from the table his mother once breakfasted at. "Run to the Palace to get the donors."

Bre was still beyond dumbfounded. He'd heard his order but couldn't react to it. With a breath of disgust, Kennen took the Tick Goblin off his mother and flung it into a corner. The creature made a brain like design of blood on the wall and landed in a fleshy heap.

With a grunt, Kennen bent and hovered over his mother. His ear hung by a single stitch now, the other stitches having snapped. The decaying piece of flesh spun around like a morbid wind chime. Paying it no heed, he whispered to his mother,

"You'll see the Day of Opening. We're not going to fail you, understand? I'll die first. Yes, *I'll die*."

That was enough to break through to Bre. In the next moment, he was running, everything whipping by in a recurring nightmare. Sultry eastern winds howled in his face as he sprinted harder for the infirmary. A colony of silver bats warred in the sky far above and he felt the same frantic mania deep inside his gut. He couldn't fail them. He had to get blood donors.

No time for hellos, Bre hurried past the pair of bleeding trees, insult shaking through their bone white leaves.

FIVE

Alisyn knew it had to be raining outside. Frozen kisses from a dark heaven, just a touch away from snow, all falling down, hissing on the sidewalks, boiling against all the windows of all the shadowy places in the city's corners where light forgot to venture. It wasn't metaphoric. It was as *dreich* as she expected.

It was Scotland.

But no amount of cold rain could chill her blood right now. She was happy. With her babies, breathing in the warmth they may have once given her, a tangible thing like the scent of soured milk drifting into her mind, she sojourned in her freezing subterranean bedroom chamber, her body draped across their coffin-tiles. It would have been a great day for a stroll through the city. She might even disregard the looks people gave her when they noticed the empty baby carriage she pushed, those warm expressions of anticipation and admiration for a young mother turned to ugly vexation and presumptive smirks. Alisyn's happiness left her suddenly. A giant light went out and a giant darkness claimed her in its place. The eclipse almost caused her to weep. Her lip trembled. She bit into it hatefully and the pain redirected her. She took a long sip from her tea cup. Mulled grape juice usually cheered her up but it wasn't working. The emptiness was too great.

At thirteen, when she left her foster home and joined the Church of Midnight, an unborn baby was the only belonging she brought with her. It was fitting, for it was the only Christmas present her foster father ever got her. He wasn't a cruel man, just poor, and addicted to everything one could find in an alley late at night. Despite his own trappings, he never seemed to give up on Alisyn being something more than him, even if he didn't provide the way. Perhaps that was why the photo of their stillborn child questioned her so intensely; it reminded her of his old question: True Son? Why would you dream things like that? You haven't gone huffing, *have you?*

She understood the implication. This was curdled fantasy, nothing more. Even the real flesh and blood children she'd carried to term were not her children. She'd let them go. In different ways, yes, but all the same, she'd let them go. It was hypocrisy to imagine any differently. Her real son would someday rule a land with her at his side as counsel. The dreams always made clear he would bring much pain to her, but she'd love him nonetheless. Perhaps the pain he brought her was even prior to his birth?

This torturous time of awaiting his arrival, this dastardly self-afflicted uncertainty?

She thought about calling Ronald. It would be nice to hear his even, reassuring Australian accent. There was a meditative quality to his vowels. His tone made her feel dreamy and hopeful sometimes. You don't need anotha man to tell you what to do, *love. You know.*

Her cell phone buzzed and clacked on the stone floor, some plastic insect struggling to right itself. She looked at the caller ID.

It wasn't Ronald.

But it was another prospective father. "Hello, Duncun."

"Meet me at King Tut's in an hour. I hae tickets fer that galoot band you like. Don't make excuses. Be there."

He hung up.

Duncun brooded as they found seats at the bar and ordered drinks at *King Tut's Wah Wah Hut.* He sat there, in his striped rugby shirt, glaring at her with his caveman eyes. She asked the bartender for straight cranberry juice and he jolted in his seat.

"You aren't pregnant. Why're you being so stupid? Get a real drink."

Alisyn ignored him. She'd gotten herself dressed in her finest white mini-skirt and blouse and wore shoes she could dance in.

Duncun hadn't made any comment about her outfit or that he hadn't seen her in a while—oblivious, just as he normally was. In many ways, she hoped his child didn't end up being the one.

The bartender dropped off their drinks. For a moment they sipped their drinks in silence. The place filled with patrons. Overhead, the bass rumbles from a sound check seemed to annoy Duncun. Everything did nowadays, including Alisyn.

"Look here," he said loudly, "I'm not some immature twit wha' believes anythin' he's told just fer a single serving of poon. Understand me? I'll no' willingly listen to all yer crap about witches an' warlocks an' killer pumpkins."

She folded her arms. The bright magenta of the cranberry juice mesmerized her. Going out was probably going to end up being a bad idea. One of her acolytes, Eric Gills, had driven her to the venue and she chose him specifically because he wouldn't blab to Camden. The plan had been for Duncun to drop her back off at Port Newark later tonight, but if this shit kept up, she might just have to call Eric to come back for her.

"Ye ain't no witch priestess or whatever, Alisyn. Ye're just nuts." Duncun appeared content with his own fervor. "I'm not going to be sucked into yer little game of house. We can screw all ye care to. I just want to get it straight that ye'll not speak of babies an' Halloween an' all this other oogie-boogie bullshite, and ye'll come to me frae now on. No the other way around. I won't be buying hotel rooms or driving across hell and back fer you. Ye know whaur my flat is."

She took a large sip of the tart tasting juice. "I don't deserve you."

He frowned, unable to determine if this was sarcastic or a true compliment. "Just 'cause I'us born on Halloween, doesn't mean I want to join no dumbfuck cult."

"I only asked you once. Forget about it."

Duncun's eyes narrowed, just as the spills of the drummer's high hat signaled the beginning of a massive crash of guitar distortion.

Alisyn drank down the rest of her drink quickly, anxious to get upstairs and hear *Future of Mankind*, one of the few metal based bands she enjoyed. Her companion noted this and drank down his beer in two long swallows. He made a face and held a hand to his mouth as he floated a belch between his fingers. "Come on then, let's go up."

The band furiously began their set, the sounds of techno, jazz and death metal blending into an uplifting roar. Some red and blue lights from the stage reflected off Duncun's thick brow ridge, making his shaved head squarish and flux like a police car beacon. She pushed against him and took his hands from behind. Duncun had nice, calloused hands. He was unemployed right now, living with his brother, but before then he'd been a carpenter. She liked the idea of him whittling off pieces of wood, looking for the right shape. She had fantasies for all her potential fathers. With Duncun, she envisioned he would one day carve his son a throne with his bare hands and paint it with the blood of lesser kings.

The thought excited her, the want to see that throne thrilled her, and Alisyn moved up and down on Duncun. His hands greedily reached for her breasts and she pushed them down before they went an entire circuit to the front. Duncun went for another try and she turned to face him, held her body close to his, crushed it against him and squirmed to the music.

You give what you give, to take what you'll take
Bloody donation, bloody donation
You live what you live, to make what you'll make
Bloody donation, filthy fucking donation

Duncun's sex had stiffened beneath his blue jeans. She worked against it, purposefully, but not with the aggression to cause him to spill. It was delicate ferocity, it was feeding a starving man bread crumbs every second, it was challenging the heavens to hold its lightning at bay while all the world's steel stretched skyward, inch by inch. Alisyn wiggled down and grazed his crotch with her lips and then shimmied back up, waving her hands to the musical blessing all around her. He took hold of the back of her hair, a large fistful of it. He grumbled, sounding like a beast of chaos over the thrumming double kick drums and jazzy lead guitar, "We're only one song in—but I damn well need ye."

"Where?"

His eyes lit up, astonished at her reply.

The journey from the club didn't take more than five minutes and then they were in the cold night air. There weren't many alleys behind King Tut's, but they found one near a research building a block down the street. Duncun hadn't thought it out too well and pushed her against the building near an open dumpster topped with shattered glass and gravel.

With how frantic he clawed at her underwear, she didn't imagine the act would last for too long and that meant perhaps they could go back to listen to the rest of the band's set.

He began clumsily biting her neck.

"Are you in?" she asked to stop his futile gnawing. Duncun whipped his head back, his eyes intense with suspicion. "Yeah, ah fucking well am." He stabbed at her with little effect.

She faked a moan to reassure him and it worked. He hiked up her right leg and he went somewhat deeper and she felt a little pleasant pressure. Duncun took big gobs of air into his lungs.

"You can stay in," she told him.

He went faster. "Fuck no, fuck no," he chanted.

His thrusts became longer, and he began to pulse inside her. She felt him slide out a little. Alisyn reached into the dumpster and found a glass shard with smooth, tempered edges. Duncun didn't notice it until she had it at his throat.

"Stay in," she ordered.

His eyes boggled at the threat. With her other hand she grasped the base of his penis. Out of sheer surprise, he ejaculated and closed his eyes. The orgasm rolled powerfully over him.

With his last shudder, Alisyn tossed the shard back in the dumpster and laughed. "Well, now that was fun."

Duncun withdrew, lazy eyed and pissed. He zipped up and she dipped down to draw her underwear from under her shoe. She almost didn't see him lunge after her.

"Ye bitch!"

She sidestepped and he caught the building with his shoulder. "Fucking fuck that hurt!" he wailed.

He caught her blouse and she slid from his grip. Now free, Alisyn took off.

And ran straight into Archbishop Camden Amherst.

The large form of Camden stood there, his eyes locked with Duncun, who had also stopped in his tracks. Duncun glanced to the limo parked behind him to the two Ekkian guards dressed in black suits that struggled against their muscular bodies.

"Wha the hell are ye, dolts?"

Alisyn sidled up to Camden. "Don't kill him, please. We can go. Let's go."

"None of these sad sacks of shite is killin' nobody!" Duncun balled his hands into bright red fists.

"One moment," said Camden, so calm it scared her. "Go to the car."

"It's nothing," she insisted.

Duncun stormed over. "Wait. Whaur are ye gaun?"

Camden deftly snatched Duncun by his shirt. The guards edged forward, surprised by their master's quickness. Camden squeezed the fabric, gritted his teeth and suddenly the shirt ignited in orange and green fire, but it didn't burn up...the shirt went away.

To the Old Domain.

Somewhere in the lands of Castletomb, the ravaged remainder of a rugby shirt would arrive and it would be anyone's guess where it came from or to whom it belonged.

"Ah, a magic trick," said Duncun, not all that astonished by being suddenly topless. "How about ye go fuck yourself wi' a wand, wizard?"

Camden punched him in the face so hard Alisyn thought she heard an echo in the alley. Duncun tumbled to the ground and fell on his back. He immediately pushed up on one hand, but went back down, overcome by dizziness. From the immediate swelling over his eye, he didn't look like he'd be getting up very soon.

Camden pulled out his billfold and stripped off a ten. He crumpled it into a ball and threw it at Duncun. The bill struck his forehead and landed on the ground. "Get some ice," he instructed. "And a shirt."

He took Alisyn by the hand and led her to the limo.

"I don't want to talk," she said and dropped into the seat. "Just take me back to the chapel."

Camden scratched at his beard thoughtfully, grasping the limo door tightly in hand. "Your acolyte did right by telling us, Priestess."

She said nothing. It would have been better to just take the damn bus. *Goddamn Eric.*

"The Day of Opening—"

"Isn't the only important thing to me," she snapped. Behind them, Duncun tried to get up and collapsed again. "And that clod is?"

"You've promised me too long, Camden. I can't wait for you. You haven't the devotion I seek."

Camden studied her and his eyes narrowed. "I gave ye a child, an' ye put it in a stupid fucking piece-o-shite box!" He slammed the door so hard Alisyn's hair blew over her eyes.

"To the Chapel," he barked.

The limo took off at once. Camden pressed the privacy window up. She could see tears welling in his eyes but she couldn't feel sorry for him.

"Our child will come some day, Alisyn. Until then, we listen to Chaplain Cloth and his children. You will be Priestess of both churches. You will have anything you desire. Think about that next time you decide to screw in some random alley where you could end up with your throat cut. We need you. The Church of Midnight isn't just running out of brethren, it's dying here. We have to win this year. *We have to.* Do you understand?"

"I could have left the Church a long time ago, Camden. I stuck by because I thought you were loyal."

"I am loyal to you."

"And to yer hoors?" she asked. "Who is catching who here?"

"You left me little choice."

Camden twisted in his seat, fire in his dark eyes. The cold Glasgow streets framed him, a sideways avalanche of darkness and streaking lights. He reached out and poked her in the forehead, hard enough to make her wince. "I told you I'm faithful! Why do you insist on calling me a liar?"

"Prove it then." Alisyn slid over on the bench seat and hiked up her mini-skirt. There was nothing sensual about the movement. This was fury and spite and she would drown him in it, make him feel a fool for ever following her tonight. "Prove your faithfulness, Archbishop. Are you a man or no'?"

Camden rapidly raised his eyebrows. "Roll around in Johnny Dumbfuck's juices? No thank ye, hen."

She stopped. "See, given the chance, you fail. You promised me devotion!"

He raised his hand, looking as though to grab her face in between his big fingers, but then thought better of it. "Devotion is caring for a young woman who has a history of mental illness and never questioning her delusions. Okay?"

Alisyn couldn't look him in the eyes. She wanted to say something to hurt him but her anger had scrambled her thoughts.

"You realize all of your True Son rubbish comes from appendices to Tomes, written by people from this world."

She faced him now, fury rising. "So?"

"So they could be false prophets."

"You're being sacrilegious."

"No, I'm being cautious. You've invested all your soul into this, Alisyn. Those passages about the Lord of Masks—most of our historians don't even treat the subject with any sincerity. It's apocryphal. Mina and Jacob Betters discussed this at length with me not long ago. Jacob suggested that even if such a person came to be, Chaplain Cloth would soundly annihilate him in little time at all."

"How lucky it is for me to hear all this now, years later. Astonishing! And you use that moldy old apothecary and some fu' bookworm to support your doubt in my role as the One Mother?"

"No, I support you. And just because I do, it disnae mean I'm going to let you throw everything away in the hopes of bearing a perfect child." He hesitated a second and then added, "I admit a part of me was glad to know you'd gone dancing tonight."

"Oh?"

"Yes, goddamn it. That was you coming to the surface again. You used to dance, you used to read, you used to listen to Japanese opera...you used to be a person, Alisyn. Now you've become just a walking womb."

"You disappoint me, Camden. But it is as I thought. I suppose I should be glad you even noticed I'd left the chapel at all." Camden sighed through his great beard. "Oh what a miserable existence you lead."

"You have no idea what it takes to be a walking womb, my love. It's not all fun an' games like it looks."

He hissed. "Fine then. You wannae see proof? I said we could start, so let's start. It seems this is all that makes you content any more."

He undid his pants and pulled himself out for her. He was already startlingly erect and all at once Alisyn remembered the feeling of him inside her, a much more dramatic and pleasing experience than Duncun.

He tilted his head. "Use me if you really wantae, Alisyn. But know this: you won't give birth on Halloween, if this takes. You'll have a summer baby."

"This is no ordinary baby," she replied, lowering her ass down into his lap. As she felt him widen her loins, Alisyn enjoyed the feeling and rocked on him. She'd missed this and at the same time dreaded having all her hopes return through someone so undependable. To allay those fears, she tried to delve back to the father fantasies she'd once dreamed of Camden.

Somehow, she'd forgotten what they'd been.

SIX

They lounged on a comfortable sofa in the lobby of the Crowne Plaza of Beverly Hills, assured their room would be ready in forty-five minutes. Waiting didn't bother Patty at all—for a change, they weren't rushing. Teresa, by and large always in rushing mode, also didn't find reason to complain. She was thankfully calm, busy eating Hershey kisses and rolling the foil into little balls. It was a habit she picked up after she'd quit smoking.

Seeing those obnoxious foil microspheres littering their hotel end tables used to drive Patty crazy, especially since Teresa hounded her about her makeup brushes and cotton balls in the bathroom. Now Patty just didn't fret over the foils and Teresa only occasionally commented on her sink area disasters. Patty supposed that was the way with most successful partnerships; eventually you had to put the trivial behind you or you'd go nuts.

For now Patty was pleased to be somewhere that wasn't inside a car, bus, subway or train. Especially not a plane. She didn't want to move an inch. She didn't want to see the outside world.

Done with her chocolate kisses, Teresa rested her head against Patty's shoulder. Patty brushed the older woman's pretty, almond-silver hair from her eyes and tucked it behind her ear. A brown hotel blanket swaddled Teresa. An unusually cold day for Southern California, the hotel lobby was drafty with the front doors constantly opening. The concierge had asked if they wanted a blanket and of course Teresa had said no, but Patty knew to say, "But I'd like one," understanding to whom the blanket would truly end up benefiting.

She placed a soft kiss on Teresa's forehead and brought the blanket closer around her. "Love you," said Patty.

Teresa smiled and squeezed her knee.

For a moment, the warmth of home spread through Patty. Teresa wasn't her mother, she was more. Since they could not claim any place in this world, Teresa *was* Patty's home. It was difficult to contemplate how much she'd come to care for the woman, after all their ups and downs on the road, the endless days up to Halloween, the Hearts of the Harvests to protect, the Church members they'd killed.

And they had killed lots of people. There was no second guessing that anymore. Patty couldn't absolve them from these deeds like she had as a younger person, when good was good and evil was evil. The Church of Midnight's followers were not innocent people by any stretch, but in body and in soul, they were weak, in many ways, wounded human beings.

Secretly, Patty believed Teresa wanted this long road trip to finally end and maybe wiping out the Church was the only logical step toward that. She understood that logic more than she wanted to admit, but still guilt pressed down. Due to the future actions of one Patty Middleton, many more people out there, right at this moment, were living on borrowed time. She often wondered if the followers had a choice to die or leave the Church, which would they take? Could she then finally spare lives, instead of extinguish them?

Pointless to even consider…it didn't matter as long as the Messenger gave them directions to kill and Teresa blindly obeyed.

Patty wondered how the blood analysis had gone, if Byron had even done the test on the letter yet. As much as she would have rather taken a nap with Teresa here on the couch, she found herself glancing around the lobby for the internet room. A big hotel like this had to have one. When Teresa went to sleep, she'd come downstairs again for a tall coffee and some LAX research. Poring over the news rarely brought her any closer to finding the Messenger—anything connected to the Old Domain seemed to dissolve from the public's eyes—but she'd pieced together some inconsistencies post-Halloween news reports had left unquestioned, never coming up with anything substantial but just enough to keep her hungry with the search. With a blast of frigid air from outside, a family of four bustled into the hotel hauling some expensive red leather luggage behind them. The daughter and son whirled around their father, a tall man with thin framed glasses and an eagle's beak nose. He was primarily focused on reaching the line to check in, while his wife, almost half as short as him and dressed in a smart business blazer and slacks took care to remind the kids to not run inside the building.

Patty felt a little sadness twist. The road had claimed all her family photos, all her keepsakes from her childhood home. Teresa told her it was probably better to forget the past, but that was just Teresa demonstrating how hard her armor had become.

Ten years ago Patty left behind two parents and a sister. Just as the Messenger's letters had foretold, Teresa had come for her the day after Halloween. Even her family preparing for it for years hadn't made that day any easier. Now that scene was a sad echo of a different life. It felt like a betrayal to let so much time go without thinking about her relatives, but it hurt too much to do so. Would they be like strangers now? Susan was an adult now. Would Patty even recognize her sister if she saw her? Would she recognize Patty? Did she still remember the Mickey Mouse dance they perfected? Could Susan still remember the tales from the Old Domain she used to tell her little sister at midnight?

Shut up, Susan. That's all made up stuff.

Like hell it is...you, me and Mom and Dad used to live in that world. Don't you remember?

Patty certainly didn't remember her brief time in the Old Domain. Not then and not now. As an infant, Patty didn't remember the trip across the gateway, but Susan had vivid stories to tell. Most of them seemed far-fetched, an older sister trying to freak out her fragile counterpart, but all the stories ended with their grandfather dying—somehow he'd given himself to open a temporary gateway. Susan's stories, while varied, always ended with, "and though there was a good chance he would survive, it was too much for his old body to handle. I think he knew it would happen. Yeah, he knew."

Her sister's whispered bedtime tales in her head, soft murmurs from a ghost behind a prison wall, and Patty would never hear that voice again. Or her mother's silly lullabies at night, the scent of garlic from her kitchen. Or her father's clapping hands when the Dodgers got on base, the glugging of his Gatorade bottles, his vanilla cherry stogies.

To deal with leaving her family, Teresa had suggested Patty write a journal and vent. After losing a few different notebooks in motels, Patty started writing an email diary. Reading them now was surprisingly fun. Well, a mix of fun and alarming at times. People did change; something you could believe in strongly one year, you could be laughing your ass off about the next.

Patty got out her cell phone and thumbed through the slow loading menus to her web browser. She hadn't looked at any of them for a while now. If she ever put the entries to actual paper, she'd be rewriting some of them, no doubt.

Choosing one at random, she clicked it open and read.

TO: pmiddleton@tvlwebplaces.com
SUBJECT: Outside Austin, TX. I am seventeen years old this year...

I feel ripped off. I see other teenagers and they look so confident, like they're immortal or something. I don't have that self-esteem, I don't have that sense of living forever. If I ever did, it'll never come back now. I've seen too much death to enjoy that viewpoint.

We saved another Heart of the Harvest this year. Always a good thing. I do think though, I mean, I have this weird feeling...over the years Chaplain Cloth improves, and I think this will keep happening, unless he dies. If he even can. I wish we could kill him for good.

I saw some of the Church of Morning through the opening in the gateway. They were trying to push a giant thing into it, I guess to wedge it open. Looked like a part of a building in a Hercules movie. The gateway shut before they had a chance to put it in place though. I told Teresa but she didn't see it for herself. I think she knew what I was talking about but didn't say much. She's so annoying about that sometimes.

We just pulled off to some stupid place. I hate BBQ. Be back in a sec...

The smoked turkey wasn't too bad. The sauce was kind of sweet and Teresa loosened up after a few Dos XX. Anywho, we do what we have to, I guess, so that everybody else in the world can keep what is normal. We give ourselves to that.

I can't think of anything else to write. I'll see you next Halloween, my journal.

Not very prolific, that's for sure, *thought Patty.*

There had been mention of the Columns though. One Church had already tried and failed. The best chance to mention this to Teresa would be tomorrow after she had some coffee in her. Still the response would likely be a lot of words just as easily communicated with a shrug. Teresa had forty Halloweens under her belt and she knew what she knew. It was difficult to introduce new concepts. But that didn't mean Patty would give up trying with her best friend. Never.

Patty put up her phone and closed her eyes. Seventeen felt so long ago. Lifetimes passed. Really it had only been four Halloweens behind the current one. In some respects she didn't understand the self-centered brat who wrote the diary, but in other ways, the longing of that young girl still burned hot as ever. Possibly, it would never go away. Not unless the Messenger was soon found, and challenged.

SEVEN

Two men died giving blood to the witch Pel'Hahr, while three more lost consciousnesses and appeared to grasp tentatively onto life. The witch regained her blood count with a scarcity of time to spare. One by one, Bre had to drag the dead men outside the cottage and pile them on the mortuary's narrow flatbed wagon.

"That all of them?" asked the driver. The man had some Ekkian features. His brown beard was thick like the warrior race, but his face far too soft, and eyes too kind, to be completely pure.

"I believe so," said Bre. "The other men are alive."

"Take the others as well," Kennen's voice came from around the wagon. He stumbled on a cluster of broken mortar and pebbles, his elegant robe tripping him more with every step. Bre caught his master around the arms just before he collapsed. The sunset blurred Kennen's deranged features but not the sleep starvation in his black eyes. Keeping at it like this was going to kill him and they hadn't even spoken of preparations for the Day of Opening.

"My gratitude, Slave." He quickly patted Bre's shoulder and moved onward, although his gait showed little improvement.

"Master, I don't understand. Those other men are still alive. You want to send them to the undertakers?"

"Get the rest into the wagon. You can help," he told the half-Ekkian driver. "Then, Slave, you need to bring the reserve bottles to the medical cache. You're dismissed to your cell after. We start again at morning's first kiss. Now get going."

So that was that.

Kennen had taken the last donor blood for reserves. All those young men had come here thinking they were making a single offering and had no idea this sunken husk of a dead troll, this sorry little witch's cottage, would be the last place they ever set foot. Fairness and decency aside, this wasn't particularly good for the chemistry of their poultice; such theft didn't make for a powerful sacrifice. Had these men understood their fate and willingly gave over their lives, the gift of noble surrender would have enriched the blood and Pel'Hahr would need fewer transfusions by less than half.

The driver jumped down and dusted his big leathery hands together. Bre stood there in the fading light, deep in morbid thought. Kennen had disappeared between the two bleeding trees.

"We have work to complete," Bre told the man.

"Work? Carrying a few bodies?" the driver laughed. "I dragged fifteen columns from Azaraith temple across marshland with only the aide of four men and five horses. Back and forth, back and forth, for three years. Now *that's* work!"

"No dispute here."

"Say, since you're close to him, has the Archbishop got his eye on any other column for the gateway? I could use some more coin for this season."

"He hasn't mentioned it in a while."

"Really? So you think one of those that we brought—?"

"Most likely is *the one*," Bre said in a hushed voice. "Now, let's get going before the sentinels come to harass us."

The man nodded knowingly and Bre went back inside the stifling little cottage. The blood pump still chugged, though it pulled nothing but air. He flipped its switch. On the bed, under a hint of creeping blue moonlight, Pel'Hahr's chest rose and fell at a sickening pace. He watched her for a moment, considering. The weak transfusions would not last her through tomorrow most likely.

Clotted blood on the tomes...Bre cursed inwardly. Kennen just hadn't thought this out very well. No sleep and worrying about the Church of Midnight's lack of leadership, *it was all coming to a head.*

Telling himself these matters shouldn't be his concern, Bre collected the bladders of blood, while the driver dragged the pale corpses outside. Some of the residual bodily fluids streaked the ground and bloodtresh flowers had sprouted up, their sharp-edged cups like tiny red decapitated necks. Before retiring to bed, Bre would have to return with the scythe and clear them out before someone's ankles got cut up. And another chore left unsaid, Kennen's robe needing ironing for tomorrow. Bre's duties never seemed to really end.

He got a better hold on the heavy sack of blood bladders. His shoulders creaked and knees sought to outdo them. In the distance, the palace loomed with its great twisting, dark orange towers, the medical cache hidden well within them.

The driver cracked the reins and glanced back at the struggling slave. "Day's almost done," he said. A half smile lighted on his bearded face. It was the kind of smile that only a free man could know.

With respect, Bre nodded and arduously carried on up the embankment.

Bre's cell had no windows but the sound of the crashing Olathu Ocean against the bone brick walls made the ill-lit dwelling a place of healing. As a child, the hissing of the salt water and the violent thrashes of the high tide kept him from many nights of much needed sleep. Now his mind wouldn't let him fall asleep without the chaotic battling of the red waves. In dreams he could still hear them sometimes. Even in dreams people would open their mouths and words would not come, just that tremendous, endless spilling roar. In his sexual dreams with Pel'Hahr, her kisses sounded like the crashing. His thrusts into her sounded like the hissing. It was the waves. Only. They cradled Bre.

And it was no surprise his concentration on the cacophony had caused him to sleep through Kennen entering his cell with an Impish Detention Box.

His mattress and basket of belongings had been removed to the hall and in their place sat the detention box, a coffin-shaped device that flourished with green accordion tubes fixed to nerve-interpreting regulators and dim blue bottles of distilled water where crystallized emotions cooked down to fluid form. Bre was overly familiar with the machine. He had helped the Archbishop put a fair share of men and women into the chamber. The subjects usually endured such suffering that they stood at the precipice of consciousness when taken out. Some had lost mental stability afterward.

The Archbishop of Morning had no other clothes on but a tan loin cloth. Kennen's body had been thoroughly pilfered like his face. He sat in the center of the cell, his back against the detention box. The ear that once dangled from his head had been removed rather than reattached by staple. Tears bloomed fast in his eyes and he had trouble speaking without breaking down. When he composed himself, he took a big breath and stared at Bre.

"If the union of worlds doesn't happen this year, if my mother is made to survive another year…I fear I'll go mad. See I, see…I think I hoped today those men wouldn't provide enough blood for her. I hoped the donations would fail her and she would drift away."

"No you didn't, master."

"I did." A tear from each eye rolled out, one stranded on a clump of scar tissue and the other split against a staple through his cheek and broke in two directions. "I know she's listening. I *know* she can still see me in her mind. I hoped she'd go quietly. Maybe all I've given to her would be recorded then. The Tomes written later would reflect my service to her power— they would express that I tried everything and that I kept her alive longer than any of the best apothecaries in the Old Domain had envisioned." Kennen's eyes sparkled like simmering tar. "I made a mistake, let my resolve go. It was my weariness that shook my faith in her. You understand that I love her, don't you, Slave? You understand that my mother is everything to me. Pel'Hahr Kennen's sacrifice will not go in vain."

Bre's eyes moved to the detention box. He used the wall to push himself up. The waves crashed outside the room, laughing.

"What will you have me do, master?"

Kennen's eyes held terror for his slave as he reached over and popped the bronze clasps to its cabinet. At once the innocent sounds of snickering and snapping made Bre's blood chill. He could hear them nesting at the bottom of the box.

Baelins.

"I need five liters to enrich the blood reserves," explained Kennen.

Each liter bottle on the side of the device looked twice larger than Bre recalled. He swallowed and nodded. Five bottles would mean a stay in the box probably well into tomorrow morning, perhaps the afternoon, depending if the incubuses took any breaks.

"I'll give you time to recover. I promise, Slave."

"As you will, master." Bre lost no time, swung his foot over the side of the box and dropped it down into the mass of baelins. At once they smacked their lips and ran frantically around inside. A gritty, wet tongue hungrily licked his ankle. He put his other foot inside and felt one of them ejaculate on his toes.

Kennen's face had never looked as disturbing as now. "You know full well what you offer."

"I know full well," replied Bre.

"And so this sacrifice is good. Your devotion sings in me, Slave."

The Archbishop started to shut the lid. Bre hunkered down, vowing to not make this easy on the den of rapists he joined, but his resolve broke quickly as the box shut and the light from his candle outside could no longer be seen.

He heard the interpreters spinning and mechanical parts moving around him. A voice from an old dream came to him and froze his core. *There is something special about you, Bre Courre. I want to use that.* Unlike his brother Kauph, the Heart of the Harvest was dead in Bre, but that did not mean he still couldn't be great, that he couldn't share some form of power with the world.

For a moment he saw a vision from his dreams: the edge of a cliff, a gathering of goat-donkeys below, felt a sharp wind on his face…

One of the baelins jumped onto his chest and forced itself inside his mouth. Bre spat and thrashed around. He tried to crush it against the wall of the box but it squirmed away. Needling fangs sunk into his thighs and another creature fought its way between his legs. Bre wailed but the sound and the emotion drew out of him like having the wind knocked from his chest.

That was only one drop in the tempest to come.

EIGHT

The mantle.

Patty saw it now, as Teresa went about dabbing her hair in the bathroom with an expensive ivory towel. The silver thing hovered there in her chest, a strange, jagged oval shape. Within, Patty could see the lump of cancer had long since died and become a fibrous powder. It perplexed her sometimes to think what would have happened had Martin not saved Teresa. She might have had Martin as her partner instead.

Teresa walked out of the bathroom and set her towel down on the little coffee table. Patty turned down the volume of the television. An on-demand advertisement for some police comedy noted that the next showing was in fifteen minutes.

Teresa looked at her. "I've been thinking about this morning with that gift shop explosion. I need reassurance you can still create mantles safely."

"You want to practice building, don't you?"

"I'll shield off the room."

"What if I...blow us up?"

"I guess the Messenger will have to go find some other slaves."

Patty raised her eyebrows. "Well, when you put it that way." Teresa had the outer world sealed off with mantles before Patty even crossed the room. The older woman was surprisingly quick in drawing them, perhaps a little quicker than Patty, but possessed nowhere near the same range or capacity. The mantles flickered golden-silver-bronze-intense white and then repeated in a mesmerizing strobe, ghost matter from the Old Domain. It was still surprising to Patty, with all of their glow,

Teresa could only sense mantles rather than be blinded by their presence.

Both Nomads brought over mantles and launched them at each other. The game was like reverse tug-a-war. Each person pressed their mantles into her opponent's. Whoever's mind let go of the mantle first would be the loser. Patty always won, but it was still a great strength exercise for both of them.

Patty drew from the cold pinpoint in her mind and brought about a perfectly square shape with blade sharp edges. Her mantle was as thin as paper. Teresa's wasn't perfectly shaped—it had frayed corners and was tilted, a most strange polyhedron, not to mention as thick as a history book. Patty's mantle struck the other, knocking it so far back it almost flew into Teresa's face. Recovering, Teresa countered, already a bead of sweat rolling down her temple, her teeth biting her lower lip in concentration. "Let me know," she said with a grunt, "when you feel like something might be wrong."

Not that that would help. Nothing had felt wrong to Patty this morning. She'd placed an insignificant mantle in that store...this one was quite a bit larger.

Suddenly something buzzed in her side. Muscle twitch? No—it felt electric—it felt to be building—she saw Teresa's eyes widen with a question.

Patty let the mantle disintegrate into the ether.

Teresa held hers for a moment, buried in thought, and then slowly did the same.

Her leg continued to buzz. Patty shook her head. "My phone," she muttered and slid the vibrating device from her pocket.

"Hold on. The Messenger said to—"

Putting a finger up, Patty hit the TALK button. "Yes, sir?" Teresa's face creased with annoyance.

The man on the phone cleared his throat. "There's a bar down the street from your hotel. *Bahama Mama's*. You want to meet up in a few?"

"How'd you know where we were staying, Byron?" Patty tried to sound as annoyed as Teresa looked. If she pulled it off, her partner didn't show it.

"I have a lot of bored agents. They already sit in cars picking their noses, might as well be for a good reason. Dontcha think?"

"Sorry, we have to leave early tomorrow."

"Well that's the pits, because I have some valuable information about the Church."

"You luring me?"

"Can you feel the hook in your lip?"

"We'll give you an hour."

"I thought it'd be just me and you. Like old times?"

"You wish," said Patty.

Teresa had grabbed one of her novels from the table and cracked it open with notable interest. She didn't object and Patty seized the moment.

"See you in a few hours."

Patty hung up. She waited a bit as Teresa turned a page from her book. The crisp sound gave her chills on top of her chills.

"He wanted me to go alone. Like a date or something," Patty said with a short guffaw. "I'll just kick back here though. Break his heart. Ha. Ha."

"Why don't you go?"

Patty didn't know what to do with the suggestion. It wasn't something that would come from her partner, not this close to Halloween.

Teresa glanced over her shoulder and laughed dryly. "Am I that much of a bitch?"

Patty smiled. "No."

"Just as long as you know this doesn't lead anywhere past tonight."

"I can't believe my ears."

"If I hold you back, you'll only want to break away, maybe get hurt. That's something I don't want you to do. He's a handsome guy. I get it. You can certainly take care of him or anything else that comes your way. Well, if you don't blow yourself up."

"That's not funny."

"You're right. Forget I said it. Maybe you shouldn't go."

"You won't be lonely here?"

Now Teresa actually snorted. "I think we see plenty of each other, don't you?"

"Suppose you're right."

Teresa went over to the bed with her book. "Now go take your shower and get gussied up. Keep in mind you can never sleep on a plane."

Patty took a couple steps toward the bathroom and stopped. She looked at her partner, for all intents and purposes, her only lasting friend in this world.

"Thank you, Teresa."

"Don't thank me, for fuck's sake. I'm not your lord and master. We're leaving tomorrow for Scotland though. That's that."

"Yes, Commander Celeste." Patty saluted.

Teresa flipped over another page and raised an eyebrow. "I can live with that."

Byron stood outside the Chase bank a few blocks from the Nomads' fancy hotel. It was a wonderfully small world. His trackers had located more than just the two women in the area. He was running into people he knew from every part of his life. Amazing what a trip to Beverly Hills could accomplish.

He opened the bank's door for a large man in a business suit and his little girl. The man grunted thanks; Byron nodded; the girl cranked up her head and pointed, "He has more gray than you do, Grandpa!"

"Alice," the man barked and looked at him apologetically. "Silver does sound better," Byron replied with a grin. "Gray is for elephants."

The man ushered the little girl to the parking lot. She glanced back, running her fingers through her stringy blonde hair, as though Byron's hair streaks were contagious.

Byron leaned forward to look at his reflection in the glass door. He hadn't paid attention this morning, but he did suddenly look twenty-eight going on fifty-eight. *Probably should go pick up some of that hair dye,* he thought. He wondered if any of his relatives had gone prematurely gray. Byron had never met any of them, so it was sort of a worthless thing to wonder.

Two chatting women drifted up to the bank door. Byron opened it for them. They didn't bother thanking him. Another group arrived, three men in casual attire, led by a man in polo shirt and slacks. The polo shirt man explained to the others, "It's not the same as flipping property, you can just—thank you, sir!" The others mumbled thanks to Byron too. He nodded to each of them. *Nobody gonna tip the door man?* He spotted the next bank departure. A younger man dressed in a black suit took long strides toward him. The man obsessed with the contents in his wallet and almost didn't notice the door.

Byron opened it for him. As the man stepped through, already giving thanks without looking up, Byron soundly struck the man in the face with the door. The impact sent the man sprawling back into the bank. Byron ducked in and pulled him up by his shirt. A button snapped off and struck the tile floor.

"Oh, so sorry, are you okay?" Byron said loudly.

A few bank tellers moved their heads sideways to look, along with several others in their lines. Taking pains to wipe down Harry Frank's suit, Byron pulled the Church of Midnight acolyte to the side of the building.

Harry still looked dazed but began grabbing at his hip. Not that there was anything to grab there anymore.

Harry focused on the gun Byron dangled in front of his face. Byron ejected the clip and winged it into the parking lot, so far no sound could be heard. Then he shed the bullet in the chamber.

Rolling his eyes in disbelief, Harry leaned against the bank and shook his head. "Fuuuuck." He shook his head again, more profoundly. "You been following me?"

"Nope, just in the neighborhood."

"Right. You shithead Arcs would put trackers on your dicks if you could find it. You better not have messed up my car's wiring."

"Now let's settle down." Byron patted him on the shoulder and handed back his gun.

Harry angrily pushed the weapon back into his suit and sniffed dramatically. "My damn nose bleeding?"

A few more people walked out of the bank. Byron gestured with a movement of his head, "Step over to the bush, friend."

They walked to the eastern side of the bank, all the while Harry muttered, "Bullshit, bullshit, bullshit."

"What did I tell you about depositing the check in person?" Harry squinted incredulously. "Nobody but you cares, Telamon."

Byron caught him by the nose and shoved him into the wall. "Jesus," Harry huffed, the air knocked from him.

"This is important," Byron said softly. "If the Glasgow information doesn't pan out, you've already seen how easily I can find you."

"You've got the Newark Chapel and you got all the Voids. That was the deal. Now let me go about my life. I ain't in the Church no more."

"Good choice! But that's not immunity. If this Void doesn't work as you suggest, it'll be ugly for you and yours."

"This is supposed to be the only Void that mutes their power. That's all I know, you lousy asshole."

Byron stepped away, reached out and grabbed Harry's hand, gave it a firm enough shake to make large tears wobble in the man's eyes. "Now then, take care of yourself, Harry. If that Void fails to take the Nomads' mantles away, consider yourself skull-fucked."

It looked like Harry believed him, which was all that Byron really wanted to accomplish. He didn't plan on killing or hurting anybody. This was all about information gathering, and he was making progress.

He released Harry's hand and the man at once massaged it with a cringe.

"Now then, have a nice evening," Byron told him. "I've got to get ready for a date."

Places like this made Patty nervous. She and Byron had sat there an hour now, but she still could not put her finger on it. Dive bars with a theme always unsettled her. Patty had no clue why it bothered her so much, but then, having been with Teresa so long, she could be suspicious about just anything. Even Disneyland dug at her the wrong way now.

The mask over what the establishment represented made

the people look trapped in a disguise they would rather shed, an unwanted prison constructed of lies.

Bahama Mama's prison, of course, was an island theme. The mural walls featured an expanse of dull blue ocean, pink sand and tall, thin palm trees that bent over everything in the small space, *ready to snatch up passerby. The bartenders had Hawaiian shirts and some of the servers wore pink and purple leis.*

"You don't like this place," Byron pointed out and took a sip of his Jameson and Coke.

Patty shrugged. "It's a bar."

"We aren't here for the atmosphere." He tapped her knuckle, lightly, and sent a thrill through her body.

She drew her hand away, in case he tried that again, and busied herself with stacking their dishes and silverware for the server. She'd only eaten a portion of her chicken nachos and he'd picked at his club sandwich and homemade potato chips. Neither one of them were getting fat any time soon.

"You don't have to tidy our stuff, you know."

"I know," she said.

"Soda's too sweet for me anymore," he commented and pushed the empty glass away. The overworked lady bartender caught the movement from behind the counter.

"Another?" she called.

Byron shook his head. "Just booze this time."

"Only booze."

"No, double booze."

The bartender grinned and a few construction workers in orange shirts chuckled at this and cast amused glances before continuing their conversation.

Byron cracked his knuckles and Patty made a face of disapproval. He ignored this and stretched like he was working a kink out of his neck. "I got to get used to this island life. Off to San Juan tomorrow. You routed that Chapel already, didn't you?"

Patty nodded silently.

Byron went on, "I'll write a report confirming that we had the wrong contact information. Oh, and blame you for everything."

Patty twisted her lips coyly. "Thank you?"

"I like my job well enough, Pat, just not the part about going after you."

"No? I thought that's what you like best."

Byron clutched his heart as though wounded. The bartender set down a large tumbler of whiskey. The overhead canned light cast brass lasers across the table as the ice jiggled around. "That's stunning!"

"Double booze can be," she said with an old smile and walked back to the bar.

He slid his drink over, "She's right," and took a deep sip.

"So other than bailing us out again, why'd you ask me here?" Patty hoped she didn't sound like she was fishing for a certain answer.

"That's a ridiculous question." He then killed half the whiskey.

"Slow down there, Bukowski."

"I'm self medicating." He winced—it looked authentic— and brought a hand to his side. After the pain passed, Byron sighed through his teeth and focus came back to his eyes.

"You ok?"

"I did ask you here for another reason besides the obvious one."

She leaned forward and he lowered his voice. "It was blood."

"What?"

"On the letter," he said. "I found a DNA match. It's from a person named R. Smith. I figure that's not a real name, but there is an assortment of Glasgow residences connected to this particular Smith. I'm trying to locate the most recent. Once I have it, I'll email it to you. Same address?"

"Are you fucking kidding me?"

"Not fucking kidding in the slightest."

It couldn't be this simple. Smith couldn't really be the Messenger. What would happen if they actually found him? Nomads had been following directions from this anonymous force since the time of the ancients. Teresa was convinced none of them had ever seen the Messenger—would she change that now? It wasn't impossible to consider; Patty had done things with mantles that no other Nomad before her had.

Byron waved his hand before her eyes. "You in there?"

"Sorry, yes, it's the same email. Please let me know as soon as you can." Patty twisted her glass of gin and tonic anxiously, only a few sips into it. She would have to get back to the hotel and definitely hit the internet.

"So do you know where the gateway will be?" Byron gulped his large drink. "Any word? You know me, I'm always curious."

"In protecting the Heart of the Harvest, our recourse is to be as far away from Cloth as we can get, not go looking for him. Where do you fail to see the logic in this?"

"You aren't afraid of Chaplain Cloth. It's the other way around."

"You couldn't be more wrong. We haven't beaten him every time. He's smarter than all of us...and I know this sounds complementary, it's not, but I think he's willing to risk more than any of us, put it all on the line."

"He's not braver than you," said Byron, shaking his head. "Or Teresa for that matter. You two are my heroes."

She let out a low laugh and appraised him, wanted to hold him. He poured the rest of his drink down his throat. Now you finish your drink," he said. "There's a halfway decent motel nearby. We could see what's on cable. Watch a movie before you head back."

"A movie. *Ha ha.*" She slid her drink toward him.

"You never ever finish." Byron studied her a moment and took her drink with a resentful swipe.

"Make it last. Sip it."

"I hate gin." In seconds he drank the drink until the ice cubes buckled and snapped in the bottom of the glass.

"You drink like this every night?"

"Just when my back is acting up. Helps me sleep."

"You going to see somebody for that?"

"That's what I'm doing right now." He grinned.

"I would like to go, you know," she told him truthfully. The bar seemed to get quiet around them. "Our last time seemed half-done. I always wondered about that, by the way. About why you disappeared and left me in the room all alone."

He acknowledged this as a fair question and pursed his lips. A drunken smile came and went. "I just...I couldn't bear having you do it to me again. Believe me, waking up beside you..." He looked down, a little embarrassed, and then chuckled. "Let's just say I wouldn't mind it at all."

She took his hand. It was clammy and cold. She placed her other hand on top of it. "That's bullshit," she said. "You're like me and Teresa. You have to be moving toward your goal, and you have to be at least a step ahead of everyone else in the race. People like that are not rooted."

He beheld her with his bloodshot eyes, about to say something. Instead he dropped his other hand on top of hers. "Dog pile," he whispered.

"I should get going. Be careful out there in San Juan. Take care of that back and catch some rays with that stressed out partner of yours. You both need a tan."

"San Juan doesn't appeal to me. I've decided to follow you to Glasgow instead."

Patty stood. "Liar."

He returned a thin smile. She took his prickly chin and planted a nice warm kiss on his full lips. It didn't matter how badly she wanted him; Teresa depended on her, and soon the Heart of the Harvest would. When she pulled away, Byron's fine-looking face had her frozen, his gray eyes turning her to stone.

"Email me," was all she got out.

As quickly as her legs could take her, Patty left the little island bar. When she got outside to call a cab, she noticed Byron hadn't followed her outside. That disappointed her, decidedly more than it should have.

Another thing left behind on the road, *she thought.*

He had to race to the bathroom as soon as Patty stepped out the door. The stall had so much graffiti it was difficult to say what color it'd been. Byron could hear the rolling twang of some country song playing in Bahama Mama's proper room, but the lyrics sounded water-bound and distant. Perched on the toilet, his thighs quivered from the strain. *So much for a romantic evening,* he thought.

He had one of these painful bowel movements once a week as a teenager, and then in his twenties two or three times a week. Now it was every day. The cramps would radiate in his gut, coils of devil shrimp chewing and pulling at his muscles and sinew. Scalding thorns would dapple his icy spine, and then this state would quickly reverse, his spinal column catching fire and volcanic daggers would then stab him from the base of his neck, down his back and into his rectum.

Byron enjoyed food but had been made a light eater because of this. He could completely forget a meal and end up ravenous some days. These bouts on the toilet made it seem otherwise, like he gorged himself day and night. Once the agony was thankfully over, he most likely flushed about four times, and it never smelled like shit—it smelled like rotting vegetation, and he could glimpse an occasional decomposed leaf in the revolting black soup in the toilet bowl. His weekly vomiting event had similar foliage, despite him rarely eating salads or any vegetable for that matter.

He could hardly remember what he was doing in this filthy bathroom, why he wasn't at his apartment getting stoned or drunk.

Patty, his mind told him. He sorted through the deep, cold wells in his brain, and tried to concentrate on her. The tension in his shoulders, *a circus strong man giving him a crushing massage. He tried to think about Patty again. She was the way out for him.*

You love her, don't you? *he asked himself.*

Byron clenched his revolver firmly in his hand, the barrel turned to his temple. He couldn't remember taking it out and aiming it. This wasn't the first time though. What would happen if the next time he pulled the trigger unconsciously? Maybe his body acted on his behalf, since his soul didn't seem to want to leave this world as badly. He stared into the barrel and imagined how a bullet could be the best medicine. One day, he figured his soul would be as threadbare as his body, and if he hadn't found Chaplain Cloth by then…maybe that would be the time to take a gunpowder pill.

In the meantime, he would continue to search for that gateway.

Byron holstered his weapon. More claws ripped through his gut. He relented and went for the photo of Chaplain Cloth in the inner pocket of his suit coat that hung over the stall. It wasn't ever instantaneous, but after glimpsing the photo, Byron's pain drew back into its hibernation, leaving only faint fingerprints of unease behind. After a few minutes, he caught his breath and wiped the sweat from his freezing cold forehead. His gaze stayed on the bone colored man in the black suit, one eye orange, one eye black. Dark trees framed the background on a blue-dark night, a young Halloween night—*how many did Cloth and his Children kill on that particular occasion?*

Back at the office there were archive films of people looking at the photo and being suddenly struck with violent seizures and the rapid onset of a poisoning-like response. When he'd gone to see if the photo was real, Byron had experienced something completely opposite. The image temporarily tamed his mystery ailment. That's when he decided to take a chance and swipe it from the evidence vault. Always a quick way out of the torment, it was easy to forget about the nightmares that would soon follow.

They were sometimes worse than the pain.

OCTOBER 27TH

NINE

That morning Alisyn had her period. It might have just been her bitter reaction to the matter, but the Newark Chapel felt colder than usual. It wasn't autumn in Glasgow; it was suddenly winter, and the iciness, the numbing madness would go on forever. She shivered and with her clean hand, raked the tears off her face. They felt cold too. She had to surface topside again. Fresh air would help, not this moist, glacial atmosphere in this freezing dungeon far below the rain-soaked Scottish soil.

She stared at the blood on her fingers for a long while. Time had stopped just to let her agonize a little more. Camden had been right. What had she expected? To give birth on Halloween to a week-old baby? Still, it put nettles in her brain, made her feel like she was at last becoming completely unhinged. Her eyes lifted to the words etched across the privy stall. *Queen Cunt.*

"That is all they think you can be," she said, "an' that's all you think of yourself..."

It was true. She was a walking womb. Being a vessel for the True Son had defined her so long she was no more a person than that wooden box that held Camden's baby.

Our baby.

Alisyn reached between her legs and took a handful of sorrowful vermillion. She smeared it across the word. After painting the wall in this fashion several times, she sat back on the toilet and cried. The word *Queen* stared back at her, but she couldn't put any credence in it anymore. It wasn't meant to be. It was a lie. It was always a lie.

For a change, she would have to resign herself to being the

Priestess of Midnight, not the mother of a God. *I'm sorry my son. Our time has not yet come.*

The apothecary snapped the last lock in place around Alisyn's wrist. A little of her skin pinched in the shackle. The woman's fumble was obvious and still she made no apology. With a savage nose looking broken a dozen times before, a salt and pepper uni-brow that always pointed down in a disapproving V shape, the Midnight Apothecary wasn't a woman to approach with trifles, especially not with Alisyn. She'd once told a cook in the lower kitchen, "That one has more interest in her litter of ghost children than anythin' else. I'd be surprised if she's even cracked open one of the Tomes."

Alisyn had made sure to come to dinner that night with a tome under her arm. She chose the *Toiling of Families*. It included her favorite poem, "Waking Miseries in the Pleasure Dream."

"It's important ye understand why I'm chainin' ye to the stone here," Mina blurted out to grab her attention. Alisyn quickly glanced up, drawn violently from her thoughts. Mina regarded her with a scientist's wonder. Her uni-brow was raised, an old dead rainbow covered in cobwebs and shadows.

"So I don't hurt myself," replied Alisyn, "or someone else I gather."

"That's the meat of it, aye. We don't want anyone residing in both worlds at once, even on the ethereal level. If ye found a place where the binding between worlds had unraveled a bit, ye'd create a gateway, and that pretty figure of yours would probably be midden afterward. Ye'd die."

"I see. Thanks for the complement."

Mina coughed raggedly. She turned her rotund frame around, old black robes shifting back and forth, sweeping the dusty stone floor. A few wheels squeaked like rodents as she brought a cart closer. The woman had laid out a variety of implements in a chaotic manner, some instruments lying across others, several jars with their lids already off, or dangling over the side.

"When will the Archbishop be here?"

"He's occupied but said he'd try to come."

Wonderful, thought Alisyn. That meant that Camden had promised his time to others and she would get the dregs. As usual. She'd be lucky to even see him at all today. So much for all that we're in this together *talk.*

Mina rearranged some the implements on the cart. "A word of caution before we start. Some of these items came from all over the Old Domain, sent just last night from the Church of Morning. They may have been waylaid in the Marrowlands for a time, so I'm handlin' them with caution. There's no telling what kind of blight they could bring back. I'm prepared though."

"The Marrowlands?"

"The other side of here and there. It is the way through, the conduit of matter, anti-matter and ethereal energies." Mina grabbed the stiff, pale cadaver of a frog with spikes running down its dotted back. The frog's eyes were closed, but judging by the sockets alone, the eyes were oversized, possibly twice as large as a human pair. Oddly, the eyelids had a fresher, greener look than the rest of the frog. Mina took a tiny paring knife and pried one open to the blank amber colored eye.

Mina delicately sliced a gelatinous layer of film from the frog's eye. She placed the cloudy piece of flesh on a small cutting board where she severed it in two. Without warning, she turned and pulled down Alisyn's eyelids. Alisyn thrashed in surprise but Mina had inserted both of the frog's lenses almost immediately. They spread out fluidly, enriching themselves over the surface of her eyes. Alisyn tried to blink, but couldn't.

"What hae ye done?"

Mina considered two cups that simmered over small flames. "Ye'll have to keep yer eyes open. Blinkin' will shut off the perception between yer body an' ethereal presence in the Old Domain. A local anesthetic would not have sufficed in this case, because ye must bear witness to an Apex Goblin, see it clearly through yer mind's eye, which will in turn be registered as visual input. With a naked eye, the goblin's magnificence will make ye lose control of yer body. Not even the powerful sight of the Voyeurs can prevent mania from setting in. This fanged-back frog, however, suffers no effect from gazing on an Apex Goblin."

Small wisps of smoke came from the blackened marrow seed oil in the pewter cups. Mina reached for a plate with several Lungbat brains. Alisyn was familiar with the brains as appetizers at Conclave several years back. They looked similar to blackberries, yet ran with orange veins and forever pulsed in the mouth until chewed completely. Despite their harvesting from the bat's skull, it was said that thoughts and ideas would continue to gather in the brains. Alisyn recalled they tasted a little less horrible than the stomach acid that rose in your throat sometimes, but they also were cold for some reason. She always wondered if the devoured thoughts had been what added the iciness.

Mina squeezed one brain into each cup. Gloves or not, she wagged each of her hands afterward, as though handling dry ice.

Alisyn watched all of this, wide-eyed. The urge to blink never set in. Going a lifetime without blinking was not only suddenly possible, it made more sense.

The layer of oil in the bowls cracked like desert earth. Black mist wiggled out of the fissures in an unbelievable torrent. Mina grabbed the bowls quickly and brought them over Alisyn's eyes. A crackling darkness surrounded her. The mist scrubbed her tear ducts like a million abrasive fingertips. She felt a few beads of tears drop out of the sides of her eyes. One reached her lips and she realized it was blood and tear together.

"Tell me when the darkness clears...do not move yer eyes side to side, no matter how they itch. Look forward always. Looking side to side will likely leave ye blind." Mina intoned the last with a bit of satisfaction.

The discomfort slowly faded. Darkness peeled back. Alisyn's body stumbled forward. Gravity should have taken her to her knees, but gravity did not come with her on this trip. She was at the base of a forest populated with black trees that reached terrifying heights into the cold sky. A clotted orange canopy of leaves stretched to infinity above. They were trees, but not. There was something too foreign about them to only make them trees.

"Can ye see?" whispered a voice on the wind. "Are ye there? In the Blakandor Forest?"

"It's hazy, but I think so," she answered, but when her lips moved she didn't hear words come, only thoughts echoed from her mind.

"Hoots! I leave ye then," answered Mina, "to the Old Domain."

Over time, images of the Old Domain became intensely real. Alisyn stood on a straw carpet. A rolling forest tapestry stretched before her, trees with bark the color of obsidian and leaves of brutal orange. Some charred implements left behind from the Church of Morning still lay on the ground, the site where Archbishop Kennen's followers had sent over the various constituents to Mina the apothecary.

Alisyn bent down on a knee. The clammy earth sent shivers through her skin, down to the bone. Alisyn tried to run her fingers through the charred remains. It was a bewildering experience, like her sense of touch flashed between nonexistent and hyper-existent. Her fingers would pass through the ash, then feel the microscopic variations in each burnt flake, then go out again. The cold in her knee was exactly the same. Come and gone, gone and come. She got up and twirled in circles. Her body was naked, but she still felt the clothing she wore back in her world. Here and not here, there and not there.

Something caught her eye and she stopped twirling.

The Apex Goblin squirmed through the trunks of two particularly thick trees. Its mighty nostrils dilated as it searched for the scent of something.

"Ghost." The word was a rumble in its smooth dark grey throat. It sniffed again.

"Ghost, come here."

It knew I was here...

She watched its gaze from behind the swinging silver hair, the crystal intelligent eyes, apple-sized sapphires, darting back and forth in its search. The beast had such beauty that beholding it for more than a minute would bless the observer's eyes with the ability to watch all life, in all worlds, all at once. Most could only see the Apex Goblin for a couple of seconds and then need to turn away.

And that was what she was doing. Turning away. This was too much. She'd seen it now. All-sight would be hers to use.

"Come, Ghost," it said again. "I have filled you with the worlds. You must fill me with a child."

Alisyn gasped. It wanted to use her. Yes, this is what she'd been denied! She would not carry the True Son. She wouldn't be its mother at all.

She was the father.

Could this work?

Alisyn carefully walked toward the gorgeous creation. With every stride she learned more of this beast's sex. The genitals grew under a massive flap in its chest. They were protected there. She could smell their musk. They needed to be milked for fluid and the hand that touched them would give of its own skin and those particles would thrive in the seminal fluid, divide into cells and become a child—hopefully a child. It had to attach inside of the chest cavity at first. If the fetus dropped out before it was ready to be planted into a tree, a sad miscarriage. The Apex Goblin's chest rose and fell in anticipation. Its breath smelled of dust and rose petals. She could feel herself weep at the thought of going under that fleshy flap, for then she would no longer see her lover, but at the same time, such closeness made her sight clarify.

The creature panted. She hadn't realized it initially but her body made her act. Pulling up the flap of skin and pushing the upper half of her body up inside, it caused the beast to have a small orgasm. Alisyn's clarity grew. That wasn't the entire height of pleasure. There was another place, a stickier place, farther up, if she could reach it, and her hands did, oh they found it, and her fingernails sunk in. The goblin screeched. The rough flesh rubbed her hands raw as she stroked down on the cavernous ridges of the organ. After only a few strokes, blood ran freely from her palms. Images of billions of people flooded into her mind and then left. For a moment, just a half a second, she thought she saw Camden sitting at a table with some acolytes, a couple of tomes opened in front of them. He looked distracted, worried. Worried for her...

But the sight was gone. Clarity was too intense for her to

focus it. Alisyn realized she needed to not only get out of this creature's womb—she needed to call out for the apothecary—she needed out of the Old Domain. She'd completed her task. This pleasure would kill her if she left it behind. No, she told herself. No, *it won't. Just leave. You have to leave.*

A gush of something chunky and cold ran down her shoulders. The goblin pushed at her. It wanted her out of its body too. The baby was trying to implant itself and she was in the way! Stuck! She was going to kill the baby!

Alisyn ducked down, tried to push out. A hand snatched her arm and she screamed. She focused down below her, near her legs.

A ghostly image of Mina peered up inside the creature. Her grip was intense with strength. "Ye hae to open yer eyes, girl! Open them! Yer body is seizing!"

"I can't!"

Mina came forward, but this drove Alisyn farther inside the beast. Her mouth slammed into a wall of mucus-covered muscle fibers. "Stop! Ye're killing it!"

"Come back," shouted Mina.

Rapidly Alisyn's eyes blinked and parted and the apothecary's laboratory grew around her like a chamber one thousand times its original size, only to shrink, constrict, deny her lungs of any of its dusty air, and then the chains around her wrists clanked as she went down to her knees and—

Intense sleep took her.

As he sat down in the throne, Camden tried to take every breath through his mouth. The stench of rot lived in the room's atmosphere like a hovering colony of fetid spirits. "There was no need to call another meeting," he said. "I was occupied. From now on, I will call when I deem it necessary...wi' respect, Archbishop Kennen."

The dirty blond corpse ignored him and twitched. Its eyes lazily opened and closed under the pressure of bloated flesh. "What have you learned about your Priestess?"

"The apothecary just informed me she has returned, much more traumatized than anticipated, but we believe it a success.

The Priestess of Midnight is in recovery now, sleeping. Now, if you don't mind. I am very busy."

The corpse's expression was blank. It sniffed a spear of brown fluid back into its nose. "I believe you've grown confused about our roles here, Camden Amherst. Let me clarify things a bit. Upon the union of worlds, the Eternal church will adopt the Church of Morning's hierarchy, by and large. You will, of course, be an auxiliary Bishop, continuing to train and delegate duties to the acolytes. But I thought you should know what to expect, and more importantly, how to speak to someone who will inevitably be your superior. In short, I will call a meeting any time I fucking well please."

Camden felt the world spinning. He wished Alisyn was here. She would have given this arrogant bastard an earful. You could too, *you know?* he thought. This wasn't the time to voice dissent though. This nonsense was all dependent on the worlds merging and if that did happen this year, hierarchy would be determined by Cloth, not by this asshole.

"It will be the Eternal Church," he simply stated, "a completely different thing."

"The members of the Church of Morning outnumber those of Midnight by a thousand to one, and that is an old estimate I created."

Camden stroked his beard and wanted to rip the hairs out of his face by the fistful. He took a deep, not so calming, breath. "I need to see to the Priestess now. I'm certain your mother needs attending to as well. Take care of her."

Maggots dropped from his eye sockets and landed on his hanging tongue. "Good luck to you. Thanksgiving to the Eternal Feast."

Saying nothing, Camden walked up to Kennen's conduit and ripped the phonograph's wiring from the exposed vocal cords.

He hovered over the decaying body for a few moments, wishing silently this dead man really was the Archbishop of Morning. Still sitting in the shadowy mezzanine level above, several people in the Inner Circle mumbled amongst themselves. A moment later the new silence made Camden realize they had left and how alone he was now, in this room hanging with the funk of rotting flesh. The decay was his only companion. The smell reminded him of the chicken stalls on his father's farm.

Camden shook his head. His eyes were watering from the horrid smell. Acolytes quietly entered the room to clean up, but something was becoming clearer in his mind and he couldn't abandon it. They shuffled awkwardly in place. They probably weren't here to clean up after all, but rather to ask something of him. How he hated these people now. They just wanted to take and take some more and he'd always went along with it, because of fear.

Let them wait...

Camden put his sweaty hands against the icy stone walls and closed his eyes. What rubbish, these bastards from the Old Domain had all their plans lined up, and what could he say, with his feeble following? Camden pinched his sinuses, feeling a headache burgeoning.

"Archbishop?" inquired a bright-eyed acolyte near the stairway. "Might we ask something of you?"

Out of the corner of his eye, Camden saw her accompanied by two strapping youths in black sweaters. Looking up, he smiled his best smile and approached them as warmly as his beleaguered heart would allow. "Brothers, sisters!"

TEN

The white bluffs over the Olathu Ocean slouched perilously like an avalanche frozen before impact. Sand both deep and snowy white swallowed Bre's legs to the knee caps. It was tough carrying the winch and ropes; his body was still sore and itchy from his revolting night with the baelins. Though he was free of the incubuses for now, the reminders of their carnal delights came sharply with every labored step. His rectum was dreadfully raw. Threaded with bright red blood, gritty yellow semen leaked from him now and then, making his ass wet and a chafe more likely. His throat was also savaged; the roof of his mouth hung with fleshy rips and his tongue throbbed with tiny razors slits from the invisible creatures forcing themselves inside. The baelins had not spared him a moment.

His pain had produced seven liters of elixir to treat the reserve blood for the spicer witch, and Kennen had confidence that it would work well as the first step in bringing his mother out of the coma. Their work didn't end with the elixir however. For the purpose of restoring Pel'Hahr's immune system, a transmungi sea squash had long been on Kennen's harvest list. Now of all days he decided to go out to the ocean to find some. Bre loved going outside the palace and casting his eyes upon more than just blood mortar, bone brick and wrought iron. Here was the most magnificent Ocean in all of the Old Domain. A deep red essence of godlike power, a great bloody kiss against the dark gray sky. Olathu was so large it terrified Bre, made his head spin, but that didn't prevent his heart from lighting with the fire of dreams. Most days he would have enjoyed every moment and stored it in his mind for later days. Today however, all he wanted to do was go back into his cell and sleep.

The sand became shallower and the ground harder under foot. As he understood it from the flora appendices in the tomes, the transmungi grew between rocks and it was said that many populated the chasms beneath the white bluffs.

"There, Slave," Kennen said, trudging up slowly behind him. The Archbishop himself was in a poor state, still weakened from his meeting with the Church of Midnight. He was trying to exert his power on the church from the Blind World. Bre didn't have to be present at the meetings to know this. He knew the man. When Kennen lacked sufficient time with his people, when he couldn't afford to coordinate more effective diplomacy, he always resorted to bullying.

Ten sentinels stood at attention about half a trollgut back, the exact spot Kennen had barked them to a halt. Up ahead the ground forked open in crevices, the largest width looking only two feet wide.

"I don't know if I'll fit down in those crevices, master." Kennen's mangled face looked dry and reptilian in the sunlight. "I cannot risk you going, Slave."

"Master, it's very narrow."

"Yes, yes it is. Also happens to be quite far down and then farther yet underwater. I'll need to take my best breath if I plan to harvest anything."

"Perhaps we should test the winch on a sentinel first?"

Kennen read his doubt. "You don't think I'd do this for my own mother?"

"You can't swim."

"This isn't swimming. I can hold my breath, *Phrey*, and that's all that need be done as long as you keep this thing from slipping." He touched the winch and took his fingers away from the burning metal.

Reluctantly Bre crept over and strapped his master into the six-buckle harness. They tested the buckles and found each held fast. Kennen slipped off his sandals. Losing no time, the Archbishop put his head into the crevice and worked his shoulder past the outcropping. Bre unwound more rope and Kennen's gnarled feet disappeared through the opening. The winch rattled at his movement and tugged forward. The rope spun around, humming a song of release.

"I'll tug twice to come up. Repeat."

"You will tug twice," Bre called down, and at the same time manually unwound the last of the rope. It took four turns.

"I'm going in," Kennen shouted.

The rope thrashed now. Bre couldn't hear any splashing over the roar of the ocean. He could feel the sentinels' gaze behind him. Ekkians needed limited excuse to make a kill. They would be cruel if this went bad...They hated slaves, so they would probably invoke the Trial of Cups, which would involve torturing him with knives while drinking their hideously strong mead. Those who survived drinking an entire bottle were given the honor of slitting the victim's throat. No, Bre decided, if the Archbishop doesn't make it, *I'm better off jumping into the ocean.*

A shiver ran through him despite the sun breaking through the clouds and turning the sky from gray to hot white. The middle support bar of the winch bent inward suddenly and the metal creased.

When he was seven years old, Vasoth Kennen nearly drowned. His mother had been watching him closely but a riptide took him away before she could even leave their picnic coverlet. He recalled the displaced sensation of his face being dragged across the salty dirt floor and water surging up his sinuses, a fluid knife to the brain. He luckily regained himself, pulling up above the waves. Pel'Hahr spotted him and retrieved his sagging body. Kennen never learned how to swim after that, but had made a point of learning how to hold his breath. Four revolutions of a clock had been his record some time ago. This morning his practice try lasted just past three revolutions.

It should have been enough time down the crevice, but groping the slimy rock walls, he'd only felt barnacles so far and already his chest burned. His hands waved out at the sides. On the right his fingertips brushed a fissure. He inspected its diameter and stuck his hand inside. He wore a ring filled with aquatic bane on each hand, so if this was an eel's den, he'd be spared any unfriendly greeting. As he probed the small tunnel, bubbles blasted from his nose in a measured fashion. Nothing. How irritating that a perfectly sized tunnel had been completely ignored.

He pulled his arm back. It came out halfway and halted. He yanked at it. Wouldn't move. His ring caught on a low hanging rock, stopping his hand. He tried to put his feet against the wall and push back, maybe slip the ring off, but the wall was too slippery to gain support. He opened his eyes to the burning red salt water. The rope floated near his trapped arm. Trying to turn his body, he twisted around in the narrow space to tug at it. His other arm became pinned behind him. With a lunge of his head, he tried to bite the rope to thrash it. Black stars joined the flowing burgundy bubbles around him. In his peripheral vision, the world dimmed.

The rope moved from side to side, just out of reach. You can't help me this time, Mother. And I can't help you.

Bre felt no tugging on the rope. It had been five minutes. That was an awfully long time to be underwater, even for Kennen. The sentinels shifted, impatiently watching from inside their scintillating orange armor, the look of them a fiery group of forge machines come to life. Some of the warriors' bearded mouths already looked to be forming coarse words for him. Bre held the support bar in one hand and the winch handle in the other. He opened his fingers to check on the bar's state. It had creased down the center and a perforation in the hollow iron threatened to snap.

The winch abruptly flew forward. Bre tried to catch it but it went sideways in his grip. Hard vibrations went through the rope and he took no more time for a signal. He brought the handle of the winch around and the small device shuddered. It was more difficult the second time, but he took up the slack. The handle cut into his hand as clean as a newly sharpened blade. He kept winding.

Kennen felt his body lift. He jerked his arm to the side and his shoulder dislocated. The angle worked and he pulled his arm free, leaving his ring behind. He grabbed for the walls to climb out, and at the same time the rope gained momentum. He grabbed at the slime and the rock and grasped onto countless tubular shapes clustered overhead. They easily tore from the walls and he took them.

When he broke the surface he didn't take a breath of air first. He vomited water from his nose and coughed so much he wondered if this were a dream and he was still drowning. He couldn't find the air. There was so much water yet to work through. He passed out and bumped his head against the stony wall.

He woke up a minute later. The slave had almost drawn him to the top again. The winch made a terrible grinding sound he hadn't heard on the way down.

"Master, hold on—the winch is failing!"

He grasped the side of the cliff. His shoulder popped back into the socket with a flare of pain that traveled into his ribs. He reached with his other hand but felt something soft flex there. Three of them. The healthiest transmungi he'd ever seen, better than any illustration had ever depicted. He was still staring at them, smiling at them, when the sentinels pulled him through the hole.

The squashes stretched their filaments eagerly toward Bre, just as Kennen had anticipated. Despite his thundering heart and the despicable taste of salt in his mouth and sinuses, he laughed with the delight he felt coursing through his harvest.

His mother would go on living.

ELEVEN

The British Airways airliner was cold. Patty had once again donated a blanket to Teresa, who had also again refused at first. Things had gotten off to bad start.

The flight was delayed a couple hours and then some technical issues caused them to wait another hour after boarding. It looked like they would be leaving just shy of four in the afternoon. With a layover at Heathrow, it would be a little over thirteen hours in the same plane. Boredom aside, the delay didn't bother Patty. They'd endured cabin fever in almost every vehicle known to man. The Nomads processed restlessness, they fed off of it now; it was the typical flow of their life, after all.

Th thing that did manage to still bother Patty had fallen from the overhead luggage compartment. Th Messenger's next letter. As usual, specifics weren't included, or necessary. Patty and Teresa were also accustomed to inexplicable delivery of this kind of news.

Go to Newark Castle in Port Glasgow. Beneath the castle a contingent of Midnight operates the last Grand Chapel. Leave none alive.

—Messenger

TWELVE

Though Alisyn hadn't gained the All-Sight yet, she did awaken with the knowledge of where the Old Domain had punched a hole through to Scotland.

Finding the gateway felt as natural as a mother's bond with child.

A prickly laugh cut through her mind as her taxi pulled in front of the unlikely location of a pub called the Marigold. She knew then. Chaplain Cloth was on the other side of its old wooden door. She paid the fare and got out. Wind bustled around her thin black blouse and rippled her silk pants. She'd expected it to be a warmer day. It was not. Her hair flowed in one direction as she stood there, considering her next step.

Camden had been running around like a headless chicken, the norm for most mornings, so it was easy to slip away, despite his instructions to stay in bed and rest. How could she rest though? After that experience in the Old Domain—after knowing that her child incubated inside the Apex Goblin's womb? Everything was different now. She wasn't scared anymore. She could face anything.

The True Son would be born.

Something swelled behind the door to the pub. She licked her lips and put her hand on the knob. Perhaps there still were things to be afraid of, after all...

Cloth would use her All-Sight to fi the Heart of the Harvest. Th e was no escaping that. If she appeased him, however, the power would remain hers, and she could watch her son, maybe fi a way to bring him into this world. Th would be amazing beyond words. Improbable, perhaps, but she would fi a way.

Her phone shook, startling her.

A text had come in from an Australian phone number:

Hello, love. Miss me?

She hesitated. These men, these silly men—they weren't even necessary anymore. Still, in the moment it was nice to hear from somebody; it spoke worlds for Ronald compared to Camden.

Hello, Ronald.

R U @ the same P.O. Box? I want to send something.

Yes, what is it?

Remember the tortoises?

How could she ever forget? All those eggs left behind on that magical Australian beach...abandoned, sacrificed for the sake of a stronger, smarter species. It was probably the most romantic thing she'd ever seen.

You sending me one? :)

You'll see. Got to go. Early day at the office tomorrow.

I will love it, I am sure.

She put her phone away and rethought this plan. What if coming here would make Cloth angry? He hadn't asked her to show. With Halloween fast approaching, how often could she break away so easily from the Chapel though?

Slowly, she took the door's cold brass knob. A vein streaked hand dropped over her wrist and clamped down. Duncun stood there, his face a violent shade of red. "Followed you, bitch-asswhore! Where's your hulking cunt of a boyfriend now?"

He lunged and pinned her to the door with his forearm. "Watch my—"

"Whit? Yer womb? Ye are no' *FUCKING PREGNANT!*" The fumes of cheap gin stung her nose.

"Get off me."

"Wha were ye texting? That magician boyfriend or someone else?"

Alisyn wormed her hand behind her back and took the door's knob.

Twisted.

The door swung open hard and they fell on top of each other into darkness. She picked herself up and tore away from him, entering a wilderness of vines and moldering debris. Duncun shouted huskily after her, but she continued on, climbing and tripping over the massive organic barricades.

The atmosphere changed the closer she got to the gateway.

Near the bar area, a giant hole sucked inward, wooden beams bent and splintered in unnatural twisting configurations, yet somehow remaining attached to the stressed construction. At Alisyn's staggering approach, bats began a nasty song that met a chorus of raw-throated wolves. A diminished chord of momentous power resonated through the pub.

She thought for sure everybody in the city would hear it and come to this place. They had to—that sound wasn't something that could go unnoticed; it would be like ignoring a tsunami raging through the streets. And yet, she saw shadows of cars coasting by the frosted windows outside. There were no doors slamming, no cries of confusion, no slamming shoes on the pavement, nobody coming to help—

Then a sicker melody played. Alisyn found the source of the sound. A man, the demon of her dreams, stood at a pipe organ inside the gateway. His bony fingers were deft on the keys while dissonant madness poured out. As the notes came, vines shot from the organ pipes and coiled along the gateway, some vanishing in the absolute darkness of the twisted tunnel and others working into the tavern. Cloth played another chord and countless vines blasted out in a snake charmer fashion, going wild against the walls.

He rubbed solemnly under his black colored eye. The orange one cut through the room, targeting Alisyn where she stood. "Your All-Sight has not developed yet."

"No."

"I can help it along. Come closer."

"Somebody followed me here."

"I know. Come closer."

She wondered where Duncun had gone. It was too dark to make out anything other than the gateway. All light pulled inside it. She tried to control her stammering but her entire body trembled. "I felt this place. So I came."

Suddenly Duncun came stumbling out between Cloth and her. He froze and studied the monster before him. It was clear he had no following words. As scared as he looked, it was sort of wonderful seeing him in the throes of shock. He edged backward. "We—We're out of this weirdo place. Come on, Alisyn."

"Alisyn," said Cloth, "come over here a little more. I need to lay my hands on you."

She approached without question. Duncun, already making his ascent over a twisted mass of vines slanting down over a sideways table, looked back.

"Hey, wait up a minute."

He launched his body backward and lurched. He regained himself and wobbling a little, started for Alisyn. "Alisyn get over here. We're gaun! Gaun now!"

Chaplain Cloth folded his black suited arms. Wind flowing through the gateway fluttered his orange handkerchief. He considered Duncun. "I've always wanted a spare. He isn't a member of the Church is he?"

Alisyn paused, not sure how she wanted to answer.

"I don't belong to her sick little worshippers. Now, Alisyn," Duncun said through heaving breaths. He snatched her arm and tugged her close. "We're out of here. Right this minute."

Cloth was suddenly before them. "What's the rush? Stay. Let's have a seat. Standing can be so loathsome."

"Awa!"

Duncun shoved Cloth and the Chaplain let himself stumble back. Empowered, Duncun bulled forward with a growl. His progress cut short though, his body flash-frozen. With a startled cry, he flipped upside-down, arms bent inward with his legs, turning him into a human table. His shirt tore away in places as bones stabbed through his skin like shark's teeth. His breathing came so fast he could hardly scream. Ribs jackknifed through his back along with his spinal column and folded into a chair rest.

Cloth strolled through a settling mist of blood and took a seat on top of his newly made chair. Duncun now let out a hair-raising screech that split the air.

Alisyn marveled at the sight. It'd all happened so quickly and with such little bloodshed. *How could Duncun still be living with all those compound fractures?*

Duncun screeched over and over again. Chaplain Cloth plucked his handkerchief from his breast pocket, leaned sideways and shoved it into Duncun's mouth.

"Now then, the monster has done his monstrous deed for the day." Cloth's two-tone eyes turned to Alisyn with some inward, devilish speculation. "I hope you weren't too crazy over this one? Have a seat." He patted his leg.

Carefully, Alisyn advanced toward Cloth and lowered down on his lap, every fiber of her being telling her how wrong this was, how suicidal it might be. Duncun growled through the handkerchief as she put all her weight down. His bones creaked but stabilized with uncanny support.

Sitting there, Alisyn couldn't look the monster in the face. But she had no choice; Cloth put his icy finger under her chin and guided her eyes to his. "As much as you are a delight my dear, I must say my new chair here could really use an ottoman. You, and that abysmal excuse for an Archbishop."

"I beg your forgiveness, Chaplain—"

A weak sob escaped through the orange fabric in Duncun's mouth. Cloth flicked him once in the eye and then continued,

"I want you to put all resources into searching for the Column. Tell Amherst."

"The Columns really exist?"

"So I keep hearing," said Cloth with a knowing smile.

Alisyn's heart thudded in delight. Many of those passages about the Column had been in the same series that made mention of the True Son. This would show Camden to doubt the later Tomes of Eternal Harvest! Oh everlasting joy, she felt like she should sing out!

Cloth studied her with a measure of subtle disgust. If he could read her mind, know her plans, he'd probably kill her right then, and the way he looked at her, as though he knew everything...her joy faded immediately.

"How do we locate the Column?" she asked, hoping to draw that look from his two-colored gaze.

"Someone close to the source always has a premonition—that's the only flaw in the Messenger's design. Find that person and you find the Column."

"What if the Nomads come for us?"

"That won't be a problem. With your sight as mine, I'll find them and kill them before the Day of Opening."

"You, Chaplain? Surely you can't leave the gateway before Halloween, can you?"

Cloth's bleached teeth were dreadfully perfect and all trace of his previous hatred for her deeply buried. "Don't worry about me. Fortune has brought me a new chair to fall back on...that's unintentionally funny when you think about it."

Cloth petted her hair and she tried to ignore the flakes of ice that settled over her scalp. Something electric passed between them for a moment. He sucked in some air with a hiss and smacked his lips. "There, the sight should come to you easier now. This is a new universe. Everything changes now. Leave it all behind, Alisyn. Destiny has come. All that is hidden within you, must be let out. Now run along, dear. I need rest, as do you."

She did as the monster demanded, not looking back. Duncun cried out in panic as she made her way out of the tavern.

Cloth was right. Things had changed for Alisyn. It was time to put all of her old demons to rest. The baby in the box. Her old madness had calmed. A funeral song she would sing for the dust that remained...

After all these years, it was genuinely bewildering how easy it was to sit there on her hallowed chamber floor and unclasp the brass locks, open the lid and peer inside the box.

There was nothing inside though. Not so much as a cobweb. No debris. No bones. No waiting baby. Had she even conceived a child with Camden? What if Alisyn dreamt about his existence and Camden just played along with her? She allowed for that awful possibility, but there was another that made far more sense.

The wee child had been set free.

OCTOBER 28TH

THIRTEEN

It was something like two hundred years ago when I realized this particular Halloween would be different than others. Despite what some may think about me, my power is not perfect. Premonitions of the future are never completely clear in my mind; foresight is more like an escaped zoo of hungry shadows, all representing potential realities, all thrashing and snarling, each fighting to win its own place in the story of Time. Amidst the bedlam, I can distinguish the dominant shadows that seem to have the best chance of becoming reality.

That's why I'm worried.

I don't often worry, but when I do it becomes obsessive. This year my obsession is Byron Telamon. I cannot see him fitting into any possible reality, and that doesn't bode well for handling all the factors to which I normally have control.

Byron is an aberration of an aberration. He doesn't belong to any world I know of. The sickness he has, I gave to his bloodline and a score of others, back at the time of the Division of Worlds. Unaided by power from the Old Domain, the sickness should have killed Byron long ago—yet he still exists. My suspicion is that he could very well be the one lingering secret Chaplain Cloth has managed to keep from me. Or he's quite possibly a secret to both myself and Cloth.

I know Byron can be dangerous, but I am not certain whether he will prove to be useful instead of disastrous. Ignorance is a most terrifying thing to me, living all this time and seeing all that I have. I used to happily seek knowledge, used to enjoy learning something new. Now I realize that the unknown can completely reconfigure everything for better or for worse. If I've been plodding along all these centuries with a misapprehension or blind faith, everything could fall into Chaplain Cloth's hands.

That I can't fit Byron into the paradigm is primarily the reason I wrote my letters to the Nomads decades in advance. One vision I've had shows a certain letter of mine being intercepted by someone other than the Nomads, but then there is a similar reality that shows they still receive the letter. The Church of Morning has shown the ability to pervert the realities before, but with Kennen so focused on his mother, I don't believe they are behind this.

Oh, so many worries. I can't leave room for any breaches in my correspondence to the Nomads, now that I know the possibility of interception. I've abandoned the text messages to Patty since I found out the government agency Byron works for has ways to recover them, although I still read her diary emails from time to time, just to remember the past and not be so consumed with the future. Strangely, I believe Patty reads them for the same reason.

In the last few hours the flight had some rowdy turbulence, so no sleep was to be had for Patty. Teresa had dozed a little, but mostly she'd been awake as well. The plane set down in Glasgow around one o'clock in the afternoon. Using their awake-time to the fullest, they studied the maps the Messenger had provided them in the overhead compartment. On the city map there were surprisingly few Void areas. Normally the city where the gateway opened had at least twenty or thirty—in the large cities it could be in the hundreds. The Voids were especially important to study and input into their portable GPS for Halloween night. Cloth's children could not tread in the Void areas. If Patty and Teresa couldn't drive out the chase, they usually found a Void to hole up in and set barriers of protection for the Heart of the Harvest. Chaplain Cloth could still go into the Voids without issue though. Still, it was better to face him alone than with his army of bloodthirsty guards.

The map of Glasgow had only four Voids inside the cities, and three outside the city. One had an asterisk next to it and a referential note on the bottom.

Incapacitation Void. Do not seek refuge here.

"Have you ever heard of one of these?"

By the look on Teresa's face, Patty could tell she hadn't. Most passengers had disembarked the plane now and Teresa took it as a cue to pull herself up from the seat. "I don't know, but I know I don't want to be sitting here anymore."

They walked, zombie-like, to the baggage claim. The calming off-white pillars of the Glasgow airport flowed by them, one after another, as though they journeyed deeper into a modern temple. Gloom spread over the airport through the long skylight. Patty glanced up through the metal webbing to the expanse of the dull sky. It had been clear when they first landed but now rain sheeted down the sloping windows; not all that different weather than L.A.

Teresa stopped into a small Tesco market to get some mouthwash and eye drops. The mouthwash was because of the long flight. The eye drops were to refresh her eyes for a rifle sight. Teresa always picked up a bottle when killing was close at hand. The reality of it happening again, so soon after the Mojave desert, drove Patty to silence. She'd read the letter but had purposely not thought about it during the flight.

"What's with the dumpy act?" Teresa said in an almostwhisper as they left the store. "This is supposedly the last Grand Chapel."

"Yes, the mass extermination is complete."

Teresa's jaw dropped. "Do you care so much for these people who given the chance would put a bullet here?" She flicked Patty in the temple.

"Don't do that. Don't ever hit me again."

"Shit, you're dramatic." Teresa followed as Patty increased her pace. "Be mad at me all you want, darling. This is a pisspoor time to change our priorities. We already reached a resolution on this."

"No, *you* did."

"What has gotten into you lately?"

Patty felt one hundred years old right then. She could hardly lift her eyes to look Teresa in the face. She lowered her voice. "If I have to explain why murdering people before they've even done anything to us—"

"Of course it's wrong," Teresa snapped, "but it's what the Messenger wants."

"Guess what, who cares?"

"You will. We both will when things start falling apart. The Messenger has a plan. It's not for you or I to ever know, but it must be followed. Every time it isn't, good people die. My last partner got himself killed because he thought he could fit his own agenda into the plan. It doesn't work that way."

"You wouldn't be here if Martin hadn't done what he had." Teresa looked away, shaking her head. Silence fell between them at the baggage claim. The luggage started falling out on the conveyor belt and Patty studied each in a self-imposed trance. Inside those containers, people kept their lives. Favorite shirts, drugs to keep them happy, keep them alive, sexy underwear to don for lovers, ugly underwear to don for comfort. And what did the Nomads carry?

The rule was to always use something bought in a store and never something that could have been tampered with— that had been the way before they killed all the Church's assassins. So this old habit left them with luggage that contained clothing they wouldn't ever wear, trail mix they wouldn't ever eat, and one travel bag of bathroom miscellany, including a tube of toothpaste that had to be seven years old. There was also the assorted rifle parts and ammo in Teresa's guitar case, all layered in permanent mantles to obscure them from security.

Patty realized she hadn't had the need to fire a gun at someone else in more than five years now. Teresa really hadn't had much need for it either, but still brought her old rifle everywhere they went. It was just like Teresa to hold onto what she knew, no matter if it made sense or not.

Two suitcases dropped out onto the conveyor. "There are yours," Teresa said, absently.

Patty approached the belt, ready to grab them as they went past.

Teresa cleared her throat. "So I never asked. How did your date with Byron go?"

Patty lugged both suitcases off the conveyor. "I should have stayed out longer."

She popped out the handles and rolled the luggage toward the exit, leaving Teresa alone at the claim.

FOURTEEN

Byron came back from the bathroom, feeling better about a whole range of different things. There was no episode with his bowels, which meant the photograph's mojo still had an effect on him. He could expect to have an attack either today or tomorrow. Right now he was feeling only minor chest pain and pins and needles below his knees, and after smoking some hash before coming to the coffee shop, he had to concentrate on the pain to even remember it being there. So his body was as ship-shape as it could be and he was in the city where the gateway would open. For a change, he'd earned the silly smile he wore.

He passed a TV mounted on the wall and was surprised to see talking heads from the American political world rather than the European. *Folks over here actually care about the world beyond their own backyards. How very bizarre...*

A pundit with hair black as a vinyl record let out a disgusted sigh before responding to the man contained in the other rectangle on the screen. "Your party has kept denying the facts, the truth, and now you've created a completely different reality! Your constituents bought into these lies about Senator Lashman, when there is absolutely no proof to the allegations. You keep lying and lying and lying and now half the country thinks this baloney is true!"

Home sweet home, thought Byron as he returned to his table. It was too bad the Messenger's letter didn't work out. That blot wasn't blood. Some sort of organic red ink made of berries and vinegar, from all he could tell. That didn't mean this frayed end couldn't be twisted back together again—as far as the Nomads were concerned, that blot could be a dab of blood. Byron had to have some way to redirect them from their primary mission. Patty had been all gung-ho about finding the Messenger, just about ever since he'd known her, *and it had become clear from their last conversation that Byron would never convince* her to lead him to the gateway.

Unless maybe he told Patty about his sickness. What if he told her everything? What if he also told her how he dreamed the gateway would cure his corrupt connection to the Old Domain and replace his terrible weakness with a terrible strength? His mind wandered. Maybe I'll be more powerful than even Patty Middleton? What would that be like? He let the dream fade and shook his head. Focus. You cannot tell them about the sickness. That will make it a starker reality, *give it more power.* It was the lie that had kept him alive all this time. For that, Byron was certain. He sipped some black coffee and its hot acidic taste flowered in his mouth. Rubbing it along his tongue, he enjoyed the minute of repose. After taking a few more hearty sips, he picked up his phone and located the cell phone number for the Priestess of Midnight.

Time to get in character.

He should have studied his Australian accent a little more, but Alisyn was a pretty easy sell. He met her when he infiltrated a conclave in Melbourne. He'd been making eyes at her that whole evening and a strike of fate came in the form of a drunken Bishop smashing joyfully into him. "Foxy, eh? Tell her your birthday's Halloween and she'll love you forever."

"Really?"

The man only hiccupped and tried to focus his eyes as he'd stumbled off.

This callousness reaffirmed what he'd gathered that night. Byron had gotten the feeling many in the Church of Midnight hadn't found much to admire in Alisyn Dunning. She was a lovely specimen of female though. Velvet black hair to her middle back, a robust yet petite figure, and soft Asian features coupled with European grace.

Juggling the Priestess and the Nomads would be pretty interesting to say the least. Perhaps it was a good thing though— all of his plans were colliding together. That could mean some kind of outcome this year. One of them had to lead him to the gateway. Most likely the Church would know where it had cropped up.

It felt right. Glasgow was meant to be. It reminded him of a particularly dreadful nightmare he'd once fought courageously through, how close my heart had felt to exploding, standing there in an old temple covered in vines, so many vines all around, slithering up the pillars and to hang in courtyards above, *winding and winding through balusters with the grace of eels through coral,* pulling him, gutting him, feeding him to the dark, and in the end he changed the nightmare into a dream of wish fulfillment, he and Patty embracing in front of a cemetery. Not the most positive or romantic setting, but holding her felt so right, so good, all the pain surged far away. That the reversal was even possible gave him hope. Byron hadn't thought too hard on it at the time, for hope could really bring someone dangerously close to accidentally exposing the complete truth, and he had to avoid that.

Something cold drip-drip-dripped in Byron's mind and he shook his head away from the recollection. If he had any fond memories of his childhood, he'd have certainly turned his thoughts there, but being a kid had been even more painful than being adult. He thought of Patty for a moment and cleared the flavor of dirty and dying vegetation from his mouth. Took another sip of coffee—he realized he'd dialed Alisyn.

"Who is this?" she said at once.

Byron tried his Ronald voice out, hoping he wouldn't overdo it. "Ga'day, love."

"I didn't expect to hear from you again so soon."

"Should I call back latah?"

"Of course not. I'm glad you cared enough to call."

"I received me delivery confirmation. Yah gift has arrived at the postal box."

"Lovely," she replied, a little focused on something else. "I'll try to get down there today."

"Promise me you'll wear it."

"Oh, so it's something to wear..?"

"You got me."

"I haven't picked out anything for you, and your birthday is only days away."

Now Byron laughed inwardly. *Poor thing.* "I don't like reminders of gettin' oldah, love. Makin' you happy makes me feel youngah though. You can buy yah friend Camden his gift instead."

She paused. "Wait. How do you know about him? He got to the Melbourne conclave late, after you left."

Byron swallowed.

"You never met him," she reinforced.

His mind raced. Holy shit, had he just given himself away? "Uh, when we ate at that beachside place, when I told you when me birthday was...you told me...that is, about his being the same day."

His accent slipped, but Alisyn couldn't dispute details of that particular occasion. Both of them had so much rum that night, they ended up sleeping on the floor of his hotel room with bits of beach sand all over their fully clothed bodies. Neither even remembered going down to the beach that night.

"That was pretty bad," she finally said. "I haven't drank like that since."

"Me neither, thank God. Anyhow, I'm sorry to rush but I need to get going. I hope you like it."

"I'd like you better."

"Until we meet again."

"Bye now."

Byron ended the call and almost forgot to sigh. A frowning teenager with sloppy hair searched an adjacent hallway of the café. He came out and asked the person behind the counter the way to the bathroom. It was tucked away in a strange place, around a bookshelf in the corner. Byron had had to ask where it was too. The teenager asked a few times but the café had become busy and nobody responded to him.

"Toilet's broken," Byron blurted out. "Pardon?" The teen turned.

"Went in there earlier," he said. "The toilet doesn't flush."

"Thanks." The teen hurried through the crowd of caffeine cravers and rushed out into the rain.

Byron sat back and felt a headache emerge behind his eyes. For several moments it didn't even strike him as odd that he felt compelled to lie to the kid about the toilet. There was no reason for it. Yet, the universe would not be harmed for such a useless transaction of falsity.

But why lie about that? Something so small and unrelated to him? Sometimes he didn't even understand the decisions he made.

He took another sip of coffee and shivered. Was he becoming so used to deceit that he couldn't bear to allow the truth any space in his life?

Or did the universe not want that kid to use the bathroom? Was he being used?

Used to hold chaos and order apart? Or together? "Needless thoughts," he said and texted his partner:

BE READY TO ACCESS GPS-7(A) POINT FOR PRIESTESS.

Byron finished his coffee and stood to leave. As he did, he heard a man inform the lady behind the counter that the toilet had overflowed.

FIFTEEN

Patty pinched the tension knot clenching between her brows. The tar fumes hung in the air from nearby road construction, smelling how she imagined a demon's body odor might smell. She crossed the street quickly when a break in the traffic finally came. Still patiently quiet, Teresa followed her, guitar case bouncing on her back as she went.

They sought shelter from the rain under a concrete balcony of what appeared to be an out-of-business dry cleaner.

"Can you make the whole thing?" Teresa asked her, palming her mouth, just in case. Always in case.

Patty turned her back to Teresa and spoke softly. "It's a strange structure—built on a downward slope under that castle. Taking out the lower supports will pancake the whole thing. The upper load bearing beams have major tree root systems entwining them, so I'll have to put a few thousand to free them up."

"A few *thousand*?" Teresa said. "I'll never get used to hearing someone talk about mantles that way, Patty."

"I'm blessed."

Teresa ignored the sarcasm. "Are there any apertures for escape?"

"There's an independent tunnel, built on a different infrastructure. I think it leads out to that gathering of trees along the road."

"How many residents?"

"Probably close to five hundred."

Teresa unslung her guitar case. Now free from their mantles, some of the rifle parts rattled around inside. Patty pulled her coat tighter and kept her expression neutral. Another argument would not move Teresa. "You're going to the trees then? You're not going to help me with the chapel?"

"I'm more useful with the rifle."

"What about my...problem with the mantles?"

"Just keep them underground, maybe an explosion will help along the collapse."

Patty set her watch, feeling as though she lived in a recurring nightmare.

"Give me ten to get down there and post," said Teresa.

Patty added the minutes and pushed start. Her watch timer commenced with a beep and when Patty glanced up, Teresa was gone. She took in a deep, cold, damp breath of Scottish autumn and rubbed her temples. A pinpoint of ice expanded from the center of her mind and traveled on fresh new cerebral highways. It was always this way with the mantles—a new, but not-new experience. Patty built a small reflective-mantle and sunk it through the ground. These mantles had the ability to enter a mass without disturbing its structure and only slightly altering its density. It also had the convenient side effect of opening a window in the builder's mind. Teresa could normally see a small range around one, but Patty, as with all other configurations, had much more scope. She could see the moldering wood beams in the damp earth, the worms and grubs and pools of subterranean water, the archaic ventilation systems that were nothing more than crumbling tubes of old plaster. And she saw the countless stone rooms of the Grand Chapel. Saw the people who lived within them.

The lowest part of the chapel was a level room compared to the others that sloped slightly with the downgrade. Largest next to a dining hall on the level above, the lowest room contained wall-to-wall bookshelves, all reaching to a vaulted ceiling. There were other shelves that made a neat thirty-one rows throughout the room. Between these, the Church had placed writing desks, some adorned with black and orange candles, more than a few with lanterns. Something like seventy acolytes read newly bound copies of the Tomes of Eternal Harvest. A great many had laptops as well. While they didn't have the garb of the Inner

Circle, these acolytes dressed in black collared shirts and jeans and slacks.

Wannabes, thought Patty grimly. They are down there studying, hoping to be something in the church someday. Her watch timer suddenly chimed. She quickly turned it off. Her eyes darted to the tree-line near the busy road. Teresa was out there, *ready to shatter the head of anybody who dared escape through the tunnel.*

After surveying the rest of the underground structure, Patty turned her mind's eye back to the library. This was the only location that she took issue with. Those rows of bookshelves would leave openings for escape. That couldn't be allowed to happen.

With a stinging, quivering breath, she began her work.

Teresa found a place between two trees to slide her rifle through and a perfect meeting of two branches to position her elbow inside, as though this tree had grown for a sniper's purpose alone. Wind kicked up through the trees and she noted its direction, though from this vantage she could probably pick anybody off with little correction.

She waited calmly. Heartbeat in her ears. In her fingertips.

Her toes.

A tremor went through the ground below and giddiness flooded her.

It had begun. The last Chapel of Midnight would soon be no more.

In the archive room, hundreds of feet below the soil's surface, a wrecking ball of a mantle crashed through the bookshelves, swiping them across the room in a terrifyingly instant domino effect. Dust clouded the room. Patty could not hear the screams, *a good thing,* and turned on the foundation beams at either side of the room. She chopped through them and the old wood shattered, the mortar blew apart like a crumbling cookie. She noticed a shape escape up the stairway right as she split the ceiling beams and the earth caved in the room. It was a man. He stumbled on the stairs when a wave of splinters struck his body and face.

In the large dining hall above, two hundred church members felt the violence from below. Inner Circle and acolytes alike scrambled for the exits like insects. And in the very next moment, were smashed like them. The impact caused a vestibule to the northeast to fold into itself. This place had one resident, an ugly woman who surrounded herself with poultices, beakers, herb jars and strange specimen containers. She was frantically gathering jars into her arms, screaming, when everything came down on her.

Patty glanced on the apartments above. The structure's cave-in had worked its way up, inevitably, and without much more assistance from any mantles. Some people died in their rooms, asleep. Some died dressing in their clothes. Two women and a man, engaged in a ménage à trois, had the misfortune of using a room beneath a rupturing sewage basin that rained down a foul sludge from the ceiling and drowned them. More than fifty others also expired in the bathhouse when the boiler ripped apart from the stress of the ceiling. It flooded other apartments where people met their fates under boiling water or falling earth and stone.

One Inner Circle man desperately tried to call out on his cell phone. He'd ducked under a large, fashionable bed. The ceiling bent above him, only moments from collapse. Patty didn't recognize him as the Archbishop of Midnight. He looked nothing like the Messenger's photos. She read the man's lips, "Come on, come on! Answer for fuck's sake! Pick up your phone, Camden!"

I pulled my eyes from that den of rats that the Church of Midnight called home and turned them to the Old Domain, to another den of rats who had the luxury of living in a palace, but were diseased rodents nonetheless.

Camden Amherst's phone rang merrily on top of Archbishop Kennen's bureau. All the slaves had gone down to the palace lunarium to begin rites, while Kennen busied himself with his slave, Bre, preparing a skin poultice for his mother. The sound of the phone's ringing would go unanswered in the empty bedroom. Since the phone had traveled from the world of the Nomads, and unconventionally spent sometime in the Marrowlands before arriving in the Old Domain, it had taken on other characteristics. The ring tone changed from the classic rotary phone Camden had chosen, to that of a squalling baby, and with every cry the phone emitted a sickening, bloodish pulse through its plastic frame. The battery had grown strong enough to outlast time itself.

In this case, such duration was unnecessary. The call was dropped from the other end, and the baby's cry silenced.

Between the trees Teresa spotted a young acolyte emerge from the underground chapel that Patty was thoroughly demolishing. A torn black shirt hung tenuously around his splinter-filled torso. Blood ran from a severely broken nose. One of his eyes had purpled and closed shut. It was amazing the man had escaped at all. Too bad for him this was the end of the road.

Teresa aligned the crosshairs with his forehead. The look in his eyes...he had the same color eyes Patty did, the same lustrous blond hair, only hanging shaggily around his ears. They're the same fucking age, *too.* The young man saw Teresa through his one remaining eye that leaked long lines of tears over his crusted face. He froze there, choking on his sobs, and shut his one eye. Teresa watched him for a moment.

"Aw shit," she muttered.

The young man continued to stand rigidly there.

Her finger pressed against the trigger. She licked her lips. *Why didn't he try to run?* A silent growl left her lips, as she pulled her eye back from the sight. "Get going," she barked.

His eye opened, amazed, and he stumbled forward. "Move your ass or lose it."

Two yards away, a tree snapped in half with twig-like ease, sending wooden fragments in all directions.

The young man started to move and two other trees split lengthwise and another twisted around itself.

Teresa hit the ground and covered her head with the oncoming explosion. The air sizzled and the scent of burning leaves and wood overcame her for a moment. She retched and her eyes flooded with tears. A tree leaned forward and she watched, completely mesmerized how it bowed so calm and slowly. It was falling. *A whole goddamn tree's going to fall on top of you!*

Teresa swiftly rolled away as it struck where she lay. Its impact with the ground made her teeth snap together and bite off a fragment of tongue. She got to her feet, head pounding and tasting iron, stumbled back and yanked her guitar case from under a fallen branch. She disassembled her rifle in three parts, all the while scanning the trees for any other sign of eruption. Her fingers shook as she closed the case's clasps.

The explosion had taken a sizeable chunk out of the wooded area, and from the scattered viscera, it looked like the young man had run straight into its center. She tried to look away from it, but it was difficult not to see the vermillion lacing the soft green leaves and traces of long golden hairs adorning meat and bones like snipped marionette strings. Teresa forced herself to concentrate on the rifle. In just minutes, she had it packed up and was heading quickly for the road.

Cars piled up at the tree-line with the police car that had stopped there. The cop leaned half in-half out of the car, talking on his radio. A thin gray plume of smoke rose from the center of the trees.

Patty jumped as Teresa moved out of the rain-streaked shadows. "Let's get," she said, and took hold of Patty's arm.

"That was another independent explosion—wasn't it?" Teresa didn't say anything, just kept moving down the sidewalk. People came up the way, some pointing, all conversations seemingly on the source of disturbance.

Patty drew her arm away from Teresa. "The explosions are happening more often now. What if they start coming with every mantle I build?"

"We'll think about that later. Keep going. Time to find a hotel. Time to shower—"

She unearthed her phone from under her raincoat to look up hotel listings. There was a text from Byron she'd missed. Patty opened it and read the message as raindrops peppered the screen.

Smith is @ Argyle St, City Centre, Z3. Property manager says tenant returns early tomorrow after a "Holiday." Good Luck. Be careful.

Teresa had read the text from over her shoulder. "Why would the Messenger stay somewhere so close to population? I don't like this, Patty."

"You're right. Best to leave it alone."

Now's not the time to argue about it, Patty thought. She was going to Argyle street. That much was clear. First thing in the morning. With Teresa, or without her. She'd worked too long and hard the past year to miss any chance. She would not be talked out of this, not with the explosions coming more often, *not with everything that had happened.*

Teresa searched for a taxi. She took a big, ragged breath. "Now that it's all over, I'm sorry."

"For?"

"Asking this of you...this Chapel...all the chapels. I'm sorry I couldn't do it all myself. I would have, you know. If I could do what you can, I would have."

Patty was quiet on this. She couldn't take the visions of those people from her head. Running for their lives from a merciless god.

"But are you sorry for smacking me?" she asked Teresa, forcing a smile.

Teresa waved a cab that passed without even slowing. "Putz," she mumbled.

"Well?"

Her partner's deep blue eyes moved to her. "No, I'm not quite there yet."

An unexpected laugh escaped Patty's mouth. She didn't want to laugh. Didn't find it at all appropriate. But she laughed again and it felt good. Selfish, but good. Teresa laughed also. They both laughed, despite the driving rain.

SIXTEEN

Camden bustled along behind Alisyn with a new baby carriage. She had caught sight of him not long after her cab dropped her off at the post office. She didn't feel like talking to him right now, and besides she'd wanted to see just how badly he wanted her, following in the rain with that stocky frame and elegant black trench coat and expensive umbrella, all the while trying to push a carriage.

"I got this for you," he said. "It's expensive. Japanese made." Alisyn happily accepted the carriage and wrapped her gloved hands around the carriage handle. In a way it made her sad. Would she ever be able to take a walk with her child? "Can I keep you company a while?" asked Camden. "Don't be silly."

He fell back a little and she turned. "That meant ye could come along."

"Oh."

She pushed along, wondering about what tortoise related gift awaited her. What would she find in that P.O. Box? For a few blocks she fantasized about swinging open the door and a newborn baby crawling out covered in birth slime and shattered placenta. What if Ronald had been being symbolic about the tortoises? What if he'd provided her a True Baby? By postal delivery...devilry...

What are you thinking? The True Son is incubating in the Old Domain. Remember?

Alisyn was getting a headache. She'd had one since she found her baby's box empty. She'd thought about asking Camden about it, but hadn't found the right approach yet.

"How'd ye manage to get out of there without a personal

guard?" she asked. "Fraser's slipping."

Camden stepped into the rain. "He's sorting through my wardrobe for conclave this year."

"The Nomads may already be in the city. It was dumb to come out alone."

"Dumb for both of us," Camden said. "But I don't think we should squabble in front of the congregation either. We need to preserve our dignity."

"I wouldn't know it if I saw it."

"Anyhow, let's head back, eh? We need to be at the chapel."

"I have a package frae my friend Ronald."

Rain dribbled through Camden's black beard. "Did you hear what I said? We're together again. You don't need affections from these other fools. You've got this fool."

"Hey!" someone called across the street. A red-headed prostitute trotted across the street, wearing a halter top, shorts and a sad poncho covering her trembling body. "Another go? I'm on sale!" As she neared, the smell of mildew overpowered them both.

Camden blushed. "I don't know ye."

"Come on, priest!"

Alisyn pushed her new baby carriage out into the street.

Camden charged after her as she continued on. Once across the street he nearly ran into her.

"Leave me be. Go back to yer church, yer hoors. I don't need ye, Camden."

He quivered and she knew by his eyes that he wanted to throttle her, but wouldn't. "Don't you see how hard you've made everything? We used to be in love, Alisyn. We didn't need one damn other soul but each other."

"That's shite."

"It isn't."

"Really? The bairn is gone, Camden. I opened the box last night. It's gone."

His face dropped.

"I thought about that some," she went on. "Maybe you let him go, gave him up to someone else in the Church, but no—you aren't man enough to do something like that."

Camden looked away. The whites of his eyes absorbed the gray of the rain.

Alisyn moved thin reeds of her wet black hair from her eyes. "That's no' whit happened. I know now there never was a baby. I fantasized the whole pregnancy an' ye went along with it. Rather than believing in me, ye humored me, because that's whit ye always do."

His eyes cast down and he gripped his umbrella tighter. "I wish that was true."

"Whit do ye mean?"

"There was a baby," he said, "an' he wouldn't wake up. He wudnae drink milk. His heart was slowing. He was...the look on his face...the look *ye* put there. He was in agony, Alisyn. The baby was ready to die, but I couldn't watch him go through that—not my son. I didn't wantae see him struggle, see when his body would move no more, an' I didn't wantae see anythin'. Too real! Too fucking real! Do ye understand? I didn't wantae know why a mother wid do such a thing. But I loved ye anyway an' that makes me worse than ye. I wanted ye happy. An' mind through all yer fickle-headed stupidity, that ye didn't think our child was the True—"

"Whit did ye do wi' him?" Alisyn took a step closer, her eyes bright and wild.

Camden met her gaze. "I sent him to the other side."

"Ye...*killed* him?"

"He was going to die anyway. At least I didn't have to see it happen. His body was sacrificed to the Old Domain. Wi' his blood an' bone, his corpse feeds its soil. He was too special to leave to this world. You must agree wi' that, if nothing else."

Alisyn felt like she'd just stumbled out of a bad car wreck. She'd seen major heights since the encounter with the Apex Goblin and now she'd fallen lower than ever. It was that moment she realized that all along she'd hoped Camden had given the child away. But he really was gone. Shattered to bits across the worlds...

Alisyn walked on to the post office. Camden followed without saying a word. Like a ghost, she drifted through the people crowding the post boxes. Kneeling, she pulled the key from her blouse pocket and put it into the bronze door. She opened the door and slid out a hand-sized cardboard box. She took her key back and brought the package over to a stationary table. There she broke through the packing tape with the serrations of the key. Inside she found a ring box.

"He must be serious," said Camden, without emotion.

She opened the box and found a rather ugly tortoise shell barrette. Alisyn wore a variety of barrettes and Ronald had remembered that. She tucked the barrette through her raven hair, moving her bangs back. The barrette felt surprisingly warm and that warmth seemed to radiate out over her head.

Camden touched her elbow. "We need to get back."

She didn't object. She followed him outside and stood next to him silently.

The cab arrived right away. For a time she tuned out Camden's apologetic prattle. Then he started in about their duty to their congregation. Her thoughts went to the Grand Chapel under Newark Castle—

Not her thoughts. Her *eyes*.

An uncountable series of eyes opened up around the world, all wide and drinking in images—they filled her mind so completely that for an instant she forgot to breathe.

The Grand Chapel was gone…buried…all of the followers… below, deep in the ground. Then Alisyn saw two women riding in a cab of their own: they were responsible. An older woman and an attractive younger woman. *The Nomads.*

Camden saw Alisyn had suffered some kind of attack. He was trying to talk to her. The cab driver was barking questions too, but Camden ignored him.

"I have the sight now," she finally said. "Well that's good news. That's great—"

"Camden—they've destroyed the Chapel. Everybody is dead. *Everybody.*"

His face went corpse white. "What? We were just there. That cannae be true."

"It's all buried." Shock numbed her mind for a minute. How strange it was to ignore all the things she could see, but ignore them, she did.

"Are you sure?" Camden insisted.

"Nobody was left alive. The Nomads took them all." Camden shook his head. "You're seeing it wrong, Alisyn."

He searched around helplessly and smacked angrily at his pockets. "No phone! I fucked myself."

He struck the door's paneling with his fist and the cab driver yelled at him.

"Whit are we gaun do?" Alisyn asked, more images of dead bodies flooding her sight.

"I fucked myself! Over this shite! Over this!" Camden's voice reached a higher tenor than she'd ever heard before.

The cabbie was fighting through cars to pull over.

Alisyn felt the great fury from Cloth reverberate through her god-eyes. After what Cloth had done to Duncun, what would befall her? And Camden?

"Cloth will blame us for this."

The cabbie was growing frantic with the traffic and the pouring rain.

Alisyn pulled at her hair. The barrette became a pressure point and she used the pain to focus. "We would have died in the chapel too."

The cab darted between a truck and a van and bumped the curb. The door opened and the cab driver tried to yank Camden out of the car. A disturbing expression fluxed through Camden's face, as it always did when he opened the marrow blossoms inside him. He reached out in annoyance and burned the cabbie. The man's mouth slid open in shock and he clutched his wrist in surprise.

He fell back and took off running. "Fuckin' lunatics!" Alisyn watched it all in numb silence. She felt like screaming, the reality of all of this falling down on her.

Camden cupped her face in his large hands. "We have to go check on the chapel. We have to confirm all these things you see."

She closed her eyes and saw every corner of the planet, and beyond that, the forming shapes of another world.

The limo in the parking lot near the Newark Castle was the only piece of property left to the Church of Midnight. Camden didn't have the keys for it, but luckily he recalled Fraser kept a spare in a magnet box near the right front wheel.

He and Alisyn sat in the car, looking through the tinted windows to the chaotic scene unraveling before them. She had mentioned it was a good idea to get going because they stuck out sorely amongst the gathering crowds, but made no further objection to Camden ogling a bit longer.

The entire area had sunken into the ground as though a moon sized meteor had plummeted down on the spot. Trees folded inward, their root systems twisting every which way like a grisly display of earthen guts. Some of the chapel's structural supports protruded from the ground and yet at this vantage it would be easy to overlook them in the mess of shredded tree trunks. Plumes of yellow steam vented up from the fissures into the atmosphere. Police had barricaded off the area with tape and were wisely not venturing into the pit that seemed to widen and drop every fifteen minutes.

In the silence, a trilling ring startled them both. The car phone had a call coming in. Only Bishops from other chapels had access to the number and for this Camden quickly grabbed the phone out of its compartment.

"Archbishop Amherst."

Alisyn could hear the voice on the other end. "Bishop Jeffrey here. I heard what happened, Archbishop. There really are no words."

Camden stretched back in the seat. "Yes—forgive me, but I thought your following disbanded last summer."

"I've kept some members. Nothing large. I had some ideas though and you'd promised me private counsel at conclave. I've been waiting all year."

"Well you can see things have changed."

The Bishop was silent for a moment. "Of course I understand, but all is not lost. I've come all the way from California and had the fortune of not being killed with the rest of our number. You can't spare me fifteen minutes?"

Camden sighed furiously through his teeth. "Not today."

"Of course."

"There is a car-park at the hotel down the street from where the Chapel...was."

"I'll find it."

"Call me in the morning and we'll set it up."

"Thanksgiving to the Eternal Feast."

Camden hung up the phone and hurled it onto the floor.

Alisyn had only been half listening to the last part of the conversation. A vision had been taking shape in her mind and suddenly blasted across her sight. Camden looked over as she beheld it in wonder.

"What is it?"

"Wait—there's something new."

"The Heart of the Harvest?"

"No—something else." A sharp impact through her sight caused her to throw her head back and shriek. Camden gripped onto her shoulders. She could feel his body trembling along with hers. When the image processed in her mind finally, she closed her eyes and held her face, spoke softly into her palms, "The Interloper's house. It has to be."

"How do you know?"

"I see—yes, yes, I think I have found it, in a way."

"*In a way*? What does that mean? Describe this place."

"It's constant motion. I see no person, only the places a person has been." She studied the slowly building structure. "I see clearly now. It will be in the country."

"Will be?"

"Yes," she said, nodding. "It sounds strange but the cottage won't exist until tomorrow morning."

The mental theater of Alisyn's mind suddenly ripped away from the cottage in the country side, and now her All-Sight was directed on the gateway within the Marigold pub. Cloth, sitting atop his Duncun-chair, turned his ghastly face up from the shadows.

Alisyn's body hitched and bucked at the traumatic changing of tableau.

"Alisyn!" Camden caught her gyrating body. "What's happening?"

Chaplain Cloth looked at Alisyn, just as she looked at him.

"Do you know how to get to this cottage?" Cloth asked calmly. "It's a place called Boghead."

"We can find it, Chaplain."

She felt Camden's body go rigid next to hers. "Do," Cloth said. "I'm curious."

"I will also continue to search for the Heart of the Harvest."

"Don't bother. I've found him. The Heart is in the Old Domain this year. His name is Kauph Courre."

"Oh," she said, swallowing hard. Images from the other world were not as clear to her yet. "And about the Chapel—"

"Yes." Cloth's black and orange eyes filled with a demented light. "How lucky for you to have been spared…"

The image abruptly blacked out in her mind. Alisyn couldn't conceive how he'd done it, but the Chaplain blocked her sight of him and the pub.

Camden looked about to explode. "What did Cloth say?"

She took a moment and swallowed. She needed a glass of water badly. "He's found the Heart of the Harvest in the Old Domain."

"In the Old Domain? I've never heard of such a thing. How can that be?"

She didn't care to answer that and added, "Cloth wants us to go to the cottage an' take a look. We can go tomorrow."

"I have that meeting with Bishop Jeffrey." Alisyn raised her eyebrows in disbelief.

"I'll keep it short, promise," Camden added, his face grim. "So, Cloth wasn't mad about losing the chapel? Was he?"

Alisyn gazed out the rain-streaked window and inhaled deeply. "We better find a place for the night."

OCTOBER 29TH

SEVENTEEN

Bre mixed the last of the tonic. He felt something terrible and vibrant in his chest. Was it pride? Hope? Love? He couldn't tell, but his well-being had improved with the simple toil. Blue-green fragments of the transmungi sea squash floated on the carbonated yellow surface. It made sense now why this tonic had the particular nickname of Filthy Ale. As he administered it down the funnel into Pel'Hahr's throat, Kennen watched from a rocking chair, a mug of typical ale in hand. It was possibly his sixth or seventh of the night.

The tonic had repaired most of Pel'Hahr's organ damage and brought a healthy glow back to her dry skin. For some time it seemed she would recover. She'd started to make sounds again and rock back and forth. But the pain returned. The old pain that caused her to ball up her body and weep through her teeth. They gave her numbing spirits and another blood transfusion enriched with the remainder of Bre's donation pulled from the detention box. It crossed his mind that the last transfusion might have been weak for the little amount of elixir solution.

Pel'Hahr made an agonized expression and grabbed at her neck. Kennen glanced at Bre with wide, drunken eyes. Bre didn't need words. He knew what would be asked of him, so he rounded the bed to the witch. With one hand he pulled back her lush silver hair and placed his other at the muscle connecting neck to shoulder. Bre enjoyed massaging the woman, not only for the simple reason of touch, but also because the repetition soothed him as well.

Kennen slurped his ale and mumbled something. Bre watched him wipe his eyes and stare up at the rain-stained straw seeping through the cracks in the troll husk ceiling. The Archbishop had slept beside the witch last night, hopeful that he'd get to speak to her again if she could only manage lucidity for a moment.

The spicer witch's flesh chilled Bre's hand. She turned over with a moan and placed her fingers on his waist. Her gray nipples hardened against his arm and Bre willed his body to be calm.

Kennen took a lengthy sip of his stout. After he licked the foam off a row of staples above his lip, he leaned forward in his rocker. "You've given much to her and I."

"Not very much, master."

"I should let you have her, Slave."

"Master?"

"Sure," he said decidedly. "I have no doubt she'd enjoy it more than writhing in pain."

Bre chuckled nervously. "You've had much to drink."

"Fuck her, Slave. Use her body. It's fair for its age, wouldn't you say?"

"I would not dishonor her, master."

Kennen stood, staggered and gripped one arm of the rocker. Creamy red ale sloshed over his hand. "Coward. Suit yourself."

"That last transfusion seemed thin," Bre said, feeling something cold and bitter grip his chest. "I could spend another night with the baelins if you need more elixir."

With soft steps, Kennen approached. Bre's eyes flickered in reflex to the slap that was about to come. Instead, a slobbery kiss pressed into his forehead. "No more, Phrey, no more. Just leave her. Let Mother be. If that tonic hasn't bought her time, nothing will."

Bre stopped massaging the witch and stood back from the bed. A cobweb tickled his neck but he didn't dare move to brush it away.

The Archbishop resumed the massaging. Pel'Hahr grunted and some tension in her naked gray body appeared to release. Kennen bent and whispered into her ear, "I hate you so much, Mother. For all I give, you give nothing in return. Do you know that the Heart of the Harvest has bloomed in our world this year? Yes, our slave's brother is out there, easy to take for a sacrifice."

Bre bowed his head at the mention of his brother. He would not show his emotions about what this Day of Opening meant to him. Honestly, he would be pleased with both outcomes, because it would be over. One way or another. But he wouldn't pray for his brother Kauph to survive the night, because somehow he knew Kennen would sense that in his heart and all the trust he'd built with the man would vanish.

Kennen's slobbery lips quivered as a quiet rage claimed him. "You listen to me, Mother. I should be minding the Heralding, preparing others for the Hunt, but instead I'm here with you in the worthless husk of a dead troll, with a spineless slave. I will know no glory unless the sacrifice falls into our lap and you somehow survive."

Tears were in Bre's eyes now, for this he could not hold back. Was this the end? Would Kennen let his mother slip away? Finally? What would their lives be like afterward? He tried to imagine an existence like that but his imagination failed to supply any visions. He and Kennen existed to care for this woman together. If she got better or if she died, neither seemed reasonable conclusions.

"I want to do more," Bre told his master. "All I can offer would be my life itself, which I *can* give. I was blessed once with the sacred fruit. It would make a good sacrifice. It could bring your mother back."

Kennen massaged Pel'Hahr fiercely now. "You have potential power that hasn't manifested yet."

"That is only a tale, master. I can offer the blood of a simple man who once had the chance for power."

The Archbishop snorted. "Did you think we harvested those transmungi easily? No, Slave—those squash will only be found by the one who holds the Heart of the Harvest."

"But...that makes no sense, master. The sacred fruit died within me."

Looking thoughtfully at the ale foam still on his knuckles, Kennen said, "*Fermented.* Your power is larger, though it cannot be used the same way. Still, the transmungi allowed themselves to be reaped only because they knew you were nearby. To them, you still carry the sacred fruit, as you did when you were born. I believe they enlivened that sleeping power in you. Be honest, you feel something different, don't you?"

"I'm not sure," Bre lied. He had felt stronger lately, more energetic, though he still didn't sense any divine power within him. "What if I give myself to Cloth's children? Can they not feast on me and open the gateway wider?"

"Your power is different than a living Heart. It is a pure concentration, but not nourishment. And why would you offer such a thing? Are you in a hurry to end your life?" Kennen drew his hand away from Pel'Hahr, who now softly snored. "No, I'll not make another mistake for the sake of shortcuts. I won't use a treasury of gold to purchase a treasury of silver. And I won't lose my only friend."

Bre's mind tried to grasp the concept. This man had punished him since childhood. This man had lived in his nightmares at times and in his revenge fantasies in others. But friends, they were. At this point, there was little choice in the matter. Kennen spent more time with him than he did with the other Bishops— much more time than he did with most of his followers.

The awkwardness of his last statement still hanging, Kennen shuffled to the rocker again and with a long sigh, took a seat, reeds straining beneath him. Bre remained in his corner like an ornamental statue.

"Go to the well and bring some water. It's too damp in this cottage this evening. I'd like you to iron the robes tomorrow morning, first thing. I need something suitable to wear to invoke the Heralding."

"Will you be ready, master? You've had no time to prepare, with how busy you've been here."

Kennen didn't bother with this and glanced down at the stitches running through his arms. He delicately traced a fresh one from the top of his forearm down to his pointer finger knuckle. "Get the water now to set in the kettle and burn off a bit. I had mineral stains on my garb last time."

There hadn't been any stains on his robes, last time or the time before, but Bre nodded and hurried for the door.

"And Phrey?" Bre turned.

"Don't take a season."

Shutting the door gently behind him, Bre's heart pounded. He couldn't place where his anxiety had come from but things had moved strangely tonight. He ran up the hill, through the bleeding trees, hello, *trees*, and then walked along the eastern palace wall to the clearing where the well stood. Four buckets were stacked at the side of the square structure of black stone.

He attached a pail and lowered down the rope. The sound of hooves on gravel took him by surprise and he nearly dropped the rope. Through the nearby glade came the half-Ekkian from the mortuary. He led a solemn brown horse with large buckets affixed to its saddle.

The man raised his hand. "Good evening to you."

"Good evening."

"The name is Sci, if you'd like to know."

Bre smiled faintly and lowered the pail farther. He heard it strike the water and he went about lowering it some more.

"You are 'He Who Might Have Saved the Worlds.' Isn't that right?"

"Just a slave, sir."

Sci leaned against the well and folded his arms. "Well, slave, are you allowed down in Hendri village?"

"Sometimes."

"There will be a great festival for the Day of Opening. The bonfire will be enormous this year. All you need to bring are two effigies of the Nomads."

"How would I do that?"

Sci's eyes boggled. "You really don't know? Well that's fine. See, these Nomads are women and so you make two straw dummies that resemble women, or as close as you can manage. You know what women look like, don't you, boy? We have our share in the village. I could introduce you to some." Sci juggled imaginary breasts for a moment.

The pail dropped then and Bre huffed. His arms were too sore to do this right now. Sci butted in and took over. He pulled the rope, hand over hand, bared teeth beyond his beard shiny in the growing darkness. A thick vein bulged across his temple and he gave Bre a look of commiseration, "You weren't lying there. This thing's loathsome."

"You never fetched at this well before?"

"The well behind the funeral home ran dry yesterday." He wiped his forehead with his embroidered tunic sleeve. "I came here for my wife. She's in the family way. You never know what night the baby will ripen."

He snorted merrily and retrieved one of the buckets off his horse. Bre stepped away. He didn't want to leave. He wanted to talk more about that festival. There were countless questions to ask but he knew if he went on, Sci would probably just insist on him coming, and that wasn't happening.

"What do you hope for? A boy or girl?"

Sci thoughtfully went about his task and at the same time looked up and pondered the question. He glanced over with a fox's grin. "The kind with ten fingers and toes I imagine."

Bre chuckled a little and nodded a goodbye, which the man returned. It would have been grand to go to the festival, but his life was not his own.

When Bre stepped back inside the cottage he half expected the Archbishop to be passed out, but instead he found Kennen still seated in the rocker, pumping the chair back and forth unnaturally fast. He didn't look in Bre's direction, but said, "Set those near the stove. I'll put them in the kettle."

"Yes, master."

He did as he was bade and returned to his place at the front door.

"Instruct the cell keeper you are to receive twenty straps tonight before bed." Kennen stopped rocking for a second, as though second thinking this, and then resumed.

"Twenty. Yes, master. Have I done something wrong?"

"No, Phrey, I have. Go along."

Bre touched the back of his head, bowed and quickly went outside. His trip up through the bleeding trees gave him no solace. Bewilderment almost had him wandering down the wrong path back to the lower palace quadrant. He wasn't afraid of the cell keeper's fat leather strap. He was afraid of not fully appreciating his punishment. Desperately, with every foot covered, he wanted to understand. When he headed into the cell block he resigned himself to the fact he may never know.

The cell keeper lay face down in a plate of mushy peas and a half eaten scoop of fireroot, his brown hair spilling everywhere and one of his fuzzy-knuckled hands resting in a bowl filled with windcherry pits.

"Keeper Oric," called Bre. When the man didn't budge, Bre poked his shoulder.

Oric lifted his head. Some peas had lodged in one of his nostrils and some mashed fireroot hung from his lanky hair like fungus. "The hell do you want?" he growled.

"I am reporting for punishment."

The cell keeper picked at his clean nostril. "Now why would you act out so...damned late?"

"Night has just fallen."

Oric looked up in the air like a gathering of bats just blew into the room. "Just fallen, oh that's for shit." He rubbed his eyes. "What's the punishment?"

Bre hesitated, then said, "Fifty straps." Suddenly Oric looked alert. "*Fifty?*"

A pair of sentinels came through the door. Their orange boots sounded heavier than the stone beneath them. Bre recognized a sentinel who harassed just about every slave when he had the opportunity. Gogg Maidmin. The man seemed to have nothing better to do at night than make himself known.

"How are you this evening, keeper?" Gogg handed over a scroll. "That's the rotation for the Day of Opening."

Oric slipped off the black band encircling the vellum and opened the scroll. He pursed his rubbery lips as he read the list of names. "This is ridiculous," he complained and took out a black and orange ledger. "Does the Inner Circle prison council even know what it takes to run this place?"

"I imagine not," Gogg stated. He glanced at Bre and nodded.

"Oh don't be nice to him," said Oric, still intent on the scroll. "That one has to be strapped. I've got all this to do now and no time to do it."

"That's a problem it seems." Gogg feigned deep thought. "You know, I'm not sure, but you could maybe pay someone to strap your prisoners. Someone particularly bored and nearly setting to rust in all this armor."

"I get it." Oric picked up a fountain pen. "Fifty Suns. One per strapping."

"One hundred," Gogg corrected. A wide leer severed his beard as his eyes found Bre. "I'm gonna use both hands."

EIGHTEEN

Byron sat on a windowsill juggling his cell phone and a Snickers bar, surveying the procession of stacked Glasgow traffic on the streets below. His partner Denis watched alongside him in silence, in the all but empty flat. The walls looked gray from the rain, but the carpet, ceiling and throw rug were all white. A fake plant near the fireplace provided the only splash of color in the room. It was a horribly dismal place, Byron decided. He'd certainly never stay long if he lived here.

Speaking of, the time to leave was at hand. A smart move would be to head off before Patty and Teresa showed. If his boys failed to tranq the Nomads, he didn't want to be around to get his head chopped off with one of those mantle things. Roberto said it might take a couple darts with his new, more effective, yet safer Ketamine-sedative cocktail. Said it would take only a few minutes—but Byron gave him a warning that a few minutes was enough time for Patty Middleton to bring down a building.

This was if they even showed. So far his rooftop position hadn't reported the Nomads arriving on the main street. Byron needed enough time to skedaddle these here parts. Toughest glitch to work out though: they had a way of seeing right through a fucking building. *I really should have thought this plan out better. Story of my damn life.*

Byron watched the marker move on the map. Ah, *my other soup's starting to cook.* The Priestess of Midnight was leaving the hotel that she and the bearded doofus checked into last night. This was a good enough excuse to bail.

He hopped off the sill and hooted. "I got to go out to the country. Girlfriend's on the move."

"You're leaving?" Denis said, moving from his position. "I thought your girlfriend was on her way here?"

"Hey, I can juggle two girlfriends and a chainsaw." Byron slapped him on the shoulder and sent Denis sprawling. Byron grabbed his coat from the sofa.

"We could use you here."

"No need to worry. The Nomads won't use deadly force. Don't give them a reason, okay? If Roberto doesn't sink his darts, and things go south—you can tell them you fed me bad information—make it look like I had no idea this was the plan."

"So you're still the good guy?"

"That's the ticket. Damn, I knew you were my partner for a reason."

He headed out.

"I hate you," Denis told him.

"Kisses, dear," sang Byron as he shut the door.

Patty wanted to grit her teeth together until they broke. She couldn't believe she'd ever had feelings for Byron Telamon. She stood in the bookstore with a very smug Teresa and just about quaked with fury. Four times she'd looked up the street to the flat where she'd placed an aperture mantle. Earlier she used the mantle to peer inside the building, thinking that the Messenger might sense the construction and flee. But at once she realized a horde of OAP agents were staked out to trap them.

Byron wasn't even with them. The damned coward had sold them out.

Teresa approached her with a romance novel in her hand.

She handed it to Patty. *Brutal Betrayal.*

"Cute." Patty placed the book on the children's rack. "So what do we do now?"

"Go back to our hotel and wait for the *real* Messenger to send us word. The Heart of the Harvest must be somewhere in this city."

Patty looked back up the street in dismay. "You don't want to kill them? They're in our way, just like the Church was."

Teresa took her gently by the elbow and led her through the front door. "Don't piss me off, Patty. Let's head up the street some."

They walked under some awnings even though the rain had let up a bit. A middle-aged woman shepherded five children up the sidewalk. The woman's face was flushed and her eyes were darting around protectively to her hyperactive brood. The sight of it made Patty forget her anger for a moment.

"Ouch!"

"What?"

Teresa searched the back of her neck. "I got stung."

"How? There's no—" Something bit into Patty's flesh just under her jaw. She grabbed at it and felt the frills of a fletching on a dart.

"Rooftop?" Teresa's eyes filled with dread. "Did you check them?"

Patty shook her head. "I didn't—thought the Messenger might notice a lot of mantles."

Teresa slammed against a parked sedan. Patty went to her. The world had become dreamy and tilted. The sensation was petrifying. Teresa's body slid down and her eyes rolled back. Patty caught her and watched as Teresa fought to open her eyes again. Patty searched around helplessly, tapping into her new hate for Byron again, hoping it would wake her up.

A group of rain-coated agents briskly approached. Patty focused on them. To hell with her good intentions, she would kill these men, *right now*. It would send a message. Her mind felt mushy though—still, she sought the cold pinpoint where mantles were drawn. The agents sidestepped the woman and her children, now only ten yards away. Patty's mind gripped the beginning of a mantle and horror flooded her. No—the woman, the children. Couldn't take the chance. Another...

Explosion... Might... No...

Can't let that happen.

Patty lowered her body as a frightening wave of exhaustion pressed down. She rested her head on her arm and felt the cold damp sidewalk against her cheek.

NINETEEN

Bre Courre took his time brushing Danur and Cortis, two of the finest horses in all of the Old Domain. In spite of enjoying his time with his equine friends, the stables smelled like death and his shoulder and back still stung terribly from the strapping.

Both geldings kept their heads together as though conjoined twins. They reminded Bre of the bleeding trees. Had he and his brother Kauph been allowed to grow up together, he wanted to believe they'd have had such a bond. Yes, he imagined despite any quarrels or differences they had, the Courre brothers would never leave each other's side.

"Slave," Kennen rasped. "Outside."

Bre dropped the brush in the stall and Danur and Cortis shifted apart, warily. He walked out to the stretching length of shadow Kennen cast across the haystacks. Kennen beckoned him to follow and they walked for a time along the north wall, in a storm channel that had long since run dry. A faint breeze drifted down the tunnel. Burning leaves fragranced its gliding touch. It was a smell Bre associated with the season and most especially the Day of Opening. Usually he savored the earthy aroma, but something today made him suspicious about its intoxicating strength; wrongness threaded through it.

"Cloth's children call me, Slave. In my restless nights when I care for mother...they see no need to pity me. They are hungry for birth. They ask for my body as a channel into this world and therefore I must be the one to invoke the Heralding. I am concerned however they are unaccustomed to the Old Domain. It has been so long since they've fed on our blood. In a sense, they need to acquire the taste to hatch with success and to thrive."

"So we give the Children what they want. We give them blood."

The tunnel ended and light flooded around them. The burning leaves intensified as they journeyed down to the gateway site. "Yes, you will."

"Master?"

Stone steps fixed into an eroded hill that led around to an open expanse of trees and broken columns from the bone temples. The gateway burned in the center of the expanse, a black abrasion in the cosmos. Thousands of deep green vines grew from its emptiness and stretched around a multitude of different columns. Bre always singled out three: a brilliant jewel encrusted ebony column, a deep green marble column with sculpted devils enfolded around its length, and then an old, crumbling column made of a brittle, ancient design faded from all detail. He thought the most appropriate would be the column with the jewels, just for its presence and majesty, but his master had never told him or anybody which one would keep the gateway opened.

Around the columns, up stone steps, even on several roofs from surrounding partitions of the palace, pumpkins bloomed, some small as a fist and some large as an asteroid, mostly a malevolent orange color, although a few were white or green with hideous bumps—these were the eggs the Children would hatch from and the shapes they would take. It was exciting, but a little frightening as well to know they would walk these grounds soon.

A row of sentinels waited at the bottom of the stairs, talking merrily until they saw the Archbishop. Beyond them, a hundred or more people writhed in the pumpkin patch. Most had superficial head injuries and blackened eye sockets from beatings. They were bound, hands and feet, and gagged with orange linen.

"Who are they?"

Kennen led Bre to the edge of the patch. Nearby a blond teenager with wild brown eyes moaned and thrashed around in a net of vines.

"Hemdri village will empower the soil," Kennen explained. "But few came willingly. That's an unfortunate truth about the lack of devotion from people today, but although it's regrettable, it doesn't have to taint our offering." He unsheathed a long dagger from a sentinel's belt. Bre winced as its handle pressed into his palm. Kennen locked eyes with him. "I know you, boy. You would never take a life willingly. That is powerful in its own right. We have to use that."

Bre's voice was dry as parchment. "You want me to kill those people?"

"Don't ask ridiculous questions."

"But somebody else—"

"I know *you*," Kennen spat. He closed the distance between them and lowered his crooked nose so that its staples nearly touched Bre's. "Though I can say you'd carelessly give yourself over to death, it would be painful for you to take a life. That is what we need. There is power in that. You understand?"

"There has to be another way."

The world around Bre ran together in splintering green shadows with blasts of manic orange bulbs. Kennen nudged him forward. Bre's body trembled so hard he feared his bowels would loosen. The knife fell from his shaking fingers. He bent to pick it up in the mess of vines, but Kennen knelt quickly and shoved the weapon back into his hand. "Pick someone who is most difficult for you, Phrey. Show me that power."

A difficult murder. Was there any other kind? That would be the mortuary wagoneer. Sci. A cold sweat soaked Bre's hairline like a winter bog. *He said to call him Sci.*

Carefully Bre stepped over the angry green cords and used several pumpkins for assistance. The blond teen thrashing around looked like he belonged to the patch. His blazing eyes and the fierce way his square yellow teeth cut into his gag made it a certainty: if this man got free he'd kill the first person who tried to stop him. This would be too easy a kill.

Several people caught Bre's eye and he stopped to consider them. A young woman, not too much younger than him, looked to have swallowed some wild terror that caused her convulsions. An older man stared back, nodding at Bre with kind, sad eyes, and it was clear he'd offer himself if everyone else could go. Then there was a child, around seven years old, unassuming, unafraid, almost curious about his capture.

"Try there." Kennen's voice startled Bre from his hideous thoughts. He looked to the place the Archbishop pointed, just around a three-foot-tall, lopsided pumpkin with green and purple barnacle-like growths at the base of its stalk. Bre trekked around it and saw a large, pale mound in the vines ahead. He stumbled sideways and knocked over a couple of little pumpkins. Ready for life, the pumpkins felt freezing cold to the touch and he ripped his hand away.

The woman's muffled moans gave his every hair attention. She was pregnant. He had no idea about these things but from the enormous bulge in her midsection. How much bigger could the pregnancy make her? The woman had to be nearly due.

Bre knelt before the woman, staring at her horrified eyes and the gleaming white belly. This wasn't just difficult.

"Impossible," he whispered.

Kennen clapped his hands anxiously. He didn't even have to raise his voice from the other side of the patch. It was quiet enough to hear everything. Not even the gentle wind that played with the pumpkin's leaves would insist on its usual song. "Wonderful choice, Slave."

Now killing Sci actually seemed much easier...*and hadn't he said his wife was with child?*

Bre placed the tip of the knife on her belly. The woman shook her head, eyes pleading, rods of muscle straining in her neck.

"Don't look at me," he told the woman. Leaning forward, Bre got a better view of her face. Her features were dark, though her brown hair had been sun-lightened. She was not unlovely, but not gorgeous either. Yet, the laughter lines near her eyes made him suspect her beauty lie in her soul, the very thing of which he sought to deprive her.

He pointed the knife at her heart instead. "Don't look at me," he said again. He pushed her face to the side and she began to sob. Dirt had temporary blinded her and she blinked spastically.

Kennen shouted, "Stop acting, Slave. I know this will be the one."

Bre couldn't believe the surly tone he replied with to his master. "Kill some whore? That makes this world better off."

"You don't—"

"She's a whore!" Bre pushed the woman's face deeper into the dirt and vines.

"Leave her alone, devils!" yelled a voice a few feet away.

Thanks to the harvest, thought Bre. He faced Kennen with firm resolve. This was his murder to make. He wouldn't be bullied. This was the one thing Bre got to take with him to his grave. It was horrible cargo, *but it was his. The Archbishop made no move to stop him as he walked over to the source of the voice.*

It was not Sci he found lying there though.

They were not identical but it was easy to tell they were twins. One had managed to untie his brother's gag using a few teeth that had slipped above his own gag. Their heads leaned against each other now, one brother's gaze averted, the other's aimed directly at Bre.

This was what Bre had missed his whole life, that other half, the person who would be there for him until the end. These two had that bond—but Bre wasn't jealous of them. No, he loved these two young men. They clarified that even in a life of constant stumbling, there could be someone who'd help you stand again. He didn't even see the young men as separate; they were a rare, beautiful, two-headed animal that shouldn't be allowed to go extinct, for if such a creature did, the world itself might as well go with it.

Over the heartbreak, the only consolation the slave had was that the brothers did not see each other die. Their eyes were pointed away from each other.

Blood erupted from the throat of the brother on the right and the cruel soil sucked it down immediately. The left brother's body flexed. He knows his brother's dying, thought Bre. There wasn't much of a sound from the fatal wound and the brother only slightly grunted. The blood didn't even have an odor above the organic pungency of the pumpkins. *He just knows.*

Bre dragged the wet blade across the surviving brother's throat and completed the job. He watched the skin open and fold back in a ragged pair of lips. The end of a mole hung on the torn flesh. Bre watched the blood baptize it, a much easier flow than the other brother's had been. The slave studied the quiet massacre and then the knife in his hand. In the next moment he remembered himself and vomited his morning porridge between the twitching bodies.

"It had to be two." Kennen crept up behind him. "And brothers at that—this wasn't out of vengeance I wager?"

Bre wiped the acid taste in his mouth across his shoulder and then bowed his head, closed his eyes. "No, master..."

Kennen found a place for the Heralding. He stooped on one knee and lowered himself to sit and then to lie down. Vines slithered around him, sensing the source of power within Kennen's body.

Bre wondered if the rite would kill his master. Heralding the Children of Cloth had done that to many Bishops in the other world. There was no way to tell how it would work in the Old Domain.

The abruptness of Kennen's voice almost brought Bre to his feet. "Sentinels! The Children ask for more. We must answer the call. Haste!"

With a succession of metallic shushes, the sentinels drew their amber sabers.

"Let it all spill," urged Kennen. "Quickly...before...I'm overrun."

A man made a great agonized groan through his gag. Bre watched as the sentinel unhoused his blade from the victim's chest. Without hesitation, other sentinels scattered on private missions.

Bre launched himself over the dead brothers, grasped onto the lopsided pumpkin and propelled himself to the pregnant woman. He worked the dagger under her restraints and they came off easily. Sacrificial blood transferred from the blade to her wrists and it disturbed him to see it paint her skin in such a colorful display.

"Hurry, you ignorant shits!" Kennen bellowed.

A sea of death calls rose everywhere. Bre worked at the binds around the woman's ankles. She struggled, still uncertain of his intentions, but he managed to slice through the rope without much hindrance. She tried to strip off her gag, but Bre grabbed her hand. "You need to run. Go!"

He hauled the woman to her feet and pushed her forward. The vines wormed around their ankles. She stumbled through the patch, stepping on and over them. Bre caught her just as she lost her center of balance and momentum carried her sideways.

The sentinel approached out of the corner of his eye, but it was too late to react. It was the one named Gogg. His body swiveled unnaturally fast and the world went black and silver and gritty. A throb down from his temple, past his eye, into his brain, had Bre almost dry heaving. In one blow the pommel of Gogg's saber had driven him to the ground. The sentinel hovered over him, seeming ready to pounce and delightfully finish the job. The woman stood frozen on the perimeter of the bloody scene before them.

Gogg didn't turn to her. "Go the hell on home, dummy," he barked.

At first she didn't move. Bre blinked at her to reinforce the statement; *go damn it*. He heard the woman amble off but couldn't see if she'd gotten into the clear because Gogg stood over him now. The tip of his saber pressed at Bre's throat. "What's this now, shit-dick? You let the chubby woman get away. That'll mean more quality time for us."

"Thank you for doing that for her."

"Suck my cock." Gogg reeled back to strike him—

In the center of chaos Kennen screeched and at once started to laugh and cry. "They've come. They've come. The Children! Theyvecometheyvecometheyvecome." He howled with renewed joy. Bre had never heard him so elated. All the murder-exhausted sentinels stood in the patch, sensing nothing at first. Bre pushed up on one arm and tried to ignore the ragged red forms throughout the pumpkin patch. Then he heard a wheeze from the lopsided pumpkin nearby. There was something moving inside. Something scratching and breathing.

The Children had arrived.

Bre moved his eyes to the two brothers, lying together in death, frozen in their tragic love. Now the slave became jealous of them. Now of all times. Not before, but now

TWENTY

Not in a ballroom, not in a lavish restaurant banquet room, not even in the dining hall of a Grand Chapel, but in a parking garage, this was probably the saddest and least attended conclave in the history of the Church of Midnight, and that history went back Before Common Era. It was pathetic. Camden should have just canceled, so he and Alisyn could get going to that cottage in the country.

To the Interloper.

He should have just told Fraser to hold off this American Bishop for a while—but Fraser wasn't around anymore, was he?

Fraser...

Camden would regret not telling him how valuable a friend he'd been. It wasn't fair that a life could be taken so quick and cold. He could see how some men might have wanted revenge on the Nomads. That would be a normal reaction, he was sure, but Camden somehow understood the Nomads' methodology. They took broad steps to make things easier. He admired that. He wished he could be a person to do the same, to crack this shell of burden around him.

At these kinds of thoughts, self-loathing flushed his skin. How could he commiserate with the enemy? Those women would have killed him and Alisyn just as well. They'd left the Church of Midnight in miserable shambles. Now it was Camden, Alisyn, and an American Bishop whom he hardly trusted. Phil Jeffery, the Bishop of an upstart chapel in the Los Angeles area, had always been someone of note because he headed the Office of Arcane Phenomenon in the United States. He'd given the church opportunities because his Washington job depended on the Church of Midnight being worthy of federal attention. *Fine line he'd toed there…*

After he got comfortable in the limo's bench seat, the white haired man bowed his head. "Thank you for meeting me, Archbishop. I know it is a…difficult time."

"Difficult disnae cover it, Bishop Jeffrey." Camden rubbed his beard slowly. "You said you had information vital to the Church. I would very much like to know what that is, so I can be off."

Jeffrey took out a photo from his suit and handed it to Camden. "You know what that is, right?"

The photograph was the Pillar of Ginsau at the St. Mungo Museum. Camden remained guarded. Only he and Fraser had discussed this. *Fraser.*

"Vaguely," he replied.

"You know what it is," said Jeffrey irritably, "and what it means to us. Now that we've located this, the merging of worlds is likely upon us. If not right away, we'll see it in our lifetimes. I'm certain." He took the photo back and studied it for a long moment. "This shot doesn't do any justice to the marble lattices at the base. I'm actually an amateur photographer myself and this lighting is for shit."

Uncertain he wanted to even indulge the man or theories about the gateway column for that matter, Camden considered how to ask the man to leave.

Jeffrey pointed to the bar. "Can I trouble you for a gin and tonic?"

Camden raised an eyebrow. "It's a might early for that."

Jeffrey's mouth peeled back in an unnatural smile. "I'm still in a different time zone."

Camden scooted over, grabbed a tumbler glass from under the bar and the bottle of gin. He opened the ice canister and was impressed to still find ice there. Fraser must have serviced the ice maker the day he died…Camden bit his lip to ward off the thought. He dropped ice in the glass and poured two fingers of gin.

"Oh, you have Maker's Mark. I'm sorry. Might I have that instead? Neat?" Jeffrey asked.

Camden put the glass of gin aside and got another tumbler out. He popped the cork off the wax-tipped bottle and was about to pour—

"Then again," said Jeffrey, "I did get a banger of a headache last I drank whiskey. I will just have some of that wine there."

With a sigh, Camden corked the whiskey bottle and reached for the wine glasses. The bishop gently grabbed his arm. "Exactly at what point, Archbishop, do you tell me to go to hell?" A chortle escaped him and it was infectious. Camden started laughing too, even though the moment was at his expense.

"Do you want anythin'? Or not? Arse." Jeffrey smirked. "You're right. It's too early." Camden softly snorted and shook his head.

"I like that you have a sense of humor. May I tell you something of myself?"

"If it pleases you," replied Camden. "But let's not footer about."

"Understood, *Archbishop*. Look this goes a bit back. When I was a boy, I had a life changing experience. I'd been taking photos all night of our neighborhood's Halloween decorations. Loved that stuff...had this little Polaroid camera and thought I was hot shit. Well there I was, worked up on candy, out too late in a Southern California suburb, pretty safe back then but without my parents' permission. Anyhow I was actually on my way home when a white faced man in a black suit comes out of nowhere, out of an enormous hole in the air. He had one black eye, one orange." Phil trailed off for a moment and looked down at his weathered hands. "I snapped his picture that night, thinking I'd seen someone pull off the greatest magic trick I'd ever seen. I knew that was just an easy explanation though. No, this was something I wasn't supposed to see. I could tell the man, or whatever he was, searched for something. Years later I would read the Tomes and come to know that search had happened every Halloween for thousands of years."

Now with Cloth in mind, Camden really needed to wake Alisyn, so they could get on their way to that cottage. He didn't have time for this man's rambling nostalgia.

Phil went on, "Before Chaplain Cloth vanished again, he bent on his knee so I could stare into his eyes…I felt like two different people stared at me. He told me I'd help him bring the Column to the gateway…and if I didn't help him, he'd enjoy destroying everything I love. Well, back then I had my parents and my cocker spaniel to worry about, and that was enough, Archbishop—believe me. But now, with children and grandchildren, you understand how getting that Column to the gateway has to involve me. We must go after the Pillar of Ginsau."

"I don't have anyone left to lend you, especially to a theory. That may not even be the right Column. The Church has been getting this wrong since Stonehenge."

"I've had dreams of this *exact* Column my entire life, ever since meeting the monster from the gateway. And unlike you, Archbishop, I have the manpower. I have agents willing to do anything to keep their jobs. It sounds like both of our organizations have crumbled through our fingers lately. Time to pick up the pieces and make something new."

"Your optimism is staggering, but one cannae rule out the Nomads stopping in to drop a building on you."

"Here's where you get happy, Archbishop."

"How so?"

Jeffrey's eyes gleamed, self-satisfied. "The Nomads are in my custody."

Camden cocked his head sideways and opened his mouth. He didn't know what to say. It was fantastical at best, a suspicious lie at worst. "Even if you're not just a *gowk*, Bishop Jeffrey, you won't have those women for long."

"By tomorrow the Nomads will no longer be in the picture. Trust me. In the end, Chaplain Cloth will owe the both of us." *I'll believe that when I see it.* "Let me know how everythin' works out. If not, it was nice knowing you. Now off with you,

Bishop. We need to be on our way."

Taking the door handle, Phil nodded. "It would be a great help if I had your presence to transition the men. Promise me you'll come to the museum tomorrow. We need to stand with each other on this. The union of the worlds depends on it. For the sake of the Church and all who came before and all who will come after."

Camden closed his eyes and saw starbursts popping on the dim tableau under his eyelids. "Certainly, for the Church. I promise I will stop by."

Phil's long face went dour, clearly not believing him. "Keep the faith, Archbishop."

Camden tried to smile. That was the one thing right now he could not do.

On the long ride out to Boghead, Alisyn watched nothing outside the windows of the limo. Her eyes were in the Old Domain, on the tree in Blakandor Forest where her True Child gestated. It didn't seem real, and perhaps it wasn't, perhaps it was only a hallucination brought on by her spiritually charged mind, but she had to believe it. She saw the baby there, writhing in amniotic tree amber. The massive Apex Goblin rested somewhere nearby, unseen for now, a guardian of considerable danger.

How she wanted to be there! It pained Alisyn to think all the apothecary's supplies had been destroyed in the Newark Chapel; she would have murdered for the chance to go back into the Old Domain, even as a ghost, to reach into that tree and touch the face of the child who would come to rule every land of humankind and enslave Chaplain Cloth.

Her son, the Lord of Masks.

Perhaps they would find a laboratory with incantation components at the Interloper's cottage—

Stop hoping. You set yourself up for disappointment.

"Did you see a sedan behind us?" Camden asked suddenly. He kept his eyes on the road, which had become uneven and bumpy.

Torn from her desperate thoughts, Alisyn snapped to, blinking.

"Can ye look?" he asked.

In her mind Alisyn searched the road around them and found no other car for miles. "I don't see anyone."

"I'm a wee nervy I think," Camden replied. "I swore we had a tail there for a moment."

They passed a small township and the cottage came into

view. It sat in a field of pure green turf, untouched by the sun. Mud and oblong puddles stretched infinitely in the rural distance. A short picket fence surrounded the cottage. Something rectangular and ornate sat on the porch.

"See that?"

"Yes."

"Is that a kennel?"

"Rather fancy for a kennel, wouldn't you say? Almost looks like a treasure chest."

"Wi' a door in the side?"

He parked the limo just outside the worst of the mud. Camden studied the cottage apprehensively. "You're positive that the Interloper has left?"

"Whoever lived here has come and gone in the blink of an eye. Let's be at it."

Alisyn slid outside into the dry air. Camden followed quickly after. From above, clouds circled the plot of land; they weren't rain clouds, they were open hands, shelter from the sky, and they approached with a chilling sense of purpose. The blaring scent of black licorice filled the air.

As they entered the gated area Camden's body tensed next to her. "We're okay," she told him. "Relax."

In the empty field, only the trilling wind and the clapping of their shoes on the concrete walkway made a sound. Camden snatched Alisyn's arm and she shouted out in surprise.

"Whit is yer problem?" She shook loose from his grip. "I saw something move in there."

"There's nothing—"

But she saw something now too. A slender black cat came from the darkness of the kennel. Its eyes were mirrored orbs— the field, the picket fence, Camden and her, all of it bent over the spherical contours. Around the black cat's neck hung a soft mane of deep orange fur, making it look like a small adaptation of a lion. Three more cats came sliding out behind the first.

"They're exotic cats."

"Don't be stupid, Camden," said Alisyn. "There's something *wrong* about them."

Streams of identical felines flooded out of the small kennel and quickly overtook the fenced area. There were, almost at once, several hundred of them and more steadily flowed out like a ruptured oil well.

The Interloper was clearly protecting something vital. Alisyn shoved Camden forward. "Chase them off."

He stood there awkwardly in the sea of writhing black fur and glittering silver eyes. Complex runes in the cats' fur glowed with the intensity of magma. Their red light made Alisyn's eyes water. Camden held a hand to his eyes.

In the very next moment Camden's entire body struck hers with such a force the air left her lungs. On a wave of luminosity and what felt and smelled of deep, soft fur, they flew backward, collided and rolled apart just on the other side of the gate.

Camden was above her, dirt and blades of grass sticking in his hair and beard. He checked her to make certain she was okay. In a dizzy madness, Alisyn coughed and drew air into her lungs as she struggled to prop herself up. The world pitched and yawed.

Using the fence to pull up on, Camden returned to his feet. Absently he brushed off his slacks and took a few steps back toward the gate again. He got no farther than those few steps before his body ignited into flames. Moving faster than Alisyn had ever seen Camden move, he reached inside his coat, grabbed the inner material and pulled it free of his arm, then pinned it to the ground with his knee, smothering the fire. He yanked his other arm out of the coat and shook it painfully. "Ah, ya bastard!"

He started forward again, angry this time, and the cats' unseen hand smacked him to the ground and shoved him back through the mud.

The cats filed back into the kennel, so quick it appeared they were being sucked back inside. In the next moment the yard had become empty again.

Camden warily got up. A pair of silver eyes followed by a black, heart-shaped face came just outside of the kennel threshold, as though to give warning. The face framed with the bright orange mane appeared too judgmental to belong to a cat.

Something struck Alisyn's brain. An image of a bone-white

colored man peering outside the gateway drowned her vision.

Chaplain Cloth looked intrigued. *"Tell Archbishop Amherst to open his marrow blossoms and stand among the Cats. They won't be prepared for it."*

Camden noticed her grabbing her head and watched her with disquiet. "Is it Cloth again?"

She nodded. A question was born within her mind and Cloth heard it just as surely if she'd used her tongue: "He will open the marrow blossoms and this will send the Cats away?"

Cloth replied impatiently, "The disruption will weaken their hold on this world. It will be...mightily helpful to me for this year's harvest. We need you to get past those cats and enter the Interloper's home."

"How long must Camden keep the blossoms open?"

"Until his heart can no longer take the force."

"He'll...die?"

"For his church," said Cloth simply. *"Have him open his connection to the Old Domain. The Cats of Delkilth will do their job and pay the price."*

She remembered lore about these cats now. They had been guardians since the Time of the Division. On Halloween they were the only thing that kept Chaplain Cloth from finding the Interloper. Without the Interloper having power on that particular day of the year, the Cats were vital for protection.

"What did he say?" asked Camden, sensing the conversation had come to a stop. His eyes were clear and full of concern, not for himself, but for her.

Alisyn immediately felt sadness grip her. It was easy to get lost in his well-meaning eyes. They'd come so far together and yet had gone nowhere. Should she just not tell him the outcome? Let him do this and perish? That would be easier, because if she did tell him, Camden might be compelled to oblige Chaplain Cloth. Yes, ignorance would be more kind.

But how would she deal with that choice? Seeing this through wouldn't help her plans. She would be in this without a partner. Cloth would use her until he didn't need her anymore and what then? She couldn't control the monster, and that wouldn't do. He'd offered her nothing in return for this. Camden's death wouldn't even guarantee entrance into the Interloper's cottage. She couldn't trust Cloth to broker a deal. This was a poor sacrifice.

"Alisyn?"

Alisyn got up and dusted herself off. "Leave them. It will kill us to go any farther."

Chaplain Cloth cut into her mind. "*What are you doing, Priestess? Did you misunderstand me? We need this. Tell him to get over there and open the blossoms!*"

She turned her third eye away. Cloth tried to force her sight back on him, but she fought the attack off, the same technique he'd earlier used on her. Thank you for teaching me that, she thought, a bit triumphantly.

"Let's get out of here," she said.

Camden's soft features grew darker as cloud-cover drifted over them. "Are you sure I cannae try again?"

She nodded and hoped she'd made the right choice. Her head began to hurt and scalp sweated under Ronald's tortoise shell barrette. With shaking fingers she pulled it out. Despite its ugliness, it was a difficult thing to let go. There was no room for others in her new life now. She tossed the barrette in the grass and stared at it for a moment.

Camden smiled at this, obviously thinking she'd done it for him. He put his large calloused hand on her shoulder. "What next?"

"We hide."

"We can't hide from these types of enemies, Alisyn."

"I can see anyone coming for us."

He cringed. "Aye, but ye have to sleep sometime—"

"The Nomads think we're dead."

"The Interloper doesn't, and it will only be a matter of time before those women are sent to kill us. If not them, then Chaplain Cloth."

"You think too highly of us. Why would either bother? You will find some kind of employment and I will search fer a new set of Tomes. In time, with study, perhaps we can find a temporary gateway to travel to the Old Domain, where we belong."

"And such research won't draw the Nomads? Seriously, Alisyn. Despite that, temporary gateways are as deadly as they are rare."

"We will figure it out," she told him firmly. "We have to. Let's leave for the States. Take whatever's left in the bank accounts an' get out of this country."

Camden gazed down at his feet, uncertainty fluxing through him. "I've got to meet Bishop Jeffrey tomorrow. There is still hope, according to him. We cannae give up yet. Cloth might still forgive our failing. We've got to try."

She gasped, exasperated. She should have just let him kill himself. "Ye're joking, right?"

"I promised." He turned with a beckoning gesture of his head. "Let's go back for the hotel. We can talk about this more after the Day of Opening."

"Talk? Is that whit you said? *Blood on the tomes,* I'm so done wi' talking. I'm sorry, Camden, but I'm no' leaving wi' you. No' anymore."

Camden whirled around. "Can we just forget about this and go?"

"I made a mistake thinking I could include ye. I shed myself of Ronald an' Duncun an' now I should shed myself of ye."

"For fuck's sake, Alisyn! What do you want from me? Tell me what it is and I'll—"

"And ye'll what? Put me in yer queue?" She paused, overwhelmed, and then proceeded in a whisper. "Our whole Church is dust an' ye still cannae commit to me."

"This is about that hoor."

"This is *not* about that hoor," she growled. "This is about ye."

"And where will ye go? Ye don't have a pot to shite in, lass. Don't be so almighty."

Alisyn started off and he grabbed her tight around the arm. "Get yer fuckin' hands off me."

"Ye wantae go to the Old Domain? Want me to do as I did wi' our son? Ye want that I should send ye there in pieces, ye ungrateful..."

"Let go of me."

Camden did. He shoved a hand into his pants pocket and brought out his wallet. "Go then. Take the rest of my money an' don't ever say I never committed to ye, this frae a half-breed girl of fourteen who had no place to go until she found me!"

His wallet fell to the ground and Alisyn reflexively knelt to pick it up. Strange, that she had never seen his driver's license before. Camden had on less weight in the photo and the smile beyond his blue-black beard was plastic-fake. Why would he even keep his license on him? *You know why*, she thought. Because somebody, somewhere, at some time, had probably told Camden to and he listened. She realized at that moment how low he really was...he was just another soul standing out in the rain, waiting for shelter, not a leader, not a great man. Then she saw his birth date.

November 17th.

Camden immediately knew why she was studying the license.

"No Halloween, yes, so I lied. The date was important to ye, and therefore important to me. I'd have said anything to keep ye, arse that I am."

Alisyn folded the wallet and handed it back to him. It took him a moment to accept it. Tears beaded on her eyelashes, Camden and the countryside behind him going smoky in her vision.

"Please, Alisyn, I cannae go on without you," he admitted.

"Well you must," she said.

His nostrils flared and he exploded, "Then go, ya bitch! Get! Leave!"

It took everything in her not to hurl a fist into his stupid face. "My True Child will rule all worlds—even Cloth will be terrified to look upon his face—I was a fool to ever believe he could be derived frae your seed, Camden. Ye're not yer own man. Ye're everybody's toy. When the worlds unite, ye will be rubbish under rubbish, ye will be a slave's slave."

Alisyn started off, praying he didn't follow. She shook her head, livid with him for not consigning himself to her at last, angry at that dumbfounded look on his face, those stupid black bows in his beard, that idiot look of love in his eyes, the sad sickness of a wasted human life.

She expected Camden to come after her one last time;
the old Camden surely would have. But no heavy footsteps
bounded after her, no coarse words rose from behind, and not
long after, as she walked aimless down the dirt road, the limo
drove past, Camden at the wheel. He didn't even look once over
his shoulder at his Priestess.

"Goodbye," she said.

Byron watched through his binoculars as the limo tumbled
down the dirt road. The GPS beacon signal remained planted
back at the cottage. It must have dropped out of her hair. Well,
that part of this was screwed. Something strange had happened
over there though—right before they got into some kind of
drawn out spat, it looked as though Alisyn and the Archbishop
disappeared for a moment and then suddenly reappeared.

"Gateway." A smile broke Byron's face. "Ho-ly shit."

The pain in his eyes and jaw and down his neck, to his ass, it
all but disappeared out of joy. How long had he waited for this?
Dreamed of it? Crouched there next to the old convalescent
home, numb in body but heart on fire, at first he could only stare
at the cottage in wonder and fear.

Byron tucked his binoculars into his raincoat and thumbed
off the holster loop to the revolver on his hip. He heard someone
walking on the road on the other side of the home and let them
pass before heading out into the field.

He listened to his feet in the rain soaked grass. The swelling
clouds tightened above. Tremors of anticipation went through
him. Would he ever see Patty again? What would happen once
he went inside it? Would the pain go, as it had in the dreams?
He touched the photo of Cloth in his chest pocket. Or would it
be like using the photo, just a constant nightmare?

Arriving at a faded picket fence, Byron decided none of
his questions mattered; he wouldn't know until he knew. He
noticed a small wooden chest on the porch. A black cat slid out
of the dark interior, rubbing itself on the threshold. It didn't spot
him at first. A wreath of fine orange hair hung around its neck.
Byron liked cats, had owned several of the outdoor models, but

this thing...he didn't trust it. He couldn't tell where the odd impulse derived from but it was obviously clear.

The cat turned a pair of silver eyes on him and his breath caught in his chest. Two similar animals came out quickly, looking surprised and out of sorts, as though they'd been more caught off guard by his presence than the other way around. A deluge of other cats left the chest and within minutes the small yard teemed with dozens of them.

"That's a hell of a cat carrier," he said with a swallow.

Cats clawed over each other, trying to gain higher purchase to look him in the eyes. It was beyond unsettling. Byron was suddenly up to his knees. He couldn't move but had no desire to either—hisses escaped like tea kettles in hell. He put his fingers to his ears and watched a domino effect of cats baring their fangs. The pain inside him, the old reliable pain, went from cold to burning. Magic symbols in the cats' fur lit to a fiery gold and their intensity matched the twisting flames of agony inside him. It was then he realized he was in a stand-off with these cats. They were assaulting him and he was assaulting them. The whole fight had gotten underway without him even thinking about it. He wasn't sure he knew when the fight had begun, or when it would end—

Then, simultaneously, in a final attempt to defeat him, the cats shrieked. Each burst into its own column of black smoke that met in a larger column, which dispersed after a few seconds in snowflakes of ash. All of it funneled back into the box where the cats had emerged. Even the bright scent of fire drew away in an instant.

Byron waited in numb silence for something else to happen. After a few minutes, he went up the porch steps, and looked inside the chest.

Empty.

And it was in his way.

The chest, or cat kennel he supposed, should have been much heavier with its fine, stout wooden making, but it was lighter than a box of tissue paper. He easily heaved it over the picket fence, where it landed in a mud puddle but made no splash. The wooden planks faded out of sight, one at a time, quicker and quicker. All that remained was a floating layer of oil on the surface of the rainwater. Gone.

Byron had come too far now and the pain had become too sharp and real to wonder about oddities outside his own. There wasn't time. He could feel another attack coming on. He believed he would find the gateway just on the other side of the door. There, he would also find the white-faced monster with black and orange eyes, the only thing in the universe that could bring him a lasting peace.

The door was unlocked. He went inside.

Byron put his hands up to his mouth.

Not a goddamn thing—just a collection of dusty furniture and a rustic writing desk. In a doorless bedroom sat a full sized bed made up with one sheet over a mattress. A closet in the corner of the room was empty.

He went back out to the small kitchen area. An old fashioned icebox with no ice—nothing inside. Growing drearier by the moment, he tested the water faucets. Nothing came. He turned back to the writing desk. Someone had piled a stack of parchment there with several jars of different colored ink. The jar of red had dried crust on its side.

Byron sighed. "—the hell is all this?"

A letter lay next to a rolled tube of longer parchment. He unrolled the tube a bit to have a look. Over the paper spread a map with strange sounding locations labeled on intricately painted banners. He had no idea about the terrain it described. Probably Scottish villages or something...

He studied the letter again. The writing was at first slightly familiar and then it struck him. The pain in his gut sank into a warm, soothing brine of hope.

The Messenger's house.

He wasn't at the gateway; he was in the Messenger's house.

Glancing back at the red ink, he nodded. Not blood at all. The Messenger had spilled some of that ink on the parchment.

"Wow," he said. "This is useful for Plan B."

Since Plan A is cluster-fucked.

He read the letter a couple times but it seemed like a riddle only for the Nomads to understand. What was this letter worth to them? He wondered.

Every other bit of leverage had to come along: paints, parchment, letter and the map. He glanced once more around the stifling little room before leaving. No gateway, but all in all, not a wasted trip. He felt like thanking someone. Since he hated the thought of any God, he instead bowed to the emptiness of the room. He left humming "Another Saturday Night" by Sam Cooke, describing that unique brand of loneliness Sam knew so well. Somehow Byron lost track of the song's melody and it suddenly became Deep Purple's "Smoke on the Water."

He envisioned a lake with a rolling carpet of dark red fog above it, and underneath it was health, normalcy, life beyond aching despair.

Oh for the moment when that fog would thin and he could dive into those waters...

TWENTY-ONE

Teresa must have opened and shut her eyes a thousand times by now. It had been a long while since she'd last been hung over, maybe a good decade ago, but this made up for it and then some. A tenuous anvil seemed to press on top of her skull and if it slid off, she would vomit. Pins and needles raced from her calves to her lower back—she twisted to relieve them and get her blood moving, although the black rubber restraints held fast to a high-backed chair.

To her left, Patty was tied in a similar fashion to another chair. She had a cut over her right eyebrow, but, snoring softly, she appeared otherwise unhurt. Through the drug-induced fog Teresa squinted to make out their surroundings. They were still in the city, outdoors between two crumbling buildings. Green and gold lichens dappled the pieces of concrete rubble. On top of a broken pillar a video camera perched atop a small tripod. A red light blinked over its shadowy lens.

The notion that she couldn't summon a mantle was not new to Teresa. As she had struggled the last hour to come fully awake, the cold spot in her mind had become stickier with every attempt to draw from it. Her connection to the Old Domain, that odd corridor in her mind, had been sealed shut. Grogginess from the tranquilizer would not have severed her from the ability—no, this wasn't the drugs in her system.

"We're in that Void," said a ragged voice.

She turned to face her young companion. From under wild blonde hair, Patty stared at her with bloodshot eyes. Teresa remembered and nodded. Th *incapacitation void* from the Messenger's map. Yes, she'd forgotten about that. It was normally a good thing when they entered a void. Most of these thin areas between both worlds affected creatures from the Old Domain and the Nomads highly benefited from using them on Halloween. Cloth's Children could not survive in most Voids. Th one here though…it prevented the manifestation of mantles. In forty years of wandering the world, Teresa had never heard of such a thing.

How had the OAP found this place? They had to have connections to the Church. But that didn't make sense.

What did?

More soft snores came from her partner and Teresa found her own eyes stinging from being open so long under all the heaviness forcing them down.

Not much later, Teresa fell back asleep.

Byron locked his rental car. He had decided to fold the Messenger's map and letter together and put them in his jacket pocket. The paint and other parchments would not be relevant to anybody but the Nomads. Still though, he didn't want to lose anything that might help him later. He suspected all these items would be free of fingerprints and DNA, just like the letter Patty gave him, but it was worth pursuing if things didn't pan out.

Amongst the rubble, he found his partner Denis chewing furiously on a wad of tobacco too large for his mouth. A couple of floodlights shined through his uncombed red hair, while the features of his face were immersed in shadow, making him look clownish and desperate.

Byron approached him carefully, sensing something was up. *Please don't tell me they got away. Tell me anything but that!*

"How's it going? Are they awake?"

Denis sat on a ribcage of protruding construction rebar. "Yeah, about ten minutes ago."

"Great, let's get them talking." Byron started past him. Suddenly Phil Jeffrey rounded a pile of rubble that cascaded from an unfathomable wound in the side of the abandoned office building. Byron tried to keep his jaw from dropping. "Why's the Director of Operations here?"

"Fabulous question," Denis muttered.

"Agent Telamon, I wondered when you would show." Jeffrey's smile and white hair floated in the darkness until he came into the muted gray floodlight.

"Thought you were transferred, Phil."

Jeffrey smirked. "You know, I'm getting that a lot lately."

"So what brings you to the United Kingdom?"

"Wow, that's funny...I was going to ask you the same."

"I got firsties."

Jeffrey glanced at Denis. "We need a private powwow. Do you mind?"

Shaking his head, Denis stood, knees popping, face wincing. He clamored over some unseen rubble hidden by the night. Byron heard him irritably spit more tobacco juice once he was out of sight.

"Touchy," observed Jeffrey.

"The touchiest," Byron replied and then straightened. "So how the hell did you find me and my men?"

Jeffrey folded his rain-flecked arms. "I recall these men belonging to Uncle Samuel America."

"God, you're still a damn riot. You know as well as I that our office went off the grid quite a while ago. If you don't remember that far back, most agencies haven't even heard of us, much less coordinate with our efforts, so that makes me wonder who tipped you off."

"Ah, well, it turns out your informant can be paid twice for the same information. The free market does extend through Church and State, it would seem."

Fucking Harry, thought Byron, *keeping his face flat of emotion.* I should have kicked his ass right there in front of the Chase bank.

Jeffrey rubbed at his eyes. "Now, let's dispense with the prattle and get to why I'm here."

"Lovely, let's."

"I want the photograph."

"Relax. Your mom talked me into it."

"Shut up with the jokes. You know which photo I'm talking about."

"What makes you think I would have that?"

"Oh let me see. For one, you accessed the vault a day before it went missing."

Byron had slipped the photo of Cloth in between the pages of a book at the hotel on the way back from the Messenger's house. It hadn't been a calculated thing to do at the time but now he was thankful for old paranoid habits.

"Where is it, Telamon?"

Byron tisked. "Oh that photo. I ripped it up and sprinkled pieces all over Newport Beach. Good riddance. Made everybody sick, you know."

"That's hilarious." Byron laughed.

Jeffrey got closer to him. His breath was hot and spearminted. "Fine then, I can play this too. If you didn't take it, this is the time to really prove yourself."

Jeffrey took out his revolver and wiggled it in front of him. Byron lifted an eyebrow. "You think that scares me, old man?"

Unease crept over the older man's features.

"Blow my brains out," Byron prompted with a grin. "Make the world a dumber place."

"Why should I waste a bullet on you?" Byron's smile faded.

Jeffrey pulled back the hammer on his revolver. "After the airport, it's pretty easy to deduce the Nomads are a walking threat to humanity. Better to take them out while we have them in this serendipitous prison, wouldn't you say?"

"I don't have your photo for chrissakes."

"And I don't believe you."

"We need them. This *world* needs them. I won't let you lay a finger on those women."

"Me? Oh I didn't get that far," said Jeffrey. *"You're* going to off them."

"Dream on."

Something cold flooded into Jeffrey's eyes. "That photo was mine since I was a kid. That photo meant we had an agency. That photo was a piece of my life. Whatever you did with it— you owe me. Blood, or the photo. I'm reasonable enough to accept one or the other and move on with my life. Make a choice."

Yeah right. Patty and Teresa won't leave here alive either way.

Gravely, Byron stared down the hill into the wreckage.

"Need this?" Jeff ey off ed his revolver. "So you know: I have men of my own here too, if you decide to go cowboy on us."

Byron brushed past him. "I have my own piece, jackass." Phil chuckled as Byron headed down the hill.

Whatever dope the agents subjected them to had almost run its course. Patty felt somewhat euphoric now, rather than the crushing hangover feeling of first waking up. It was like being drunk in reverse. Her failure to resolve her feelings made her much worse off in battling the wooziness.

It didn't make sense. There wasn't a good reason why Byron had done this to them. If he worked for the Church he had plenty of opportunities last year to set them up, and the year before for that matter. Had he spent all this time just to build their trust? She'd looked him in the eyes and saw no deceit there. After dealing with the Church's double-dealing spies and informants over the years, she could spot a liar. Byron didn't strike her as one.

Or maybe he was the greatest liar of all time…

It was scary how much she'd let her guard down. Teresa had been right to not trust him. Patty still fought against that reality, until she spotted Byron sliding down a steep pile of gravel, gun in his hand and a lifeless expression on his face. Patty had never expected to see anything but a glint in his eyes and a well meaning smile there.

"I'm sorry for this," she told Teresa.

Teresa wasn't listening. She watched Byron with hawkish eyes. Two other men came down the hill, an older man in excellent physical shape with snow white hair and a cruel set of ingot eyes, and behind him Byron's out of sorts partner, Denis, who fiercely chewed a mouthful of something like it was going out of style.

"Can you explain this directive again, sir," asked Denis. "I'm not understanding this situation."

The white haired man stood before the Nomads, appraising Patty and Teresa with an iciness that brought Patty's hair on end. "You don't have to understand, agent. This is from above."

"Above?" Denis let out a dubious laugh, "An executive order?"

The man glared over his shoulder. "If you want to puss out, Boyle, you can go over and weep in the car. There are still plenty of DHS field jobs across the border, lots of trips down south where decapitations have become en vogue. I thought you wanted to keep your position with us? Christ almighty, you young people depress me. This directive amounts to keeping our country safe. The other men get it, so get a fucking hold of yourself, agent."

Denis fixed a tragic look on Patty and then on Teresa and shook his head. "We aren't the CIA for crying out loud. We just brought them here for interrogation."

The man raised a frosty eyebrow. "And have they answered anything? No, you agents have got a time-bomb running around here, and you're treating her to all the freedom she can stand."

Byron waited in the shadows, gun resting on his hip.

The man leaned over Patty. It wasn't a gesture saved for her; she got the feeling he got within an inch of everybody he spoke to. Bullshit intimidation. He locked eyes with her. For his age and ugly demeanor, he was actually quite handsome.

"Don't blame me," he whispered, "this is Byron's idea. He can call it off anytime."

Byron took a ragged breath and coughed miserably into his fist.

Phil glanced back with some amusement. "Nothing to say, ah?" His eyes found Patty again. "The smartasses never do once they're soakin' their drawers. Fear's twisting his gonads right about now girl, because...yes, I get it. Byron likes you a whole lot. And why wouldn't he? Too bad a man's got to do what a man's gotta do."

Patty really wished she could bring just one mantle, a small one, the size of a pebble—she'd rattle it through his body until he bled to death on the inside.

"Oh, you're pretty mad at me, aren't you? But shouldn't it be him?" Phil nodded at Byron. "He's a thief and liar. Nobody likes that. Nope. It's a damn shame you're stuck here without that little magic trick of yours, Ms. Middleton. If you could kill us, who would you start with? Him or me?" The man chuckled joyously and slapped his legs, swinging his head to both of them now. "Yep, without your mojo you're just a dumb little girlie with her washed up Grammy."

Patty took advantage of the man's wide stance and kicked his legs out from under him. He dropped to his hands and knees, and as he scrambled to stand, Teresa brought her forehead down into his eye. The man cried out and went backward on his elbow. Dizzily, he fought to get back up and hadn't made much progress before Teresa slammed her head down again into the same eye. He went prostrate before agents materialized from the shadows to drag him out of harm's way.

Byron continued to stare at the scene without expression.

Denis stifled a laugh. "Are you okay, Director Jeffrey?"

Holding his eye, Jeffrey got in front of Byron, chest to chest, and shouted, "You still have a choice, asshole. But time's about to run out."

"I told you the photo is in the ocean," Byron replied.

Gaining sudden animation, as though awakening from a trance, Byron walked around Jeffrey and spoke to the agents. "We'll need the women in that building over there, not out in the open like this. Don't untie them though. Carry them on the chairs. And one of you bring me a silencer."

Jeffrey and Denis watched the agents quickly leave, looking a little taken aback by Byron's order. Neither had thought he would go through with it. There must have been a good reason why Byron was doing this, but Patty supposed she would never know.

She wasn't scared. And she knew Teresa wasn't either. They'd faced worse kinds of death. If this was the end, it was certainly not the terrifying sort Chaplain Cloth might have imparted on them. In a way, there was a sad relief, as two agents hefted Patty up into the air on her chair. The world, still blurry from the tranquilizer, grew quieter, bricked in cotton and mortared in dull heartbeats. At her side Teresa bounced in her own chair as they carried them up the noisy rock hill into the interior of an abandoned building.

"Check that their bindings are tight," Byron reminded the men.

The agents tugged on their cords. Patty tried not to react to the sting. Jeffrey came into the half-destroyed room with a cold pack held to his eye. Teresa smirked. Despite the situation, she apparently couldn't help herself.

Once they were made to sit down, Byron stood before them, gun in both hands, rested against his right leg. "This isn't personal. I'm so sorry, you two...We've been friends and I don't believe you are the real enemy. But there is a problem I can't ignore any longer. Maybe I ignored it for this long because of my own selfish reasons but that has to be put right now." He swallowed slowly and gave them a deathly serious look. "You are dangerous. Maybe even more dangerous than the Church—volatile, I guess would be the word."

"Only me," Patty told him. "There's no reason Teresa needs to be here."

"Hush," Teresa said.

Byron shook his head. "How do we know Teresa won't become just like you? How do we know she won't be walking down the street one day and bring down a skyscraper? Whether you mean to, or not."

Jeffrey looked on, pleased. Denis turned away and bit at his lip. The other agents gathered around, a silent mob standing by for the execution. Byron brought the hammer back on his semi-automatic.

"Again I'm sorry," he said, voice breaking, "really...truly, for what has happened. Outside of this Void, we have no control of you. With the Church gone, you are the only threat that exists."

"You know that isn't true."

"We have to take this chance. You gals are too powerful. Out there, outside the Void. Only a few steps away and you are a pair of goddesses..." Byron turned his back to his colleagues. "We have to take the advantage here, because we're within the boundaries of the Void. You understand? You'd do the same, right? Take the advantage I mean."

"Stop stalling, Telamon," barked Jeffrey. He took the ice pack away and his swollen eyelid half-blinked. He grimaced at its movement.

Byron focused on the Nomads and raised his eyebrows

higher. "So yes, time for you to die."

Jeffrey let out a gasp. At once his body hitched back and flew up into the air. Agents tried to respond and were suddenly grasped by invisible fists. Three handguns fired and the white-red flashes lit the darkened space. Byron's partner Denis turned sideways before he was ripped into the air, crying, "Awwwww shhhhiiiiit!"

Denis, Jeffrey and the rest of the agents jammed against the concrete ceiling, stuck like human magnets. Some squealed girlishly, others squirmed to no avail, and a few calmly checked the ceiling for something unseen that might free them.

Byron lunged after Teresa, but his body flew sideways through a ragged hole in the wall. He tumbled to the ground outside in a clattering of pebbles and stone.

With two quick scissor mantles, their bindings snapped off. They were free.

"What hap—"

"Come on." Teresa grabbed Patty's shoulder and pulled her out the hole in the wall.

Outside, Byron dusted off his slacks. He looked up. "Ladies," he whispered.

"You did that back there?" Patty asked Teresa. "How?"

Teresa walked, putting distance between them and the building. Patty and Byron slowly crept after her.

"Teresa?" Patty implored.

Her partner stopped and turned. "He moved us just outside the Void's boundaries. Didn't you feel when we crossed over?"

Patty gasped. No, she hadn't felt it, and she hadn't even tried to bring a mantle in there. She'd given up after so many attempts before.

"She can take a hint, Patty." Byron rubbed his elbow ruefully. "Thought I was gonna have to write it across a banner or something."

It was too much to control. Patty struck out with a mantle. Fifteen feet away, Byron dropped on the ground and twisted onto his side. Strangely, he didn't call out in surprise or pain. He had the odd posture of an abused rag-doll. He attempted to rise but Patty pressed down on him with another mantle. Teresa watched with concern, yet made no move to stop her.

Byron took a quick breath through his teeth. "Can I explain before you squash me...there...uh...Pat..."

"I should have never trusted you."

"I knew about the trap, but...didn't...think...they'd... actually—catch you."

"Sure." Patty eased up a bit to let him talk.

Byron forced his face toward her as much as the mantle would allow. "I found a letter...from the Messenger."

"Bullshit," said Teresa.

Pressure built from somewhere inside the mantle. Patty eased up even more.

Byron looked closer to passing out. "I have a letter and a map, right here in my coat. See for yourself."

Teresa slid a mantle of her own through his coat and used it to mirror an image into her mind. "Something's there. Take a look."

Stooping over, Teresa opened his jacket and took two pages out. She unfolded them and examined their inscriptions for a moment and then sighed in disgust. "Shit, we better bring him."

Patty let go of the mantle. Byron gritted his teeth and cringed, looking to be in more pain out of the invisible restraint. Patty leaned over him, ready to tear his head from its shoulders. "Where did you find this?"

"Let me know where the gateway is first."

"You don't *get* to bargain!"

"Shut up, both of you," Teresa said. "Byron, take us to your hotel."

"Why?" asked Patty.

Byron looked at Teresa. "Yeah, why?"

"If he's holding back letters from the Messenger, what else does he have? We should search his place and keep him for questioning until we're satisfied."

Patty gave him a sidelong glance. "I guess that's a good point."

"Yeah, I hadn't thought of that either," Byron replied. "Let's hurry. I don't want to hold that mantle all night, and I'm sure his friends would rather be earthbound again."

"You can leave Jeffrey up there."

"They wanted us dead. Why not kill them?" Patty looked back to the building and then to Teresa. For a change the question wasn't to bait her partner, even though it might have come off that way.

Byron sputtered. "Really, Pat?"

Teresa took off, doing her fast-walk, which could outpace some runners. Once she was far enough away, Patty shoved Byron with a flash mantle to his back. He stumbled forward, tittering. "I get it," he said, "you're cross with me."

"I should deprive you of your head."

"Easy now. Losing out on head is a pretty harsh punishment."

Another mantle clipped his cranium and Byron pitched forward onto the ground. Patty watched his head snap back as his face struck a dirt clod. He grunted, pushed up on one arm, then collapsed. Something metallic dropped out of his pocket then and struck the gravel.

Patty waited there, somewhat happy and ashamed simultaneously. Calls from the men stuck on the ceiling could be heard in the immediate distance. Was Byron Telamon any different? Maybe he should be up there with them.

She knelt. Byron must have blacked out because he lay still, softly breathing. Patty swept up the metal object and brushed some dirt from it. A map of the Scottish countryside showed a small town named Boghead. A beacon pulsed there. At the bottom of the screen a question asked, *Route a trip?*

"What's going on back there?" Teresa called. Her indistinct form started back after them.

Patty stuffed the GPS device in her pocket and pulled Byron to his feet. He groggily searched around.

Patty shouted back, "Bastard tripped."

Byron shook his head. "Nice. You really have no sense of humor, Pat."

She nudged him forward. He obediently walked on. When he patted his pocket and found something missing there, he glanced over. Teresa was upon them now, breathless and approaching the end of her wick. "Come on, you klutz."

Byron frantically rummaged through his coat. Patty

imagined him a crooked gambler searching for that hidden ace that had fallen out somewhere on the way to the casino.

"Lose your shit?" She smiled.

His face dropped. "Yeah, yeah I guess I did." Patty looked at Teresa. "We need to talk."

"Can it wait?"

"I think we have a way to track the Messenger."

"No we don't."

"But Teresa—"

"Patty, goddamn it, this is no time for your side projects. This has got to end now before we get wrapped up in something and botch another Halloween. We ended up here because of your unattainable goal and I'm never letting that happen again. I'm putting my foot down."

"Oh, not the foot."

Teresa huffed, her eyes wide with annoyance. "I swear to God, I'm never going to let you go to an internet café again."

"It isn't about that! Will you just listen please?"

"Stop it, okay? Just stop. This is not why we're taking Byron with us and you know it."

"Look, let me just talk for one friggin' moment."

"No, I don't think I will." Teresa gestured them on.

Patty let out an irate sigh and pushed Byron forward. They walked into the night, in silence.

Cloth had felt the Cats of Delkilth thin out over the entire universe—but how? Those imbeciles from the Church of Midnight fled and the Cats hadn't been displaced at the time... They wouldn't have been able to get rid of the Cats completely anyway.

But who had managed the feat? In Cloth's mind he'd seen nobody else approach the cottage. He hadn't sensed the movements of the Interloper either, but someone certainly had exorcised the Cats.

Someone of great power.

Who?

This was interesting. Since Cloth had been abandoned by his humans, new moves had to be played. Mindful of disastrous outings from the gateway he'd taken in the past, he would still go to the cottage. Killing the Nomads would have to wait, unfortunately. The Interloper wasn't far. He couldn't miss out on whatever that meant. Above all, in his weakened state, Cloth would more than likely ruin his physical form, but he had a back-up body right here in the gateway.

"Tomorrow you're gonna hold the fort," he told Duncun.

The man went into another fit of begging and pleading for death. "Tomorrow? Just end this now...I cannae stand this... any longer...I beg ye, let me die."

"You think I enjoy your company? I need your body to keep residence, Mr. Selfish."

"Whit does that mean?" Duncun stammered. One of his eyeballs ruptured from a clotted vessel and pinkish fluid ran from the socket down the slope of a nearby pumpkin vine. He didn't even notice this amid the rest of his distress. "My body's no good now. Let me die! *Please!*"

"Your body is perfect." Cloth grinned. He reclined in his Duncun-chair and the man screeched at the succession of vertebrae separating. Chucking, *glurping* sounds came as Duncun gasped to fill the lungs that sagged out of his ribcage like popped balloons.

The Chaplain tuned out his miseries. And rested for tomorrow.

OCTOBER 30TH

TWENTY-TWO

Bre found Kennen in the dark cylindrical council chamber in the palace where the inter-world meetings took place. No Bishops from other lands had made a connection. Or if they had, they'd long abandoned it after Kennen fainted from exhaustion and pain. The man had hooked up his body to the machines but lay on the floor in a heap of cables. Sentinels had been directed to other duties, so there wasn't anyone to check in on him. This was how disconnected things had become lately with all of their attention focused on Pel'Hahr.

Bre painstakingly detached the cables and hauled the Archbishop out of there, clear through the palace and down the dirt road leading to that special space near the city wall where his mother's cottage sat. The trip was close to twenty trollguts but he never paused.

The Heralding had thoroughly ravaged Kennen's body with its poison. His eyes frequently rolled back into his head and he went in and out of consciousness. Bre gagged at the smell of his body, pumpkin guts and earth.

"There was no answer, Phrey..." he muttered. Some of the staples running along the left side of his face had snapped and fresh blood oozed out. "The Church of Midnight is gone. Dead. All of them. I feel...it's all up to us now. The Nomads are coming for us. Patty Middleton...should have watched her better."

"Master, they are the burden of the Church of Midnight, not ours."

"No," he rasped. "If they find a way into this world...we're doomed."

Bre returned Kennen to his cot near his mother's bedside,

but did not tidy up his facial wounds, as he normally would have. Before the man passed out again he demanded Bre iron another week's worth of robes and undergarments, extra starch on the runic hems. Two weeks' worth of robes had already been ironed, folded in neat squares and set atop Pel'Hahr's bureau, and it was more than the Archbishop ever had at the ready, but this chore was his attempt to keep the slave focused on work.

Bre wasn't focused though. In fact, he burned his palm three times on the flat iron. The events of the Heralding wouldn't unfix themselves from his head. Although he was caught in the flow of his old life, he was a different person now. The small flame of decency he'd coveted as his own, for as long as he could remember, had been extinguished. It wasn't coming back. In its place a hole bored deep inside him and just when he thought it could go no deeper, it went on. The faces of those two young brothers stared at him from the pumpkin patch of his subconscious. They smiled. Their necks smiled. The blood laughingly spilled out of them forever. In his memory, it had been him and his brother Kauph. He'd slain them both, when he should have saved them both.

Things would never be the same.

So this was the perfect time to take advantage of the change. After the ritual Kennen could only stay awake for moments at a time, and with feasts, festivals, the sentinels gathering for strategic talks of fortifying Church-held lands, the palace seemed in perpetual motion in preparation for the Day of Opening. Nobody was looking in his direction and this was exactly what he needed.

That morning, after Bre had spoon-fed the dying witch her stew, he went to the supply wagon and packed it with everything he could think of taking: dried pepper pork and eight large jugs of water, all the clothes he owned and some of Kennen's, his favorite volumes from the Tomes of Eternal Harvest, and other important miscellanea. He covered his stockpile of crates with one of Pel'Hahr's patchwork quilts that had the least staining. Bre imagined he'd forgotten something. After all, he'd lived on palace grounds essentially his entire life and had no idea about the needs and wants of normal life. It would have to do.

He walked the Clydesdales back to the stables and collected Danur and Cortis. The horses seemed to sense something great awaiting them in the future, for they almost pranced back to the cottage with him. He wished for the same thrill of impending liberation, but in truth, he was terrified. No other option afforded itself though; this last part had to have follow-through. He always knew that if he made an escape, his largest tie to the palace had to be cleanly severed.

That part of the plan seemed easiest when he considered how Kennen laughed while he cut those men's throat, as well as all those punishments he doled out time and time again, but then when Bre thought about the man he'd spent nearly his entire life with, his only guidepost amongst all these miserable years, it broke his heart in a million pieces to think about ending his life.

Bre's arms shook as he finished the last orange robe and stripped it from the stone board, moved it to find more creases. There were few. This one's silk had a blood-honey color and the shine of the material unsettled him.

When he finished the ceremony of completing his very last chore as Kennen's slave, he had two things left. Break open the Archbishop's head with this flat iron and then board the wagon and flee. Simple actions with difficult consequences. Or was it the other way around?

There were no wrinkles in the robe for some time now, but he persisted until the stone had to be reheated. He went to the cauldron and stopped. No, *this is finished. I'm done here. I've completed the last thing he'll ever ask me to do.*

Bre stood motionless and gripped tight the sweat-soaked linen wrapped handle of the flat iron. His feet moved him forward, first a shuffle and then a few steps. Over the coals, the cauldron hissed with venomous anticipation. The universe seemed to know what he intended.

Suddenly Kennen put his withered hand up and shaded his eyes from the sunlight. He had propped himself up on both arms. He absently draped his loincloth back over half of his revealed buttocks, the only part of his body that seemed unscarred by past sacrifice.

Pel'Hahr groaned from her bed. She'd been doing that throughout last night and into the morning. Kennen drowsily nodded in her direction, to himself. He knew she needed him now more than ever, but it wouldn't happen this time.

"My mother is in need of assistance and I cannot stay awake..." He broke into a long, spraying yawn that ended with a thrashing of his head. "...Long enough to give that to her." His eyes rolled around a bit; a dizzy spell had suddenly taken him. "Mind her, Slave! Don't let me sleep past the Opening, Slave. Don't...you dare. Nomads...coming. Middleton...too dangerous."

A light snort rolled up from Kennen's throat and through his nose. He shifted on his side and under the pasty flesh his mole-speckled ribs flexed with his slow breathing.

Bre hovered over his master's cot. Kennen's back was turned. This was almost wonderfully lucky. Bre stared at the coarse hair at the back of Kennen's skull and the bald pockets that cropped up here and there, the cowlick that swirled in a galaxy of dying roots. He knew what it felt like now to kill. He'd done it to two people who were aware. This was so much easier. One well-placed strike and all the pathetic memories of this creature would die on this cot along with the body that housed them.

Bre's blood felt colder with the moment, the iron heavier in his hand, and his heart beating that cold blood faster, a machine powered with ice water and murderous thoughts. What would come of this crime? Would the sentinels catch him? Could they propagate anything more vicious or horrible on the lowly slave's body that had not already been done?

He lifted the iron and a prayer went through his mind. Strange...but it was a prayer of emotions, not of words. He took a deep breath and stepped forward.

"Vasoth, my son!"

Bre's frantic reaction made no sense to him, as though another person swiftly acted in his place. He watched this other person whip around and unconsciously fling the flat iron with supernatural might at the direction of the voice. The iron wobbled in its flight, but struck the now-standing witch. She was right there! On her feet, naked young-old breasts heaving with more life than Bre had seen in a long time. But it was only momentary. The point of the flat iron met with Pel'Hahr's left eye with such a force it snapped her head backward and sent her toppling behind the bureau.

Kennen rolled about and muttered, trying to will himself awake. Bre watched in absolute horror as his eyes opened and stared at him.

Then they shut again and he began snoring.

Bre rushed to the side of the bureau. Under a fallen heap of freshly ironed orange robes, Pel'Hahr's shapely female form lay in a crumpled horseshoe position. The iron had pushed her eyeball into her brain and the impact of the ground had farther shattered the left side of her head. Blood gushed from her nose and mouth. Bre reached down and put a hand over her chest. She wasn't taking much air into her lungs. He pressed harder on her chest and touched her wrist. The faint heartbeat faded and a foul odor hit him as her bowels slowly emptied.

Bre backed out of the room. His heart boomed in his ears. A volcano seemed to tremble eagerly in his stomach. He cracked open the door to check the outside. No sentinels lingered. At least none he could see. Suddenly wooziness claimed him. He'd forgotten to breathe. He woke from a blackout as his back struck the wall. The troll husk cottage shuddered.

Kennen rattled around on his cot and strangled his pillow in his jaundice-knuckled hands. It was impossible now. He had to go. This...couldn't be happening.

Bre slipped outside, into the gray sunshine. Phantom tears stung his eyes. This was the end. Was it the end? Pel'Hahr was dead. Pel'Hahr was *dead*? Terror and joy became one. He could leave now. This was really finished. Not finished—destroyed.

Reality was deformed. Time to leave. Time to run from this and everything else.

First things first. The bleeding trees...

It took no time to climb up the first tier of branches, for he'd done so most of his life when imagining playing with his brother Kauph. It was second nature to Bre. He'd set up the tinder in between the branches earlier that morning and it still looked well-packed, but he wasn't certain if the lantern oil he applied would be enough fuel to get a good fire going. Nevertheless, he had to try and get something to distract the sentinels from the main gate.

"What are you doing?"

Bre froze. His eyes slowly moved down.

Sci, the mortician stood below. Black rings orbited his eyes and his beard looked oily, unwashed.

With a dry swallow, Bre nodded a greeting. "Is your wife okay? Are the babies—?"

"Yes, they are fine, thanks to you." Sci looked down at his worn boots and his skin flushed. Saying thanks must have been hard for the man. He almost looked angry, as though disappointment in himself climbed unheeded to the surface. "I should have been there during the Heralding."

"I'm glad you weren't. Many died."

"Are you leaving with the Day of Opening upon us?" Sci asked, eyes wide. "I see the wagon packed."

"The sentinels will come. It will buy me time. Trying at least, not having much luck with this tinder."

"Oh," said Sci, suddenly realizing, "you aren't just leaving for supplies. You're *really* leaving."

"Yes."

"In that case," the mortician said starting to climb the tree, "let me start this for you. I craft all the bonfires in my village. I'll get this good and roasting, send all the sentinels from their hiding spots."

"Really?

"Yes, but keep a lookout, or it's my hide too."

"I appreciate that, really."

"No time for that shit." Sci climbed past him as Bre made the descent back to the ground. "You aren't thinking of going out the main gate are you?"

"Supply gate."

Sci tisked. "That's still taking a chance from the posts at the shorter turrets. I know another route. I'll show you, if you want."

"If it's better."

Bre got into the wagon set. The horses shifted nervously. Smoke already plumed out around the man. Leaves and small twigs crackled in the branches above.

"Luck?"

"It's taking." Sci quickly shimmied back down the tree and bounded up into the wagon. He took the reins from Bre. "It's just south of the gate, along the Hendri boundaries. You know where I mean?"

Of course Bre didn't know. His routes were limited in the palace grounds. He handed the reins over to Sci. With a snap, the horses took off at a fast gallop.

Bre couldn't believe this was happening. He'd always imagined living here until he died, or Kennen died. Yet, here he was, leaving, and the Archbishop was every bit still alive, though his quest to save his mother had come to an end.

This was surreal. Bre looked back at the trees with some trepidation. Smoke thinned to wisps at the top and no flames rose.

"I don't think it's catching! Damn it. We have to go back." He turned around and blinked at the new scene before him, unable to believe where the wagon headed. "Sci, you're leading us right for the main gate!"

Sci's face was stone. He raised his voice above the pounding hooves. "You think I should thank you when it was the sentinels who saved my wife? You slit my nephews' throats. Is thanks what you expect from me, slave? Mardra saw the whole thing. I hope the sentinels cleave your balls in twine."

The main gate was before them, a looming brutal collision of darkwood banded in orange ropes, the spikes at the top webbed together with Ekkian carpentry.

Bre spotted four hulking sentinels. It didn't appear that Gogg was one of them...until the wagon got closer and he recognized the man's infamous scowl. Sci started reining in the horses, slowing the pace. There was nowhere to go. Even in armor, these men would catch him now.

Gogg crossed his armored arms and sniffed. A pocked face sentinel leaned into his ear. Gogg nodded and smiled, listening to the man's snide diatribe. Pock Face shrugged and shook his head when Gogg asked a question. The wagon drew near and Bre halted the horses.

"Stand by," Gogg told Pock face. He came around to the wagon's side, almost beaming. "I didn't expect to see you out and about so close to the Day of Opening."

Sci jumped from the wagon, almost slipping. "This slave was going to escape! He planned to rob the Archbishop."

"Ah! That's the finest tale I ever heard. Come on down from there, you wet little clit."

"Shall we drink mead and knife this one's asshole?" sang Pock Face.

Gogg, beaming with delight, gestured to Bre with his head. "Let's see what you were planning to take." He narrowed his eyes and shifted his weight on one foot to look at the back of the wagon. "An awful lot in the rear there—I think we should take a gander."

One of the other sentinels snorted and Gogg glanced icily at him. "All of you, back of the wagon. Open this thing, slave." Bre glanced at the peaceful dirt road slithering down the hill beyond the main gate. How he would like to be on that road right now. He wouldn't let tears come to his eyes. He had no fear left in him. Why fear something when one is already dead?

He dropped out of the wagon and the bracing impact of his sandals on the ground sent his teeth lathing off each other. It fed his anger, but he would not show these louts any of that.

Everybody went around back. Bre pushed the bolt over and let the wagon door drop. In the front he packed three crates of bitter cordroot for kindling, two of the sand apples that grew on a bush behind the cottage, a few bundles of firewood, all Pel'Hahr's pots and pans and kettle, and several stacks of pepper pork.

"Looks like a camping trip to me," Pock Face commented. "In-fucking-deedy it does," replied Gogg, face absolutely brimming with mirth.

"You can see the fire he tried to set back there by the cottage. There's still smoke," said Sci, looking back, eyes tired and wild.

"You're dismissed to the mortuary," said Gogg. "Move along villager."

Sci's face darkened. "I want to see what you do to him."

Gogg pushed Sci aside and rifled through a few things in the back of the wagon. He pointed a sharp finger at the Impish Detention box, which rested away from the other items. Bre had heard that baelins made the best deterrent in the forest for predators. The smell of one would even drive insects away.

"That's an expensive piece of equipment, looks like. Where did you plan on selling it?" Gogg smacked the top of the box and a flurry of tiny claws came from within. Gogg blinked in bewilderment. "And what in the salty fuck do you have in there?"

"They sounds like the butter-ear rabbits," a stunted sentinel said, licking his greasy lips. "Look there. Slave took and reined some bred horses. They ain't no supply mounts. That's from our prize stable. If he's takin' those, he may be takin' from the sacred larder."

"Like hell that was rabbits," his companion disagreed.

Obviously less skeptical, Pock Face took his sword's hilt in hand. "That's blasphemous to take blessed beasts outside the palace."

"What are they, shitbrain?" Gogg leaned closer. Before Bre could say anything, he said, "I suppose we should just go and wake up the Archbishop and tell him something wonderful and new about you, in a way that only I could tell it. Or we can see this now?"

Bre took a step back and gestured. "Mind the bottles looped on the sides, they are fragile."

"I'm not opening the damned thing, you sorry little shit." Gogg snatched Bre by the shoulder.

"I'm not opening it."

"That's funny," Gogg shoved him face-first into the detention box, "because I think *you are* going to open it."

"Bash in his skull," said Sci with a tremor in his voice. "You shut that throat of yours, or I'll plug it with my Ekkian cock!" Gogg shoved Bre again. "Last time I ask you, slave. Open it!"

Sighing in defeat, Bre reached out with numb fingers and took one of the brass claps. He unsnapped the left and then the center and then the right.

"You're doing an excellent job," Pock Face observed. Gogg snorted.

Bre's mind had given up on this. Whatever happened, happened. It was out of his control now. So he didn't hesitate. He took the side of the lid and pushed up. The other sentinels closed in and peered over the side.

Pock Face squinted into the dark opening. "What's this bullshit?"

Gogg had a look. He glared back at Bre. "Explain this."

Bre cautiously glanced over the side. There wasn't anything visible inside except the cold riveted steel bottom of the detention box. Bre grabbed onto the lip with one hand, stood on his toes and took a harder look.

"No rabbits," said the stunted sentinel, who was quickly clouted on the back of the helmet by his companion. "Ow."

Gogg flicked Bre's earlobe with a gauntleted finger. "Stop being a jackass. There's nothing in there to see. Where'd the sounds come from?"

Gogg looked very near to punching him in the face. His fist went back. Pock Face intercepted his arm though and guided Gogg over with the other two sentinels. Their voices were lowered, but not so much Bre couldn't hear snatches of conversation. *"He's running."*

"You...the one to answer?"

"Better then to

...Archbishop up and ask."

"I'd stake my saber on it."

Sci stared daggers into him. "I hope they stomp your guts, boy."

Frozen there, still gripping the side of the detention box, Bre almost ignored the feeling at first. A slick baelin tongue traced a line down the side of one of his fingers and started sucking the end. The sentinels grouped together. Bre took a wide step to the right. Gogg swiveled his head at the movement and his mouth opened to say something, but it was too late. Bre pulled down the box on its side and the contents spilled out. Sensing danger, Sci scrambled up into the wagon.

The baelins worked so quickly Bre hadn't returned to the

horses when he heard pieces of armor clacking on the ground, the leather ties swiftly bitten through. Men fell fast and miserably. Gogg, thrashing and shrieking, was the last to go. He dropped to his bare knees and his hands. His small-clothes tore away and blood sprayed copiously from his ass. His terrified eyes swelled—his mouth opened wide for an invisible phallus and a horrible gurgle followed as he collapsed.

Bre sped to the wagon seat. A force from behind sent him hard to the ground. He twisted around and saw the belly of a Tick Goblin lowering toward his face. He screamed and caught Sci's wrist. The man must have discovered the goblin in the supplies.

"You aren't getting away, killer."

"Archbishop...made me."

Sci's eyes lit. "That's no better! Die, you! Die!"

Bre lunged and bit one of the hanging organs from the goblin's underbelly. A proboscis swung out to strike. Sci veered back in surprise and dropped the creature. As it fell the proboscis flung back and sunk into his left eye socket. Sci let out a wail that sent vibrations through every bone in Bre's body.

The man dropped heavily and his hands went to the throbbing cord connected to his eye. The goblin doubled its effort and latched onto his chest through his tunic, bright blood striping the sides.

Bre pulled up his adrenaline-shot body and climbed into the wagon seat. Once there, he took and cracked the reins hard. The horses passionately responded. He took another look, morbidly fascinated with the scene he'd created. He heard himself weeping as the wagon charged through the open gate, down the main road.

He took a deep breath. It seemed the first he'd taken in hours.

Yes, in death, things would never be the same.

TWENTY-THREE

Sunshine Meadows convalescent home bustled in the early morning. The shift had just about turned over for her, so Mallory Aguirre let the residents bicker about television channels and the mediocre English breakfast they'd served them. Most days, this remaining hour she would be at her tensest, all her patience dwindled from the pair of insomniacs in room ten and the pervert in room thirteen. Today however, she was going home to sleep and her daughter was visiting her father in London. No more hip-hop thumping on the walls, no more being woken up every twenty minutes to be asked a question that could wait for later.

Most of the residents were up and about, a surprising display for some of the sicklier. Only Brian McLeod still slept. Mallory rapped at his door, gave a sparing couple moments and then opened it, as all the nurses did. Privacy wasn't really an issue after you'd scrubbed diarrhea off of someone's leg while they masturbated and aimed for your face. Brian had severe dementia and she wouldn't be surprised if she found him dead in his bed. He wasn't dead though. Anything but. Brian sat up straight-backed, fully dressed in the sweater and slacks he wore when his son brought him there last month. Wild eyebrows extending like feathery hands, he stared out the window to a field.

"Ready for breakfast, Mr. McLeod?"

Brian gave her a sidelong glance. "I cannae eat the food here. It's that rubbery sausage again?"

"Aye it is, but I had some myself and it's—"

"Awful," he finished and then pointed to the window. "I

don't remember that house out there, do ye?"

Mallory leaned past him to see, expecting something every day. Brian was right. A cottage sat out in the field. Boghead wasn't large enough for something like that to go unnoticed during construction.

"I'll be," she muttered. "No, I haven't. Well now. Looks like we have a new neighbor."

Brian hissed and jumped unnaturally to his feet. His body struck Mallory and she staggered back, meeting the wall. "Mr. Mc—"

The old man's eyes rolled in his head and something horrible ground in his throat. His body quaked and jittered. Mallory opened her mouth to scream. Brian leapt into the air and dropped to the ground. The fall had an echo that repeated throughout the old wood floor, through the entire home.

A startled gasp caught in her throat—that was no echo. Other people had fallen.

She bent to check on Brian. Steam rolled off his graying skin and moistened the air. She put two fingers under his jaw for a pulse. Nothing.

"Daniel!" Mallory yelled and pulled herself up. She took to the hallway, accidentally tearing off the room's clipboard from the wall. Through hyperventilating wheezes, she managed to call out for the orderly again. What had she seen? An attack of some sort? What made him jump up in the air like that? And the steam?

Bodies slumped over folding chairs in the common room and others lay crumpled in the hall, all of them writhing in hot steam, as though their old bones had boiled their flesh. She shoved open the bathroom door and found the orderly, Daniel, lying next to his mop bucket. A supernova of radiant blood came from the back of his head and reached out across the tile.

Mallory fell back into the hallway to call for help.

The front door squeaked open. A man in an elegant black suit and silken orange tie walked in. His skin was the color of snow under a witching moon. His hair, the color of a night sky without stars. The eyes: one a pit of churning tar, one a radioactive inferno. Black and Orange.

She felt herself collapse and her tailbone slammed to the ground. The scene faded around her as the strange man stepped lightly toward her, his loafers padding on the wooden planks with wild grace. He knelt and she heard someone, some other woman that lived in this moment, make a plaintive sound. It wasn't her. She couldn't be the person staring at this thing. Surely she was watching this from elsewhere. Things like this don't happen. Shouldn't happen.

The man leaned back on his haunches and regarded her silently a moment, clasping his chin thoughtfully.

"Say, have you seen a cottage around here? I'm an out-of-towner."

Mallory found herself nodding.

The man's face brightened and he grabbed her by the ankle. "Show me."

She screamed as he hauled her across the floor. Her head hit the porch outside and darkness wavered around her. Then her head slammed down one more step and she blacked out. Something pulled her consciousness back though...something from *him*. She felt tired. So damned tired and weak. Like her entire body had been put through a ringer and brought back in the next moment. Brittle.

"Oh, I see it now," she heard him say, from what seemed like miles above her.

A few moments later, Mallory propped herself up. The man was already far away, heading toward the cottage. She sat there for a minute, dizzy and terrified. It was almost impossible to breathe. Her body sagged. She rubbed at her eyes. Her heart thumped weakly in her chest, an overworked contraption on the verge of failure. A stiff wind kicked up as she fought to stand. It occurred to her that she was in a place she'd never been before. She thought of her name and it sounded foreign. All the memories of her life had been encased in sticky black gauze.

There was a man in a dark suit walking in the distance. He was a stranger.

No concern of hers.

Mallory wandered off then, her destination, her life, unknown.

Chaplain Cloth approached the cottage, feeling invigorated. It wasn't wise to waste such power before the Day of Opening, but in this weakened state he needed reassurance his ability to loosen reality's hold was possible.

And if the Interloper had returned to the cottage, there would be need of such power.

Right off, Cloth noted a series of decomposed mantles in a mud puddle nearby. They were shaped like a cage of sorts—so that's where the Cats had lived. He wondered who had been able to move their home from the foundation in such a way. Thankfully, *it was done before he arrived. His temporary constitution didn't need such challenges. The retirement home was his hunger getting the best of him. It wasn't Halloween yet. He had to remember that.*

He stepped up on the porch and considered the vast field of green behind him. The white sedan he'd stolen appeared toy-like in the distance. Driving had come naturally to him, though he couldn't remember ever doing it before. On Halloween the gateway took him wherever he wanted, so such vehicles never mattered. Getting behind the wheel had been…interesting. Just like all these silly appurtenances of human life.

He pondered the cat cage again and something anxious settled in his hollow gut. A puzzling event happened here between the Cats and some other party. The Interloper's guardians pulled power directly from the marrow springs, just as he did…not enough to do anything but slow him down, and certainly not enough to even pause that terror, Patrice Middleton. But nobody else should have been able to displace the Cats.

Strange. What did the Interloper have going on here?

Unless…the thought crystallized in the ancient winter that was Cloth's brain. Was it possible one of *them* found this place? That would be really disheartening, not to mention amazing with all the pain they endured.

Cloth pushed open the unlocked cottage door. He stepped inside the small space of the Interloper's false façade. Millions on millions of mantles stacked the air in ornate spiral staircases leading up past ten mezzanines.

All was silent, but that didn't matter. The Interloper could keep quiet as death, if warranted. It had been a long time since they'd met. Hesitant, Cloth swam his tongue across his teeth. This was a bold step, doing this before Halloween, his body's bones already calcifying from wear. It would be more than worth it though, if he could pull this off.

"I'm coming to get you," Cloth told the Interloper, as he took the stairs.

TWENTY-FOUR

Once the cottage came into sight, Patty pulled off the road next to a dusty white sedan. The beacon continued to flash on the GPS unit. She got out and followed it into a wide grassy field slashed with mud runnels. The beacon intensified as she neared a small tortoise shell barrette in the grass. She took a knee and examined the beacon for a moment. Not knowing what to make of it, she slipped it in her pocket. The cottage in the distance was foremost on her mind.

What if the Messenger had returned since Byron came here? What would she say to him or her if that happened? Or better yet, what *wouldn't* she say?

As Patty made her way through the rain-soupy grass, a startling thought crossed her mind. How would the Messenger react to this discovery? After sneaking out on Teresa this morning, leaving her downtown with that backstabber Byron, it had never occurred to Patty that she might not return.

No, Teresa can take care of herself if something happens to me.

She's dealt with it before.

Something else hit Patty as she continued on. There were mantles here. Thousands—millions. She could feel them hanging in the air, building a fortress above. She smiled. This was it. Only the Messenger could build something so unbelievably immense.

She'd arrived. She'd finally arrived.

The cottage door was open a crack already, maybe how Byron last left it, or maybe from the Messenger returning? Patty's heartbeat skipped in her throat. She pushed the door with her elbow and peered inside to the stunning construction that lay within.

A glutinous stomach-acid and blood cocktail burped from Duncun's throat and painted his chin. He retched at the taste of it but had nothing else to vomit. Since the monster named Cloth had left this morning, the gateway's presence sucked at his mangled body. It reminded him of adjusting to the pressure of deep sea diving, which he had done once with his step-father on a holiday in Greece. He'd hated that fucking bastard shithead—at the time. That was then though.

Now, Duncun had a new perspective on life. Hating was for people with energy and focus. He had neither and he wasn't afraid of how the world saw him anymore. The world could take all his dignity, log the memory of his existence as an absolute disgrace and rob him of every joy life once offered, if only the anguish would go away.

Leafy vines, pumpkin vines, slithered out of the darkness of the gateway and coiled around his hands and feet. They'd been doing this for a while now. Something on the other side of this gateway had given life to the twitching earthy things in the darkness.

Unlike previous times, the movement of the vines wasn't a violent, protective gesture, just a curious probing...Duncun couldn't readily explain this new evolution, yet invisible things he'd sensed once before now had a fullness to them. Indeed, a pregnancy in the shadows had come to term and children were born. They might be seen by more splendid eyes but for now they could be felt, and at times...understood.

Bats tittered for their direction. Jackals growled their obeisance. And somewhere nearby, just at the corners of Duncun's vision, perverse people prayed for the creatures to find release. Duncun, his body a twisted throne for a twisted monster, could only remain there before the gaping maw between the worlds, and listen to the Children sing.

Pull the muscle from its kernel Bring us the Feast Eternal!
Power scorned is weakness born— It is, it is, it is.

Loam the tread, tread the loam Slit throat chorus on your tome
Passage sought, darkness wrought— It is, it is, it is.

Tear apart the ever weeping skies Suck the eyeball fruit, free its lies Pain endured, treasure absurd— It is, it is, it is.

Icy tears, larger than Duncun thought his tear ducts capable of creating, drafted out the sides of his eyes and cooled his hot face. He called for Alisyn. He wasn't mad at her anymore. He loved her. He wanted to show her how afraid he'd been. It wasn't too late. If he could survive this long, with this many sickeningly compound fractures, perhaps it wasn't his time. But he had to get out of this place before Cloth returned.

"Help," he rasped and broke down weeping. "Fer chrissakes, help me."

The pub was quiet and would remain so. People didn't pay attention to it; they walked by all day as though this was the single least important location in the universe. But while the pub was quiet, the gateway was anything but.

"Please help!" Duncun shouted, louder than he thought himself capable of now.

Then he heard a response. Far inside the tunnel, claws scraped against the obsidian space below and started to move.

Patty had never seen a construction so complex. Most ghost matter brought over from the Old Domain came out in flat panels that could be warped and reconfigured into shapes— the Messenger had woven singular strands of matter in helixes that locked sequentially to create an individual panel, and they were everywhere!

It'd seemed like overkill when Patty first began climbing the spiral staircases to each mezzanine, but as she went on, studying, deconstructing the mantles, pulling apart their links of connection and placement, she saw a form of reinforcement that achieved something rather remarkable. She'd once read a science magazine on the road about hyper-diamonds and how their nano-crystalline structure made them the hardest known structure in the world. She had used mantles to peer inside the diamond in a heart necklace her mother had given her, now long since lost on the road—but examining the diamond's structure and reading that article, she could imagine how a larger compression would be. This structure seemed to be superior to that of a hyper-diamond—

It'd take me twenty years just to remove one of these steps from the staircase, she thought in awe. The place hadn't been built out of power, *but out of patience.*

The intensity of structure overwhelmed Patty, each empty floor she arrived at. What was the purpose of this empty fortress? There was no furniture, no décor, nothing but space. The Messenger must have taken everything from this place. Always a step ahead of them. Always—

A rattling came overhead. The sound echoed and Patty's heart went still for a second. She hadn't come here to be fooled yet again. She couldn't do it anymore. She couldn't be like Teresa and continue on, wandering, wandering, wandering, wander—

Grating.

A thud reverberated against the layer of mantles above.

Patty raced up the staircase, the cold déjà vu in her mind deepening to make her whole body shiver. Deprived of youth, of freedom, of love, left in the dark, made an indentured servant, a murderer…she heard footsteps quickening above.

"Who's there?" she called. "Show yourself!"

The next floor was second to last. She stopped at the stairs and scanned the room. It looked much like the others; ghost matter only had color if you put color into it, and the Messenger had left all of it the typical hue of wet slate. Disappointed, Patty almost grabbed the railing to head up to the next floor. The far wall looked different though. Someone had cut panels away from it.

She strode across the room, her footsteps plinking on the unnatural surface. Disconnected ghost matter littered the floor in small squares and unbroken strands. She dipped down quickly to pick up a piece. The small square felt magnetized to the floor—just so damned heavy she couldn't pick it up with her fingers. That must have been the sound...these pieces falling out of the wall.

Taken from the wall. But why?

Patty regarded the hole. Why would the Messenger try to take this apart here?

Why else, but to escape her?

A breeze blew down the staircase. She turned around. It'd been fast but a mantle had dropped over the side of the mezzanine. Someone had been inside it, hiding.

"You can't hide," she shouted.

Abruptly, thousands of foreign mantles sprang up throughout the fortress. They weren't the intricate building blocks of this place though. No, more like the kind she or Cloth would summon. Taking the advantage, her mind immediately went to breaking down all of them. More sprouted up in place, but they were thinner—yes, the Messenger was weakening.

Patty went to strike out with another wave of destruction.

But then a rusted hook caught in her consciousness and tore at the tissue of her thoughts.

Thousands of mantles remained, but one had an explosion hidden inside it.

"Son of a bitch," she whispered.

She unwittingly put it there and though she felt the mantle-bomb's presence, could not discover in where it'd made its home. The Messenger must have sensed this too, because no new mantles formed.

Tears of rage formed in her eyes. Not here, *not now.*

This structure had just become a colossal house of death that she herself had made. How would she get outside without an explosion causing a reaction from the other mantles? All at once it would be like the sharpest panes of glass raining down from heaven. There would be no stopping it.

Patty sat down on the cool expanse of the shimmering floor. Tearing down the mantles had to be done in only one sequence. The correct one. She would have to figure out what that was, and carefully.

It was nearly an hour before Patty began her careful work. Taking apart the bonded ghost matter couldn't be done prudently, it just had to be done, and she recognized that for better or for worse.

She sorted through mantles hovering over the staircase. Any of them could explode—she really had no clue. They all looked the same. A sickening taste flooded her mouth as she brought a mantle of her own to serve as a blast shield.

Then she methodically deconstructed scores of mantles. Nothing happened.

It may have been her mind playing tricks, but in the absolute quiet she could have sworn she heard breathing from below.

She walked out onto the landing and down the stairs. The massive collection of other mantles had formed on the lowest level, so it would seem the Messenger reached the bottom floor before constructing them.

Quick, but not quick enough, she thought miserably.

With every new mantle she brought down, she felt a little better, but it was still a lottery that might have a terrible outcome. Hundreds were down now, and she stood on the second floor, looking at the wooden space of the cottage's ground level below. A forest of mantles shined like slick gray monoliths. Under one was a disaster; under one was the Messenger. They might be interchangeable for all she knew. Or the Messenger might be hiding inside a bomb with no way out...

Patty melted away a reckless trail of them leading down the last spiral course of stairs and took a long breath as she came down the final step. With a mental swipe, she took away around three hundred. Twice as many remained. She'd have to go slower now, the odds lessening.

"Glad you finally came down."

Patty recoiled. She knew that voice. It had been a fixture of her dreams since she was a little girl and she heard it almost every Halloween since leaving her family.

"It's near the door, if you're wondering."

How could Cloth be out of the gateway? Patty checked the mantles near the door. Around twenty or so there—but she could remove the rest in the room before even touching them.

"Right by the cotton-picking door," said Cloth with a cluck of his tongue. "Well done, Middleton."

He'd been trying to escape and the mantle-bomb had stopped him from running outside.

"Why the rush?" she asked, taking a few more steps down. Carefully.

Cloth didn't answer. She could see him from behind, his dark suit, his white fists clenching. He knew what she planned for the likes of him.

"You mangled the wall pretty good upstairs," she told him and took a few steps out onto the wooden planks.

Cloth snorted. "Yes, well, the Interloper apparently builds them like they used to."

"How'd you find this place? Who told you?"

"Aren't you going to blow us up? I'm eager to see how that goes."

"You are?" asked Patty with feigned alarm. "And go and miss Halloween?"

"It would be rather dull without me, wouldn't it?"

Patty slowly dissolved mantles in groups of ten. She didn't get through them all before she revealed the Chaplain standing on the west side of the room.

He smiled grimly. "I guess you're *it* now."

She drew a mantle to cut him in half, but light burst across the room—

The force of the explosion sent Patty's blast shield into her body. Her hands lifted in time to feel it connect. Out of instinct, she brought another mantle to shelter her fall against the unyielding stairs. Staffs of yellow sunlight cut through the giant wound in the side of the cottage. Fiery bits of mantle scorched the ground and silvery particles snowed down.

Cloth stumbled diagonally outside the opening, holding a raging torrent of blood flowing from his stomach. His black suit had torn away and smoked at its singed ends. Patty tried to catch her breath and regain her feet. Sunbursts sword-fought before her eyes as she clawed at the railing. This was her chance. She just had to get to her damned feet already!

Wound forgotten, Cloth limped his way across the field,

gaining speed toward the road. Patty pushed up on her hands with a growl and lunged outside. A happy hungriness enlivened her. She made giant strides, her chest burning and the smell of singed hair rushing through her nostrils.

As he accelerated away, mud drops went scattershot from behind Cloth's white sedan. She couldn't let him escape to the gateway. *Not this close*, she thought. She had an opportunity like none other, to kill him before Halloween even began.

She got into the car, turned the keys and the engine screamed. She pressed into the accelerator as though to drive it through the floor, all needles climbing on the display.

The gently curving roads swayed around Patty but she concentrated only on the car before her and the dark figure at its wheel.

The speedometer touched 112 km/hr and climbed.

The countryside flowed past unnaturally. Green. A smattering of trees along the roadside. The round brown-white shapes of cows raking across her peripheral vision. She narrowed her eyes. Found the cold spot in her mind to summon mantles. Watched Cloth's car. She thought about bringing a mantle, but suddenly the road went into a meeting of buildings elevated on brick risers. It wouldn't be a good idea to take his car out in such close quarters.

Slower moving cars flew by on the right in frenzied screams of air. Cloth veered left and Patty read a sign as quickly as she could, trying to get a sense of where the city would be.

Kilmarnock (A71)
East Kilbride Paisley (A723)

She couldn't allow Cloth to get back in Glasgow. It'd get a whole lot more complicated in the city. The Chaplain may have had the power to make people forget his deeds in this world, but that was a gift the Nomads had never been given.

At once a blue van appeared before them, merging into their lane. Patty felt a mantle release from Cloth—and the next moment the van had turned perpendicular to her car. She jammed on the brake and the whirring sound in the tires set her teeth on edge. The van slid rearward from the mantle's impact. Ripping a mantle from her own mind, Patty fired it back to soften the blow. Her aim was off and the van disappeared down an embankment.

"You fuck!" She drove her foot back down on the gas.

To the freezing womb in her mind, that tundra-place where mantles came from the Old Domain to be born into this world, Patty brought hundreds of them, her own private arsenal, and lobbed them mercilessly ahead. They struck Cloth's car and forced it sideways into a skid. His trajectory headed for upcoming road construction. Workers near a machine marked Civil Engineering scattered. Patty slammed a solid wall of mantles in front of Cloth and his hood flew up at the crash. Astonishingly, the car continued forward.

Patty caught up to the sedan again and shoved another mantle into it. The engine compartment in his car seethed in black smoke. An SUV came upon them suddenly. Cloth's passenger door flew off without warning. Patty reflexively yanked her wheel to dodge it. She jacked the steering wheel to the side as the SUV's driver door also came hurtling at her. The door struck the ground, spinning up in the air on a runner of sparks. The white sedan trailed off the road and plowed into a brick riser. Patty swerved to miss it as the car rolled back into the street. Cloth hurled an older woman in a gray dress out of the SUV. It was so quick Patty almost didn't believe what she saw.

She locked eyes on the twirling form of the woman's body— she padded the woman with the softest mantles she could create on the spot and gave her a smooth landing on a nearby sidewalk. As Patty did this though, she felt another of Cloth's mantles approach with startling velocity.

A street lamp crashed down in front of her and she wheeled right, going into a spin. The back tires walloped the lamp post and she heard its metal rolling over the road. She continued to turn into the spin, doing a complete circle, the right front tire bringing her over the top of the post.

Up the road the SUV erratically changed lanes and passed

other cars. Patty punched the gas. It would take time to catch up again, but she hadn't lost sight of him. Cloth wasn't getting away this time.

Teresa smoothed the Messenger's letter out over the bed and read it again. Besides inventorying the contents of the suitcase the Messenger had left in their hotel room, she had to do something to take her mind off of worrying about Patty.

She pulled her eyes off the letter and looked once again at the bundles of British pounds, Euros, and American currency, as well as the row of ten shiny, black M67 grenades. All of it would help, she supposed. They hadn't needed to use much ordnance with Patty's abilities maturing to such staggering heights, but it was better to have other options besides waiting for Patty's own brand of explosions.

The letter again. Teresa couldn't keep her mind off it. Byron assured her the Messenger's house was abandoned.

And of course it had been. The Messenger did not want to be found. Teresa had come to accept that. There was no way to change a law of nature. She had given up wondering about their mysterious boss a long time ago, but for some reason she'd never been able to get her younger partners to ever buy off on that. Still though, she had to wonder what Patty would find that perhaps Byron overlooked. Whatever it was, Teresa hoped she would return soon and put both their troubled minds at ease. They had to be at Glasgow Necropolis tonight. That meant there would be some security and evasion concerns to work through.

She held up the dusty, delicate letter again.

The Heart of the Harvest has ripened in a young man named Kauph Courre. He lives in the Old Domain. When the clock turns over to the 31st, you must seek the tomb of the heart you won and lost in the city necropolis. A temporary gateway there will be found, but only through personal sacrifice shall the way open.

—Messenger

Why had the Messenger been even more cryptic than usual? The Tomb of the Heart you Won and Lost? Perhaps the Messenger knew that someone else had been reading the message. That hadn't, in all her years on the road, ever happened. And that map of the Old Domain made this all the more real. They really would be going to the other world...

Byron walked out of his bedroom, black and gray streaked hair messed from restless sleeping. "Do you have any scotch around here?"

Teresa slipped her arms together. "Didn't you take two bottles of booze from your room last night?"

"Well I'm fresh out."

The search of Byron's hotel room hadn't proven helpful. Her first impulse had been to cut him loose, but something wasn't right here. She wanted to keep an eye on Byron a while longer. It made no sense, him having found that letter. The Messenger only let Nomads find them.

"Earth to Teresa," said Byron with his hands cupped over his mouth. "Come in, come in?"

"You shouldn't be drinking this early in the morning."

"I have a headache," he added quickly.

"There's aspirin in my bag in the bathroom."

"Do you have anything stronger? Tylenol-3 or something?"

"Nope."

This agitated him. "You Nomads need to know how to pack, for crying out loud. What if you get injured on the Halloween? You should have that stuff with you. You should keep your supply handy, you should—"

"Should?" Teresa went to the hotel table and smoothed out the map of the Old Domain again. "I should have let Patty squash you last night, that's what I *should* have done."

Byron's eyes settled on the map. "You two really going to that gateway tonight then? To the Old Domain?"

Teresa traced a finger down the route marked in dark red. "I'd like to go too."

"What a surprise, but I'm about to turn you loose, if my intrepid partner doesn't show her ass up."

Byron bit at a fingernail for a few seconds, then abandoned

it and clicked his teeth together nervously. "I got that blood work done for you two—put my job on the line scouting out the Messenger's house. My superior, Phil Jeffrey, is going to put together why I wasn't stuck to a roof with him and then others. Not to mention, my partner Denis is a paranoid guy. He'll bring more attention to me when I go back. I made my bed when I decided to help you out of that Void. You have to let me go with you to that gateway."

When she didn't reply, Byron sighed and headed back for his room. Teresa blurted, "You really don't want aspirin?"

"Nah," he answered. "I'll just read. It seems to help." He plopped down on the bed with a grunt and reached for his book. "You think Patty's okay?"

Teresa slowly nodded, but for a nagging old superstition, she didn't want to answer the question aloud.

They were getting closer to the city. Patty had closed the distance between her car and the skittish SUV, which had taken massive damage from her attacks. Cloth's driving was unfocused now, almost careless. His power must have been waning. Anticipation clutched Patty's heart. She would go back to Teresa with some unexpected news indeed. Chaplain Cloth's corporeal body destroyed before the Day of Opening! That would go a long way to protecting the Heart this year, not having the monster constantly at their heel.

A sign blew by:

Towncentre, The Murray Westwood Hairmyres

None of those places sounded familiar. She should have studied the Scotland map better on the plane.

Just then they entered a roundabout and Patty lost her bearing. The SUV hopped a curb and crossed over to another lane. She wheeled that way and gunned it. This had to end here, while no other cars were around.

Patty sent down a mantle like an anvil and the impact made the SUV's back tires lift. Cloth tried to force the vehicle on, going faster, but inky plumes came out of the engine compartment.

She got ready to throw another mantle, when flames leapt from the front end. Chaplain Cloth fell out of the doorless driver side, smacked the ground, rolling. The impact almost looked fatal, but he pushed up immediately from the ground. His hand was bright red with blood and desperation weighed in those black and orange eyes. He turned to run for a group of tall, elegant houses up the street—but he was too late. She had no idea before it happened. The anvil that Patty had dropped on the SUV contained another of her miserable defects. A mantle-bomb detonated and scattered Cloth's body in a hailstorm of red-black pieces.

Sitting there at the wheel, breathing in a pungent cloud of burnt rubber and oil, Patty wanted to smile, to laugh, or sing, but she could only stare at the fiery fragments cast across the road. Traffic behind her approached, but she was in a haze. It would take a few minutes to pull herself together and drive away from the scene.

Cloth was gone.

Not forever, but maybe for this Halloween. "Fuckin' wow," she whispered, shaking her head.

The car approaching behind roared as the driver pushed its speed to the limit. Patty glanced in the rear view and saw a taxi cab approaching at a deadly pace. The sound of its engine peaked in her ears. *What the hell was this lunatic doing?* Reacting, she threw a mantle that burst the windshield and sent the cab lurching. She braced for the impact as her car went sideways.

Everything had become too silent too quickly.

Patty couldn't figure out what had just happened. She hadn't gotten over her shock of destroying Cloth, and now this...

It pissed her off.

She got out of her car and roughly rubbed at her neck. Steam billowed from the front of the taxi cab. Byron's rental car had some scratches but was otherwise still drivable. The cab opened and an attractive dark haired woman held her stomach protectively with a gory hand deprived of thumb and pointer finger. Patty noticed the tearing of the taxi's fabric ceiling and the bisected steering wheel looking like a welder artist's rendition of a butterfly in flight; the mantle sawed through the woman's fingers and just missed cutting her arm off.

The young woman's chest heaved as she stared at Patty defiantly. Though the woman was several years older than she had been in the Messenger's photo, it took only another moment for Patty to recognize her.

The Priestess of Midnight.

"Why are ye just standing there?" she demanded. "Alisyn Dunning?"

"Go on an' finish me, Nomad."

Patty noticed a dead cabbie slumped in the back seat, multiple stab wounds in his chest and face, a dagger sticking out of his right temple, the nearby eye shattered red pulp. "Like you did to him?"

The Priestess took a step forward and her pale face colored. "Don't talk to me of murder—she who kills innocent people in their place of worship."

Patty wrapped a mantle around the woman's throat and saw a milky vein rise up on her neck. The Priestess fought to speak. Patty increased the pressure of the mantle, just to be through with it—she had to commit to going quickly now, severing the Priestess' head from that slender neck and...

Patty loosened the grip and the Priestess sucked in some air gratefully. The sound of another car cresting the hill came from a couple miles away. Patty carefully created a probe mantle and dipped into the woman's head.

It was as she suspected. Another mantle, an impossibly strange mantle of such design Patty had never encountered, grew on the Priestess's brain and connected to her eyes. It was a projection device, but of an organic make—and *she saw things with it.*

All things.

Patty glanced through the projections and saw the entire world at once, as well as a foreign place, the Old Domain, trapped across a vile membrane of darkness. This place contained plants, animals, people she'd never seen before. She even beheld a young man in a forest, before a campfire. There was something special about the boy. Patty knew it right away. The Heart of the Harvest. She'd found him. She knew where he was. It was too much to process, so she took her probe away from the Priestess's mind and cried out in surprise.

"So that's how you found me," Patty said.

The woman swayed from her blood loss. She closed her eyes. "I'm sorry, my son."

"Who?" Patty heard the distant sound of a siren and decided to drop it.

Hoping for no more unexpected bombs, Patty inserted a mantle to barrier the flow at the Priestess's severed thumb and pointer finger. She then bound the Priestess's hands together and prodded her over to the rental car.

"Get inside, you lucky witch. You're not dying today."

Cloth's essence forced its way through this world's thin ether toward the gateway, formless, weak, but not defeated. This wasn't the end he'd hoped for, but it was better that Middleton hadn't found the gateway, and especially good she hadn't found his reserve body.

The Marigold's door flew open and soundly smacked the wall. The Chaplain could not afford to lose time. He shot over the heaps of vines and overturned tables, seeking out the pile of abused flesh named Duncun.

The man had collapsed and hardly took the twisted chairform Cloth had left him in. Over his gorged throat, a Child buried its orange jack-o'-lantern face. Blood and ichor coated its fanged mouth.

NO! *Cloth's mind roared.* NO! NO! NO!

A slight smile of relief was painted on Duncun's dead face. Chaplain Cloth flowed back into the gateway. He could only hold a physical form inside. He could not walk outside now, not even the few steps usually permitted to him while holding a flesh form.

Bending down, he grasped a vine connected to his Child's stem. The pumpkin shaped being rolled back off its meal with a gurgle of surprise. It was medium sized with an oblong body throbbing with fat orange veins, its dark green vine legs and arms thrashing about, its hidden black claws under its leaves slicing invisible victims in the air.

Cloth grasped the sharp stem atop its head, pulled the

Child up and dashed it against the ground. The skull split and jellied tangerine brains slipped out over his loafers. He cast the dead creature aside. A gathering of other Children claimed the body a few moments later. Cloth could hear them fighting and killing for their fair share.

He gazed despondently to the Blind World. The mirror across the bar held a reflection of Chaplain Cloth in the gateway. Never in all its millennia, had the pale face seemed so out of sorts. And it should be. He'd taken a great risk and failed monumentally. It was useless now. Even if he could find another mortal, and break him, there wasn't enough time to transfer enough of his soul into the flesh. His power would be limited and Patrice Middleton would certainly give him another thrashing.

No, this Halloween he would remain trapped in this gateway.

It was up to the Church of Morning to bring the sacrifice. While the Old Domain was less hospitable than this world and the Church of Morning with greater number and ability, the truth was they hadn't been on the Hunt in a very long time. They were human…blessed in power, but still perhaps the most flawed creature in the universe to ever rely upon.

Cloth touched a droplet of orange blood that had splattered on his cheek. He rubbed it between his bony fingers, examining it solemnly. "It's enough to make you cry," he told the darkness.

TWENTY-FIVE

On the drive back to the Radisson Blu hotel, Patty had time to think. The Priestess was stone silent from the backseat, which made the whole strange conclusion to Patty's morning somewhat more bearable. Periodically, Patty would probe the bizarre organ on the Priestess's brain and gaze into that projection. Viewing was hazy, possibly clearer to the Priestess since it grew right into her eyes, but still, Patty could see both worlds. It was amazing on too many levels to describe.

Patty purposely avoided looking on the Old Domain for long periods though; it required too much focus while driving. This world was enough. She watched all people, all places, all at once.

As they got farther down Argyle Street, she used the AllSight to search their hotel. Patty had left in a hurry and had to comb a few floors before remembering where their room was found. It was like what she'd done with projection mantles in the Grand Chapel she destroyed, but this experience was so much more inclusive. She could concentrate on a layer of dust over a window sill, or a beam of light through blinds, or a puddle of water left on the floor of a shower.

An unconscious smile caught on Patty's face as she mentally entered their room. Teresa sat on the bed, a mound of Hershey kisses wrappers near the reading lamp. Byron wasn't in the room with her. Had she let him go?

Patty tapped into the Priestess's mind and searched for him. Byron wasn't anywhere on Earth.

Her eyes went back to Teresa, who chewing another chocolate kiss, studied the Messenger's last note. Patty hadn't really thought about the letter that much, being too concentrated on finding the Messenger's house. Now she used the Priestess's god-eyes to peer over Teresa's shoulder and read along with her.

The Tomb of the Heart they Won and Lost.

It was at once obvious to Patty who that would be. The man's name had been Bran Drummond. He was one of the many Hearts of the Harvest they had been tasked with protecting. Years had passed since the event, but the pain left behind was still crisp for Patty. That Halloween, on the way to seeking safety in a Void located in an abandoned warehouse, Bran had been taken by a bullet in the head, meant for one of the Nomads. The Church of Midnight had some lousy thugs working the Hunt that year.

All the Hearts had been told that if something should ever befall the Nomads, taking their own lives would be better than the future Cloth and his Children had in store for them. Strange that Patty and Teresa had never considered the ramifications of the opposite happening. What it would be like if the Heart died before Cloth even got his hands on them?

Patty and Teresa got to see exactly what happened the night they lost Bran. They had to guard the corpse. Even with Bran dead the sacred fruit kept them emotionally tied to him; they still felt that awful love that manifested with all Hearts of the Harvest.

The Nomads had been mourning in the worst way imaginable. Patty pled with Teresa, begged her to put a bullet through her temple. They fought insanity and fought each other. She remembered scratching Teresa across the face with a claw mantle, and in return getting punched so hard in the stomach, Patty thought she'd die. Luckily the pain from her punch grounded Patty before she conjured something worse, but not much. To this day, Teresa had a thin scar through her left eyebrow from that and Patty was quick to protect her abdomen.

That time with Bran was a freakish night. After somewhat getting control on their emotions, she and Teresa struggled to keep their mantle barriers from Chaplain Cloth's constant assault. He sat outside the main barrier, cross-legged and grinning like a starving ghost. If he couldn't have the Heart of the Harvest, he would have them.

In the end, they made it through that night. Their minds returned to normal with the new day. The Heart of the Harvest had not been reaped, but neither had it been saved. They had won and lost, essentially.

Bran's body was flown back to his family in the UK. Patty never would have dreamed of a reunion with him. Especially not this way.

Byron rested on the bed, taking one final look at the photo of Cloth tucked inside the book he brought from his hotel room. The Nomads had searched his other belongings, even, to his horror, flipped through the pages of the book, but luckily didn't catch the photo. Had they taken it away, he'd be in a world of hurt. Literally. As it was, his nightmares would be intense tonight, but the pain would be bearable for a good day or so, hopefully.

It was all good though; he had the feeling he wouldn't be sleeping tonight anyway.

The door to the hotel room shimmied in its frame. He sat up in bed for a second, listening to Teresa's reaction. Nothing came. He was about to lay back down when he heard the door being unlocked.

Teresa's voice sounded awe struck. "What the hell? *Patty?*"

"Sit down," Patty ordered, but it didn't sound like she was speaking to Teresa.

Byron slipped off the side of the bed and cautiously went to look around the door. A young girl with raven hair sat on the couch. Her hand was mangled, though it didn't seem to be bleeding profusely. He studied her profile a moment and his heart sunk in his chest.

Alisyn...

She must have gone back to the Messenger's house somehow. Shit, he had to get out of here before this whole thing blew up on him.

"Where did Byron go?" asked Patty.

"He's in the room," Teresa said. "Hey are you going to tell me why the hell the Priestess is here? No, hold on, are you first going to tell me why the hell you left this morning?"

Byron inched back and glanced out the window, wondering how far the fall was.

"I had a good location for the Messenger."

"Patty—"

"Of course, you were right, there was no Messenger," Patty flatly responded.

Byron tried to sneak another peek. Suddenly a force drove into his back and sent him flying through the doorway. He crashed to the floor in front of a coffee table. With the quick jab of a mantle, he was on display for all three women.

"Easy," Teresa told Patty. "Talk to me before you beat up on him. Okay?"

Patty's face went red, her eyes killer cold. "Chaplain Cloth was waiting for me instead."

"Holy shit…"

"I didn't ask you to take my GPS. *Steal*, rather." Byron tried to push up on one arm and flinched as his insides coiled. He glanced over his shoulder and Alisyn's faintly Asian eyes held him before looking away. "The Priestess of Midnight, huh?" he said cautiously.

Alisyn pursed her lips and said nothing.

"Patty, finish what happened out there." Teresa tried to stand between them.

Patty's eyes flitted to her partner. "I chased Cloth down and destroyed him."

Teresa's head dropped slightly and she looked up, speechless. Patty nodded with a smile. "He was looking for the Messenger too. One of my explosions took him out."

"He's gone then?"

"For now anyway. There's something else too." Patty's eyes moved to the Priestess. "Slide a probe through the center of this one's brain. Tell me what you see."

The Priestess looked over in alarm and went rigid.

Teresa went about the invisible operation and quivered with the task. "I feel some type of growth there. It creates a projection much like my probe does. It's too complicated for me to discern though. What is it that you see there, Patty?"

"Everything, Teresa…that mantle is a projection of both worlds. We don't even need the Messenger's map! I know exactly where the Heart of the Harvest is, just as long as we take Snow White here with us to the Old Domain. No backtracking, no getting lost, we can get in, get the Heart, and get out."

Alisyn scowled.

Byron noted Teresa's frazzled expression. Silence ensued and he finally said, "So can we get that bourbon now?"

Patty walked over to the Priestess and threw her head in Byron's direction. "Can you see that scumbag through that Third Eye of yours? Because I can't. It's like he's invisible."

Alisyn craned her neck up and blinked purposefully. "You are right. Invisible."

"That's what I thought." Patty turned to Byron. *"What the hell are you?"*

Byron shot a glance to Teresa. "Can you call her off?"

Teresa watched them both like a referee who wanted to escape the ring. "Let's think on this a moment."

"As far as he goes, I say we split him in two," said Patty.

Byron wasn't afraid of dying. He knew it would look that way; he really feared going on living with Patty looking at him like that. "Hey, just because Cloth found that place too, doesn't mean—"

"Shut up."

"Wait up, that's not a bad idea," said the Priestess suddenly. Byron didn't risk a look over in Alisyn's direction. Why wasn't she saying anything about him? This was madness. Did she not recognize him as her dear old Aussie boyfriend Ronald? "Let's be calm," Teresa told Patty. "Byron saved us in that

Void, or have you forgotten?"

"He saved himself," said Patty. "He was the reason we were there in the first place."

"Might I make a suggestion?" Alisyn said.

"Oh yes, let's hear the Church's take," Patty said.

Alisyn looked tired but resolve hardened in her pretty face. The look she gave Byron told him enough. She did remember him and yet she kept it to herself.

"The letter from the Interloper says the gateway opens

through a personal sacrifice. He would prove useful for our safe passage to the other side."

"How did *you* see the letter?" asked Teresa suspiciously. "We can see everything," Patty explained with a sigh and glanced at Byron. "Except for that asshole." Byron shrugged.

"She could be right though," Patty continued. "The Messenger doesn't intend for us to sacrifice ourselves. This group came together for a reason..."

Silence fell and all eyes were on Byron. He licked his lips and rubbed at his stubbly jaw. "I've wanted to see one of these gateways for a while."

Teresa gave him a hard stare. "Patty's grandfather was disfigured when he opened a temporary gateway. He died soon after. From my understanding, that result is by no means unique. Byron, this is no small thing you're being asked to do. It is likely that the gateway will ultimately—"

"Kill you," Patty finished.

Her voice wasn't cruel though. It was frightened. Byron realized that all of her talk before wasn't authentic. She had no intention of doing anything but making him frightened, because she'd just been through something terrible and she was taking it out on him. In spite of everything, that made him feel better.

Even if the end was approaching.

They arrived at the Glasgow Necropolis an hour before dark. Patty created a mantle to hide them, from the time they left Byron's rental car, their walk across the Bridge of Sighs, all the way to the freshly uncovered grave of Bran Drummond. The graveyard was impressive. Countless stone monuments decorated the gravesites, a much more traditional feel than the golf course style cemeteries of today.

As they approached the grave, Patty let go of her mantle. The Messenger had evidently placed many around the area to redirect the attention of any of the Necropolis' visitors. Just beyond that, Patty constructed her own barrier, an outer ring three feet thick and around fifty feet tall. Nobody could get inside to the special area, and with concern for the Priestess, nobody could *get out.*

Building the mantles was a refreshing break from the thoughts and images that polluted her mind. Patty was in full denial mode.

The group looked down at the coffin for several silent minutes. This was the way. Down there. In the coffin. The Heart they had won. The Heart they had lost. All the years of hearing and reading about the Old Domain, and this man made pit was a shortcut past Chaplain Cloth and the monstrous gateway he lived inside. It seemed easy and normally anything easy had to be cause for serious thought for the Nomads.

But Patty was tired of thinking. Despite her age, despite, perhaps, her lack of wisdom, she just wanted to bull through this china shop, so she could shake off the shards of glass and breathe fresh air on the other side. It was time. It was past time. Teresa probably knew that too, but so many years of thinking the dynamic would never change, that the Heart would always be of this world, had made this all too confusing.

That was why, without any discussion, Patty clamored down inside the perfectly cut shaft in the ground. Not hesitating like most girls her age might have, Patty opened, with surprising ease, the lid of Drummond's coffin.

Teresa hardly remembered how the man had looked in life. She did remember the suicidal feeling of failure that one Halloween though, and the near-impossible night that followed his accidental death. Peering over Patty's shoulder, Teresa studied Bran's dried blue-black corpse resting inside a pale suit. The coat had been pulled away, the dusty shirt beneath unbuttoned to reveal a brittle dark gray ribcage that appeared to bend inward.

Shoulder to shoulder with the Priestess, Byron leaned over and beheld the dead man. "Lovely," he muttered. "So this is where the gateway will be. I'd heard it was larger."

Patty took a slip of parchment tucked beneath the corpse's shoulder. She handed it up to Teresa and nimbly climbed out of the hole. Teresa unfolded the letter and had to fight her annoyance as Byron and the Priestess edged closer to read. *They're in this too now, I guess*, she thought. But it didn't mean she had to feel good about it.

Pull forth the rotten fruit with only the *right* hand, crush it fully and press it over a living, beating heart. The gateway will not last beyond the Day of Opening. I have one more note for you, left in the Old Domain. Expect its arrival after you find Kauph Courre.

—Messenger

"I guess whatever it takes to get this thing open, huh," said Byron solemnly.

"Let's go study that map." Patty bumped past him and grabbed the Priestess's shoulder. "You, come close, I need that tumor in your brain."

"Tumor?" the Priestess said, a little alarmed.

Patty took the map out of the backpack she'd set against a rectangular monument speckled with green lichen and gone rhombus with time.

Teresa went to Patty. "We need to talk."

The younger woman spread out the map. Tracing the route with her finger, Patty pretended to be intent on what she saw. "We don't have to go far to get the Heart—Kauph Courre will be close to our cross over point. That's easy enough to see." Patty whirled around to the Priestess, who approached warily. "Hey! Hurry and get your ass over here."

Teresa guided Patty around the monument and pressed her firmly against the stone.

"You going to slap me again?"

"Would it help?" Teresa asked her sharply.

Patty took a deep breath and pressed some fingers into her eyes. "It was a mistake. I made a mistake in thinking we could bring her. Byron's more useful to us over there. His training—"

"Hey, stop, ok?"

"I've got the map internalized. Why not make the Priestess open the gateway? Crushing a rotting heart sounds like something she'd probably like."

"The Priestess won't be crushing anything anytime soon. Or hadn't you noticed when you took off half of her right hand?"

This struck Patty like a bag of bricks to the face.

"There are only three people here who can open that gateway. Two of them are needed to shepherd the Heart of the Harvest out of the Old Domain. The remaining person has offered, gladly even. Why? I don't know, but as you always tell me: do we really want to let this chance go?"

Patty moved her head around the side of the monument and considered the Priestess, who leaned her slender body against another tall piece of stone. A light breeze ruffled her black dress, making her look spectral. Byron stood on the other side of the grave, massaging his neck as he listened to his iPod.

"It was meant to be," Patty mumbled.

Teresa sighed. "I know there is more to this for you. I get that."

"You've made me kill before—and I've never liked it, but I always did as I was told."

"Say it. Go on."

"Why him, Teresa?" Patty looked down to the ground, eyes filling. Her voice broke. "Why in the hell him?"

For longer than she could ever remember doing before, Teresa hugged Patty tight. Kissed her cheek more than a few times and petted her hair. In times past, she would hum Sam Cooke's *Hem of his Garment*, but that was consolation for a little girl. Part of Teresa longed to do it anyway, just to show her that she did understand.

"Listen a sec, will you?" she whispered. "Remember Vancouver? You were twelve. Back then I didn't tell you everything, didn't think you should worry about what I had to. The Church had that second band of Colombians on us. A few of them proved to be pretty damned good at what they did. Found us a few times."

"I remember them."

"The Messenger instructed us to get some distance. Pulled a fourteen hour stretch and I started falling asleep. I heard the car drifting off the road and I managed to get control just in time. I was so mad at myself...so very mad. After that I sat there, adrenalin racing, watching you sleep."

"Why are you telling me this?"

"I wanted to know who that girl sleeping in my car would turn out to be. I wanted to make a mental image of the moment I came close to driving her into a tree, because seeing her grow up was all that mattered to me." Teresa pressed her lips together a moment. "We hadn't gotten half as far as we needed to, but I refused to drive any farther that night. I said to hell with the Messenger. Remember what happened?"

"In the morning they had our car surrounded. HK416s on us."

"Serious shit. You almost didn't get us shielded before they opened fire," said Teresa. "I remember."

"So you now see, it doesn't matter how great our intentions. Orders are orders."

"Maybe this risk is worth it."

Teresa sighed. "No honey, it's not. Believe me."

"What else do we have? What is there to leave behind? I wish for once you could see things that way, Teresa. Just once."

Patty broke off from her. Teresa watched as she went back to the map again, to pretend and concentrate, to bury her worst thoughts, to act as if tonight wasn't going to happen. Teresa felt the dread right along with her. Just like that kid she was going to snipe at the Grand Chapel—resigned to destiny.

Byron walked up. His steps were light, either of a thief, or a child seeking forgiveness. "Teresa?"

"Yes, Byron."

"Is she going to be okay with this?"

Teresa looked away from his querying eyes and shook her head. "She'll be okay. Eventually."

"I see."

"And how about you?"

"What?"

"How well do you follow orders, Byron?"

He pursed his lips for a moment. "When I believe in their worth."

"You're a brave guy."

"Hardly…" he answered.

She left him there and walked back to Patty. *Let duty and obligation stomp you into the ground until you're an older woman with a soul worn thin and nothing to show for it.* She didn't want to think her little girl would carry that around with her the rest of her life.

She's not your little girl. She's your partner.

Teresa shook her head. No, *she's always been more than that.*

Patty was what Teresa would leave behind. She had known that all along.

But how could she ever let go?

The hours had not dragged on like Patty required. Each of them had time to themselves, thinking and thinking some more. All, except for the Priestess, who ate peppered beef jerky and drank cans of iced tea—this was a Nomad style meal if there'd ever been one, Patty mused. Funny to see a member of the Church enjoy the same spoils of the road.

It was a quarter past eleven o'clock and darkness had soaked through everything in the silent land of graves and ghosts.

Byron leaned against a dark piece of limestone deformed from rain. He stood there, hands tucked in his suit pockets, tall, handsome, and all alone. Mistrust should have made her hate him. It would be easier if it did.

"Do you have any cigarettes?" he asked, realizing she'd been watching him.

"No."

"You aren't going to slam a mantle into my face, are you?"

"I just came over to talk a little before you...do this thing." His face had an ashen quality to it now, almost appearing like stone; he belonged in this yard of morbid statues and death, but the moonlight refused to take the attractiveness from his pained face. "What do you want me to say, Pat?"

Patty shrugged. Her shoulders felt so heavy. "It doesn't matter what I want."

Softly, he pushed away from the headstone and took her face between his hands. The warmth from them was almost feverish to the touch.

"Don't kiss me," she warned.

He forced his lips into hers and she let it happen, all at once hating and enjoying it. When he drew away, she halfheartedly pulled him back.

He chuckled. "Remember, it doesn't matter what you want."

"Goddamnit...you just act like this is nothing."

"Wrong," said Byron, "this is something—probably the most important moment in all my life. I wish that made sense." He turned his face down, then closed his eyes and took deep breaths, willing something horrible away.

"Tell me the truth," she insisted. "Tell me something, Byron! Who's side are you on? Do you care about me? At all? Even a little?"

He met her gaze. "I'm sorry, I don't."

"No, that's not what your eyes say."

"Don't trust them to tell the right story."

"You're always in some kind of agony, but I don't know from what. Is this like a suicide?"

"That's perceptive enough."

"You won't tell me then?"

He stared up at the starless sky. "I cannot tell you the truth, not in a way that wouldn't sound like a lie. I wasn't given the tools to deal with this in another way. I can't afford twisting the moment."

"You're afraid I'll get hurt?"

"No," he replied, shaking his head frantically, "no, I'm afraid the truth will become a lie. I don't know if we can live with that."

Patty rubbed her left temple, trying to ward off the headache cultivating there. "Not even for closure?"

"All I want to say is thank you."

"*Thank you?*"

"Yes. You're what got me this far...that's better than anyone else has done for me. I've been drowning a long, long time now, Patty. Thinking you'd be up there at the surface, waiting for me, it's helped get me here. I might die just before I reach that sweet air, but at least you'll be with me. At least I didn't quit or give up hope. Because believe me, I was close many times."

"You know how much patience I have for riddles?"

Byron gestured an inch with his thumb and pointer finger. Patty turned from him. When she did, she came face to face with the Priestess of Midnight. Coyly watching them both, the exotically beautiful woman stood there, hair flowing over her bosom, twin falls of black silk. Her eyes flitted to Byron. "You two would make beautiful children together. Such wonderfully strong features."

"What do you want?" Patty demanded.

The Priestess stared at her passively. "The older Nomad has gone down into the grave. She said we need to gather around quickly. The time draws near."

"What? You're insane." Patty almost bowled her over. Teresa was nowhere in sight. Patty broke into a sprint. Byron was already running and reached the grave first. Dirt slid out from beneath his shoes as he stopped and caught himself.

They all stood around the opening in the ground. Patty watched as her partner straddled the coffin and squeezed something black to her chest. Rich red and brown dirt fell away from it.

"Teresa! What the fuck are you doing?"

"To hell with the Messenger," Teresa called over her shoulder, just as the ground began sinking beneath. The coffin and earth fell away to nothing. A pit formed beneath, endless, cold and dark, straight into oblivion.

"No! You can't leave me!" Patty shouted and reached down.

Byron immediately restrained her.

Teresa pressed her eyes closed. "Don't say...I never...did anything...for you."

Teresa's body pitched into space. The dead Heart made her fist glow with rich orange light. That energy crept into her knuckles and slipped into her own heart and spread through the veins and arteries, which immediately raced with the same glow, through her skin, through her yellow blouse, through the tips of her silver streaked almond hair. Her muscles rippled and crashed like a frenzied ocean storm.

Patty reached forward again but now the Priestess clutched her arm. "Don't interfere."

Teresa's torso twisted unnaturally around. Waves of dark purple, almost filthy looking steam pushed around her. She dropped into the pit, vanishing completely with a hissing sound.

Byron jumped in after, his arms banging against the earthen wall, sending errant mud clumps down with him into nothingness. The Priestess glanced challengingly at Patty, then stepped off the side.

Gone with the others.

In the next moment, Patty found herself leaping down into the hole.

Through Teresa.

Teresa was the gateway.

Patty could smell her Oil of Olay scent on her own skin, her scream was with Teresa's voice, her gasps came from Teresa's abused lungs—this was a Teresa-Ladder into another place.

The world Patty knew was left behind.

OCTOBER 31ST

TWENTY-SIX

There was a different eclipse in both of Alisyn's eyes. Her body still felt the sensation of falling, even though the journey through the gateway had only been momentary. She fought a dizzy spell and sour saliva filled the back of her throat. Her hand with missing fingers pulsed angrily to insist on reminding her it hadn't healed. That seemed to help displace the pressurized feeling of the Old Domain.

The four of them writhed in dead grass the color of cigarette ash. The sky above was a drape of storm clouds, a dark electric blue from the obscured moon. They all appeared to experience the same uncomfortable crushing feeling as she did, but Ronald had a different look in his eyes, an expectancy that stretched into disappointment.

Alisyn still couldn't figure out why he'd lied to the other women. It wasn't a good idea to reveal him, although she'd come close when she saw him sharing a moment with that Middleton bitch. But it was just as well. Alisyn had no claim on him, Camden or any other man; she was free now. For now, whatever scam Ronald ran on the Nomads, she would play along with, for leverage. She had to use something. *That phony American accent is so transparent. It went to show how dense these two women were.*

Her body acclimatized and her limbs, all pins and needles, craved to move. She rolled over and attempted to push up on her shaking hands. Middleton cared after the older Nomad, who lay still and silent. Her sight still hazy, Alisyn noticed enormous shapes towering over the dead field around them. She lowered her eyes and met Byron's gaze. He looked so perfectly confused she wanted to smile.

"Where was Cloth?" he asked. He closed his eyes as wooziness consumed him.

"That was a gateway, no' *the* gateway."

"Is it close?"

She shrugged, but thought *I hope not*. With nowhere else to go, with coming painfully close to thinking Camden had been right, Alisyn had tried to prove herself worthy to Chaplain Cloth. And failed. Who would've imagined her capture would lead her right to the place she so longed to go?

She filled her lungs with the burnt leaf air of the Old Domain.

This proved what she'd always known about the True Son.

They were meant to be together.

A sob escaped the Middleton girl. Byron crawled over to her side. Alisyn got to her knees for a better look. The older Nomad, the one called Teresa, was ravaged. The skin of her face hung limply to one side and pulled back on the other like bad plastic surgery. Her blouse had burnt away at the area she'd held the dead Heart. The skin there and elsewhere rippled with blisters. Middleton held the woman's scaly red hand in hers and kissed it in torment.

Teresa's eyelids dropped.

"Don't you fucking dare!" Middleton yelled.

Teresa's eyes shot open and a sound came from her that sent Alisyn's hair on end. The Nomad began screeching, over and over, each primal sound making her wince. She didn't think it could be any worse but then the pitch changed to an almost infant like wail.

Ronald got down beside Middleton and took the frantic woman by her face, made her look into his eyes. "Teresa!" he hollered over her calls. "Teresa!"

Alisyn looked out in the distance to a copse of dark trees. Earthen figures moved around between their roots, peering at them inquisitively with milky red eyes.

"Concentrate on where the pain is, Teresa," said Ronald. "Think about it—"

Teresa quieted, taking big gulps of air.

"Distract yourself from *all* of it and just deal with a piece at a time."

Back and forth, the woman thrashed her now fully silver-haired head.

"Sometimes, you can stop believing in the pain," he said. "Convince yourself it doesn't exist. Think about it, like it's a lie, discover it was never there to begin with. Do you understand?"

Teresa calmed a little more, blinking, breathing, a grimace still firmly fixed to her face. "Is that like Zen bullshit?"

Ronald laughed. "Yeah, exactly."

Middleton leaned over her. "Are you a little better?"

"A *little*, yes."

"Why? Why did you do that? Why? You have to tell me why, Teresa!"

A hoarse, smoky voice came from the older woman's blanched lips. "Didn't count on it hurting this much..."

"Goddamn you! You can't just go sacrificing yourself without checking first." Tears dropped from Middleton's eyes.

"Death doesn't come easy for the likes of Teresa Celeste.

You wanted me to take a risk, for Pete's sake." Patty gasped. "Not one that big."

"Well, I figured I've had my time. You and Byron haven't." Byron put his hand up to his eyes. "Oh Teresa..."

The Nomad's eyes seemed hyper-white. As far as Alisyn could tell, it was the only piece of her left untouched by the gateway's twisting. Teresa sat up, despite Middleton's urgings.

"I'm dying of thirst."

"Teresa keep still—"

"Patty," she snapped. "Feel sorry for me later. Let's bring the Heart of the Harvest back to this gateway."

"Okay...yes, okay."

Teresa touched the burnt area on her chest. "Patty—is Martin's mantle still inside me? I don't sense it."

Middleton examined her, seeming to see something nobody else could. "It isn't...Teresa, it's gone."

A look of sadness passed over the woman's disturbing new face. "It did something on the way through, got caught on something, like a hook. It pulled out of me. I felt it happen. The mantle stayed behind in the gateway but became one with me

too. I feel it tugging on me, and I don't feel real, Patty. I feel like
I am a MANTLE."

A large gush of blood spilled from Teresa's mouth. "Shit—
you're bleeding inside. I'm patching you up." Middleton bowed
her head, engaging in her invisible work. "It's strange here—
I'm not bringing mantles, I'm using your own tissue to seal the
wounds."

Teresa spit out some more blood, looking less bothered by it
than having all these people gathered around her.

Alisyn drank in their surroundings with her mind's sight.
The shapes she'd seen before at a distance now she could study
with detail. Scarecrows—a dozen or more, towering scarecrows
with horned heads. Nothing grew here though and that meant
they were boundary guardians of some kind. Throughout the
field she spotted trigger discs to set off some sort of alarm from
them.

"Mind the plates in the ground," she told the group. "Or the
scarecrows will be activated."

"What will they do?" asked Ronald. "Best no' to experiment."

Extending her sight farther northward, she found a road
leading into a dead little village. She roamed a bit beyond that.
A barn sat in the shadows of two coiling black trees. Several
water cisterns were along the back wall. She peered through
their wax seals. The water inside was fresh. That meant they'd
been filled recently. Humans were nearby. Calling them human,
however, might have been a stretch.

Middleton grabbed her head in surprise and gritted her
teeth. She'd been sharing the All-Sight with Alisyn. "It hurts
when I look into her mind. It didn't before...not in our world."
Alisyn's heart thumped faster and adrenaline ran hot in her
face. If they couldn't find a use for her here, what would they
do? Likely what they did to the rest of your Church, *fool.*

Patty wagged her head. "I see everything so clearly it's
painful. Teresa, there's water in a barn. Let's head that way
and avoid those plates in the ground. It's not en route with the
Messenger's path but I think we should continue on up the hill."

"That's a dangerous route, Nomad. We should find water

elsewhere," said Alisyn. "You may no' believe me—"

"That's not the point. Those hills over there aren't as steep. It will be easier to take Teresa around the bank of trees. From there, it's only a couple of miles to the camp where the Heart is waiting."

"Don't detour for me," Teresa said.

"Look!" Byron pointed. Across the field, where the terrain sloped upward to a gathering of black foothills, a wave of pumpkin shapes crested an adjacent series of foothills, all flooding from a deep black pit in the air. The pit snapped shut and the pumpkins were gone almost as suddenly as they'd appeared.

"The Children," said Teresa. "We've got to get moving to the Heart of the Harvest."

"So that's the gateway?" Byron asked. "The real one?"

"It goes where Cloth tells it to," said Patty. She hoisted Teresa up to stand. "But I suspect this year, he's going where the Children take him."

"Enough chitchat," Teresa said pointedly.

Chaplain Cloth stood at the precipice of the gateway and watched the surge of Children wander the lands of the Old Domain. It had been so long since he'd been close to the fertile lands of this world. Tremors of need went through him. There was a slave out there who might fit his purposes wonderfully, but Bre Courre was miles away, in a forest the Nomads would never venture into. Oh, *to just set foot out there and feel the power well up from the blood blessed dirt.*

The Children returned in a rush, an avalanche of orange. Then the gateway opened a moment later to a new location and they flooded back outside. There was no rhyme or reason, no methodology to their hunt. Just smelling the air like blind, hungry dogs. And he was tied to the dog sled.

"Swell," Cloth whispered.

Patty could hear Teresa's pained breathing, so close to her it felt like her own lungs struggling for air. Trying to get her mind off what had happened to her partner, Patty attempted to build a mantle, just to see how it would feel in this new world.

It was...*off.*

Just like when she'd attended to the various perforations of Teresa's internal organs and could apply the typical mantle bandaging, but had to loosen the tissue and spread it thinly over the wounds, making a flesh slurry, which actually clotted quite well, even if it left Teresa's body in a fragile state.

Once more, she checked her ability to draw mantles from farther away. Patty's mind tugged on something; she brought it closer, first gradually, than faster, anything to take her thoughts off the chilling creepiness of this shadowy world.

A rumble beneath the dirt came down the road. The Priestess and Byron froze. Patty saw it and let her mind relax. Dirt clods flung into the air in a shower of pebbles and the noodle shapes of oversized earthworms. She held the disruption there for a moment and let it drop back to the earth.

"You tried to build," Teresa said, sedately raising her head from Patty's shoulder.

Patty glanced down. It hardly looked like Teresa anymore. The almond-silver hair had become kinky and flat gray. Her Latina complexion had bleached away and blood vessels ran blue and purple just beneath tenuous skin.

"Oh you did that?" Byron asked, grasping his chest, blinking and shaking his head. "Holy shit..."

"As I said, it's different. It doesn't work the same way here," Teresa replied. "The matter we control are not astral-projections, not ghost matter, but *actual matter.* Come let's go, I'm so thirsty..."

They went on. The gopher tunnel Patty's mind had dug creased the road through a small town of pine board buildings. From the disrepair all around, it didn't look like the residents would care much. Long, sneering weeds with glossy chandelier heads buffered the dark porches and stabbed through the planks. No glass remained in any windows, but some crystal fangs remained in the frames.

At first there was no other sound but their footsteps on the dirt road.

Then the muttering began. Along with the soft drumming of hearts all around them.

Hundreds of pairs of bleeding eyes drifted from the absolute darkness behind the windows to touch the grim light of the clouded moon. Glowing red outlines pulsed in some of the windows. When Patty stared at it, she felt as though she might become sick to her stomach.

The hidden people took her thoughts and turned it into a chant.

"Ill, ill, ill, ill, yes, we are. Feast and feast. The pageant's about to start. Come and rot with us."

"I told you this way wasn't safe. This is a town belonging to the Clan of Sickness…" the Priestess of Midnight told them. "Keep to the road. They will not engage unless we set forth inside their quarantine. We must hurry."

Decaying smells rolled thick from the houses: cold metal blood odors, sharply sweet feces aromas, overpowering ammonia piss.

Teresa got her footing and took her arm from Patty's shoulder. She limped faster toward the end of the small row of homes. The old barn waited in between two outcroppings of rock from the foothills. Patty saw four water cisterns against the far wall. She let Teresa go first and tear through the wax seals. Byron helped lift the cistern and pour the fresh water in Teresa's palm. She smelled it and slurped some up. After a moment, she nodded. "Good."

Byron put the edge of the cistern near her open mouth and poured. After four long draughts, Teresa waved him to stop. She turned and collapsed.

Patty went to her. *What had she been thinking? Why had I gone on about Byron? I should have never told her. This is all my fault.*

"Got tipsy," said Teresa defensively. "I'll be over it in a second."

Byron took a hand-scythe from a rusted nail on the wall. "This makes me feel slightly better…"

"Something's wrong." The Priestess of Midnight stood outside, her curvy body outlined in the night's soft illumination. "Middleton, look to the north."

Patty sought out the reflection in the woman's mind. It felt like a bolt of migraine pain to both of her eyes, but she still saw everything in both worlds, laughing, crying, loving, hating, births, deaths. She didn't seek detail in any of it however. Looking north, as the Priestess had suggested, she found a disturbance in the tall grasses. Something tall shifted back and forth and it was stepping quicker. It was like this thing knew they had discovered it and decided to hasten its pursuit.

Beyond this terrible Thing, a couple of miles away, Kauph Courre waited in his camp, a boy in his late teens, perhaps early twenties. The Heart didn't realize that, not far from his camp, the gateway had opened and Cloth's Children clamored forth to hunt him. They were deadly close now.

"We've got to get going," Patty said. "Teresa, can you stand?"

Teresa swayed as she stood. A hard look of disappointment caught in her face. "I'll get it. Don't worry."

Patty looked to the Priestess. "What is that thing up ahead?"

"A Voyeur," replied the Priestess, her typically serene speech fractured. "The Clan of Sickness alerted it to our presence. We have to run. If it gets sight of us, it'll be worse than death."

"Leave me here, Patty," said Teresa.

"Like hell."

Byron studied his new found weapon. "Guess I'll get to try this out."

"I wouldn't count on that," said the Priestess.

TWENTY-SEVEN

Phil Jeffrey cursed as he took a right turn. Since they'd left this morning for the St. Mungo Museum, he'd had difficulty driving a stick shift on the left side and steering with an arm bound in a sling.

"It was a nice dream, having the Nomads and all," Camden said, trying to keep his spikiness at a minimum.

After playing with the radio and finding only commercials, Jeffrey jabbed the power button. He smoothed his white torch of hair back a moment and angrily scratched the base of his head. Camden was happy somebody was as miserable as he was. "You look nervous, Bishop Jeffrey."

"I was stuck to a ceiling for most of the night like a fucking fly on fucking flypaper. I'm not nervous, I'm pissed off." Phil took a calming breath. "But the Nomads aren't important."

"Oh?"

"I knew I'd make it here some day. I knew you would too, Archbishop."

"I keep my word, bishop."

"No, I'm talking foresight. I've seen how everything goes down here. I've dreamed about this Halloween most of my life.

You and I are in the vision with the Pillar of Ginsau."

"That so?" Camden tried not to sound too skeptical. He should have gone with Alisyn. This was a waste. Even if the Column were real, this wasn't the path he'd wished to take. But you didn't want to go with Alisyn either, *did you? That wouldn't have made you any happier. You don't know what you want. Never have.*

Camden recognized his internal voice. It was his father. He hadn't thought about that blowhard in days now. So much for his streak.

The other OAP agents found parking places outside the museum. Only one car was here, possibly the night watchman. Jeffrey killed the engine and got a package of gum from his suit pocket. He peeled off the wrapper and popped the purple stick in his mouth. The smell was sickly sweet to Camden and he moved to open the door.

"Wait!" said Jeffrey.

A tall man with thin brown hair, in his mid-forties, stepped outside the museum with a large jumble of keys in hand. A girl, maybe ten, dressed in a karate uniform came out with him, followed by a woman, probably the man's wife and her mother. "Fuck me in the eye—looks like daddy needed a ride home. There's our easy ticket inside. This is going better than I planned for." Phil thumbed off the strap of his gun holster and pushed his door open so quickly he had to shield himself with his sling as it returned violently.

Camden went numb and quickly ducked out of the car. "Stop, police," yelled Jeffrey, "stop right there!"

The family went rigid. They put their hands in the air and looked at each other, puzzled and frightened. Other OAP agents ran toward them, gripping gun handles.

The family was ushered back inside the museum.

"Who are ye people?" Camden heard the man ask. "Please show us ID."

"We work in tandem with the United States Central Intelligence Agency. Now where's the curator? Where's the other staff?" Jeffrey's voice echoed in the hall.

Camden stepped into the museum and felt chill. There was something faintly strange about this location, as though it was surrounded by an unseen, disturbing oddity.

"I can call her," explained the man. "Wait, where's that identification?"

"What about shift change?"

"There is no shift during the day."

"Who's working tonight?" Jeffrey demanded. "Daddy," squeaked the girl in the karate uniform.

"It's okay, darling," Jeffrey assured her and then looked pointedly at the man. "We're here to protect you. I need to alert the next shift coming in tonight."

"We're closed for three days. I'm the only watchman. All the rest are at the convention in London. Now please—"

"Oh wonderful." Jeffrey patted the man on the back and nodded to an agent with an oily goatee. The agent took out zip ties and the others closed in on the family. "Lock the door and keep someone posted."

"Wait!" called the woman. "Who are you?"

Jeffrey glared at her. "Do we really have to gag you, lady?" The family's protests trailed off.

"What now?" Camden asked.

"Put them out of sight for a bit, then we can figure it out together. Right now, I'm going to see the Column."

"That's what this is about? The Pillar of Ginsau?" the watchman asked suddenly. When everyone stared at him, he added, "Are ye 'ere about the singing?"

"Singing?" Camden put his hand lightly under the man's arm.

"It's remote, aye...I hear them sometimes, like they're behind the walls. Others have heard it too, but everyone here disnae want to talk about it."

"Marvelous!" Jeffrey clapped Camden's shoulder. He pointed to the showcase room. "I'll be in there, admiring our destiny, Archbishop."

Camden felt the watchman's arm hair rise, and as though the chill transferred between them, his own hairs followed. Carefully, he led the man and his family toward the curator's office.

The man leaned into Camden's ear and whispered, "I have savings. We could go to a cashpoint and withdraw as much as it will let me—"

"I won't let anythin' happen to ye."

Sweat beaded on the man's furrowed brow. He had coffee breath and stained teeth to match. Genuine fear cooked in his panicked eyes. "I appreciate that but—"

"I promise ye," said Camden and opened the office door.

TWENTY-EIGHT

The Voyeur found them.

Byron thought they left the creature behind in a small swampland area, because he couldn't hear its heavy feet splashing in the water behind them. But the Voyeur flanked them, completely without warning. His first thought was, *what is this creature?*

And an answer abruptly shoved itself into his mind:

You are a creature too.

Creatures, different. Creatures, same. Creatures, all of us.

"Don't look at it! Keep moving!" said Alisyn. He could hear the terror in her voice. She knew her words were frivolous. Byron could tell.

Their group tried to change course into a maze of ugly corn—kernels like dead fish eyes and stalks with the blackened ash quality of coordinated arson—but the Voyeur moved twice as fast as them. It was no wonder: Teresa could hardly stand and Patty had to help her, Alisyn wasn't used to walking through tall grasses with mud in her glossy black shoes, and then there was Byron, of course, well, he had to deal with the old pain again, and in this place it was an entirely different type of suffering. Normally he felt like his organs were being tied into messy knots; the struggle was internal. In the Old Domain, his skin pulled and wrenched and stung every pore like white hot needles dipped in hatred. Each hair on his head was a micron worm eating into his skull.

Teresa growled and pushed harder, leaving Patty's side. The group turned from the corn into the surrounding gray plain dotted with transparent weeds. Wide, stretching crimson symbols bedecked the plain. Byron noticed the symbols hadn't been painted but occurred through the growing of red grass. He couldn't focus on the designs—he was about to double over. For relief, he reached for the photo of Cloth in his back pocket. A cluster of glassine weeds bent in a succession of crackles, like bones shattering, as a tremendous foot came down. "Don't let it—" Alisyn shouted. Her words hung in the air and died.

The Voyeur's head was ten times the size of a human being's, but it had no face. The head was a massive bloodshot eye with an oil-dark retina, pierced by a lantern glow in its center. Ruby veins trailed from the base of the eyeball to form spindly arms and legs. It took three lengthy strides closer to the frozen group and wobbled a bit on its gory stilts.

Byron couldn't turn his head. His body was free to move but he didn't want to do anything except match the Voyeur's gaze. The stillness of his companions told him they were under its thrall as well.

Moaning rolled through every hemisphere of Byron's mind. It was the orgasmic call of this creature as it sorted through his head like a burglar tossing unwanted items out of drawers and closets. The mental fingers touched memories that could easily be twisted to make Byron a gibbering idiot, or a psychopath, or the bravest soul the universe had ever seen. It was all there for the manipulation, but the Voyeur wasn't interested in any of that. It hungered for memories and connections built into those memories. This process petrified Byron but in some ways brought respite from the pain. He heard the women around him, recognizing each of their voices. Teresa grunted and breathed angrily through her nose. Patty whimpered and sought to dampen a scream. Alisyn was already screaming, although it was a small sound in an endless hissing acid storm.

Byron locked onto that word.

Endless.

It very well could seem like that.

The geography of his mind the Voyeur had covered was practically insignificant compared to the entire field of memories and emotions found there.

It became clear then how Byron would die. *How they would all die.*

Starvation.

Teresa's breathing sounded hitched, like she'd forgotten how to inhale. The sound recalled Byron to his own bodily needs and he let out a ragged cough. Maybe starvation was wishful thinking. He'd just forgotten to breathe a moment ago while the Voyeur tinkered with his respiratory system. Darkness dabbed the edges of his vision.

Alisyn exhaled with a shriek. Teresa fell to her knees. Patty kept silent, her blinking eyes filling with hateful tears.

Dull edged knives plunged up through Byron's throat and sobered him to the Voyeur's probe. The pain had cut through this trance. It was the only time in his life he could remember welcoming his strange disease. The photo of Cloth was in his hand and he longed to focus his eyes on it instead of that giant retina that stared into the reaches of his soul. His arm quaked from fingers to shoulder as he lifted the photo.

And handed it to the Voyeur.

Patty fell against Alisyn and they both tumbled over Teresa. Byron slammed down on his rear, caving in one of the glasslike weeds with a crunch.

The Voyeurs' vein-twisted hands greedily clenched the photo of Cloth. The moaning the creature made inside Byron's mind turned to panting and screaming. What little white of the eye there had been now burst red with ruptured vessels. The black retina cracked, watery fluid escaping and pumping out of the fissures. The Voyeur's screams were interrupted with frantic giggles. It would never let go of that photo. It would always behold it, study it, cherish it.

Patty tugged Teresa to her feet, and Byron took Alisyn's pale hand. As soon as she regained herself, she let his hold go and charged up the sharp grade after the other women.

He followed. The old pain renewing itself inside him all at once, an ocean pulling back to reveal a beach littered with razorblades. And they were all Byron's to walk barefoot across, once again.

Nobody mentioned the Voyeur. Nobody asked Byron what he'd given.

What had been sacrificed...

What had he been thinking? That photo was his only protection. Panicked thoughts of running back for it flooded his mind. They ran down a steep hill into an immense collection of burnt orange cacti with jacketed black needles. Everybody was trying to catch their breath when Alisyn spoke, "Middleton, do you see? Ahead. Look."

Patty touched a place above her temple, then gritted her teeth. "Oh shit."

"What?" Byron managed. *"What?"*

Patty looked deathly ill. "The Children found the Heart's camp."

TWENTY-NINE

Teresa should have been thinking about the Heart of the Harvest but other jagged thoughts tore through her mind. Was she here? Was she really a part of this chase? She'd thought opening the gateway had been to spare Patty and Byron, but when she looked into the eye of that Voyeur, it changed how she saw it. In the thrall of its gaze, she'd stubbornly refused to succumb to the gateway, as though she had a choice, but now, all her thoughts reconfigured, the dark truth whispered: You were tired, and you didn't want to go on. Your sacrifice was selfishness. Nothing more, *nothing less.*

She fought this. *Not true. I've seen how I die in dreams before—I knew I was safe.*

You hoped to be wrong, that the dreams had been wrong.

Teresa told her mind to shut up and limped on. Please don't be dead before we find you, *Kauph Courre.* More of the painful looking orange cacti swelled from the ground, black needles extending over a foot long. Their blossoms were black and dusty, like something taken from a fireplace. The cacti became more frequent and taller, forming a forest that leaned over them, shadowy desert gods.

Wind whistled around them. Patty had a broken look on her face. The Priestess looked pensive. Byron was ghostly white. As mangled as Teresa's own body had become from the gateway's twisting, he seemed worse off by far. He'd done something to the Voyeur that saved them, but Halloween wasn't a day to answer all questions. It was a day to protect—

"There!" Patty whispered.

The cacti ahead did not resemble the rest of the perverse

lofty shapes they'd traveled through this far. The presence of the Heart of the Harvest had changed them, given them light from within. Radiance welled from the orange flesh of the cactustrees. Each needle shined with a polished onyx glow. Even the gray dirt floor scintillated, a mixed substance of soot and diamond powder. A lullaby came from the influenced cacti.

Heart preserve us, Heart serve us,
Oh Heart, be with us today Oh Heart, never ever go away
Oh Heart I beg you, ever do I beg you, never go away...

A tremulous sigh came from the group, equal wonder spreading across each face. Teresa tried to get a grip for the sake of them all.

"The Children are near. We have to move quick and quiet." They approached the thatch of vibrancy from the surrounding darkness. Teresa wasn't sure if she could conjure a mantle, or whatever it was they did here. That was the good thing about Patty though, she'd always had enough power for both of them and then some. She had to wonder about the mantle-bombs. What would they do here?

As they entered the clearing, Teresa braced herself to be overcome by the Heart's influence. Depending on its potency, the power could overwhelm them for a few minutes. That was the case in their world, but in this one...she felt different. *Good.* Great, even. Rather than zap the life from them, she saw Patty stand straighter and smile unconsciously. Teresa felt she could stand without help and even beyond that, she could run for days without tiring. The energetic euphoria would most likely go away soon, just like the fatigue they experienced in their world, but Teresa would enjoy it while it lasted.

"Byron?" asked Patty.

Teresa looked over and saw that Byron's entire body took on the vividness of the area. Godlike, he stood there, every contour of his skin heated with blinding perfection.

"That man is a part of the power that springs between worlds," said a charred voice from above, "and Kauph is reflecting that power."

No sooner had they looked up when a figure dropped from the arm of a cactus above. The man's boots hit the ground but his landing was impressively soft. Dark blue bandages mummified him. Only a slit for the eyes and mouth opened through the wrappings. Teresa felt Patty reach out with her mind. A cactus began to shudder from behind her. Extending one bandaged hand, the mummy said, "I am Widdah, the Heart Bearer."

"Then where's the Heart?" Teresa asked.

"Above us," Patty told her, not taking her eyes off the mummy. Teresa glanced up. Around the cactus's arm, a burlap mat hung, and sitting on that mat was a skinny teenager dressed in a thin gray robe.

Widdah eased a bit. "We camped here because the scent of cactus blossoms confuse the Children. Just west of here I have a transport that can survive the journey through Cauldron Valley. I can drive you back to the gateway."

"That wasn't a part of our instructions," said Patty. "You can drive then. As long as the boy is safe." Kauph Courre grunted from above.

"They won't hurt you," said Widdah. "Come down from there, Kauph."

Immediately the boy slipped off the side of the mat and landed awkwardly, almost falling on Byron. With care, Byron helped the boy gain his balance and Kauph bowed his head, backed away a couple steps and said nothing. Byron's skin had lost some of its luster. They were beginning to adjust to the Heart's influence.

"What do you think?" Patty asked Teresa. "About this transport?"

Teresa found that she was in no place to make decisions. The intense color had already faded from the prickly forest and the boundless energy she'd had moments ago had fled. Still, she felt better than before. "I don't know."

Snarling sounds in the distance caused them to jerk around. The boy named Kauph walked over and stood between her and Patty.

"He's been waiting for you for a long while now," Widdah said, eyes glinting through the bandages. "I will do everything

I can to help you get him to the other world."

Kauph leaned against Teresa's arm. She was surprised her appearance didn't scare him, but then he had a sinister looking mummy as a guardian.

Patty turned back to Widdah. "We will take the transport, and you will show us how to drive it."

The mummy nodded.

"Now," said Patty, eyes closing to slits as she searched the Priestess's mind, "where are the Children now?"

Suddenly Widdah whipped around, unsheathing an indigo machete from his back, and brought down the blade, slicing a pumpkin body in half.

"Go!" he shouted.

The gateway split open the atmosphere just to the right of them, bending all the cacti into a dark orange infinity. A lethal, roaring machine of growls and snarls and smacking lips, the Children poured out. Behind them Chaplain Cloth stood in the murky shadows amid twisting vines.

"The boy!" Cloth ordered.

Teresa snatched the teenager's hand and her strength came from the deep unknown. Walls of cacti closed in from both sides. Kauph held her speed rather easily. Good, *he's a strong kid.* That would help.

The gateway pulled open just ahead. She took a sharp right and tore her shoulders on some needles. Patty and the others made the turn with them, but Byron must not have noticed their change of course.

He ran straight for the gateway.

Byron surged ahead, sprinting past everything. Past the women and boy. Past the cacti. Past this world. Past life. Past pain. Thrashing pumpkins fell from the tops of the cacti above and obscured his sight of the gateway in a wave of gnashing black fangs and disturbing orange faces. Green claws clicked together in anticipation of his flesh. Would they pull him toward the gateway? Or would they pull him apart?

Byron put his arms out and let the wave come.

The world snapped sideways and he felt his shoulder pop

out and then pop back in the socket. His head struck the dirt and a scattering of black butterflies went over his vision. When they cleared, he saw Alisyn yell at him, though he couldn't hear her words. At first. Then they came screaming into his head. "Get up, Ronald! Get up!"

He couldn't remember where he was, but he did as she said. Something clawed through his suit coat and ripped the skin of his lower back. He let out a yelp and ran faster. The enveloping cacti broke away to a pit of pebbles and softer sand. A vehicle sat there, looking somewhat like an oversized black hearse with tank treads. In the cabin he could see Patty situating Teresa and some boy—

The boy, the Heart, the gateway...

Byron almost stopped running. He'd been knocked silly, but he was fleeing from what he'd come here for.

Patty left the vehicle and rushed down the hill. "Priestess, get into the driver's seat," she ordered.

Alisyn gave her a suspicious glance and then slid away from them.

"You okay?" Patty asked him. "Sure."

A chorus of shrieks flung into the air. Most of the cacti suddenly collapsed. Green arms wiggled between the cracks and buried glowing eyes stared out murderously. Something had brought all of the cacti crashing down on the Children.

"You?" Byron inquired of Patty.

"Me," she replied and tugged on his shirt to get going.

As soon as they stepped into the cabin of the tank, Teresa shut the rail door and latched it shut. Through the blast window Byron could see the gateway forming again in the distance. He fell into his seat and rubbed his head.

Alisyn glanced back from the driver's seat. She looked apprehensive and amused at the same time. "You're no' much for gratitude."

"Nicely done," he replied.

In what would have been the copilot's area, the mummy bent over a metal tray on the dash that streamed with wires running to multiple holes in the ceiling. A struggling animal, a bat of some kind, fought there, tied down and clamped with wires. Widdah brought out one wire from under the dash. A sharp crystal key was attached to the end. Byron didn't get to ask him what it was for—the mummy drove the key into the bat's stomach. The key glowed orange. He twisted it, the flesh grotesquely turning with the key, and the orange deepened to black. The hearse tank rumbled like twenty diesel engines roaring to life for the very first time.

"Head north," said Widdah without looking at Alisyn. Teresa piped up, "No, we were headed back east."

Something sparkled in the mummy's masked eyes. "Of course, but north is safer right now. We are in a tank for a reason. This world isn't like yours."

"East."

"Indulge me just a moment. Climb this hill," he instructed Alisyn. "I want to show you something, Nomads. It is the reason why the gateway hasn't opened here."

Alisyn pressed a quivering pedal underneath the deck and tentatively put her mangled hand on the steering wheel. The hearse scaled the sand pit easily. Through the cockpit shield they could see a vast expanse leading to another grassy area beset with weeds. The Children congregated there around the gateway, which floated in the middle of space. Some of the Children had grown in size...in fact, one of the pumpkin creatures could easily be compared to a small house.

"A Void." Patty nodded, as though understanding. "We don't seem to be encountering any this year that benefit *us*."

Widdah tightened one of the bandages around his forearm. "Beyond that Void you will also find territories owned by the Church of Morning. I don't believe we should press our good fortune. There are worse things than the Church in these lands. Let us go north a few trollguts and perhaps we can get back through Blakandor Forest."

"Let's get some distance and then we'll have a look over the map, and *we* will decide," Teresa said.

Kauph scooted closer to her. The kid looked scared, although more calm now inside the tank. Patty sidled protectively closer to him also. The love the two Nomads felt for him had been instant, just as they'd described it before. Byron also felt a strange connection to the kid, as though they were relatives or something. It was especially weird because Kauph hadn't said anything yet, but still, Byron had a sense of his character, maybe even the sad life he'd lived up until now, only to become the most important sacrifice in the universe.

Maybe he related to that kind of uncertainty.

Byron was about to ask Kauph something, just to break the ice a little, when his body lit with fire and his muscles clenched into knots of barbwire. He turned away from everybody and bit his fist. The taste of his blood was bittersweet. He considered tasting this for years to come, feeling these attacks bombard him again and again, and he knew he'd always think back to that moment with the Voyeur, to what he'd given away to save himself and his friends.

Goddamn it...

How the hell was he going to get into that gateway?

THIRTY

It was happening again. Any authority Camden might have possessed had dwindled to nothing. How could he continue to sink lower? He had promised he'd stop asking himself what he was doing here, in this museum, in this paper cluttered office, with his family of hostages, when they could have put a field agent in here.

Where the hell was Jeffrey? The minutes were days. Had he confirmed the Pillar of Ginsau, or not? Camden should have been the one to study the runes. Scholar he wasn't, but he could tell the script of the Archbishops of old. He owned some of the original tomes they wrote in soot, oil and blood.

Used to have, anyway.

He remembered again how everything was crushed, buried, forgotten.

"What're ye gonnae do?" the watchman asked. "Please, please speak."

Camden ignored the man's constant braying and turned his eyes to the child in the karate uniform. She hugged onto her mother.

"It's a little early in the morning for martial arts, i'n'it?" he asked.

The girl's eyes flicked to her father.

"She sleeps in her uniform some nights…when tournaments go late," he said carefully.

"A tournament?" Camden lifted the end of her belt. "Red belt—I reckon that's high up there. Isn't black next?"

The girl buried her eyes into her mother's hip.

Camden went to the door and cracked it open. Two gray

suited agents walked past a tapestry hanging in space beyond the guard railing. They seemed to be joking with each other and not taking any of this seriously. Camden wondered what Jeffrey had told them about this particular mission.

The door to the inner showcase room opened and the white haired old fuck strode out with a smug look on his over-tanned face. Camden opened the door as he approached.

"I've been seeing that same old piece of marble in my dreams...forever now. It took me a while to convince myself I wasn't dreaming."

"I'd like to see."

"Wait a moment and listen."

"I wantae see it," insisted Camden. "I'm risking much if I take Cloth the wrong artifact. He isn't exactly pleased wi' me right now."

"Wait a moment *and listen*." Jeffrey leveled his eyes. "I phoned my driver. The rig took a shit just outside the industrial park. They're bringing another. It shouldn't be long—it better not be—in the mean time we'll drive the forklifts in the back through the service gate and get the column on the forks. We'll need all the help we can get." Jeffrey glanced at the huddling family. "You'll help us, right?"

The watchman and his wife nodded fiercely.

Jeffrey rubbed his chin and shook his head. "Naah, scratch that. We'll all be occupied and one of you will run. We can't deal with that shit right now. In fact...I'm not so sure I like the idea of you being here. No, that wasn't exactly how I dreamed it. Let's think about this some."

He strolled off toward the tapestry and three agents joined them. They looked bored. Impulsively, Camden crept outside the room and the family, still one big beast of burden closely tailed him. "We can tie them up and leave them in the office."

Phil looked over his shoulder. "That wasn't what I meant. In my dream, they were lying on the floor, dead as dirt. Right over there by the front door. We can't mess this up, Archbishop."

The family gripped tightly to one another and created a sudden cacophony of frightened protests and sounds of alarm. Camden felt sick down to the lowest pit in his gut. He took hold of a support beam holding up a tapestry and braced himself to fight his instant queasiness. "They aren't a problem, Phil. Let's concentrate on the Column."

Three of the agents began to walk off, relieved.

"Stay right here, if you still want your money," Jeffrey ordered. The men exchanged glances and appraised the family with distress. Jeffrey stepped back from them and rapped his fingers on his arm in the sling. "I guess my brain is imbalanced, right? I'm the sick asshole in the room. Jesus, Camden, you never fail to disappoint. You can't rise to these occasions when it's called for."

"This makes no sense. You're doing this to protect *your family*, aren't you?"

Jeffrey pointed at the huddled gathering with a trace of disgust curling his lip. "Last time I checked, they don't look a goddamned thing like my family. Shit, I knew you'd make this weird instead of taking care of business. Don't they teach priorities to Scots?"

Camden opened his mouth and got no words out.

The little girl in the karate uniform snapped her leg out and kicked Jeffrey in his bad arm. The old man hollered in surprise and swiftly pulled his firearm. "Ah fuck this."

Camden did it without thinking. Marrow blossoms, thousands inside his lungs, opened like a universe of brand new stars, filled and drew power, and in his hand the tapestry's aluminum support beam splintered and vanished. The tapestry swung sideways and collapsed on Jeffrey and the other agents.

"Run, eejits!" Camden screamed at the family.

The three flew for the front entrance, feet thundering on the floor. Jeffrey's voice was behind them, shouting amid the whispering movement of the tapestry being thrashed to and fro. Jeffrey got around it, took aim and fired. The watchman's head bucked and he fell to the ground in a cyclone of red mist. His wife went down right after him. Part of her ragged skull cap struck the low ceiling. The young girl ducked as shots peppered the wall over her head.

"Cease fire!" cried one agent.

The girl got to the door, grabbed the handle, pulled, and at once her karate uniform flowered with numerous bloody holes. She dropped to the floor on her right shoulder, blue eyes open with astonishment.

Phil Jeffrey let his empty magazine hit the floor and pulled out another. Camden ran headlong into him and sent the man sprawling. Another gun fired somewhere and the bullets caromed off of something. Camden darted past the open door to the showcase room. The hollers of Jeffrey and his agents came closer, a surging tide of madness and terror.

Camden slammed closed the doors to the showcase room and placed a palm over the divide between them to allow the blossoms to release again. He sent a displaced area of the door to the Old Domain. The metal frame twisted and locked together in an ugly mess. The door rattled at once and a fist drove down on it hard. It wouldn't budge, for now at least.

"What are you doing, Archbishop?" Jeffrey heaved with uncontrolled breaths. "Have you swallowed that pea-brain of yours? We're knocking this shit in."

"I wouldnae do that," Camden cautioned.

His mind raced. What could he do to prevent them?

The door rocked furiously again. Camden turned and in the center of the room caught sight of the twenty foot tall pillar, accented in swaths of soft blue illuminated by recessed lights.

"Knock it off," he shouted, "or I'll send the Column over to the Old Domain. Ye know I can do it."

Suddenly the door ceased. "I know you could, but *why* would you?"

Camden didn't have the answer for that at the moment. "Are you crazy? A fucking kid?" yelled an agent outside.

Another shouted hysterically.

"Focus, men! Focus!" replied Jeffrey. "Trust me, goddamn it, or we'll all die today. A couple lives for billions. Think about your kids and remember that well."

Camden could only chuckle. Dead. All of them. He couldn't keep his promise. Again.

Through the sick feeling of another failure in his gut, something new was born. He'd been wrong this whole time. It was a loneliness he'd felt for a long time but it was unfounded until now. All he'd ever wanted was to be with Alisyn, but it wasn't her he really craved. It was that old feeling she'd brought him when she brought news of her pregnancy, it was the reason he became Archbishop in the first place. To be part of something, to know himself, be certain of it.

Did he even want the worlds to merge? Did he want bullies like Archbishop Kennen and Phil Jeffrey to win?

Alisyn? No.

The answer was too simple.

He was Camden Amherst, a man, only a man, and that idea gave him butterflies. For the first time since losing his father, he was soaring over all his fears and laughing. Camden was obligated to only his desires. It was beautiful.

Massively beautiful.

Jeffrey whispered through the door, "I was hasty with the family, okay? I admit that. It was cowardice and I'm fucking sorry as shit, really. But the scene is now exactly how I dreamed it. We are standing together when Cloth comes for the Column—"

"That was another reality," said Camden. "I'm inclined on making a new one. Wonder how long it would take to send something this big to the other world?"

"No, don't! Please, listen. Believe me, you don't want to do that."

Indeed, thought Camden, sending the Pillar of Ginsau to the Old Domain would probably kill me.

"Let's just talk this over." Jeffrey sounded terrified. "We can decide what to do together. You and I, Camden."

Again, no. There wasn't a *we*. Camden was on his own now; he would go forth in life or in death to do what was right by him first.

Jeffrey growled impatiently. "Are you going to let me in?"

"No," said Camden with a smile. "Ye can go to hell."

THIRTY-ONE

Alisyn focused on the gray-dark land rolling before her. She missed Camden, longed for the privacy of her chamber below Newark Castle, and desired to once more be in the comfortable surroundings of her dead babies and her dreams. Moving on wasn't going to be easy. In times like these, when she was completely alone, her heart would call out to that better time. Funny, that while she lived through it she'd felt so miserably alone, but now looking back it was something she'd actually cherished.

Light from a low hanging orange moon cut through the cloud bank ahead. Tall structures jutted from the ground of varying size and height, but they seemed to be part of an old temple that had collapsed, while no other debris was present.

"Stop up there," the mummy instructed. "Near the ruins?"

"This is a deserted dumping ground of the Church of Morning."

"Columns," stated Teresa. The older Nomad looked pensive beyond her mask of defacement.

"Yes," Widdah said. "Vasoth Kennen spent years looking for the column that would support the Gateway forever, for he knew sacrificing the Heart of the Harvest was only the first step to merging the worlds."

Kauph Courre closed his eyes and dropped his head back on the worn leather headrest. Ronald mussed his hair and smiled. "But fuck them, right?"

The young man returned his smile, though it was closemouthed and dubious.

"Kennen has located a column he believes will work, says

some outcast Ekkians I've spoken with. And what of your Church, love?" The mummy turned his head to Alisyn. His voice had a peculiar coyness to it that she didn't care for, "Care to enlighten us on your discoveries?"

"She won't say," Middleton replied.

Alisyn pushed down the throttle one last time and came to a grinding halt near a column with blue and purple studs that reflected the moonlight in uncanny wavelengths.

"You sure she should be driving?" Teresa asked Patty. Patty glared at her partner.

"I didn't mean to shake the hive. Finding the Columns doesn't matter," said Widdah absently. He had his midnight blue machete on his lap and ran a bandaged finger over its edge. "Such things are new dogma. The Churches of the past left the Columns to Chaplain Cloth. Now it's all human power-grabbing. People want to be more significant than they really are."

"I'm getting some air," said Teresa suddenly. She grasped the latch on the door. Her twisted appearance had not softened on the eyes, only worsened. The old Nomad looked caught between leprosy and death.

"Bring the map," Middleton instructed.

Teresa lifted the tube out of her backpack and held it aloft. "I've got it, Mom."

Middleton ignored her and told Ronald, "Don't go running into any gateways. We need you to keep the Priestess from running off. I'm going to have to trust you again, I guess."

"What if I have to piss?"

Middleton regarded him for a moment with narrowed eyes. They all piled out. The Nomads, Heart of the Harvest and the mummy congregated in the back of the hearse tank, which contained the vehicle's engine rather than a coffin. Teresa spread out the map on a maintenance step in the rear and began to study it.

"We have the tank and can travel through Cauldron Valley with little issue, but I suggest this route though Blakandor Forest," said Widdah. "We'll need to leave the tank though, for it's only passable on foot."

"It's a forest," Middleton said, clearing some of her golden hair behind her ears. "Back with those cacti I had to wait for us to get in the clear before I could defend the position. I can't bring trees down with us underneath them. No, I think we should stick to the Messenger's route."

"I don't need to bring down any trees to defend us." The mummy tapped the hilt of his machete.

"No," said Middleton firmly. "What of those marshes?"

"A number of Goblin races infest those marshes. It would be trying and we would, again, need to leave the tank. Not much of a short cut."

"The Messenger knows best," said Teresa.

"Hey, you're bleeding!" Middleton pressed a thumb to a ruptured boil on Teresa's forehead.

Kauph Courre's eyes grew large with concern.

"She's alright," Middleton told him and then addressed the mummy again. "Care to spare a bandage, Widdah?"

"The Blue Quarter considers an insignificant unraveling tantamount to a mortal sin."

"We're not religious."

His submerged eyes flicked up at her. *"But I am.* So, no, unfortunately I cannot spare any of my shroud. I do have an apothecary's supply inside. I'll show you. Take what you need." Middleton gently took Kauph under the arm and guided him back inside the tank, after Widdah. Teresa put her hand to the wound and went back to studying the map.

Alisyn went around the tank and rested against its hot metal frame. She checked to see if Ronald was watching her—silly, as though she'd really venture on alone in this place with no protectors.

Only, Ronald wasn't there.

She caught sight of him at once. He was walking rapidly for a gathering of wooden columns inscribed with golden script flowing up their sides.

He did need to take a piss.

And Alisyn may have casually accepted that and turned away, had she not spotted the rolled up parchment clenched in his fist.

Byron read the note over again. The sapphire light from a series of runes within the wooden column made the paper look like the thin pelt of a sea animal. He felt cold inside, colder than he'd felt in some time. The note was definitely authentic. Same parchment he'd taken from the Messenger's house. Same hybrid printing and cursive handwriting: T-bar analysis identical, g and *y* stems sharp and angular, breaking and spacing almost anal in its consistency and ending strokes full on flourishes. This was the Messenger's handwriting. To think he'd found it tucked in one of the hearse's treads...

"Whit is that?"

Byron closed the parchment and whipped around to Alisyn. "Toilet paper. Why aren't you up with the doomsday crew?"

"The old Nomad has a head wound—"

Byron looked around her. It appeared he did care for those women. *How gentlemanly of him.*

"It'll be fine," added Alisyn. "Bleeding freely, but minor, and fortunate for us in that it will need tending. Ye have a note from the Interloper. Let me see it."

He uncoiled the letter and re-read it again along with the Priestess of Midnight.

Return to the gateway through the Azaraith passage. Avoid Blakandor Forest at all costs.

Also, you travel with an imposter. Rid yourselves of this person.

—Messenger

Alisyn pursed her lips in thought momentarily. "Ye're safe, Ronald. I won't let them know who ye really are."

Byron flinched at the name. *She really doesn't think she was lied to. She thinks it was the other way around.* Could he use that?

"I don't like seeing ye live this lie for the Middleton girl. The Voyeur made me realize something, Ronald. Ye might not be *the* father, but ye're special to me. These women will kill us both if they find out we were ever together—"

His voice fell into an Australian accent quite instinctively. "Blackmailing me won't work, love."

"Why do ye want inside the Gateway?"

Byron heard Patty in the distance. Was she calling for them? It was too difficult to make out. He waited but there was nothing. If she found them together...

"Let's head back. This isn't any of your business." He turned to leave but Alisyn grabbed his arm with her injured hand. There was still strength there.

"It doesn't have to be this way. We don't all have to wander, Ronald. We can take a path together."

"I'm on my own."

"Aye," said Alisyn, apparently feigning defeat, "well, good luck. To get into that gateway, ye'll have to go through Cloth's Children first—the way ye went about it before, ye might as well jump into an industrial meat grinder."

Byron glowered.

"There is only one creature in this world that would pose the Children a threat, and that creature is no' you."

He peered around the column and saw the group standing near the back of the hearse tank. Patty methodically wrapped a bandage around Teresa's head. The mummy and the Heart of the Harvest looked on.

"Out with it then," said Byron. "What creature?"

Alisyn's voice trembled. "The Apex Goblin has no love for creatures born from the dirt and has a legendary hatred for Cloth's Children. The distraction will help me escape, an' help ye get to the gateway wi'out being chewed to wee bits. We must get the Nomads to change routes to Blakandor Forest."

Byron felt a panic-induced headache settling in above the high frequency pain vibrating in his bone marrow, skull and sinuses. "What if the Children don't show?"

"Then we're in the same place as we are right now, but if ye let the Nomads have that letter..."

"Patty will use your All-Sight thingy and see this goblin of yours a mile off. She won't risk the Heart of the Harvest. Just forget it. Sorry, I'm not going to be conspiring with you today, no thanks. You and I…this isn't our year."

"The Apex Goblin is invisible, until it manifests." She noted his skeptical silence and added, "As the mummy said, Blakandor is actually a quicker route—wi'out knowing the danger involved, this path will make sense."

The silence was unnerving. He scratched his cheek. Damn, he needed to shave badly.

"Okay then. It was only a thought. May I ask you something before we return?"

"No," he told her.

Alisyn's expression was grave. "Were you really born on Halloween?"

"March 5th." He chuckled. "Still mates?"

She folded her arms and if she was disappointed, she didn't show it. "Ye're all I have now."

Truth was, Byron didn't know when his birthday was. He took another glimpse at the letter and shook his head. Promptly, he ripped it up. Pieces littered the ground, which rolled with the oceanic light of the nearby runes. With inward prayer to a nothing-God, Byron turned his foot sideways and kicked dirt over the fragments.

With another quick look to the hearse, Byron reached in his suit and thankfully found one of the folded parchments, along with the jar of red ink and the featherless quill.

"Good thing I was taught to never throw anything away."

He pressed the parchment against the column with his shoulder and unscrewed the cap on the ink jar. Alisyn took a quick look to see if the coast was clear to return up the hill. "So did your mother and father teach you forgery then?"

He dipped the quill in the blood red ink. "I taught myself everything I know, and the first thing was to forget all about them."

"Aye, but I wouldae loved being your parent," said Alisyn.

He said nothing. Shortly after, she slipped away. Patty and the others seemed to be finishing up. Shit, *have to do this quick on the job.*

The quill shook in his hand. Byron tried to make every line count, tried to be precise to the Messenger's script. This decision would take him on one of many possible paths. He just hoped that whichever one that was, Cloth's gateway stood at the end.

THIRTY-TWO

According to the Priestess, the Children were in a different hemisphere of the Old Domain, terrorizing a farming village and eating their fill of livestock.

The distance didn't provide any comfort for Teresa though. The gateway could show up in front of them at any minute if they happened to catch a smell of Kauph Courre on the breeze.

The tank gradually descended a sand bank, heading to the shore of a vast crimson ocean. Its bloodiness stretched to the limit of the Old Domain with strains of moonlight forging a volcanic plateau to the eyes. Teresa had read of this red sea, *Olathu*, before—from one of the books she and her partner Martin had confiscated. Fondly, she often dreamed if there was an afterlife, he'd be waiting near an ocean for her. The man had been most at peace on a beach.

This wasn't a peaceful ocean though. Black kelp washed up in the dark sand in swirls, looking like the severed heads of mermaids with raven hair. The surrounding rocks had a coarseness painful to behold, among their flame-like peaks that contrasted against the brightening sky.

"What's the deal with this kid?" asked Byron. "I haven't gotten a word out of him this entire time."

Kauph looked expectantly at the mummy. Widdah did not turn around. He was busy reading the Messenger's map. Teresa couldn't imagine why he was so interested. The route was agreed on and they were well on their way.

"The boy was born without a tongue," said the mummy.

Kauph made a whining, squeaking sound and turned his beleaguered eyes to Byron.

"I didn't know. I'm sorry, kid."

The Heart of the Harvest patted him reassuringly on the knee and leaned back to rest, seeming satisfied they knew he wasn't simply being rude.

For a while, they were all silent, listening to the humming treads of the hearse tank outside and the occasional rock it cracked or spit sideways. It made Teresa tired to listen to the repetition. She'd almost nodded off when Patty nudged her. "Do you sense that? God damn...Do you know what this place is?"

Teresa concentrated. She still felt her odd connection with the temporary gateway but she sidelined that and tapped into her ability. There was something nearby that brought overwhelming nostalgia—it made her scalp tighten, as though an old familiar hat had lowered down on her head. It took a few minutes to understand this new feeling.

They'd arrived to the origin of all the mantles they'd ever drawn out of this world and into theirs. This place near the ocean, this ugly beach—it was where the raw materials came from, where the ghost matter wasn't *ghost* at all, but real.

"The Village of the Unpaid Harvest, an extremely deadly place," said Widdah. "Stop at the gates up ahead," he instructed the Priestess, who immediately eased the engines. The mummy swiveled in his copilot chair and regarded them. "Everybody must eat an offering to pass through. The villagers believe it brings them fortune and keeps visitors from harm. It's a custom and should only take as long as we make it take."

Teresa could tell Patty had also discovered what this place was. "People live here? Why? I mean—if it's dangerous?"

"They believe they're the chosen few who will bring about the merging of worlds. Several times they've faced extinction, only to have defectors return to take on the responsibility of keeping their bloodlines going."

Teresa made out a shambling group of people ducking out of kelp covered huts. The sky brightened slightly behind the hilltops. At first the surrounding hills appeared dappled with similar boulders and slanting shadows of the coming light. After squinting a bit with her failing eyes, Teresa noted they were not boulders.

They'd come to another necropolis.

Thousands of burial sites lined the lower and upper regions of the level areas of the hills. Caves of every size filled the towering rocks above, as though mighty stone termites had feasted for millions of years. We are those termites, *Patty and I.*

When Patty once described how a mantle looked, she'd said they normally looked the color of slate. Normally.

How many of those holes are mine? Teresa asked herself. Some of those had been made by her last partner, Martin, and others by her first partner, *David. And all the Nomads before them.*

It wouldn't surprise her to learn the lion's share of the large holes Patty had made.

Widdah opened the hatch and they all quietly exited the vehicle. Teresa saw big tears wobbling in Patty's eyes. She put an arm around her and held her tight. "What's the matter?"

Patty said nothing and dropped her head down.

One side of the mountain had almost collapsed from their mantle harvesting and crude wooden supports and rocks supported some of the most egregious wounds. The destruction of this particular mountainside had a systematic look to it.

"Greet them and eat their food. We must be cautious here," Widdah warned.

Sad as it was, Teresa didn't think a group of destitute villagers would pose much danger for them, especially considering the Nomad's connection to the matter here was intense and they could take this place apart like a child's building blocks. It should be quickly done. Teresa didn't mind eating. She was starving right now, but this wasn't the time to hang out.

The group of villagers, around twelve adults, approached with more confidence than would be expected from people in such a formidable environment. Teresa noticed then, the source of that confidence. Around their waists, seven of the villagers were strapped with three gleaming dynamite sticks.

Sunlight just peering through smoky layers of clouds and affording them more visibility, Byron followed the group to a series of driftwood tables near an outcropping of rocks. He didn't understand why the Nomads had become so solemn.

Something about this place really upset them, other than the obvious hideousness of the mountainside and the deformed villagers.

Widdah spoke in a guttural language with a young man with a half-dissolved face, one arm and a serious chunk missing from his leg. He was one of those with the terrorist corset around his waist. Whatever conversation they had, it ended almost as soon as it began. Teresa inquired what they'd said. "They wondered if you were of their bloodline," he said, "and I explained that your injuries are not the same."

Teresa unconsciously touched her face, and let her hand drop almost immediately. "What else did you speak of?"

"I asked why they wear explosives. He told me that some of the badly injured have decided to pay full sacrifice rather than live in suffering. Once the fathers of the village consented to this, some have taken up the practice."

The one armed man added something, as though understanding some English. Widdah listened and nodded. He translated, "These devices will only explode if the inner belt is damaged. The villagers are not allowed to set off the explosives. The Unseen Harvester chooses. They are on the ready now, because the Day of Opening always brings more harvesting."

"Whit about others?" asked Alisyn. "They aren't worried about being harmed in an explosion?"

The one armed man turned. A ten-year-old girl with a collapsed jaw sidled up next to him affectionately. "We...all of us...sacrifices. You eat. On way then—Please, before hurt?"

They sat at the tables and waited for whatever food these destitute people might bring. Byron watched several villagers, young and old, all covered in bloodied cloths, going to and from the kelp covered huts. It was obvious: they were excited to have visitors, even in the face of their unhappiness. The words came to his mind and they twisted at Byron's tired heart. Such bravery. They were resolved to live with their pain, not try to outdo it. He put a knuckle to his eye to stop a tear from emerging. Getting soft in your old age, buddy.

A young woman came to the table with several driftwood platters on her arms. It was almost comical to Byron, because she looked so much like a waitress from some road stop diner, and yet this girl had probably never seen or heard of such a place. She was a pretty thing and made some eyes at Kauph, who promptly blushed. Plate after plate, the young girl smiled at the person receiving. The wind picked up and blew back her lengthy, rust colored hair. She was missing an ear. Kauph saw this and politely smiled.

On the other side of the table, the woman put Byron's platter down. A large ash colored moth rested there with a slim bone handled carving knife. The body was the size of a moderate lobster and each of the wings about the length and width of a sheet of writing paper. He could tell the moth had been lightly roasted from the singe marks around the edges of the powdery wings.

"Dig in," he muttered.

Widdah lowered some of his bandages around his mouth to reveal a pair of veiny, bloodshot lips. He lost no time breaking pieces off the wings and stuffing his face. The crunching made Byron's stomach quiver. He glanced over to the others. Kauph, Teresa and Patty had begun eating as well. Alisyn sliced the body of the moth apart with a look of morbid interest on her face. Why had he even entertained her madness? The pain was making him desperate.

Thoughts aside, Byron ate. The wings tasted like orange peel, perhaps slightly sweeter, surprisingly. The body, however, wasn't as pleasant. With a minor, tasteless, exoskeleton, the inner part of the moth had the texture of trail-mix soaked in soured yogurt. Occasional sharp flavors would take over and in part reminded Byron of curry, but at the same time tasted like how chlorine smelled.

Kauph, most likely having eaten any matter of dish on the road with Widdah, finished his meal first and nodded thanks as the girl collected his platter. The girl's mane of hair had crossed behind her shoulder to reveal that her other ear had gone missing also and a large scar went from its absence all the way to her jaw.

"You name?" she asked and her eyes focused hard on reading Kauph's lips.

Growing a shade redder, Kauph pointed to his mouth and shook his head.

The girl's head turned in confusion. Kauph slowly opened his mouth to reveal the nub that was his tongue. Her mouth opened partway in a fascinated grin. Actually, the girl beamed. "We match. Fate has you. Has me. Match made. No speak, no listen. You...back here...soon?"

Kauph looked sheepishly to his comrades. He shrugged.

Patty pushed the last piece of moth into her mouth and stood up. "Excuse me. I have something to do."

Teresa glanced at Byron and he took the hint. He wasn't finished with his food but hopefully he'd eaten enough to satisfy the requirement.

"Hey, wait up," he called. Tears streamed down Patty's face but she looked pissed. Very pissed.

"Stand back," she warned.

She stopped in the center of the village and closed her eyes. Byron slowed his pace and approached carefully. Out of the corner of his eye he saw something rush at him and intuitively he ducked. A boulder, large enough to kill fifty. It rolled through the air and slid into the gaping side of the mountain. Hundreds, and soon thousands, of other rocks pulled from the shoreline and ripped from the ocean in giant gurgling splashes. Dirt followed in cosmic brown ribbons gliding through the air.

Byron felt like curling into a ball for protection, yet everything seemed in a firm hand of control.

In moments, Patty had filled the craters in the hilltops with rock and earth, and then these patch-jobs superheated all at once, glowing yellow, red, molten, and then cooling as quickly as they heated, great curtains of steam lifting from their perimeters.

It took a moment for Byron to remember to breathe.

It all looked so beautiful. Maybe the most beautiful thing Byron had ever witnessed. This woman, *she had healed this sad place*...The thought of such healing, the thought of miracles, empowered every feeling he'd ever had for Patty. The Voyeur had shown Byron this was the truth, though he'd been ignoring it until now. This act just went farther to demonstrate how foolish he'd been for not telling her everything about his sickness. This was who she was and what she had to do; she healed things.

Patty's shoulders drooped as she turned from him. Not looking exhausted in the least from rebuilding an entire mountainside, she headed back to the table. Byron took her hand before she got by him completely. She moved her eyes to him but said nothing. After a moment she squeezed his hand and managed a small smile. It was a more mature smile than the one she'd given him a few years back when they first met.

The villagers approached, mouths wide and hanging, eyes bulging in incredulity.

"The Unpaid Harvest is over," Patty told them in a measured tone. "You must leave from this place at once."

Widdah translated at the same cadence. Byron noticed Teresa still sat at the table and mildly picked at the moth, not looking in Patty's direction.

Now alone, Byron stood near a hut, wondering about the gateway. The children hadn't come back yet. Maybe they wouldn't show in the forest? Maybe the Apex Goblin would hurt someone?

Two kids ran from a hut across the way. A boy with a scab riddled face, a girl with no arms.

Byron took out his fake letter. A wreath of black kelp leaned against the hut. He dropped the letter there and kicked the kelp on top of it. With that, he returned to finish his moth entrée.

Teresa decided not to address Patty's miraculous renovations of the coastline. She was through scolding the girl for being impulsive. It was a decent thing she did for the villagers, and hopefully they would listen to her and leave this area. Because despite Patty's patching everything up, if they needed a mantle, this place was the well they drew from. It always had and probably always would.

Their group had somewhat more energy, despite the unsavory meal. Widdah went up into the tank, followed by the Priestess and Byron. Kauph was led over by a very quiet Patty. The serving girl from earlier met up with him. She had a black kelp brassiere on with a skirt of matching aquatic leaves and bulbs. She gave Kauph a long kiss on the cheek.

"You eh return? This...dress...for weddings."

Without any bashfulness, Kauph leaned forward to hug her. Teresa spotted something in her hand and pointed. "Miss, what is that?"

The girl held forward a parchment, which Patty noted darkly from where she stood near the tank. "Yours?" the girl asked.

"Ours." Teresa slowly took the letter and read it.

When they got inside the hearse, Byron noted the letter in surprise. "The Messenger?" he asked suddenly.

"We were told we'd get another once we had Kauph." Byron looked dismal.

The Priestess of Midnight arched a raven eyebrow. "Whit does this one say?"

"We're going the Blakandor Forest route," Teresa said, trying to hide her frustration. "You get your wish, mummy."

"It isn't far from here," replied Widdah.

Patty checked Kauph's seatbelt and said nothing. She didn't even bother looking at the letter. Teresa thought about pressing her to acknowledge the new situation, but let it go. She sighed and ignored the spinning in her head. Right about then, Teresa felt older and more worthless than ever. It might have been better had that gateway just ripped her apart.

Byron shivered next to her. Teresa nudged him. "You okay?"

"Maybe," he answered.

THIRTY-THREE

Alisyn had noticed her breasts were tender now. Since arriving in the Old Domain they'd gradually swollen with milk. Now that they were far into

Blakandor Forest, the end of her nipples had gone damp in her bra. It was uncomfortable, but a gift nonetheless.

Blakandor Forest looked altogether different in the sunlight and having a physical presence here rather than an ethereal one. Black apples littered the ground, some trodden under the feet on large forest animals, some sun-dried and malformed like twisted charcoal faces peering up through the fires of the past. The shelter of orange leaves above caught the sunlight from Altar, the first sun. The two distant suns of Bloodeye and Joint had not shown yet in the cloud occupied sky. Alisyn hoped they might show so she and her child could behold all three suns on his birthday. Such a thing boded well for the life he would live. A trilling, clicking bird song rose up behind them. They didn't stop, but Kauph Courre, Ronald, Teresa and the Middleton woman all chose their steps more carefully. The mummy Widdah had taken the outer perimeter. Now and again he would disappear, only to return, fiercely weaving around sepia bushes and tree trunks the color of fresh lain tar. Alisyn wondered when he would alert them about the Apex Goblin. The beast's home was not a secret, not even in the Church of Midnight's collection she'd studied years ago. Widdah had made no comment though, and he had not led them away from the nest either. He might have led a sheltered life taking care of the boy, but she doubted the creature's whereabouts had eluded him. No, there was more to this. The mummy was up to something. She would keep her eye out for him.

"How much farther?" Teresa asked.

If they passed right by the nest and kept on, it would be a few miles to the field of scarecrows. Her plans would be ruined. "A little more than two," said Middleton with a huff. She helped Teresa up a natural staircase of half buried rocks and fallen branches. After a few more steps, she stopped. Kauph and Ronald turned and watched her inquisitively. "There's something big out there."

"We'll kill it if we have to. Let's go," Teresa prodded.

Alisyn could see the beast now. The other parent of her child had come out of its home under its tree. It would be upon them any minute now. Still, the gateway had not shown.

The Children were not here.

This could end horribly for them all.

"This thing is too big to kill without weapons." Patty searched desperately around them, possibly for climbable trees, of which there were definitely none.

"We don't need weapons, Patty," Teresa told her firmly. "You can draw right here. You don't have to draw from that village—"

"I'm not using our power anymore. We don't know the repercussions. We never have."

"This is no time to argue—"

"I agree," Patty snapped. She glanced around. "Where the hell is the mummy?"

In a blink, the young Nomad dropped down to a knee as enormous claws swiped overhead and half-uprooted a tree behind her.

The Apex Goblin moved its stunning muscular body with swiftness for something so large. Its silver hair fanned out as it jumped and struck the ground, causing a tremor through the forest bed. The large cobalt eyes found the other intruders at once and it howled.

Everybody, including Alisyn, cast their eyes away—unlike the enticement of the Voyeur, the sight of this beast was too much for the eyes to process.

"Get going!" cried Widdah as he fell from above. He landed on top of the beast's shoulder, machete raised high overhead.

"Go!" ordered Teresa. The others sprinted for the trees.

I must leave you to the worst my love, *thought Alisyn to her monstrous lover*. Forgive me.

Alisyn took several steps back and hid behind the fuzzy butterscotch pods of a plant that smelled like sweet blood. She pushed them away at the acrid odor and accidentally caught sight of the goblin.

She couldn't move anymore.

She saw doubles of both worlds—saw two Olathu Oceans, two Old Domains, two pairs of Nomads, two Kauph Courres, and saw two Earths, two Pacific Oceans, two Atlantics, two Scotlands, two Camdens inside two dimly lit museum rooms.

Alisyn gasped as her inner visions collided into one.

Her All-Sight vanished then, forever...the power, revoked. Through the trees ahead she saw a brilliant white fist lower with Widdah in its grip. The mummy struggled slightly but couldn't do much to prevent what happened next. The grip tightened and snakes of pink and gray flesh slithered out from behind the mummy's bandages with a flow of red like a newfound oil well. Clabbery brains unfurled from the wrappings around Widdah's head, chunks of slate colored cauliflower and pieces of bone and teeth tumbling over the Goblin's powerful fingers.

Just as the unsightly mat of gristle and blue bandages met the forest floor, Alisyn tore off into the forest as fast as her feet could take her. The missing digits in her hand pulsed painfully and her breasts felt like stinging water balloons about to rupture, but none of that mattered right now. She was well on her way to the nest when she realized the Apex Goblin hadn't followed her.

Patty pushed Kauph forward, standing between her and the pursuing monster. Kauph pitched over a rock and crashed to the ground. He recovered quickly and Patty grabbed him under the arms to pull him along. He glanced back.

"Don't look at it again!" Patty warned.

Teresa was lagging behind and Byron all but carried her up the rocky path. They both slipped and caught each other.

The beast growled lustfully as it closed the distance. Patty spared a glance. Dark red blood painted the goblin's hand and some of its leg. A few slips of blue bandage hung from the grisly mess. Widdah had not escaped. The beast reached down for something on the ground and winged it.

Head-sized rocks atomized against tree trunks around them. Dust from their explosions filled the air and their lungs.

Kauph gagged and spit as one brilliant white detonation went off inches from him.

The beast took up another handful and pulled back its arm, then suddenly shielded its face— from an eclipse— in the trees beside it— the gateway.

Cloth's children burst from the opening. The pumpkin creatures swarmed over the goblin like vicious ants. With swipes of its long arms and stomps of its powerful legs, the beast fought back, still coming forward, as though it hadn't given up on its pursuit of them.

Byron released Teresa and stopped. Patty turned to look at him in wonder. "Come on!" she called.

A confused look crossed Byron's face. He looked on the scene behind them.

"Come on you asshole!"

Something hummed through the air and Byron flinched.

Buried in the tree trunk beside him: a hand-axe with flaring black tassels.

Silver arrows flew everywhere in the forest, unseen whispers of death. Two penetrated a tree trunk near Teresa. The arrows' fletching moved and sang in tiny voices, as though each fiber was a living organism. Patty felt Teresa try to move something in the forest, but Patty already knew what would happen. They couldn't draw matter without recalling the seaside village. That was the known source now and their minds could not avoid it. And that was miles and miles away. Their power was now as useless as it was cruel.

They would have to be a human shield for Kauph.

Patty increased her pace. Lungs and head burned ferociously. Some half a mile back, she saw the Church of Morning had brought an army into the forest. Some donned orange cloaks and others in armor the color of autumn. They charged around the trees with dangerous grace.

Byron was suddenly by Patty's side, a hatchet in his hand. He put his body at the other side of Kauph and pushed Teresa on with his free hand. If he died here...losing him this way would drive Patty into a madness she'd never escape from.

He gasped for air and looked at her with poise. "We're getting through this."

Behind him, the beautiful goblin raised a pleading arm, but its forearm had become bare bone, as well as bones in the neck, and more than half of its ribs were showing. The muscles glopped down to be quickly eaten by the Children. The goblin took one more step and collapsed under the weight of its feasting adversaries.

The Apex Goblin had deposited the fetus in the large, swirling hole in a tremendous, leaning tree. Alisyn could hear a distant war going on somewhere in the forest, but the chaos was lost on her. She could only see her child, breathing under gallons of rippling amber. The True Child stirred a little and moved its slender pink hand to its mouth. A thin branch from the tree coiled inside the amber with the child and planted into its belly. Alisyn's breasts tightened and her heart pounded with the love she knew had always been there but could never manifest for a child other than this one. She reached for the amber womb in the tree with hands shaking in delight.

"He's beautiful, isn't he?" She froze at the voice.

A hand forced her around and she came face to face with the blood-soaked mummy.

"Widdah—you died."

"Not really possible, Mother," replied the mummy. "You already killed me long ago."

A long tape-like stream of blood slipped from below the mummy's exposed mouth. His shattered and hanging teeth were glossy red. "I believe you know."

"You are—Camden's son?"

"And yours, Mother. But the *Marrowlands* was the only parent I ever needed. I was shown how it happened, how Father sent me there when I was near death. He must have thought it would shatter me across this world. Yes, he thought it would finish me, but instead it made me. Forever."

Alisyn shook and instant dementia set in. Nothing was real anymore. She wanted to deny it. Had to. "But ye're too auld to be mine..."

"The Marrowlands is not in the service of time. It works different for everyone. I aged thirty years before I crossed over to this world."

"How did *ye* become the Heart Bearer—"

Widdah gave a gurgling breath of disgust. "Incidentally."

A disturbing pang of regret went through Alisyn's gut. All the surmounting joy she'd felt a moment ago had grown cold in her chest. She'd given up on this man, this son of hers. The baby in the box. *He shouldn't be here!*

By the moment, Widdah's posture corrected as the destruction to his body seemed to repair itself. "I found them in Cauldron Valley four and a half years ago. On the Day of Opening, when the Interloper had no power and little sight, I slew the mummy and took his vehicle. There was nothing left but to watch over the boy and wait, because the songs told of your coming this year, Mother.

"It was difficult to delude the boy and their small band of confidants, not to mention the Interloper. Much was sacrificed to hide myself in these wraps—they are a lifetime commitment. I've since learned the ways of the Blue Quarter and it has been beneficial. Regrettably, I had to take the boy's tongue when he discovered my identity...but it worked out well, and was as it should be. Everything ends as it should be, Mother."

"I don't understand."

"Yes you do." The bandages around the bloody mouth lifted in a distorted smile. "I'm your waiting baby. I've always waited for this moment, just like you have."

Warm tears spilled over Alisyn's face as she considered this long-sought moment. "I tried to preserve ye. It was Camden's fault whit happened."

A blood-flecked wheeze came from the bandages. "I adore your madness, Mother. Don't apologize for the most beautiful part of you. Come, take my brother now. I would like to witness his birth."

When Alisyn didn't move, Widdah stepped forward and his voice took a savage tone, breath like blood wine, "Do it now, Mother. This world is not a safe place for dallying."

She turned to the tree's womb. Carefully, she pushed her fingers through the thick honey amber. Even with Widdah watching her, she cried out in delight as her hands wrapped around the baby. He thrashed around as she pulled him toward her. When the baby came through the barrier, his cries filled the forest. He coughed out the amber and briefly opened his glimmering tangerine eyes to see his mother.

Widdah's machete came out and Alisyn's body went limp.

What did he intend?

The blade severed the thin umbilical branch from the baby's belly. Alisyn wept now. She couldn't help it. This was all too tremendous. "I cried like this, for ye too, you know," she told the mummy. Her voice quivered and sounded unconvincing.

"I'm certain you did," he answered dryly. He unraveled some of his bandages from his left arm, exposing cracked bones and leathery black veins beneath. With the machete he sliced through the end of the bandages. He put a finger on the bandages and whispered something to them. Alisyn didn't hear all of what he said, just the last part, *"And this I do release."*

He handed the bandages to Alisyn. "For now, to keep him warm."

The baby continued to wail, as she wrapped him in the blood stained blue bandages. "Thank you," she said.

"You are welcome, Mother." Widdah's dark eyes roamed the forest. "It begins today. Let us go now together."

Alisyn could feel the baby rooting and chewing at her with splintered teeth. She would have to feed him now. "Where will we go?"

"The Marrowlands is a place with more brutal love and cruel beauty than any of the two worlds together. I'd like to spend time there with you and my new Lord brother, before he comes back to rule. I can show you, Mother, what the universe will soon become. I need you to bear witness to my upbringing, for your sake and the Lord of Masks. The Marrowlands is the land of birth and of pain and of boundless knowledge and dreams."

Widdah laughed and a few saturated bandages fluttered over his red mouth.

"No," said Alisyn. "I wouldn't take the bairn to such a place."

The mummy lifted the machete and pointed it at her, at the baby. "Perhaps this isn't the cycle it occurs then. Will you have me wait for the next True Child?"

She shook her head quickly.

"Do not worry. I have enough bravery for the both of us. Oh Mother, you will scream and laugh, you will wail and feel joy so loud when you discover where we fit into the scheme of everything. You'll want to die for all the pleasure you feel. Let us begin that journey."

With a chill passing deep through her soul, Alisyn started off through Blakandor Forest, the first steps of her new life, following one son and holding the other.

The All-Sight ability had left Cloth's mind, which meant the Priestess of Midnight had either died or had the power taken from her. He supposed it was just as well. This was turning out to be a miserable holiday.

Having finished with their meal, Chaplain Cloth watched as the formation of his Children scrambled around and headed in the opposite direction of the Heart of the Harvest.

"Wait!" he screamed. "Where are you going? He's *that way*! The Heart is over there! Stop! You ignorant fiends! *Why?*"

He knew his pleas would go unheard. The Children followed instinct and with all the new smells the Church of Morning army had introduced into the forest, they had lost the scent of the young man who would feed them what they truly yearned for.

Cloth shook his head and sat down on a large vine in the wretched gateway.

THIRTY-FOUR

Patty tried to tap into the cold place in her mind again. Every time she did though, she saw those pitiful villagers and the lives she'd created for them. And the Messenger had allowed them to do this. It would be impossible to not see those deformed children in her mind before Patty went to sleep at night. It would be impossible to ever use her ability again without abject terror.

And it would be impossible to protect the Heart of the Harvest every year without using mantles...

Having lost the Priestess, Patty had also lost touch with seeing the two worlds as well, but the loss made her feel content somehow. She didn't want the burden that came with such things. It was nice to be rid of it.

Byron helped Teresa over a fallen tree that Patty and Kauph had avoided altogether by taking higher ground. Once they left the deep forest, the Church of Morning split into two divisions to flank them. It was silent now but they would need to run like hell through the field to get to the gateway. Problem was they'd already been running like hell for a mile and half. Teresa had collapsed and Byron looked ravaged.

Blakandor Forest thinned. Patty saw the field of immense scarecrows a quarter mile off, beyond bare rolling hills occasionally dappled with a black sapling with miniature orange leaves. "We're almost there," she told Kauph.

The young man nodded to Teresa and Byron. "They'll be okay."

Something whistled on the air and Kauph suddenly fell to his knees. His hand touched a thread of blood spilling from above his temple. More rocks started flying past. A barrage struck Patty in the back as she helped Kauph to his feet. The Heart of the Harvest staggered, his eyes rolled back.

"No!" Patty yelled. She pulled his arm over her neck and plowed on.

"Help her, Byron," Teresa said.

Byron let go of Teresa and pulled Kauph's other arm over his shoulder. Teresa stumbled behind them, trying to keep up. The temporary gateway had done the greatest damage to her gait and it hadn't improved.

The thundering of hooves approached from the west. Battle cries of the hooded men and women came from the east. They were, as Patty had feared, wedged off. No other route presented a way out except the gateway, and that was still off a ways.

Stones and hatchets rained over them. Patty tapped that forbidden place in her mind again. She'd told the villagers to leave and she wouldn't be drawing from the beach, but how did she know? Nobody could tell her what disturbing matter in this world would do to the other world? Was she killing innocent people back home? What?

There wasn't enough time to think about it—the power just couldn't be used anymore. In her mind, she could hear Teresa lecturing her: the Heart of the Harvest is always more valuable than an ordinary life, even ours. Losing the Heart could lead to losing the world, *the universe.*

Byron quickened his pace. Patty's whole body burned but she did the same. The sound of the horses and armor drew near, the snorting of steam engines and the clacking of enormous warring insects.

Teresa went face down in the dirt. Patty kept forward. Her partner would eat her alive for attempting to go back with the Heart at risk. She, the Heart and Byron continued to the shimmering spot in the ground where they would return home.

The skyscraper-tall scarecrows watched them in silence. "Shit, look," Byron rasped.

Another Church of Morning cavalry appeared right over the ridge before them. Giant dual bladed axes glinted in the shafts of sunlight through the clouds. They stopped, gasping for air, out of options. Teresa seemed to have gained her feet again but made no move.

"You're going to have to do it, Patty," Byron whispered. "I don't think Teresa's got it in her."

A large stone struck Byron's hip and knocked him to his knees.

Patty blinked through the madness before her. The row of horses came down the fiercely steep grade, warriors shouting wicked things in a cacophonic charge. One of the riders shouted a command to halt but the horse's momentum had already taken. The mounted warriors passed over something black and circular in the ashen grass. Two wooden rods sprung from the ground. Purple points of light charged on their tops and a brief arc of electricity went between them.

A heart-stopping hiss came from the innards of the nearest scarecrow. Purple eyes fired to light under the enormous straw hat. Its arms drew off the cross beam and the scarecrow pulled out a scythe with a blade that had to be over forty feet long.

Patty didn't wait for a show and neither did Byron, but as they reached the gateway, Teresa just behind them, it was impossible not to see the blade's path. The large weapon sent a flurry of tall grass up into the air and then beheaded an entire row of Church riders with one swing. Dozens of helmeted heads were sent out in all directions on lassos of blood. The horses reared and collided in sudden chaos.

Kauph moaned. He'd come to, just as the mass decapitation occurred. Byron let go of him and Patty pulled him into the sparkling grass. They fell through the gateway, in an upside down, sideways, twisting moment, she heard Byron and Teresa passing through the gateways as well, only seconds behind them.

They made it.

In the fading light of the afternoon, Teresa checked Kauph Courre for injuries. The Heart of the Harvest, save for the nick on his upper brow and possibly a terrible headache, was well. Teresa wished she could say the same for herself. Any beauty she'd managed to take with her to sixty had been viciously replaced with a contortion of skin and crooked bones. The mantle her partner Martin had put inside her had not returned and beyond that, she still felt oddly fixed to the hole in the ground, like from its dark depths an invisible rope had been wrapped around her soul. As Byron went about hotwiring a car in the Glasgow Necropolis parking lot, she wondered if this connection to the temporary gateway would always be there, even after Halloween.

As they rushed him around, Kauph Courre marveled at his new surroundings. Time had moved differently in the Old Domain and Halloween night was already fast approaching here in Scotland. In some fashion, being closer to November 1st was a gift, but in another way it gave them less time to settle into a Void for the rest of the night. Facing the Children en route was never a welcomed scenario.

Byron ducked out of the car. "I need a screwdriver from my car. It'll turn the ignition."

He opened his rental car, which Patty had banged up pretty good on her outing to the Messenger's house. Teresa watched as Byron frantically emptied his suit pockets into the center console. The man was sick as hell and still acting like a jumpy business man with too much filling his agenda. She wished he'd just rest himself for a moment.

"We have to look up directions to the Voids. Do you have a map?"

Byron coughed and put his arm to his mouth, carefully checked it. "Got a GPS unit."

"That'll do."

He slid out of the car with the device and the screwdriver. Teresa noted his ashen face. His eyes were monstrously crimson and blood had crusted in his nostrils and ears. Somewhere along the way he must have been hurt but wasn't saying anything. She related to that, and in her desire to be left alone, she gave him the same consideration.

Nervously tapping his foot, he waited for the GPS to boot up. Immediately a pinging sound came from its speaker.

"The hell?" He checked it for a moment. "How is that possible...?"

He bent back into his car again. After a moment's searching, he pulled forth a hair-clip of some kind, looked to be made of turtle shell or something.

Byron held it up for Patty to see. "You brought this back?" She shrugged. "Your barrette? I found it outside the Messenger's house. I never got a chance to ask about it. What's the deal?"

He closed his eyes a moment and sighed. "Goddamn... They've registered this trace on the network now. They're probably already on their way. See this?" He pointed to other green dots that had floating banners with letters and numbers denoting code names, apparently. "These other agents are nearby, not far from here and they have people monitoring this."

With a grimace, Byron searched the air in thought. Patty went to say something and he held up a hand. Again he went back into his car and this time pulled forth a revolver. "There's only the one." He handed it to Teresa. Its weight felt wonderful in her hand.

"If we leave my car behind, they'll have to search it, and the Necropolis, but they have other scouts checking routes out of here. We need to go right now." Looking at the turtle shell in his hand, Byron rethought this, "No, no, wait, I can head out on foot and lose the tracker on a bus or something. That'll really goose them."

"Just leave it here." Patty turned for the car. "We're staying together."

Byron shook his head. "No, Pat, I can help more if I take the OAP out of the picture. We only have one gun for all of us."

Teresa had not experienced anything good from splitting up in the past, but the point that Byron wasn't a Nomad still stood. It made this plan sensible.

"We can handle it," Patty pressed him.

"He's right," said Teresa. "If you're not willing to build mantles, we can't take chances. The agents spot him, they'll be on us too. This can't happen now. We need to protect Kauph from the Children by getting to a Void."

She studied the GPS. Two different Voids were in proximity to them. One in a place called Temple that had few routes in and out, and one in another place called Bishopbriggs, which was slightly closer and would give them time to dig in.

"So these are Voids that'll keep you safe?" Byron looked at Kauph, who touched the concrete curb with astonishing interest. "Keep *him* safe?"

"According to the Messenger's information." She looked at Patty. "Bishopbriggs is closest."

Patty nodded. "I was thinking of Bishopbriggs as well."

"Can we take this GPS?" Teresa asked.

Byron put his hand on her hunched shoulder. "You'd take it even if I said no."

Teresa leaned forward, put a gray arm around his neck. She was surprised when he gave her a big hug in return. "Take care of yourself, Byron."

"You too, Ms. Celeste."

He stuck his hands in his pockets for a moment, then awkwardly went to Kauph. He put out his hand. Teresa half expected the gesture to provoke confusion, but it seemed the worlds shared this courtesy. The Heart shook his hand and smiled a gummy smile. Byron mussed the young man's untidy brown hair. "Maybe some day you'll find a girl like that one in the village. You never know, kid. This is a wonderful world... you're gonna love it."

Patty stood there, looking left to right. An expression of self-doubt crossed her face but sadness ate through the façade.

Byron went and embraced her. She pulled away from him with an impatient sigh. "So when the hell do I see you again?"

"When I can be fair to you," he replied. "When's that?"

He laughed sadly. "There's no saving me. You know that by now, right?"

"That doesn't change that I love you. I wish it did." He touched her face. "I know how you feel."

Without another word, Byron took off running for a nearby alleyway. It wasn't long before he was out of sight.

"We need to get to Bishopbriggs." Teresa rubbed her slackened face. "This is one Halloween that can't end soon enough for me."

Patty guided Kauph to the car. Teresa got in and inserted the screwdriver into the hole where the ignition used to be. She turned it and reached to put it in reverse. A horn blared on and off and the dash lights flashed.

"Shit, security alarm."

Kauph glanced around, terrified and Patty reassured him. Teresa withdrew the screwdriver but the alarm continued to sound. "Great job, Byron."

Patty popped open her door and let Kauph out. "Gotta take the rental car. I hope it holds up after its last trip."

"And I hope the agents don't make us in this car."

"Byron will take care of them," Patty replied simply. "We can trust that much from him."

Byron wasn't going to make it to a bus station.

The car he found down the street had one thing going for it. Keys hung in the ignition. It was a small car, probably the smallest he'd ever driven, definitely the smallest he'd ever stolen, and that list was long. He dropped inside and inhaled the ghost of a thousand cigarettes plaguing the car's interior. That would have been nice right now. Take a drag, sit back. What he really wanted was strawberry shortcake. Yeah, get the dusty moth taste out of his mouth.

Did they have strawberry shortcake in Scotland?

It was just as well. He supposed there wasn't time for any last meals.

His thoughts led back to Patty. What if he'd told her everything? Would that have changed anything? Would she have tried to sort his problem out? How could she? Taking care of him wasn't her job, and Byron hardly had patience left to spend another minute making himself right with this affliction, especially now that he no longer had the photo of Cloth to get him through the roughest spots.

Buildings flew past. A couple blips on his GPS chimed. There were agents in the vicinity. Byron found a broad alley with graffiti painting its length and thought about how to give them the slip.

Then light broke over his mind. His old comrades weren't the ones he needed to give the slip.

Byron Telamon had to give Byron Telamon the slip.

That was the only way. It was cowardly, cold, and not how he wanted it to end up, but this thing inside him wasn't going to change; he wasn't going to get close to that gateway without dying anyway. All his hope had been foolish. The whole idea...

Foolish. Sad.

Wasted optimism.

Byron turned down the alley and stared into the brick side of a building that bisected its path, less than a mile away. He took off his seat belt and inhaled a deep breath. The wheels screeched and he opened the little car up as much as it could go. Despite his initial criticism of the car, it sped down the alley frighteningly fast. That brick wall came closer. He imagined what it would be like slamming headfirst into it. Could the pain of a broken spine be any worse than all he'd gone through? What if it didn't kill him? What if he was an invalid that continued to suffer and had no possibility of ending it on his own?

He stomped the gas harder and started laughing. The brick building loomed before him and then—

A car cut through a cross-alley.

Byron stomped the brake down with both feet, one pressing on top of the other in a mad effort to slow. The end of his little car fishtailed and odorous smoke billowed out of the brakes and filled the alley. The front end scraped a wall and sparks flew out over the hood.

His car was still now. He had to blink a few seconds to get any kind of focus from his eyes. A tinted window slid down from the other car. Denis's red face came out like a disembodied head. "Byron, man! Holy shit! You were going to run into me."

Scrubbing at his sweaty brow, Byron tried to catch his breath. "Not until you got in the way."

"What?"

Byron opened the door and staggered outside. The air was bracing and chilled his stomach as though his guts were exposed to the elements.

"I thought you were dead! Jeffrey is after you and your friends." His partner caught a better look at him. "Christ, you might as well be dead. What the hell happened? You look like warmed over shit."

Byron stood there dumbly and stared in the side mirror. His nose ran with blood, as did the corners of his boiling red eyes. The face that stared back was solid white like a statue's. Dark spots floated in his vision. This was it. He would pass out, maybe go into a coma and then die.

"Come on, man. Get in. I'll take us somewhere far from them." Denis moved his head, indicating for Byron to jump in. "I don't think so. Not this time, buddy. Thanks. I'm sorry I was a lousy partner."

Byron took a step and suddenly someone wrenched his arm behind his back. Denis sprung from the car with cell phone in hand. The other agent cuffed Byron's other hand behind his back. Byron tried to slam his head into the buffoon, but this agent, a newer guy with a stringy goatee, sidestepped and clucked his tongue. "Easy, By," he crooned.

After a moment Denis said into his phone, "Jeffrey, yep, signal was correct. We found Agent Telamon."

THIRTY-FIVE

Bre knew that the horses wouldn't survive much longer. He'd pushed them harder than they could take and if he carried on the same way, Danur and Cortis would be another one of his casualties on this bloody escape. They'd taken him to a place of absolute beauty, and according to the wagon's wheel counter, some 160 trollguts from the palace. Bre'd never seen an unraveled troll intestine and had no frame of reference, but they must have been long, for he felt a universe away now.

The opening in the forest led to a black, rocky ascent dappled in orange lichen. A pale waterfall droned around the craggy bend and a brook curled protectively around his little camp. Danur and Cortis sipped from the brook and ate the high, starchy grasses that sprung between the boulders. They shared the area with an inundation of goat-donkeys.

Bre couldn't think about sitting in that wagon right now. Stretching out on this rock felt more comfortable. He would sleep for a bit, but he had to keep moving. Soon Kennen wouldn't have the Hunt to occupy his time. That would mean settling unfinished business with his slave.

Bre slipped into a gentle slumber. An hour later a goatdonkey woke him as it tried to nip at his tunic. Bre pushed it away and went back to sleep. He couldn't say how long the next stretch was, but when he awoke he felt colder and wondered if that might be because of the great hole that had appeared in the meadow. Was this death come for him?

Hundreds of pumpkins with terrible clasping fangs flooded the area. They were sniffing the ground and the air, some were singing, a few were tearing each other apart. They came near

Bre, sniffing him, sniffing him, sniffing him, salivating insanely. But they retreated, unappeased, and continued to search the forest.

The gateway had opened several feet away. He'd know that empty black hole anywhere, having lived so close to it for the last year. The brook carelessly bent inside the gateway, several tree trunks pulled within its gravity like stretched brown silk, and in the void's center an orange eye glowed and a black eye deepened. Although Bre had never spoken with Chaplain Cloth, he had been present several times during his conversations with the Archbishop. That he'd seen Cloth before, didn't make this time any easier.

"You escaped the palace. What was it that scrubbed the yellow from your back?"

Bre moved away. "How did you find me?"

"My Children caught a whiff of you somewhere in the forest. I imagine…because you are the brother to Kauph Courre? Aren't you?"

"He's no brother to me."

"Oh I'm not without my brain today, even though I am a bit trapped at the moment. You've long been on my potential list, Bre, and while the power inside you has fermented, it always needed a catalyst. Ah, transmungi squash!" Cloth said happily.

Bre considered the small convex shape of light behind Cloth. That was the other world. A better world.

"You're free to come inside and try your luck. It might be easier than you think."

"You're trying to lure me," said Bre.

"The truth is, your brother died a very long time ago. There is no Heart of the Harvest this year."

"I don't believe you."

"Fine by me." Cloth's silver white smile faded back into the emptiness. "But I suppose I should level with you about something else."

"No, thank you. Goodbye."

"Don't be stubborn. I've watched you at Kennen's side. You aren't like him—"

Bre found a spot through the trees and thought about

running for it. Then he noticed a swarm of Children pillaging the forest beyond it.

"Doing my utmost to not sound Faustian here, it makes no sense to remain a mortal when you can easily have unlimited power. I just need a way out. That's the only price you pay and it costs nothing save for a small series of steps in this direction." Chaplain Cloth studied him a moment. "But if that doesn't seem to make sense to you, Bre, then hear this, for I deteriorate with all this talk and you may soon lose this opportunity..."

"What?" Bre snapped.

"You've earned this, boy. You've paid more than your fair share of dues. This will be your only chance for a new life. Once I'm gone, your life resumes as it did before."

"Is my brother really dead?"

Cloth's eyes narrowed. "I like to play ahead in this game, Bre. You want to know the truth, come with me. I see the truth in all things."

"All that you say is too good to be true. That means I can't trust you."

With a sigh of resignation, Cloth said, "So you've made up your mind?"

Bre walked back to his camp, careful not to fully keep his back to the gateway. Everything was in stasis. Everything was silent. The calmness worked on him. The enormous silence left behind pushed on his spirit. The spicer witch was dead. Kennen would seek his revenge...

Bre could fight for that not to happen. He was the One Who Might Have Saved the World. All that talk of residual power from the fermentation inside him—it had all been another unfulfilled promise—it made him facile and submissive—it was there to lead him on, as though something special could be salvaged from a common slave. But his life was an empty pit already, and at least Cloth's pit promised something, even if it ended badly.

It wasn't death, and it wasn't serving the Archbishop of Morning.

But did that make it the right decision? Did fate really love him?

As Bre returned to the gateway, Cloth's pale face slid into the muted light of the forest. "You've done what's best for all of us," he said.

Bre couldn't tell how much time had passed, but he found himself climbing up the rocks and working sideways along the ridge, just shy of reaching the waterfall. From dreams he remembered this view, looking down at the brook, seeing the horses grazing, the lazy goat-donkeys perched on outcroppings, and the gateway—that break in the world that sat inside the landscape like the teardrop of a demon god.

Try to get us closer to it, *Cloth told him.*

The voice in his head even felt familiar. Had Bre heard this in his dream as well?

Bre sighted a long stretch of grimy brown rocks that resembled a natural buttress to the surrounding formations. There, said Cloth. *And hurry. Your body must be broken before you are useful to me.*

Using his hands more than his feet to move his body, Bre went up to the buttress. The waterfall's sound rang like an old lullaby. He remembered it too, just as he remembered every ant on every rock and every blade of grass or golden thistle that worked through the rocks. Edging out to the end of the buttress, peering over the side and staring at the soft blanket of grass far below, it all rang of déjà vu. As did what Cloth said next.

There is something special about you, Bre Courre, *said Cloth.*

I want to use that.

Bre stepped to the very limit of gravity's sanctuary and a footfall from its execution.

I haven't figured out what to do with your mind yet. At this point I let go the tangible spirit, absorb it into my consciousness, but I feel...grateful you've come to me.

Shivering at the vertigo below, Bre closed his eyes. "You owe me nothing. I've given you freedom. You should give me the same."

You must ready your body for me.

Bre jumped from the ledge.

The world spun around and the wind made little noise.

The drop was quick. Bre's body met the ground and chaos twisted throughout him. In all parts of his body, pain raged like instantaneous psychosis. He spat out blood, felt it running from his nose and ears, felt it running between his guts, felt it bubbling out his rectum.

His slighted eyes caught a hazy view of the gateway. The black rip had drifted a few boulders higher. The rock formations were flat, almost like steps, but with a body like a maze of muscles contortions and compound fractures, Bre couldn't figure out where his arms began and his legs ended.

We have to pull ourselves up to it, Bre. Hurry the Children are returning!

Despite everything Bre roared with laughter. It was shortlived as he gagged on blood. The gobbling, thrashing sounds of the Children flooding back toward the gateway just yards away contrasted with his mangled heartbeats.

Cloth/Bre compelled his right arm to move. Blood whistled out of the hole his clavicle punched through his flesh. Bre gritted his teeth but found he had few left to do so. Cloth/Bre grappled onto a ridge in the first boulder and slid his body several inches. Several pumpkin beasts clawed past them and flung their oblong forms into the blackness.

Blood loss was taking its toll, but Cloth/Bre's lungs unnaturally filled with air and hungrily fed his body. Curses streamed inside him. Cloth/Bre tried to move again but found no decent hold in the rock.

"And so I fail one last time." Bre smiled and relished death's icy approach.

Something nibbled at his ear. He looked up to the goatdonkey busy at him. "Leave me be," said Bre.

Cloth snatched the goat-donkey by the leg. He dug Bre's fingers into the matted fur and broke the skin beneath. The animal yelped and dragged him (them) forward. Cloth used every ounce of adrenaline Bre hadn't called upon. A meaningful bray came from the goat-donkey as two Children latched onto its back.

"Get away!" roared Cloth.

The goat-donkey nipped at the hand locked around its leg,

but Cloth held fast and dug deeper. They thrust forward. Bre's body bounced up the lips of the natural stairs. He hadn't noticed until now that his jaw had completely unhinged.

Chaplain Cloth let go of the miserable animal. The goatdonkey shuffled down a small rockslide, trying to fight off the pursuing Children, which seemed only vaguely interested in eating the animal.

Cloth extended the slave's only functional limb, stretched the pounding, bleeding thing as far as it could go, and dipped a finger inside the gateway.

In the next moment the gateway folded around them, caught Bre's brutalized body and stitched together its champion with shadows and light. And this time, Cloth's form developed with an insight he'd never been granted before. The fermented juice of the sacred fruit fired through his muscles like the creation of a new sun.

At once his Children caught Kauph Courre's scent from the other world. Savory, close, almost touchable. Cloth's army had regained their target.

This wouldn't be such a bad year after all.

THIRTY-SIX

Teresa drove the quiet motorway, occasionally looking in the rearview to check on Kauph. A van with children drove by. They were dressed in Halloween costumes: witches, pumpkins, ghouls, ghosts. She felt self-conscious when other cars passed and longed to wear a cap to at least shadow her new ugliness. A half smile came to Kauph's face when he saw the children. Teresa would have loved to know what his thoughts had been at that moment.

Patty took out an M67 grenade from the suitcase. After checking its safety clip and pin were secure, she leaned over the seat. "Do you know what a bomb is?"

Kauph blinked a couple times, then nodded.

"This is one, right here," said Patty. She pointed to the pin. "This won't come off easily, you have to rip it off...then see this?"

He leaned closer, slowly, eyes wide like ponds that had never seen a ripple. Teresa looked back to the road and bit her lip. "This is the safety lever. Pull this up and then you've got about four or five seconds before it explodes." Patty paused and then met Kauph's gaze. "Do you know why I'm going to give you this?"

Kauph's already light complexion went milky pale. He swallowed and gave a short nod.

"If something were to happen, if we were...gone, and the Children found you..."

Kauph looked down at his lap.

"We're not going to let it get to that point, kid. This is just in case," Teresa butted in. "Don't worry, okay?"

"You've seen how the Children eat..." added Patty. "This is better than the alternative, right?"

Kauph slid his hand over the center divider. Patty took off the safety clip and rested the grenade on his palm. "Remember, pull the pin, then lift the lever. Understand?"

He carefully placed the grenade next to him on the seat.

Patty turned around and expelled a great breath. "What are we going to do with him after this is over?"

Teresa glanced back at Kauph, whose curious gaze was now constant out the rain spotted window.

"Something we're going to have to think about. The Church is destroyed here, but that doesn't mean Cloth won't return like he always does. Maybe Kauph can learn what we do."

The yellow blip on the map that showed the turtle shell beacon returned onto the GPS screen, just to the left of the Necropolis.

"Byron's gone back."

"Or been captured," Teresa put plainly. "They might be able to track this unit. Get out the map." She reached out and held down the GPS power button.

Patty opened the center console and reached inside for the map.

Froze.

"I put it in the glove box. It's not in there. That's probably Byron's junk." Teresa spared a glance but didn't want to take her eyes long off the road.

From within, Patty drew out several sheets of folded parchment and ink jar with crusted red around its lid. Her eyes narrowed.

"What is that?"

Dumb question. She recognized that parchment. It was the same kind she'd been receiving from the Messenger for forty years now.

Patty dug in the compartment again and found a slender quill with dried red on its nib. One of the parchments had been lined in several different letters like a practice sheet.

A blob of the red ink had been dabbed at the top left. "That letter we got in the Old Domain was written in red ink, wasn't it?"

Teresa looked back and forth, from the road to Patty. "Yeah, so?"

"So it wasn't blood we saw on that letter from the Messenger, it was this stuff." Patty lifted the jar and let it fall back into the console with an exasperated breath.

"But how did Byron trace the Messenger's location?"

Patty thought for a moment, blinking, unsure. "Oh no... Teresa, pull the car over!"

Kauph Courre grunted as she brought the car into the dirt. "Don't worry, Kauph. Everything is okay," Teresa said.

"We're almost to the Void."

Holding her forehead in her hand, Patty visibly trembled with hate. "Oh shit."

"What?"

"Son of a bitch."

"*What?*"

"I don't believe," Patty whispered to herself. "What a first rate asshole I am."

"If you don't tell me right now, I'm gonna clout you again, girl."

Patty took a deep breath and shook her head. "Byron got the paper and ink from the Messenger's house, but that barrette with the beacon was left behind—it probably belonged to the Priestess. We both know how she found the location."

Teresa nodded slowly. "She can see everything..."

"In both worlds," Patty added.

"How did he figure out it was the Messenger's place?"

"The Priestess probably told him."

"And after he saved us in that Void, he lied about the blood trace to get us to trust him again."

"Yes, and who saved him in the cactus forest?" Patty pinched her eyes.

"You think they were in this together?"

"Completely?" Patty shrugged. "With Byron, who knows? But don't you find it odd that the Messenger would send us into the forest with an Apex Goblin and give no warning whatsoever? The Priestess conveniently escaped when it attacked. That thing came out of nowhere. It was hidden from our AllSight. She had to know beforehand to slip away at the perfect time like that."

"She forged the letter then?"

"I don't think so. Byron had experience deciphering handwriting, and nobody has ever been able to find the Messenger's letters, with the exception of him. He found one and switched it with his fake."

"That's too weird."

"Do you still have the letter?"

Teresa checked her pocket. Nothing was there.

Patty's mouth bent into a disgusted smile. "That was a nice long hug he gave you just before we left him, wasn't it? He wouldn't want us scrutinizing the letter too closely, not after what happened in the forest."

"He needed it in the gateway, didn't he?"

This was too crazy to accept. Would Byron actually put them in danger just to get to that gateway? She supposed he had done so before when he let the OAP abduct them, but he'd had some control over that. Sending them in the forest with that goblin, sending Kauph, it didn't seem like something he would do.

"But Byron helped us get back here," said Teresa.

"He probably wasn't counting on the Church of Morning attacking us." Patty's teeth came together and clenched. "We have to do something about this."

"Calm down, think."

"There's no time to think anymore. This day isn't over yet and I'm not building another mantle unless I really have to."

"Don't overreact."

Patty popped open the glove box and grabbed the Messenger's map. "We can't have any other surprises. Byron knows we're going to Bishopbriggs now and that can still be dangerous for us."

"I agree, but we're almost there—"

"No, it's not safe. We're going to the Void in Temple." When nothing else was said, Patty turned to her. "We need to turn around goddamn it, so go!"

Teresa put the car in reverse.

"Agent Telamon! I see you've decided to join us again." Phil Jeffrey extended a hand, which Byron limply shook. "What did those girls do to you, son?"

"Nothing I wouldn't have done myself."

Denis bent over the dead body of a girl in a karate uniform. "What the hell happened while I was out?"

Jeffrey ignored this, "Carry on, agent, secure that doorway. There's still a situation here."

Denis slowly stood, a look of disquiet settling over him. "Are any law enforcement arriving?"

"Eventually. Now get to the door."

Denis drifted uneasily away from the body, as Jeffrey guided Byron to double doors in the center of the ill-lit museum. He was about to say something when a call came through. He plucked his cell phone from its holster. "Phil Jeffrey," he greeted. After another moment he said. "It's the last number I called him, right? Back in the States? Yeah? Send me that one. Thanks."

After putting the phone away, Jeffrey placed his hand on Byron's neck. "You got the flu? Fuck, you're like ice."

Byron shrugged.

"Cut to the chase here. We've got the Archbishop of Midnight holed up in that room. I got people around the building, so he won't be using those fancy hands of his to melt a hole in the building and escape, but I do need someone to go in there and… chase him off the Pillar of Ginsau."

"What pillar?"

"Securing such a relic would mean a great deal to the department—"

"Fuck the department."

They stared at each other for a moment. Jeffrey's phone chimed as he received a text message.

"I guess you're wondering why I'd ask your help after I ordered you cuffed?" Jeffrey raised an eyebrow. "I'm going to call the Archbishop in a moment. While this happens, I'm going to blow the charges we've set on the hinges. I need the first one through the door to be you, Byron, to distract him. That'll give us enough time to tranq him. I know it's hard to believe, but I've dreamt about this day. Camden Amherst is alive in my dream, with me and the pillar."

"You dreamed this, huh?" Byron asked. He felt he'd reached his limit on wonder.

"Am I in the dream?"

The old man's eyes thinned. "No," he said resolutely. "But that shouldn't matter."

"I'm not complaining. Dying sounds like great fun."

"Good, because I was going to push your sorry ass in there anyway." Jeffrey took out his phone and dialed.

The Archbishop Vasoth Kennen knelt at the bedside, staring at the brown blood staining the quilts. His mother's blood. He'd carried her to his private chamber and held vigil over her ever since. He couldn't believe Bre had done what he had. Hadn't they been friends? Hadn't their lives been devoted to keeping this woman alive?

Madness buzzed in his ears. He didn't want to live any longer. Not after being so close to victory, not through this shame. When the head of his Ekkian guard reported the Nomads had escaped with the Heart of the Harvest, he might have once felt dread and terror over it, but it was smaller in his mind than anything he experienced at the moment.

The buzzing madness continued.

The sound wasn't from his mind though, but instead from the communication device Camden Amherst had sent him from the other world.

Kennen stood, his knees cracking under his spent body, staples and stitches straining across his stomach and groin area, all his flesh sacrifices to his mother—wasted. He went over to his collection from the other world: a baseball glove, a can of hairspray, a pair of horn-rimmed glasses, and a broken disc with writing on the side and an illustration of a man with a guitar slung around his neck. Kennen used to wonder about each of these items and dream of the world they came from, but now, none of it mattered anymore.

All that he had sacrificed, for this emptiness.

Nevertheless, he picked up the phone. Purple light emanated from its smooth material. A green button glowed there with other symbols. Kennen pushed it. A miniature voice escaped from the device.

"Archbishop, we must talk about this Column," a man said.

Kennen looked down at it, felt like throwing the thing into the wall. *"What do you know of it?"*

A cold hand clutched Kennen's wrist. He yelped in surprise and wheeled around to face Chaplain Cloth.

The gateway had torn through the back wall of his bedroom, but had come in complete silence. Several of Cloth's children roamed the room already.

"Let me see that phone," said Cloth. No hint of the usual sardonic humor on his face.

Kennen handed him the device. Cloth looked slightly taller and more built, stronger than he had in the past, the white of his face more luminescent, the black of his eye deeper, and the orange of his other eye like volcanic fuel. Cloth nodded before placing the phone back down. "Outstanding."

Kennen's heart quickened when the Chaplain headed back for the gateway and glanced at Pel'Hahr. He continued on, not stopping. "You've done well keeping her alive, Kennen. She looks better than she ever has. I will return after some business."

The gateway shut and the room was empty again. Kennen hadn't been able to say a word. Hadn't been able to utter the truth. He glanced at the dead body of his mother. Cloth wasn't lying. She really did look better in death than she had during her last few years of life.

Reality gripped him again and Kennen collapsed on the floor, sobbing.

It would be any second now. Camden could not take down all of the agents. He might get lucky and burn a couple, maybe a few, but his body would be getting pretty lead-heavy with bullets by then. He could hear talking outside the door. Jeffrey was planning something.

Let him, *thought Camden with a shiver.* I'm ready.

It was better this way, he kept telling himself. It was better than facing—

With a vicious-sudden pull, like atmospheric decompression, the door and wall of the museum bent inward and dissolved into black infinity. Vibrant green vines forced out with the greedy probing of tentacles. From the absence it created in the wall, Camden could see Phil Jeffrey standing in the other room, stock-still with a cell phone poised at his ear. Smoke erupted from the phone and he dropped it, unable to tear his eyes from the gateway. Another agent stood beside him, hands cuffed behind his back. The sight must have really worked on the cuffed man because he was white as snow and appeared injured; blood coursed from his eyes and nose and made a sick beard.

Cloth's maniacal living horde of jack-o'-lanterns frolicked into the corners of the room. They sang and growled impatiently. Wearing a grin, Chaplain Cloth, black suited with a fiery orange handkerchief pluming out his breast pocket, stepped through their number and glanced around the museum with great interest. Several agents ran through the front door, took aim and fired. Something flashed in the air as the bullets ricocheted off an invisible barrier.

"Hold your fire, jackasses!" shouted Jeffrey.

The panicked agents stopped near cover, confusion permeating their expressions.

One with a goatee put a gun to his forehead and fired. Another with shaggy, dirty blond hair pointed under his jaw and discharged a round. And one more agent, bald and well-muscled, rushed inside, studied the scene, and then robotically lifted his own gun, stuck the barrel into one ear and sent a graypink jelly stream of brains out the other.

Cloth didn't pay attention to this collective suicide. He mused, looking around the museum again and then to someplace distant. "That's how the Interloper got them to the other side! There's a temporary gateway in the graveyard out here— surprising I didn't hear the echoes of my Children singing through it. The Interloper did well to hide it from me."

He must be talking about the Necropolis. What did that have to do with anything?

Cloth bowed to the sickly man near Jeffrey. "I suppose it's much more astonishing to find you here, on your own two feet. The Interloper's disease wasn't enough to keep you down, I wager. Very surprising indeed. How do you do, Mr. Telamon?"

The man's eyes drifted to the gateway. He looked like an

addict, the hungry face begging for a fix.

"Patience," said Cloth, black and orange eyes dazzling. "You'll be inside soon enough."

Phil Jeffrey took a cautious, but jubilant step closer. The white haired man quivered with joy. "Chaplain Cloth. Do you remember me? I was that boy who took your photo, years ago."

Chaplain Cloth smiled. "Ah yes, the photo. I'll never forget that idiocy."

Jeffrey swallowed uncomfortably before brightening. "And there it is! After all these years, I brought you the Column! The Pillar of Ginsau. You promised to spare my family if I brought you to it…remember, you said this, in my dreams. You *promised.*"

Cloth was more interested in the man named Telamon, but replied, "I must meet this dream version of myself, such an interesting guy, always making deals."

The older man's face burned red with excitement as he ran for the Pillar of Ginsau, his arm in the sling swaying absurdly. He reached beyond the velvet rope and gently patted its marble face. "I brought you here, Chaplain Cloth, to the Column. I did it. Just like you asked."

Now Cloth turned. "So you did, sir. Thank you for calling that phone, and well done, you've saved me a most laborious search. Your family, from hereon, is safe."

Cloth flicked his bone white fingers. The Pillar of Ginsau rocked violently one way. Jeffrey gave a fleeting look behind just as the forward momentum brought the heavy stone down on him. Jeffrey's good arm was all that made it out of the way. The pillar cut off the limb neatly at the elbow joint and forced the arm across the floor on a blast of blood, where it crashed into a nearby wall.

Camden watched as blood spread from under the massively cracked marble. *Why would Cloth destroy the Column?*

"Thanksgiving to the Feast," Cloth said with a snort. "If I had a hat, I'd take it off, truly. I should get a hat."

Cloth returned to his immediate interest and took Telamon's shoulders. "Byron, my boy, there are two places the Nomads are likely to go, given their time: Bishopbriggs and Temple. You're chums, so tell me please, which Void?"

The man cast a guilty look to his feet. He dropped to his knees and vomited something that resembled a stew of entrails and sage leaves.

What was that shit?

Pressing his palms to his ears, mess still unwiped from his lips, Byron cried out and arched his body. The Children in the room swayed and sang a myriad of different songs, a colossal hornet's nest-buzz of lunacy and longing.

Cloth took a knee in the puddle of vomit and squeezed Byron's chin. An agent came running out of the darkness with his gun drawn.

"Denis!" Byron shouted. "Don't!"

All at once the agent's bones pulled through his body and tore through his clothes. His ribs ripped through his shirt, femurs pulled through his slacks, skull tore through the soft skin in the back of his head, and that was just what Camden could see in the instant—it seemed every bone, from small to large, left through a grisly red exit, sent flying on coils of blood, only to land on the floor, clattering musically. A few seconds later and all that remained was a layer of ripped fabric and soft organic matter on the ground.

Cloth turned back to Byron. "So, yeah, like I was saying, the gateway is just over there, the end to this bad, bad journey of yours. Go ahead and tell me where the Nomads are camping out."

Byron swallowed something hard and looked away.

"I don't know why you didn't collapse in a coma like the other with your affliction," said Cloth. "I don't know what compelled you on—one who is kept alive, and the other who refuses to die." Realization fluxed with the shadows cast across Cloth's bone white face. "Did you think a gateway would make you a Nomad? Eh? No, Byron, no, you're far more special than those fools that inelegantly molest the fabric of the worlds. Your purpose is a grand, agonizing one, but you can find some resolve. Just tell me which Void."

Tears commingled with blood and the sides of Byron's face ran pink. His lips sputtered. He tried to get the words out—the man looked delirious in pain and wretchedness. Camden almost wanted to just shout at him to say something, anything, but then the word was formed.

"Bishopbriggs."

Byron hunched over and retched. He wagged his head and mumbled incoherently now.

"That's a nice start." Chaplain Cloth tweaked his ear in thought. "But I hate these types of decisions. This is tricky." Cloth reviewed again the tormented man. "See, Byron, I don't believe you'd sacrifice those you love so easily. Middleton meant more to you than that."

"It's the truth," he croaked. "What can I say? I'm a risk taker."

Vines shot over and caught Byron's leg. He made no move and let the gateway yank him through the gory mess into the blackness in the wall. Cloth called after, though the man was long gone, "You can come along for the show in Temple, where I think the Nomads are really headed."

The man's screams intensified in the gateway. Chaplain Cloth allowed his Children to flow back inside. Swift of step, he returned for the gateway himself.

"I'll be consulting with you later, Archbishop," he said to Camden before also vanishing inside.

THIRTY-SEVEN

Kauph Courre dug his nails into his palms. The vehicle was going too fast. He could see trees and strange buildings zipping past them, faster and faster.

Teresa, the malformed Nomad who piloted the vehicle, tightened her warped hands around the wheel, her wrinkled arms dotted with sweat. The growl of the engine got louder.

Kauph took the bomb in his hand and recited Patty's instructions how to activate it. Pull the pin, *then the lever.* If those things killed the Nomads and found him, yes, it would be better to end things all at once. With everything in him, he didn't want to, but this wasn't about Kauph Courre. This was about the Old Domain. This was about the Blind World.

Oh, but what a poor name for such an amazing place! They passed other vehicles of different sizes and interesting gradients of color. None were going as fast as they were. Kauph didn't like such speed. It reminded him of the Heart Bearer's old horse they used to ride on, *before the Blue Quarter built him that tank to protect them in Cauldron Valley. The horse had been powerful and fast and in the beginning Kauph had taken several painful spills off the back of it. He'd wished the* mummy would have left him behind, but Kauph was never that fortunate.

Then Widdah came one night and hacked the mummy up into little pieces, took his bandages and tank, and took Kauph. Now Widdah was gone and another group had collected Kauph. Maybe for good. But the reckless, dangerous speed of escape had remained. He was always moving. He'd been on the run his whole life and he'd thought to have become accustomed to it by now, but the Nomads' vehicle was worse. It brought him closer to something he didn't want to see, although he'd known it was waiting for him for some time.

Patty cried, "Sonuvabitch! How?"

Teresa wrenched the wheel to the side. The vehicle spun and the world flowed with it, trees a green arc through the storm cloud sky. Orange faces, insane eyes and gnashing fangs filled the windows in a wall.

The Children of the gateway had found them.

The vehicle still moved and Teresa struggled to gain control of it, already ragged pieces of steel tossing into the air from the Children's claws.

Chaplain Cloth stood ahead of them in the road. Kauph stared at the man in the black suit and orange necktie. The creature that had terrified him in his sleep for his whole life—now, it was before him, but only for a blink, half a blink, the ground, the wet black concrete of the road, Kauph could see, could see the lines in the road, he didn't know how, and then it was clearer, it made sense, the way sense could come quickly at the confusion of time's flow, and the shock of a single person's life registering as an element to be here at one moment and the next to be gone; yes, Kauph knew, knew that Cloth had struck the car and sent it into the air, spinning around, like a village dancer, perhaps how that earless beauty might have danced for Kauph had he stayed behind in the Village of the Unpaid Harvest.

He yelled.

He saw Teresa throw her arms up to her face.

He felt Patty reach back and press a hand into his abdomen. It was for protection. But it was too late. The vehicle's glass shield splintered and rained over them in the half-darkness like mirrored snowflakes. The last revolution sent two of the side doors open, Kauph's and Patty's.

Two white bags popped out in front of Patty and Teresa. A foul odor and smoke escaped them. A sheet of blood came down from a ruptured boil in Teresa's forehead. "Get out, Kauph! Run!"

He stabbed the button on his restraint, which had cut a wide bar of pain across his chest. The restraint unbuckled and rattled against the doorframe.

Everything was dizziness. Everything, sideways.

Cloth walked toward the car, seemingly on a different axis.

Kauph pulled the handle and the door opened. He grabbed the hand-held bomb off the ground.

A squat, wart-spotted Child jumped off the vehicle from above him. Kauph threw his hands over his head—saw the pumpkin beast strike something invisible and slide off him. The Nomads had put barriers around him.

Patty poked out of the vehicle, one of her eye sockets purpled by an impact with the door. "There, Kauph, across the field. Go to that shack."

Chaplain Cloth increased his pace, the swelling gateway flowing behind him. More Children piled out of its dark heart, some as large as their vehicle, some the size of wild dogs.

Patty and Teresa faced the surging wave of evil. "Are you building?" Teresa asked Patty.

"Yes," she replied quietly.

Kauph's vision cleared then, and he ran.

Another of Cloth's Children flew at him. This one's vine wrapped arms clasped around his neck. He grabbed for it and swung it off him with all of his might.

What had happened to the barriers?

More Children came at him. Kauph closed his eyes. They slammed into an invisible wall.

"He's tearing them down fast," yelled Teresa.

"I know," Patty hollered back. The pretty blonde woman closed her eyes.

In an instant, hundreds of Children fell to the ground, orange fountains of blood erupting from their heads, as though Patty had swept the air with a high powered crossbow. A monstrous Child emerged from the gateway, this one house-sized, with fangs as long as fence posts.

Something unseen split the large creature in two halves like an enormous butcher's knife cleaved down. The two parts fell neatly sideways under rainbows of vibrant orange blood and connecting tissues.

Well done, Patty.

Kauph stumbled on. Everything wobbled in his vision.

The world had become a ship dipping through the waves of a tempest. As many Children that had fallen, more came barreling out of the gateway.

"The shack!" one of the Nomads called to him.

He ran now through the high grass, the children not giving up their fruitless attack. Chaplain Cloth walked at an even, but determined pace. Kauph almost stopped when he saw Patty take a frightened step backward.

"Teresa! He's still tearing them down! All of them!"

Teresa hobbled over. "More mantles," she ordered. "No hesitation!"

"I am. He's destroying all of them. Oh shit, I'm so sorry! I can't stop this. I can't!"

Kauph did slow now, despite the hammering of pumpkins all around him. He wanted to yell at the women to run. He wanted a tongue so he could shout at them. Chaplain Cloth was getting closer.

They did move then. Patty grabbed hold of Teresa and they turned away from the wreckage of the car. Kauph waved his hand frantically for them. In the distance, Chaplain Cloth raised his hand as well and he blinked his black and orange eyes.

Patty and Teresa collapsed together on the ground.

Teresa tried to force herself to build more mantles, but her connection to the gateway pulled her mind away. It was even more intense when she sensed Patty building. The sensation was magnetic in nature. She could feel both of them tugged in every direction.

Thousands of mantles came to be.

All of that reconstruction back in the village, and Patty had probably devastated it again.

Long trails of tears went down her partner's face. She was failing everybody and there was nothing she could do about it.

Chaplain Cloth moved closer and extended his hand.

Patty concentrated, but all of her mantles immediately came crashing down.

He was more powerful than they'd ever seen him. How had this happened?

Teresa began crying too, because she knew what was coming next.

Their tenure was over.

Teresa grabbed hold of her little girl and told her she loved her.

It ended here.

The Nomads' bodies dispersed into a red mist that spread through the air like a chemical bomb. No bones, no muscle, no evidence of life, save for the falling red dust in the moonlight. From behind the door of the old barn, Kauph wailed. *"No! No! No!" his mind shouted.*

Protection gone, the Children poured from the rotting rafters above. Their thorny green hands grappled Kauph's wrists and ankles, and pulled him through the door outside. The sky of this beautiful new world darkened overhead. Up in the storm clouds above, he saw a small patch of blue sky. He'd never seen a blue sky before. The Children pinned Kauph to the wet grass. He struggled, but they firmly held him.

Someone walked up. The face was airbrushed in the scarlet blood of the Nomads, but this was not Chaplain Cloth.

It was his brother. It was Bre Courre. "Let him up for a moment," Bre ordered.

The Children snarled all at once in a frightening refrain. "Let him up!" Bre's intensity matched their growling hunger.

Gradually the Children let go and fell back a couple feet.

Bre offered his hand. Kauph stared at him dumbly for a moment. He hardly remembered his younger brother. The face was not entirely unlike his own, though a little leaner around the eyes, and his hair had an ashen quality instead of a luster. He'd had a difficult life as well it appeared.

Kauph took his hand and let his brother pull him to his feet.

Bre embraced him tightly and Kauph let him. "I missed you. My whole life, brother."

Kauph briefly touched his face, since he could not respond.

Pools formed up in Bre's eyes. "We were robbed of each other, weren't we?"

Kauph let his forehead drop on his brother's shoulder. He

wanted to cry too, but he knew this wasn't real. His pulled the pin from the hand bomb. His brother backed up. Kauph lifted the safety lever. When he pulled away to take another look at his own flesh and blood, Chaplain Cloth stood in his brother's place now.

"You're welcome, boys," he said, snatching away the bomb. Kauph lunged to get it back but halted at once as Chaplain Cloth's mouth opened in a disturbing cavern of blood soaked teeth. He forced the explosive inside and swallowed. His throat bulged only momentarily as the bomb went down into his gullet. A gray slug of a tongue peeked out, and Chaplain Cloth licked his lips. No explosion came.

Kauph backed away, every muscle in his body quavering with a mania of its own. The orange sea of Children swept in around him.

Cloth harvested the bloody fruit from Kauph's chest and put it down for the Children to eat. Laughing in absolute enchantment, he watched them race back into the gateway, alive with the Heart of the Harvest's power. They exploded inside the gateway and the opening to the Old Domain swelled large enough to pass an army through.

Chaplain Cloth returned to where Byron Telamon huddled in the vine-writhing shadows. "Do you feel that power? It's time to begin. Are you ready?"

Byron mumbled something that sounded like, "*It was all a lie.*"

Cloth helped the man to his feet.

Swaying, Byron stood amongst the vines, belonging to the gateway more than the Children, more than Cloth himself. He was a nexus between worlds, a God that would ultimately bridge the gap there, a Column to carry the burden of two struggling worlds.

In the next moment, that notion became reality. Byron's fingers split apart and his hands reached skyward as they exploded off the wrists. Great, powerful black vines roared from the stumps and twisted to the vaulted ceiling of the gateway where they tied to other vines and anchored there with the fierce sounds of guillotines falling in succession all over the universe.

Byron's shoes burst off in leathery ribbons and his feet popped like enormous blisters, letting forth blood with gray-dark roots that deftly planted into the floor, gagging sounds like serpents choking on their tails.

Byron swayed for a few breathless seconds and then his body twisted and clothing shed in bloody fragments. The skin sloughed off the skeleton as vines wormed through the ribcage and wound around and around.

Chaplain Cloth stood there watching the glory. Happy. So, so happy. After all this time, he'd seen this day. For millennia he had the notion that the universe would end on its own before he had his way with it.

Now, this.

He wiped a tear from his eye and chuckled at it on his pale finger.

The Telamon Column quivered at the stress from the gateway, the vines flexing like thousands of twined ropes. He could not see the brain and the pair of eyes that remained from the man named Byron, but Cloth knew they lay somewhere buried inside the column of vines. The man's mind would continue to have thoughts and feel a pain unknown to anybody, even to Cloth, all the cosmic torture the universe could inflict, but it would not be in silence. A music device had wrapped inside the vines and the sounds could still be perceived by Byron. The device would never lose power from all that raw energy coursing through the great column.

Blissfully, the voice of the singer Sam Cooke would hum against the muscular vines going from the depths of the gateway up to its vaulted heights.

Cloth almost became emotional again when the Children surged forth. He laughed, a parent seeing his younglings finally become adults. They raced out across the Scottish countryside to begin the feast.

May they never grow full.

EPILOGUE

The Eternal Feast

It has been some time since I've been to the Old Domain. I could look upon it whenever I chose, but it's different to be standing here, in the flesh. As I waited in Kennen's chambers in the Palace of Morning, one of the few places the Children had not destroyed, I thought about what might be occurring on the other side. All of the worries of before, falling economies, random acts of terrorism, genocide, famine, disease: these were reflections of a harsher reality to come.

I have no power on Halloween. It's been this way since the beginning and will remain this way until the Last Moment. Now that the gateway was kept open, the worlds caught in a perpetual October 31st, I was caught in perpetual weakness. I'd done my best to avoid this very thing from happening, but there were too many things against me this year. I lost the Heart of the Harvest. I lost my Nomads. I lost everything.

Chaplain Cloth had sent a group of Ekkian sentinels to collect and bring me to the palace. He didn't bother doing the honors himself because he hoped this would make me feel defeated. I want to say that he failed, but I've been on my own for so long, powerful for every day out of every year, out of every decade, century, millennium—I would have been false with my own inclinations, if I didn't feel like a wounded rodent dragged from its den by the hand of a God.

I gazed out the window. From this vantage, I could see the gateway stretching to the limit of the sky, and through it I could see a city in Scotland. The Children flowed over everything, like an undulating orange moss. A building shuddered and slid sideways in the distance. A dirt cloud rose up with its fall.

I felt the need to watch it all. My failure. If the Earth had to suffer, I would not turn my eyes away from it. I would share the suffering in whatever way I could.

The door to the chamber opened. The bishops of Midnight and Morning walked in. Despite fresh clean robes, Vasoth Kennen looked as unsightly and deformed as always and Camden Amherst looked as though a cement truck had backed over him.

"Archbishop Cloth is on his way," Camden informed me. I said nothing. When the two men sensed I wouldn't speak, they turned to each other. Kennen's uneven eyes bulged and hasty stitches in his face flexed, likely to break soon. "I thought Cloth had other matters to attend?"

"No, he communed with me just an hour ago."

Kennen frowned despite his next words, "My congratulations to your victory, Arch—I mean, Bishop."

Camden shook his hand without looking Kennen in the eyes. "I was lucky."

The chamber door burst open. "We all were."

Cloth came through the door. He had on his typical garb of black suit and orange tie, but to signify his ascension, now donned a top hat with dark orange band. "Every day is Halloween and I no longer have to wander the worlds!"

He clapped his hands and gave Kennen a good-natured tug of the shoulders. "Ah, the one who is on top of everything! Your toils at keeping that miserable mother of yours alive will now see fruit. I need you to transport her to the gateway at once. Byron Telamon cannot carry the entire burden forever!" Cloth looked to the bed. The body had been removed for burial by Ekkian guards an hour ago. "You moved Pel'Hahr?"

Kennen looked as though he were about to cry. "That's what I've meant to tell you earlier, Chap—Archbishop Cloth. Something truly terrible has happened."

Cloth poked his top hat back. Under the shadow of the brim, his black eye consumed, his orange eye cooked. "Terrible?"

"She's passed on."

Cloth's face dropped. "But how can that be? I fed all the components into your brain. With those transmungi, she should have lived months longer."

Kennen's voice broke. "I thank you for all you did for us, Archbishop Cloth. I'm ever in your servitude, but it wasn't our efforts that...led to my mother's end. My slave, he...murdered my mother while I was unconscious from the Heralding."

Cloth suddenly looked bewildered, frightened. "Bre Courre?"

Kennen lowered his head. "I couldn't bring her back. She was already gone when I awoke. I can't believe, I—"

Cloth turned away, his suit swishing. He took off the top hat and tossed it on the bed. *"He Who Might Have Saved the Worlds...* such a revoltingly ambiguous nickname."

Kennen stepped forward. "Archbishop Cloth? I beg forgiveness."

"You need to leave."

When the man made no move, Cloth turned and his eyes stared black and orange daggers at him. "Quickly," he added.

Kennen dipped his head thankfully.

"Fuck off now," Cloth snapped, "before I reconsider your usefulness."

The former Archbishop of Morning almost collapsed as he escaped through the door of his own chambers.

Cloth clenched his fists and closed his eyes, thinking. It was a wonder how he still contained such emotion after so long. I'd lost the ability to express my feelings much longer ago. Sensing my evaluation, he gave me a brief look of disgusted annoyance before motioning Camden over.

"Listen, Amherst...I'm giving you another chance. Will you fail me again?"

He bravely looked Cloth eyes to eyes. "I promise I won't," Camden said.

"Very well. The Heart of the Harvest grows in many people now. Every moon I must harvest it to feed the Children, or they will devour each other. They must thrive, for I need them in the Last Moment. I will ensure the Children eat the sacred fruit, while you search for the next Column. Understand?"

"Fine...aye, okay."

"A single Column in the gateway will last for generations, but I don't want generations, I want permanence. Without balance there will eventually be a breakdown. It will not be easy to find one of these afflicted, because they either die of the pain, or exist outside physical and spiritual logic, but search for the same traits of illness detailed in the appendices of your holy books."

"I understand."

"You will find that person, you will plant them in the gateway, and then the Last Moment shall be upon us."

Before Camden could ask a question, Cloth went to the armoire and snatched up a phone. It had the residue of marrow pulsing through it, which Cloth knew very well would make it more than a simple device. He strode over to me and pressed the phone in my hand.

Moving a tress of my orange hair away from my eyes, I smiled at him.

"I know you've kept track of all your afflicted," said Cloth. "Contact them by any means necessary and direct Bishop Amherst to them." Cloth spoke to Camden again, but his gaze didn't leave me. "When you find one of the afflicted, tell him or her to come to the gateway at once, tell them it will make the pain go away."

This was another strange display of emotion from him. Cloth knew I wouldn't call any of my afflicted. Keeping people like Pel'Hahr and Byron Telamon in the throes of disease and disillusion was the way I'd prevented the Church from ever taking this shortcut to keeping the gateway open. It was the only piece of leverage I possessed now.

"Start calling," Cloth insisted.

Everything had gone so perfectly wrong. The tragedy of it made me chuckle.

"Do you think I'm joking with you, *sister*?" Cloth asked, a murderous light widening in his eyes.

I slid my hands down my hips, making him wait a moment longer. "And how long has it been since you've called me sister, rather than Interloper? Are we family again now, *brother*?"

Cloth whirled back to Camden, startling the man. "She is your best compass to guide you to the next Column. Use her at your will."

"Of course, Archbishop," Camden replied with a slight bow. "But how do I—? Where are you going?"

"To rip open the universe," Cloth hissed as he reached the door.

Camden waited until the monster was gone. Afterward, for several moments he scratched under his black beard and studied me quietly.

"You are his sister?" he finally asked. I nodded with a grim smile.

"And you are the Interloper?" Camden pulled anxiously at his beard. "The same one who the Nomads call *the Messenger?*"

"Amongst other things," I replied.

The man looked flabbergasted. "Why would Cloth leave you here without guard?"

"I am not a problem to him any longer," I told him. "Cloth can go anywhere, be anything. The game of life and death is his to toy with until the Last Moment. Until then, the worlds will bleed together, people will suffer and struggle, and he will have his way. My freedom isn't real in the shadow of such power."

I moved the trains of my black dress away from my feet as I stepped toward the window. It was so dark outside.

Camden looked at me with disquiet. "He can listen to everything we say, can't he?"

"If he wishes to. His mind, I suspect is elsewhere at present though. After he works through the shock of losing the other Column, I would choose what I said about him in a whisper. If I were you."

Camden moved closer and said in a hushed voice, "I made a mistake taking the path I did. I know that now."

"You are too late for redemption, I'm afraid."

"Aye, I know. But I'm helping anyway. We can gather others—you can show me how. He thinks I'm out looking for the Column, but I'm working with you instead. We can turn this around on him. Can't we?"

I shook my head.

"I won't give up," Camden assured me. "We're in this together."

With an awkward step back, he found the handle to the bedroom door. "I'll return when I can," he said closing the door.

I only half processed what he'd said. I was looking at the impression on the bed where Pel'Hahr had rested. She was the last piece that fell through for Cloth. This year was the closest he'd ever come to the Last Moment. All in one swoop.

Closing my eyes, I attempted to brace myself for the horrible reality of what had happened. Cloth, my wretched monster of a brother, possibly hadn't come to terms with everything either. But it wouldn't be this way for long.

I moved to the bed and sat there in bewilderment. It was always tragic when I lost my Nomads. Throughout time I'd had hundreds of pairs of them, but each held a place in my memories. Much of the joys and defeats they shared, I had as well.

I took the cell phone Cloth had given me and maneuvered through the menus to select a web browser. Looking outside, it was conceivable that internet service would not be available anymore. The Children had multiplied and spread through every metropolis, city, town and village by now. I was shocked to find I had a signal, even in the Old Domain—this phone must have been imbued with more power than I'd realized.

I logged onto Patty's emails. For years I'd done this to study her mind and predict how she would react in certain situations. It was so surprising that she'd agreed to destroy all those Chapels and kill all the Church members. She hated doing it but then she probably believed she would be free of this life, one day.

And now she was.

Thumbing the keys I noticed a new message. Actually, it was from Patty herself. I looked at the date.

October 31st.

Narrowing my eyes, I read the subject. My heart began to race.

TO: pmiddleton@tvlwebplaces.com
SUBJECT: Parts unknown. I am twenty-one years old this year…

We have both sustained serious injuries. I've used my jeans for bandages but I'm going to have to find something else soon. It's too dark to go now, and I hear things moving out there, so I'll wait for some kind of light.

The Heart of the Harvest has been lost, the gateway opened and we narrowly escaped being killed. I don't quite understand why we're still alive, or where we went—this is not our world, and something tells me this is not the Old Domain either.

I have internet access on my phone, however possible that is, so I will add to this journal when I can to document what has become of us, for anyone who might care. I must go now and check Teresa again. She is the worse off between us both. She might even be dying, but after the mistake I made to lead us here, I'll be damned if I let that happen.

I will heal her, even if it kills me in the process.

I pushed off the cell with a trembling finger.

Yes, foolish me. I should have known. The truth, it is always moving.

Leaves on the wind; wind on the leaves.

I took a moment to theorize what tremendous forces had shaped this outcome. It made sense in an abstract way, only because I'd never seen it happen before. Two massive collisions of ghost matter, pushing together had ripped open the seam between the worlds. That would be possible by only Patty and somebody equally or more powerful than her. This new manifestation of my brother was every bit of that—

But only a suitable vehicle could have safely taken two human beings caught in the center of that collision without tearing them completely to ribbons. They would have had to touch something that existed in the space between.

My mouth dropped a little. It was astonishing I could still feel surprised.

Teresa's mantle, lost in the gateway, still tethered to her.

She'd been their vehicle.

That meant they were in the Marrowlands then, but the Nomads were alive!

I braced myself on the bedpost and pushed away to the window again. The land throbbed with frantic movement. Shouts and screams and snarls. More buildings fell in on each other and dust swirled into the fire-lit darkness above. Some places on Earth would now become as dangerous as the Old Domain. This partial merge of worlds would somewhat prolong the eventual misery to come but in some cases also show what the future had in store.

Unfortunately, Camden had been wrong. We weren't in this together anymore. The universe was on its own now. All of us, alone, left to roam these homicidal lands and hope for temporary shelter. Some would have a destination and some would not. But in the face of long odds, there were a pair who could still bring us back together. That was my only comfort. My Nomads were out there, somewhere on the other side of here and there, making this journey, fighting through the madness of the forever-road, no use for wanderlust or fond thoughts of the path ahead, giving up their bodies, giving up their spirits, searching for those very last scraps of light.

I prayed for their return.

ABOUT THE AUTHOR

Benjamin Kane Ethridge is the Bram Stoker Award-winning author of the novel *Black & Orange*, as well *Bottled Abyss, Nightmare Ballad,* and other novels. For his master's thesis he wrote, "Causes of Unease: The Rhetoric of Horror Fiction and Film." Available in an ivory tower near you. He lives in Southern California with his family. When Benjamin isn't writing, he's defending California's rivers and streams from pollution.

Curious about other Crossroad Press books?
Stop by our site:
http://store.crossroadpress.com
We offer quality writing
in digital, audio, and print formats.

www.ingramcontent.com/pod-product-compliance
Lightning Source LLC
Chambersburg PA
CBHW031133260626
47153CB00021B/160